She Said/He Said

A Journey from Forgiveness to Reconciliation

Rose Kuo

authorHOUSE®

AuthorHouse™
1663 Liberty Drive
Bloomington, IN 47403
www.authorhouse.com
Phone: 1-800-839-8640

Published by AuthorHouse 03/24/2014

ISBN: 978-1-4918-9971-7 (sc)
ISBN: 978-1-4918-9970-0 (e)

Library of Congress Control Number: 2014905547

This Book is lovingly dedicated to my mom, Anne Leuzzi. She provided the funds for this endeavor and the encouragement for me to finally finish something that I'd been taking way too long to complete. I love you, Mom.

Preface

This book, though fiction, is based on real issues that plague the church today: sexual immorality, lack of forgiveness and reconciliation, legalism and spiritual abuse, and churches that are run like corporations.

Church leaders wring their hands and wonder why the number of Christians is decreasing. They wonder why, with all of their programs and outreaches, people are not clamoring at their doors, to become believers.

Until the Church understands that it must clean house and learn the art of repentance; this decrease in people coming to Christ will only continue.

It is only through repentance, forgiveness, and reconciliation, that the hypocrisy which the world sees all too clearly, will be removed.

When hypocrisy and sin are rooted out of the Church; then and only then will people finally be able to see and know Jesus. The church will be a haven of healing and not a place to become wounded. The world can sometimes see more clearly than the Church. Will the Church remain stubbornly blind?

The love of God is to be the main focal point of the Church. Showing the love of Jesus to the wounded and sin weary is the only way to see lives healed and restored.

We can't show the world Jesus or the love of God if our "stuff" is obstructing the view. If people who are Christians are no better than the world and do not manifest the love of God, then why should people ever want to know Him? They can be miserable without the Church.

Chapter 1

My wife was out of town, visiting her relatives, so I decided to take the Bart to my office, early one morning, on the last Saturday in February. I have a midsized office in a renovated office building near the Embarcadero Station area, in downtown San Francisco. During the 1930's the whole floor we are on was a large office suite for a railroad baron. About ten years ago the building was renovated and I was lucky to get the office that still had the old fellow's custom built extremely ornate fireplace. In my mind, I could just see the giant desk he must have had in front of it and all of the lavish furnishings, kind of like in the movie Citizen Kane. My office is much more humble. I basically have a used desk (that my wife refinished), two huge comfy overstuffed arm chairs (for my clients), a small couch, a hot plate, a microwave, a tiny apartment refrigerator, and a large leather office chair with matching ottoman. My desk and the leather chair are right in front of the fireplace, so I can face the door when folks come in. My wife, Anne, put up a few framed sketches of local bridges and some folk art decorations. The office screams, "Simple and cozy", when you enter. San Francisco, being what it is: chilly, means my fireplace is burning for about nine months out of the year. Oh yes, I forgot to mention I have a big gray cat, that I named Max, who lives in here year round. I find him to be a comfort to me and he puts the clients at ease. I'm on the third floor overlooking a little courtyard with cherry trees, which are just starting to bloom.

I am a licensed therapist and my first name is Mark. I have my Doctorate in Clinical Therapy; but I choose to downplay this, a bit, so I don't intimidate my clients. My wife and I live in a new home up in the hills of Dublin, CA. and we have one daughter who is away at college in Eureka, CA. She visits mainly for holidays. My wife teaches the fifth grade at a local school near our home. We often go for little side trips around the Bay Area, and the rest of our spare time is devoted to our church. My wife enjoys doing pottery and I made her a studio in our garage. I enjoy doing little carpentry projects. Though I'm an extremely dedicated Christian, I chose to run a secular practice, for a variety of reasons. But many of my clients are Christian and are actually referred to me by Christians, from my own church and churches in the area.

Which brings me back to my Saturday morning trip to my office: if my wife were home I'd have worked, from home, to catch up on my paper work. But since she was out of town I felt like a little adventure. So I drove to the Dublin Bart Station at about 5:30am and took the empty train downtown to my office, grabbed a Mocha and a cream cheese bagel, from a local shop, and walked the two blocks from the station to my "home away from home". The building was deserted and I quickly built a fire in the old fireplace to get the chill out of the air. Max came and sat on the desk watching me as I worked on the insurance papers for my clients and filled in a few charts. This took me till about 11am and then I made myself a big cup of cocoa, lit my pipe, and gazed into the fireplace. When no one is there I can face my chair towards the fire and remove my shoes and place the ottoman inches from the fire. Max came and cuddled in my lap and sat gazing at the flames, with me, until I drifted into unconsciousness.

I could have stayed that way for a few hours, but a light cough brought me back to the real world. I turned and saw a middle-aged woman with curly red hair that hung in wet ringlets down to her shoulders. It had obviously begun to rain harder than when I had arrived. She was wearing a wet olive green raincoat, with a matching floral scarf around her neck, a pair of black clogs with black stockings, and a large black messenger bag was slung across her body. She was a little overweight and appeared to be in her early fifties. She seemed quite nervous and kept fidgeting with her

2

scarf. I motioned for her to sit down, got up, and held out my hands for her wet coat. She handed me the coat and I made her a cup of tea to help her warm up and settle down a bit. Max went over to her and lay on her shoe and this caused her to smile and relax a bit. I smiled wryly and put on my therapist face, as I waited for her to begin.

Her eyes were a bit moist as she cleared her throat to speak, "Do you know Ralph from your church?" I nodded and motioned with my head for her to continue. "He is my cousin and he recommended you as a therapist that I could trust. By the way, my name is Rhoda Cohen Du. My family are converted Jewish Christians. I don't go to your church; I'm in a Messianic Jewish congregation, in Alameda. I teach school, the third grade, part-time, at a little grade school near my home. So coming to see you was a bit of a drive. I hope you will be willing to take my 'case'. Being a teacher, I don't have too much money and this might be one of those long term treatment experiences. I was told by Ralph that you sometimes give 'believer' discounts."

I leaned back in my chair and studied her for awhile. I could tell she was sincere and in a lot of emotional pain. I also had a feeling her story was not going to be simple. "Now why don't you just tell me what happened and we can worry about payment issues later. I can sense God sent you here. Why not just start at the beginning and I'll stop you if I have any questions. Just tell me what you are comfortable with, the rest we can work out later."

She watched me for a few moments, trying to gage in her mind if I was trustworthy or not. "My married last name is Du, my husband is Vietnamese. How he and I met is a long story and though he is involved in this story; he is not why I'm here. I'm here concerning a friend, Alex. This is also not about some affair or something, my husband and I are happily married. I just wanted to clarify that from the get go."

I reached out my hand and introduced myself to her, "My name is Mark" and motioned for her to continue.

"Well, we used to live in Texas during the early part of our marriage and about sixteen years ago we decided to move out here to the Bay Area. My husband is a computer geek and wanted to be near Silicon Valley. I had no real preference about where to live and let him pick the city. This is how we ended up in Alameda.

I found some tutoring jobs right away and then I got a part time job at a school near our home teaching reading. I decided to work part time, since we have a daughter Lelani. She was quite young at the time, around nine. I had not been in a formal church environment, for years, and because I wanted her to be involved in Christian children's groups, I decided to look for a church in my area. We bought a little home about two blocks from a big mega-church and began attending. My husband is not saved yet, another long story, and so he only came with me to church, on occasion. But Lelani and I enjoyed the church very much. She got enrolled in Children's church and I began a ladies Bible Study class. Most of the folks there were rather wealthy and a bit reserved, but I soon had a few lady friends and my daughter, also, began to make friends. I eventually decided to stop working part-time and decided it would be nice to begin to volunteer at church, though I didn't know how to do so. I asked the church secretary and she said I should wait about a year before getting involved. So I just went on Sundays and to the women's Bible study on Thursdays. During that time, the Bible study I was attending was life changing for me; it stressed the importance of serving God. The study's author said we need to keep our eyes open for opportunities. I have always been one of those 'on fire' Christians and really wanted to serve God at my new church, but couldn't see any opportunity. I asked one of my new girlfriends about how she would go about trying to find a niche job at the church. She said to me there was a pastor, whom she knew of, who was looking for a part time assistant, on a volunteer basis. I found out he was my daughter's Sunday school teacher and he had seemed pleasant enough, when I'd meet him in the hallways on the way to my daughter's class. I was not sure what he did, at the church, but later discovered he was the coordinating pastor for the children's ministry. I was thinking I'd like to work for someone like this and since I had been a teacher, children's ministry was right up my alley."

By this time it was getting close to 3pm and I decided to stop her there. "Mrs. Du, let's stop there and I'll make you an appointment for later in the week. What's a good day for you? Is Thursday alright, about 2pm? (She nodded.) Let's try and keep our sessions to about an hour from now on and I'll start asking more questions as time goes on. How's that?

"That would be great. My job hours are flexible, only a couple of hours per week. So I can arrange them around the sessions and I can still get home in time to make dinner for my husband and even beat the traffic. I know my story is a bit tedious, but I think telling you some of the background will help you understand me more, when we get into the meat of the story. Thanks for letting me speak with you like this on your day off." She hugged the cat and gave him a nuzzle and then proceeded to get ready to go out into the misty afternoon. I shook her hand, gave her her now dry raincoat and led her to the door. I then went to the appointment book to make a note, for my secretary, to call her for a good time to schedule in her session.

Then I proceeded to tidy the office and wash the dishes. I double fed and watered the cat, since he wouldn't be seeing me again till Monday and I had forgotten to do so on Friday, put away my papers, put on my outer rain gear and locked the office. It was one of those misty mid afternoons and I took my time walking to the Bart station. I entered the station and pondered the woman who I had just met. I tried to guess what her real reason was for seeing me. Before I knew it I was back to my town. The weather was sunny and warmer in Dublin, but rather than taking off all my gear I turned on the air. Then I picked up a couple of movies from the Library and a steak to barbecue on the grill. When I got back home, I barbecued my steak, poured a glass of wine, and watched a film that my wife would call a guy movie. I don't remember the name of it, now, just that it had car chases and lots of karate. I watched almost the whole thing and went to bed. I spent most of Sunday at my church and had a late dinner with my wife at our favorite bistro, when she returned home from her trip.

My wife and I had an early breakfast on Monday since both of us had full schedules and we both ran out the door together to get to our destinations, only stopping to kiss each other in the driveway. I parked at the Bart station and made my way, with all of the other suburbanites, into the city. As soon as I got into my office, Helen, my secretary, told me that Rhoda had called about her appointment and wanted to know if we had any cancellations, so she could come in as soon as possible. We did and my secretary scheduled her in the cancellation's place. I thanked my secretary and went into my office prepared to meet my 9am. To my surprise it was Rhoda, since Mrs. Thomas had cancelled; she said she could not wait till Thursday to come in. I was glad she could come in sooner. She had only been a minute or two away shopping at the Embarcadero Center Mall, when she decided to call the office and check for a cancellation so she could come in sooner. The secretary told her she could come in in five minutes if she hurried from the Embarcadero Mall. She dashed right over.

I asked her if she wanted a cup of tea and she declined. After a few pleasantries I decided to get into the meat of the appointment. I leaned back in my chair and tapped my pen on the desk, then I said, "I need you to continue from where you left off at our last session. So you began to work for the Children's pastor?"

"Not exactly...he told me to pray about my working for him, for about a month, and then after that month we'd meet again to see if both of us got the same message from God about whether I was to work there or not. Believe me that was a hard month because I like doing things right away and waiting is not my style." She then smiled and said, "Something funny happened around that time, about a week before I was to work for him. I fell in a hole downtown and ripped my tendons in my ankle. I was with my daughter and tried to hop to a pay phone; those were the days before everyone had a cell phone. Alex was driving by at that moment and I tried to flag him down because I needed help. Instead he thought I was waving, waved back, and kept going. A kind stranger eventually helped me and my daughter get home. But I ended up on crutches right before starting my job. His office was on the second floor and I guess my actually getting up the stairs showed him I wanted the job. So I was hired at that meeting and even started working on his files while on crutches. He and a pastor's wife prayed for the healing of my ankle. Since I was no longer teaching, I told him I could work about 30 hours per week for him and even would do some work at home in the evenings for him, if necessary. His office was that extremely messy and chaotic. I knew he needed help and lots of it."

"Were you paid for your work?"

"No it was volunteer work; but another lady at church had told me the only way to get on staff at that church was to volunteer first and then they'd think about hiring me, on a permanent basis, after seeing my performance. Also the Children's pastor told me that he wanted to train me to think like him and learn how to be a pastor. He said he'd teach me computer skills and that he wanted me to arrange a seminar for him. So I saw the time as a preparation for being officially on staff."

"Had you ever done work like that before?"

"Well I'd worked in offices in the past, but I never got too heavily into the computer. The actual job really didn't scare me. It was the having to totally design and arrange a seminar for him that made me nervous. I thought this was a lot of responsibility for a new employee. He seemed to think I could do this and so I began to undertake the giant task from square one. This seminar was going to be for over three hundred churches and their children's ministry workers. While I was to receive some guidance from him and his wife, the majority of the thing was 'my baby'. I can't believe I was asked to do this, now, especially since I had no previous model to work off of and had to do a large part of the work from my home computer, which caused me to not have immediate access to the office information, when I needed it. That eventually caused lots of problems. For the most part I was left to figure out the details on my own. He was never available to give me direction for the seminar."

"Why didn't you express your apprehensions to him? You had a lot of responsibility and little direction."

"Yes, this is true. But he kept telling me how talented I was and I knew too little about the whole project to even know what I didn't know. You know what I mean? (I nodded.) So I proceeded forward with the project, doing the seminar work mainly at night from home. During the day I worked on lesser projects like the volunteer program, curriculum for the Children's classes, paperwork of all sorts, and even janitorial projects. We'd meet for a half hour every morning, during the week, and he'd often come into my office to see how the little projects were coming along. But there was very little talk about the big project, the seminar. Again I knew too little to know what to ask. It was quite stressful and my husband was not thrilled that I was working so much for no pay. Yet he often helped me with computer problems that arose. There was always the promise of being on staff, someday, that kept me going. But the real reason I stayed was a bit more complex."

"Let's just go into this in a light manner today and we can get more into it at our next session, alright? So what were you going to say in a general sense?"

"Well the main reason I stayed on, in spite of his inability to clearly communicate was..." I broke in at that moment.

"Can you give me an example of his not being able to communicate well with you? Something not related to the seminar."

"Well, one day he wanted me to get a poster for a Children's ministry event made. He handed me an eight by ten piece of paper that was a mock up of the poster and told me to go to Kinkos and get a poster made. I had seen his other posters and he had said the shop knew the details of what he wanted. So I went to Kinkos and told them to make a poster and do it according to the previously noted specifications. (He told me they'd made similar posters for him in the past.) They finished it, I then gave it to him and he was very upset and said it should have been 18x24 inches. He made me cut it down to that size and then complained all day that it looked ugly. He said he'd never send me to do that again. I wanted to smack him; but I controlled myself. That type of thing happened about twenty times, but he blamed me each time. Later he'd apologize; but it was always a few days afterward. I learned to forgive this character flaw. But it did frustrate me."

"Please go back to what you saying before; I get what you mean much better now."

"Well, as I was saying, I was becoming his friend a little at a time. He had a really funny sense of humor and this made work fun. He would tell me little stories about his family, his dreams, his difficulties, and in the matter of a few months I felt I'd known him all of my life. He also was a very patient teacher with many of the job skills he needed to teach me. He often told me how I'd go beyond him in the ministry someday. Basically, he told me he wanted me to learn his job and kept telling me how I was doing such great work. He'd let me try my hand at all types of tasks: new computer skills, writing reports, designing volunteer programs, planning events, hiring contractors, on and on. Each task was out of my comfort zone, but I was able to pull them off. This and his praise built up my confidence level and other people began to respect my work. But mainly we were just friends. He went to dinner with my husband and I a few times and he and his family came to our house. His son even pet sat our rabbit during our vacation. My husband had no insecurity about our friendship and laughed at all the stories I told about our day at work and Alex's wild humor. I could go on and on. I guess I'll stop here now. It is kinda weird remembering all of that."

"How so?"

"I guess I have had a bit of amnesia about that time. But I really do have to go. I have to bring my cat to the vet today. Yes, I have a cat too. Wow, I guess I spoke a lot, sorry."

I stood up and picked up Max, who was sleeping on her lap. "Well, I guess this is the point of you coming to see someone like me. You are supposed to open up. You are just doing what you should be doing in an office like this. Let me get the door for you. Why not make another appointment for later in the week with my secretary." I was still holding the cat and I lead her to the door. She shook my hand and thanked me, then with a nuzzle for the cat, she left.

I watched her go to the Bart, from my window and jotted a few notes about our meeting. Then a quiet rapping was coming from my door and my secretary showed Mrs. Finkle, the hypochondriac, in. To be honest I was still thinking about Rhoda, as Mrs. Finkle, rambled on.

Chapter 2

Rhoda couldn't come in until that next Friday. I had an early morning breakfast appointment with a friend and was afraid I'd be late for Rhoda's appointment at 9am. But I got to the office at 8:45am and my secretary handed me my mail and a cup of tea, just as Rhoda walked in the door. I could tell she was chilly so I handed her the tea since I had just come from breakfast and had had about five cups of coffee. I let her get settled while I answered "the call of nature". With that finished, I started up the fireplace and sat down with my wool scarf still draped around my neck. She seemed a bit excited, like she had something to tell me. But instead she calmed herself and said, "Doc, remind me to tell you something at the end of our session. I'm just bursting." I assured her I'd remind her and was a bit bemused that she called me "Doc".

She gathered her thoughts and said, "Now where did I leave off last time...hmmm. Oh yeah, okay. I remember. I was telling you about what a good friendship Alex and I were having and how we worked so well together, except for a few communication problems. Right? (I nodded and she continued.) Well, we were working very hard on the normal daily tasks and on the preparation for the upcoming seminar event. When the date of the seminar got nearer I did start to do more of the work at the office, but still was only allowed to use my home computer. He never told me why. As I mentioned, the event was a huge Bay Area wide workshop for those involved in Children's Ministry programs. It was to run three days and had a few dozen speakers. There also was the setup for each room and the catering for snacks and lunches. I also had to arrange hotel accommodations for the speakers, as well as collect all of the money from each group and do the daily estimates on how many people would be attending. Some of these things changed from day to day and even hour to hour. So it was quite a lot of work and my husband was very patient since it took up a lot of our family time. But it was such a challenge that I enjoyed the whole process immensely. I was working at the church for about thirty hours per week and in the evenings at home till the wee hours of the morning. Yet I hardly noticed since I felt I was really involved in ministry. Everyone told me how wonderfully I was doing."

"What about your daughter, how did you swing caring for her at the same time?"

"Well, her school was next door to the church and if I was not done, she'd just come to the church, otherwise I'd pick her up from school and walk her home. She'd do her homework next to me as I worked, and since other moms had their kids at church, she'd often play with them in one of the classrooms. I'd leave at about 4pm and go home and cook dinner and do a few chores. My husband did start to ask me, more and more, when they were going to pay me for all of my dedication and the head pastor told me if the workshop went well, they'd consider giving me a paid position in the Spring. This seemed more than reasonable to me, since the work was something that fulfilled me. I wanted to do a job where I felt I was in the ministry somehow and also many staff people also taught bible studies and gave other classes, so I thought this job would be a spring board into even greater ministry opportunities. Anyway, I tried to help my husband see he only needed to be patient and then we'd both be happy. He'd get the money from a second income and I'd be fulfilled."

"I assume Alex was married. (She nodded.) So how did Alex's wife appear to take your friendship with her husband and your working for him? Did she seem jealous of all the time you were spending together?"

"Actually she seemed quite comfortable. I am not glamorous, by any means, and I think she saw me as no threat. She'd even give me hints at how to make her husband happier. But she appeared to have no interest in getting to know me. My husband also did not seem to want to know Alex, though I tried to get them to like each other. They seemed to have nothing in common. Oh except they did have the same first name. They both have Alex for a first name. Funny, huh?" She paused as if musing on something, like she was a million light years away.

Then she continued, "Around Thanksgiving I invited Alex and his family over for dinner. His oldest daughter, Lana, did not come, but the two younger sons, Stan and Glen, came, as did his wife, Liz. We had a roaring fire in the fireplace and games for the kids. I cooked the worst dinner of my life, which their five year old son decided to mention. In spite of this, the adults drank wine and we had a nice evening, speaking about superficial aspects of our lives. I was hopeful we might all become friends, but I could see our spouses were just being social and had no real interest in forming friendships."

"Do you think that they cared if you and Alex had a friendship?"

"It didn't appear to bother either of them. Alex loved the holidays and as soon as Thanksgiving time was on the horizon, he became quite cheery. This was not usual for him. Though he often liked to play while he worked, he had a dark side. He seemed borderline bipolar, at times. He could go from a funny playful mood to a dark brooding mood in a matter of minutes. I accepted this character flaw and this acceptance often bewildered him since he had lost many assistants who could not take his mood swings. I always was pretty even keeled and upbeat, in my personality and so I kept being constant in my friendship feelings even when he went up and down. He told me I was one of the longest lasting of his assistants and I had only been there a couple of months. So it was interesting to see him in the totally up mode during the holiday season. As Christmas approached we had extra holiday duties to add to our hectic schedule and this made me feel a bit overwhelmed. There was so much to do and so little time. I also noticed that he and his wife were arguing a lot and that he was staying at the office till past 11pm. I felt sorry for his wife and kids not seeing him. He seemed to feel a sense of freedom at work. His wife would come by to help out, on occasion, and he would seem totally uncomfortable like when you are a kid and your mom comes to school. He also never let me talk to her or would send me home early if she was going to be in the office for a long time. I think she also worked part time as a teacher, at a local Christian school. She seemed to do a lot with their children, but did not seem to be a friend to her husband, like I was to my husband. My husband and I had a great friendship on top of being married. In their case it looked like they were married, but not really friends. Anyway, though I noticed these things, I had a self imposed rule to never talk about our marriages, since I felt that kind of talk might lead to an office romance or something. I made sure that anything I spoke to him about was something I could speak about if my husband was there. Now this is where my story is going to get a bit wild and I hope that you will suspend any judgment, for the time being. Promise me that you'll let me speak openly without judging me or Alex too soon. Promise?"

"Of course, Rhoda, that is the whole point of this profession of mine--objectivity. Don't worry; anything you say now will not shock me. I have heard many wild stories in my time. Please continue." I started to get an inkling about what she was going to say, but I know enough to not jump to conclusions, sometimes there are twists and turns in what might seem to be a run of the mill tale. Also I did promise I wouldn't judge. So I bit the bullet and held back on trying to figure out what she'd say.

She studied my face carefully for a hint of prejudgment and seemingly satisfied; she gathered her strength and continued. "Well, things went on in a pretty mundane fashion until Christmas season. For pastors, Christmas is like Homecoming. It is second to Easter holidays, in importance, and Children's pastors especially get to prove their worth to the church at that time. It seems that head pastors are always looking for ways to trim their budgets and firing a junior pastor or two is always one of their first choices, to help trim the fat. So the junior pastors are always trying to prove how invaluable they are to the corporation. Alex was no different, and so he had to practically perform miracles every year in putting on these Christmas extravaganzas. He used them to show the talents of his kids in Children's Ministry and his ability to be a director and choreographer, with help from the other talented members of the church. Whenever there were

13

other presentations he'd volunteer to put them together; he had this artistic streak. So considering all the work involved, he was given free rein to choose the theme, songs, and performers. This meant long hours spent in his church office and still more hours spent in his home office. He truly had no time to pray and no time to see his wife and kids. This was on top of his daily duties and that seminar. The other pastors, we had seven, seemed to be strangely absent during that time, leaving him with all the work. I don't know how he did it.

The big children's event I was working on was to be held in January and I was working far over my 30hr a week commitment. His work on the Christmas project made him even more inaccessible to answer questions on the Seminar and so I tried, with my husband's help, to figure things out on my own. Alex was very protective of the computers at work and so when we got closer to the event, I was writing all the information I had to download on to the computer on dozens of yellow tablet. I ended up doing my usual office work and reports, plus fielding calls for reservations and making calls to set up hotels and all that type of thing at work, the rest I downloaded at night on my computer. Did I mention, I was also in charge of getting volunteers to do Children's Ministry work, like classes and crafts, and miscellaneous other jobs around the church? That alone was a huge workload. So we were both beyond busy. But he would still take time to come into my office and get a hug, give about two minutes of direction, and have a bit of light banter before the day began. I began to notice, as Christmas approached, that he was more and more depressed. His wife, and rightly so I might add, was a bit upset that she was taking care of their three kids, without any help from him, preparing for the holidays, working at the neighboring church school, and helping him at night with his paperwork. I think she thought with all of that sacrifice he could at least give her and the kids a bit of affection now and again. She was absolutely right, of course, and yet he withdrew from them more and more and when he did interact it was always with an angry spirit. I could see this, but since I had that rule about not discussing our marriages, I kept quiet and prayed for them. I even tried to help him more so that he had a few moments to spend with his family, yet he would just fill in the free time I won for him with even more work. I noticed she did not help him with his paperwork at the office, as much, since he was so snappy during this time. It was not fun for me to be around him, either. I had to forgive him about ten times a day for his insensitivity; I wondered how much more his wife had to put up with, when he wasn't at the office. But we all trudged on and he'd use me as his emotional outlet. He'd sometimes just come and sit in my office, as I worked, silently, to get his head clear and return to work on the Christmas show. I tried to ignore him and keep working. But he'd occasionally joke about how crazy the show process was or how he wasn't sure he'd make it until the children's workshop seminar. I'd listen to him and then tell him, we had better get back to work or we'd never be done with either project. He seemed to need this social interaction time since he was too busy to spend time with family and friends; he was only home to sleep for a few hours each day.

We were speaking about how it was only three days to Christmas and that the ladies group was not even finished decorating the church. He was supposed to have had this all taken care of right after Thanksgiving. But he had trusted them too much and now he'd have to finish it himself before Christmas Eve service. So to give him more family time I volunteered to help him. Christmas Eve morning we went into the storage room and carried out boxes of decorations and candles for the service that evening. You know the candlelight service, that most churches have on Christmas Eve night? So while he strung garland on the ceiling, I put a candle on each chair and finished the trees. Then we both put up these huge angel medallions. This went on nonstop all day. No time for lunch or to sit down. But my energy matched his and I did not complain. A few of the ladies came after school to help us complete our task. My daughter came and I asked her to play with the other church kids while I finished up helping Alex. She skipped off to be with her friends." Rhoda paused and looked a bit sheepish. "I'm speaking too much. Huh? Do you want me to stop?"

I told her that no other clients were coming for a few hours so she should continue and finish her train of thought. I did have my secretary get us a couple of sandwiches and more tea. After we got settled, she continued. I was getting interested and so I didn't really know what time it was and didn't care. I knew my secretary would give me a head's up when another client had arrived.

"As we were working, I looked at my watch and was surprised that it was already 4pm and I had planned to make my husband a special dinner. So I practically jumped off the ladder, gathered my belongings, and ran down the hall to get my daughter. She came bounding out of the room, where she'd been playing with the other kids and ran out the back door to skip in the parking lot area. It was a nice day. I was rushing after her when Alex came up beside me. I told him I had to run home because my husband was coming home soon and I had to make Christmas Eve dinner for him. Alex then began to say how lucky my husband was to have a good wife like me and how he hoped my husband appreciated me, etc. Compliments about what a good wife and mother I was kept pouring out as we walked toward the door. Though in normal circumstances I'd have been glad someone noticed, in this situation I began to feel like this was a little creepy. I actually got tears in my eyes because I could sense he was not himself and maybe not too stable. I thought that I'd try to talk to him after the holiday about how he needed to spend more time with his wife and possibly see a therapist or someone similar. I was a teacher and he seemed a bit needy, like a few of the students that were not really feeling the love at home and so they'd cling to me during the day at school. He reminded me of them at that moment. I didn't want him to see how upset I was, so I walked a bit quicker to get outside before him and find my daughter. As soon as I got out the door into the cool air I felt a bit better and was motioning to my daughter to come with me, but she was too into playing a jumping game. Alex caught my arm and said, 'you're not leaving without a hug for Christmas, are you?' I felt a bit unsafe for some reason and reluctantly gave him a cool hug. But then I realized he was not letting me go. I thought that this was not a funny joke and began to push him away; but he had one of my hands behind my back and my other arm was in a weird position. Also I was off balance and falling backwards, a bit. I didn't want to fall in the parking lot and so a struggle ensued. He was trying to tip me backwards and kiss me and I was trying not to fall and to not be kissed. This was not romantic to me in anyway; it was terrifying. Many thoughts rushed through my mind, 'should I scream', 'should I kick him and beat the living tar out of my boss and friend' (who was obviously crazy), 'will my daughter see this', 'I love my husband', 'this guy is my best friend; what is he doing', 'this doesn't happen to someone like me', on and on. Then I prayed, 'Lord help me'. As all of this struggle, outwardly and inwardly, was taking place he was whispering, 'I love you, Rhoda, I love you.' I thought, 'Is he crazy? I love my husband and have never given him any signals that I felt anything, for him, but friendship." Now I was really afraid, since this was so out of character for him and so I asked God again for help. I then said, for some reason, in a baby voice, that wasn't mine, 'I love you too.' I didn't mean that, but at the speaking of that phrase, he let me go and said, 'Really?' 'Oh yes really', I said as I picked up my belongings and ran and grabbed, my still out of it, daughter, by the arm. I was totally unhinged. I had to pass him to get out of the parking lot and run home and he said, in a chipper voice, 'see you Monday'. He said that statement, like what just happened, hadn't happened. I grabbed my daughter's arm and literally ran the few blocks home, stopping to throw up twice, crying my eyes out, the whole way. My daughter kept saying, 'is something wrong, Mom?' I told her I was sick and had to get to bed and that she should tell Dad, when he came home, I didn't feel well. To be honest I didn't feel well. I was nauseous and dizzy and I fell into a deep sleep as soon as my head hit the pillow. I was awoken a few hours later by my husband who could tell I was not myself and I apologized for missing dinner. He said he'd taken my daughter out for a burger and then I fell into a deep sleep again.

Christmas morning my husband and I went to the church service and I tried to pretend everything was okay. But it wasn't obviously. I spent the day, robotically, doing all the Christmas things, opening gifts, making cookies with my daughter, and making a big dinner. I was a shell of myself. I did all the things on the outside normally; but inside I was dying. My mind was spinning and in turmoil. 'My best friend tried to hurt me?' 'Did I do anything to encourage this behavior?' 'I'm not that cute. Why would he pick me?' These and many thoughts swam through my head. I finished cleaning up from the day about 8pm and went to bed again falling into a deep stupor. I woke about 1am to violent crying and shaking. But I could not tell my husband about what happened. I didn't want him to hate Alex, make me leave my church career, and hate Christianity. I decided I had to cover up the mess and figure out how to deal with it. I kept getting up to weep and shake and pray for a few days. In the meantime I had to perform as usual in all of my daily tasks. I tried to be a good actress and succeeded. My daughter was the only one who knew her mom was not her normal self. I was not sure how much she had seen if anything. I decided to pretend the incident never happened and tried to forget about it. But I could not and was now weeping during the day. as I worked, as well as during the night." She brushed away a couple of stray tears and I wondered what I was going to say about this seduction scene, she had presented. I handed her a Kleenex and began to rub my chin and think of how I should approach a subject like this. Then she spoke again, "Speaking of time, I have to stop here with my story and get home to prepare my husband's dinner again. Can I see you again next week and tell you the rest?"

"Of course", I said quietly. "Oh yes, before you go, you said you wanted to tell me something, remember?"

"Oh yes. Right before I came here today Alex called and told me he wanted to finally reconcile." I'm not sure how he wants to do this yet. I'll let you know when I know. She seemed genuinely happy and this concerned me in light of what she just shared.

"Are you sure this is wise, I mean do you feel safe to do this?"

"Oh, so sorry Doc," she chuckled a bit, "I'm leaving you in the middle of my story. I guess I'd say the same thing you just said, if I only had the info you have up to now. But don't worry when you know more of the story you'll agree this is a good, no, a great thing. Really." She stood up and put on her coat. It was raining again and I handed her one of my spare umbrellas. She squeezed my elbow and gave the cat a pat on the head and I opened the door for her. She went over to my secretary's desk to make an appointment and gave me a little wave. I nodded and went back to my office to pray for wisdom, both for her meeting with Alex and for me to help her heal.

The next Wednesday I had barely gotten off my coat, when my secretary popped her head in the office, "There is a call for you on line two. The guy's name is Alex. Would you like me to get you coffee and a bagel with lox smear, next door?"

"Yes, but make that a soy chai, okay? Thanks." I got comfortable, even lighting the fire and putting on my slippers before I pushed the button for line two. Alex was clearing his throat and stuttering a bit. So I said, "I know this is a hard call for you to make, but just relax. You are safe here." I could actually hear his sigh of relief on the other side of the phone. "I suppose you are making this call as a response to the call you had with Rhoda earlier? By the way, it is only eight-thirty. Are you both going to meet?"

"Hello, my name is Alex. I had wanted to meet with Rhoda but I bumped into her in a dark coffee shop and she mentioned I might want to do it the right way, by meeting with you as our go between."

"Well, first of all won't you be putting your job in jeopardy? Aren't you forbidden to speak to me?

"Did Rhoda tell you this?" He sounded a bit betrayed. "She said she'd told very little of the story."

"Actually she didn't say anything about this issue. I just worked in churches in the past and I know how controlling they can be. So I just guessed. Is this what is going on with you?" I tried to sound reassuring so he wouldn't get skittish. I could feel him getting more relaxed again.

"Funny you'd ask. Just last week the pastor that was my main controller, Stan, retired. That's actually why I finally called Rhoda. I don't have to be subject to him anymore. So I don't have that obstacle in my way any longer. Also we have a new head pastor and some of the other lower level pastors have also left. So I don't feel any restrictions in that area. But I still need to keep this hush hush just in case. Okay? I'll tell you more when I meet you. How should we set this up, anyway? I've never seen a therapist. My church believes it is a sign of spiritual weakness to see one of you guys."

"Alex, I'd like to wait a week to see you. Will you promise me you won't change your mind in the meantime? You see I'd like to see Rhoda one more time alone first. It will help me have better questions for you.

How is next week on Wednesday? I think I have a block of time open from 8-10am. Will that work for you?" I hoped it would since I didn't want to schedule him out too far. I thought he might have a change of heart.

"Wednesday at 8am, hmmm, yeah that would work. My work insurance covers this sort of thing and so I won't have to break the bank to see you. Should I schedule a time with your secretary?"

"No, don't bother I'll let her know. Oh yes, one more thing don't speak to Rhoda till after your appointment. It can muddy things up a bit. I'll tell her I told you not to contact her till after next Wednesday. I think that's it. Can't wait to meet you." He said good-bye and then he hung up the phone. I got up and told my secretary to schedule him for 8am the following Wednesday.

My secretary did so right in front of me and as I turned to go into the office to prepare for my next patient, she said, "I just wanted to tell you that Rhoda will be coming in this Friday, at 10am." My secretary knows me so well that even if I do not speak with her about a client (I can't really anyway because of client confidentiality laws) she is able to pick out those that are of a special interest to me and she gives me a heads up.

I smiled and said, "Thanks, Helen," and plodded back to my desk. I just had time to flush the cat's business before my first "in person" client arrived. Yes, it was the hypochondriac. Her husband was quite wealthy and traveled a lot for business, so she was a frequent visitor. I truly think she came in more out of loneliness than anything else. She was seventy-five and healthy as a horse. But she needed a friend and paid for me to be that. She had no intention to change her health fixations at her age. She enjoyed visiting with me and the other doctors in our area too much. We were her paid friends. Actually, most therapy is a substitute for a good friend.

Chapter 3

$\mathcal{M}$rs. Kent, a mother of a troubled teen, had an appointment at 9am that Friday. She was quite emotional during her visit and it took a lot out of me. So I was actually happy that Rhoda was ten minutes late. It was just enough time for me to grab a cup of cocoa and make one for her. I covered it with a napkin to keep it warm. I stood to turn up the fire and as I was placing a couple of logs on fire, Rhoda came in out of breath and flushed. I hung her coat by the fire to dry and handed her a cup of cocoa. She gratefully accepted it. "The bridge was packed, there must have been an accident, and so this is why I'm totally late. Sorry, doc. I didn't take Bart today 'cause I've got loads of errands to run after I see you." I understood about the traffic, but wasn't too happy about the errands. I prefer if clients have a light day after a session so that they can mull over what we talk about. I think it reinforces the time. But I didn't say anything to her since she was already stressed.

"Rhoda, what I'm looking for today is a general picture of what occurred after the *attack*." (I purposely used a strong word here to see her reaction to it.) If you can start from Christmas day and proceed from there till today, in a general fashion, that would be great. I want to get the full picture and then we can break it down into bits in our following sessions." I felt like the father from that old show "Father Knows Best", for some reason. But though we were similar in age, I had a fatherly/big brotherly feeling towards her and somehow more so on that day.

"Before I start, I gotta know. Did Alex call you and is he willing to meet with you?"

"Yes, he called. We are meeting next Wednesday at 8am. I did tell him not to call you till after we meet so don't get all nervous that he hasn't called. He called me at 8:30am on Wednesday. We had a nice little chat. He sounds like a kind man."

"Uh, oh, yeah, he is. Just wanted to know. Okay, so Christmas morning I got up early and my husband, daughter, and I went to church. Alex looked over my way, but did not come and greet us. I was thankful for that and determined I'd speak to him about the incident on Monday. But when Monday came I found out from the church secretary that Alex and his wife were in LA on some sort of pastor's retreat or something. I tried to reach him on his cell phone and he answered and said, rather shortly, he didn't want to talk about anything until he got back. So I tried to keep going on with my work on the Seminar project, I kept up a frantic pace until he returned a few days later. He called me into his office for a meeting to see how the project was going and I told him a few points and then stared at him in disbelief, wondering if what had happened really happened. He did not bring up the subject and his impersonal manner caused me to start to cry. I could not stop and he had the audacity to say I was bothering him with my crying and maybe I should go home. I told him I needed all of my papers. So I remained in the office and we stayed in our own corners for a few days, coming into work and not speaking. I tried to put it out of my mind, as though it didn't happen and tried to speak to him without crying. That was hard, I'd do well for most of our meeting and then I'd break down and cry again and this would bug him. But on we trudged through our project and I even was able to forgive him and go forward. Until...(she swallowed hard and cleared her throat) about two weeks into January. I always went to the office before him. It opened at 8am and he came in at nine. I got there at 8am; I think it was a Tuesday. I went into my office to pray, as was my custom before beginning work for the day, and began to cry my heart out to God and was asking God why (concerning the whole situation). When he quietly came downstairs and tapped me on the shoulder. I was so sad I started crying and he gave me a hug which I thought was normal, in the situation. But then it turned ugly because he got 'excited' and I broke free from the situation and jumped back. I said, 'No!' and tried to change the situation around. 'We need to go and set up the chairs for this morning's women's meeting.' He got all flushed and said he couldn't walk yet and I should go and start setting up the chairs. I sat in the chair behind me and just stared at him for a moment. I kept shaking my head since I could see he was in a bit of pain, but at the same time I wanted to belt him. But he was my boss and I was having a battle within myself. 'If I start to shout at him I'll probably get fired, the Children's workshop wouldn't get done, all of my hard work will go down the drain, my proposal for real full-time employment was on the head pastor's desk, our spouses will hear about this, there'll be a church investigation, he might get fired, on and on.' And to top it off I was really mad, but still his friend. So I went upstairs and set up the chairs and back to my office to finish my work for the day. Before leaving I again prayed and started to cry. I began to feel a bit despondent and realized I was trembling." She stopped there, wiping a few tears from her eyes.

"So why didn't you just quit right there and then? Why was working at the church so important?"

She looked at me for a few moments and began to shake her head. "You know, Doc, that is a perfectly rational question; but at the time I was not a rational person. The church made a big thing about being on staff. If you were on staff and had an in with the pastors, it was like you walked on water or something. I did not want to lose that possible position that I was applying for with the head pastor. He kept hinting to me that it was only a matter of time before I joined, "the elite". Just working for Alex as a volunteer had a certain status and I liked that feeling of having others look up to me. One mother at church, pointed me out to her little daughter and said, "That is Rhoda, she gives her life for the church and God's people. She works for Pastor Alex." I was being noticed for my service. So I tried to again go forward as if nothing happened. My daughter was on school break and I had her sit in my office, as a kind of protection for me, hoping

Alex would cool down and go back to his old self. He would come in my office and try to get me to go out with him into the hallway or whatever, but I'd use my daughter as an excuse or say that I was really trying to get the project done. I made sure he and I were never alone. Yet I was still considering him as a friend, as a friend I was momentarily ticked with. But I started to not be able to sleep, I lost weight from not eating, I kept crying, and I started to feel like I was losing it. I even began to consider suicide because I was so despondent and depressed. I was also sad because I did not feel I could share this with my husband for a variety of reasons. And yes I still had that blankety-blank project to finish. How I was even able to concentrate on that job, I can't figure it out now, but I did. Kind of." Again she started to shake her head in unbelief. She picked up Max, began stroking him and stared out the window. It was like she was looking back over the plains of time.

"Rhoda, what do you mean by kind of?"

"Well...this is kind of funny, now, but churches would call in daily and say how many people they had that were attending the workshop, then they'd give their church's name and they did not have to give an address until the actual day of the workshop when they registered. We kept a running toll of the funds that each church was going to pay and the amount of food that would be needed. This may sound efficient. But... two things did not work: first the amounts of the funds were hard to compute because some churches had three even four names, for example: New Life, Abundant Life, Life Abundant, etc. and to make things more confusing, a new person from that church would call in each time, which would make it seem like a new church was calling in each time. Each person who called, called the church a different name and didn't know that others had called us from their church. Ugh. Then Alex did not let me use the office computers for the project. So I did the work at home not knowing the church was Windows95 and we were Windows97 and that the two were not compatible. So on registration day there were many less people and thus less funds and less need of food. And the down loaded programs from the Windows97 computer at my home did not connect with the church's Windows 95 and so all of the data was off. We did not know any of this until we began the registration process that morning. What confusion it caused. Some churches also decided to bring extra people with and the whole thing got out of control. Since he was not speaking with me daily neither of us caught this. I even got accused of stealing the missing funds for awhile. To be honest he dropped the ball on this one; but I bore the brunt of the whole mess. Man!"

I could see this still bothered her. "Why do you think this still bothers you?"

"I never got to explain myself and was accused of something that was really his fault. I felt that he did not respect me enough to sit down and ask me what happened. I felt he wanted to get to know me better sexually, but did not want to get to know me as a person. Anyway when the workshop was over I had less work and was more able to think on all the things that had recently happened. Then I really began to get depressed because I had waited for an apology and none came. So I decided to make a formal meeting with him in his office. But he didn't want to meet. I was crying whenever we sat down to have our morning assignment meetings and he was getting nervous. My home life, my faith, my job at the church, everything was affected. I wasn't sleeping; it was a hard time for me, and my best friend, Alex, couldn't even speak with me about this. So I decided to go and see another pastor at the church and get some guidance because this was all beyond me. I did not understand the implications of church politics or I would have never done this. I was very naive. So I went into the office of a pastor that seemed to like both Alex and myself, and I was looking for a possible bridge, if you will, to link us back together. It was Pastor Stan. He was a tall, lean, and a bit of a cool (cold) person, whom I thought would be able to help us without getting too emotionally involved. I went into his office and had a hard time beginning since he had a scowl on his face and such cold gray eyes. I immediately wanted to run out of his office. I started to feel I had better choose my words carefully around this fellow. I told him that I was having trouble with one of the people from the office and needed his advice. He asked me what it could be, thinking it was a little women's issue maybe about some sort of office trivia. I told him that one of the people in the office had made unwanted sexual advances towards me. When I said that, he jumped out of his chair and demanded to know who it was. He guessed several of the janitors. I kind of got a bit angry that it would have had to be a janitor. I'm not gorgeous; but why were janitors the only possible culprits? Funny, I could tell that he wasn't mad, on my behalf; he was mad that someone had done something he could not control. I said I did not come to turn anyone in, but to speak about how to deal with the situation on my side. He then sat down looking at me intently and said I should make a formal appointment to speak to the man and confront him. I told him I would do that and rose to leave. He kept staring at me and said he wanted me to come and see him after the appointment and that he thought he knew who it was, already. I left and began to tremble seeing that this man would not help me and my friend. I wanted Alex to learn to act correctly; but I did not wish to harm him or his career. I knew if I took this one step further my friend would be in danger of losing his job. That was not my intention. I made the appointment to see Alex but I determined to never speak to Stan again. Wow I haven't remembered that for ages."

I had figured the story might go this way, but I again stopped myself from being judgmental and said, "So you made the appointment and how did that go?" From working at church, I knew that Stan would have gone immediately to Alex and warned him not to say anything real to Rhoda and then he would have put the fear of God in Alex about the possible loss of his job. The old me would have done this, too. I have been free from legalism for years now. I wondered if Rhoda would have caught on to this behind the scenes drama.

"Well, I went into Alex's office and he did not face me when we talked and on top of this he was trembling. It was obvious that Stan had threatened him, prior to my arrival. I knew nothing of value would come from that meeting. And do you know what he said? (I shook my head and she continued.) He said, 'I'm sorry if you are upset and I apologize if I ever did anything that could have hurt you.' First of all those were not his words and secondly I could tell he was lying. I began to shake and cry. I said, 'What are you talking about? You know what you did. Did Stan talk to you?' He turned to me and said under his breath, 'I'm really sorry.' He got beet red and made a sign with his eyes that someone was listening in the hallway. I got up and left. I was hurt and angry for his lack of ability to stand up for me. I did cool down and thought I'd give the matter some time to work itself out. I did not hear anything for about a week, except that the church had assigned a woman to work over me in my office. She was to be a go-between between me and Alex and to keep us from speaking to each other. She told me I could only communicate to him through her. But Alex always made sure to bump into me in the halls or speak to me when she wasn't at work. But I wasn't in the speaking mode, especially since she had what I had wanted, a paid position. I still wanted a chance to speak honestly with him and make things right; but it was not looking like that would ever happen.

Then one day Stan called me into his office and told me I was never to speak to Alex again. He said that Alex had said he no longer wanted to talk to me, yet he had tried three times earlier that day. When I saw that Stan was not only a liar, but not for me in any way; I tried to get out of the situation. But Stan told me that he might let me speak to Alex in a year if I agreed to let him (Stan) counsel me and take a class called Cleansing Stream. I wanted to speak to my friend again and so I agreed thinking that they'd let me speak to Alex once they saw that I was innocent on my side and willing to do their ridiculous counseling and class. I also thought that Alex would eventually repent and help make things right. Little did I know what lay ahead of me." She looked sad and was staring out the window.

Our time had already gone over and I could guess the rest from being in church situations myself, in the past. She'd never be given permission to speak with her friend and they'd make life miserable for her. But I wanted to hear her spin on this all too common story. However I did have another client coming, so I said, "Rhoda, I'm so sorry we have to end this session. I have another client coming in a few minutes. I have the gist of the thing. Let's meet after my time with Alex and we can get more specific. I was involved in church situations for years and I kind of see where this will be going. I want to hear your unique take on this; but I think I've gone enough into this to start my sessions with Alex. Over the next few months we will dig deeper into the whole matter and when the time is right I'll have the both of you come in together. Please know you can trust me and that I have confidence to help you both out." I helped her on with her coat and she made an appointment with my secretary. I then escorted my next client into my office.

I didn't have any other clients to see, after the client I saw, who came in after Rhoda. So after working on my notes for the day, I asked my secretary to go and get me a Chai and a lox and cream cheese bagel. When she returned I told her she could set up the answering machine and go home early if she liked. She thanked me because her daughter had a school play that evening and this way she would be able to help her get ready. I wasn't being as generous as she thought. I had wanted to be able to rev up the fireplace, eat my snack in peace, and be alone with my thoughts. When you are a therapist some clients are more than just cases; there is a connection. We often ponder their cases a bit more than the average case. That afternoon I thought about Rhoda and her sad situation. Her trust had been broken on so many levels: her friendship with Alex, Pastor Stan's not supporting her, and her relationship to her church. All three relationships were supposed to be safe, and though I had not heard the full story yet, I could tell from past experiences that she'd been betrayed on each level. Sadly this type of situation is too common in the church and no one ever stands with these victims. They've become the modern version of lepers and no one will go near them to protect their own ministries. After praying for her and Alex, who was also a victim of the system, I closed the office and stepped out into the soft but chilly rain.

Chapter 4

Meeting Alex was a bit of a surprise for me. I expected some glitzy Hollywood type of pastor.

Someone who was super attractive; who would sweep women off of their feet. But in front of me stood a rather short (about 5'4") slight man. He was athletic, but not in a muscle bound way, but more of a wiry, hyper type way. He had blond, surfer dyed hair and a pleasant face that was wrinkled from being outdoors a lot. He did have mesmerizing brown eyes that were the Latin lover type and yet he was Caucasian probably of British decent. Not your typical Lothario, for sure; but I could see how ladies would go for his eyes. He was very nervous and kept fidgeting, so I asked him to sit down, gave him a little stool for his feet, and offered him an afghan. I also gave him a cup of cocoa, hoping he'd soon relax. When I saw him pick up Max, that is when I finally spoke. "Now Alex, I sort of know why you are here; but I'd like to hear you speak for yourself. Rhoda is a nice woman and all; but she only knows one side of the story-- hers. The old saying is correct, there really are two sides to every story and each is equally valid. From what Rhoda told me you never felt quite safe at your church to speak out, but here you can feel safe. I'm not quick to judge someone and even if I do, inwardly, that is nothing for you to worry about. I am a true professional and know how to separate my feelings from my desire to do what is best for my client. Also nothing you say here will ever get back to your church; unless you tell them. I don't recommend that, because I'm not sure they have your best interest at heart. Do you see where I'm coming from and are you comfortable with this?" He nodded and seemed to tear up a bit. "Now why don't you start on how you got to be a pastor at your church; just a brief summary will do."

He cleared his throat and kept staring at Max. "Well, I got into trouble with the law for petty crimes when I was a teenager. I was saved as an older teen and from the beginning felt I had a call on my life. I knew my dad would not think that Christian service was a real job. So I decided to work for awhile and send myself to school to be a Forest Ranger, since I love the outdoors so much. I did that for a few years and then I went to the University of California, at Humboldt. It was in school, that I met my wife, Liz, she was a year younger than me and there for Christian education. I honestly married her thinking that marriage would help me settle down. I always had a thing for the ladies and was seeing multiple girlfriends, at the same time, for years. I have to admit they were not pure relationships and, being a Christian, I always felt a bit guilty about that. I thought a good girl would help me fly straight. She and I had gotten a bit closer than she liked and I thought I should marry her. I was afraid she might become pregnant without the benefit of marriage and I needed a break from my partying ways. I stayed on an extra year at school to get a minor in Christian education. But my real love was being a ranger and when school ended I got an assignment in Northern California and we went and lived in the ranger housing unit there. I had a real hard time adjusting to marriage; it took me at least seven years to feel comfortable. (My daughter was born during that time.) I felt Liz, was controlling me all the time. I have to admit I have had a bit of a roving eye and over the years I did cheat on her a few times; they weren't anything serious. But somehow we always got back together. People have said over the years, "Why didn't you just divorce her and be single?" I've thought about it many times and even though I strayed a few times, something about her always drew me back. Maybe I do love her and that's why I can't make a clean break.

We moved to a little town near San Francisco and I worked at a factory for Clorox Bleach, for a time, while I also worked part time for a small church. I eventually got into working with the kids there and became a friend to the head pastor. I don't know why I did so well with kids. I, myself, eventually, had three kids and they always felt like a bit of a burden to me. Don't get me wrong I loved to take them on trips and tried to spend time with them, but I started to feel kind of tied down and like I couldn't be as free as I had been. So in a way I did better with other people's kids. Like the old saying goes, 'you can send them home at the end of the day'."

He seemed to feel a bit ashamed at admitting this and looked out the window caught up in his own thoughts.

I broke in for a moment, by clearing my throat, and looked at him. He was obviously in his fifties; but was trying to look younger by the way he dressed, he wore clothes like a seventeen year old skate boarder, right down to the way he bleached his hair. He also tried to carry himself like a younger man and tried to talk like he was in his twenties. He was ultra clean and didn't have an extra ounce of fat anywhere on his body. You could tell from this that he liked outdoor sports and excelled at them. I thought he seemed like he either rode a bike or rollerbladed. He seemed to be someone who wanted to stay forever young.

So I asked him, "Did you feel more secure in your marriage as you got more towards middle age?"

He said, rather thoughtfully, "Well just when I was getting used to the whole parenting thing, with the older two kids, we had another surprise baby. This threw a wrench in my dream of going with my wife on long trips and finally getting free from the responsibilities of fatherhood. This third child is a great kid, don't get me wrong; but he came just when I thought I was going to be free and young enough to enjoy life. It was at that time that I began to get more involved in ministry at my church. I was working, doing more ministry in that small church, and not home much. I was surrounded by women and many of them seemed like they thought I was the greatest thing, kind of a rock star. I liked all the hero worship and I again started to stray. I soon had a little woman on the side, which I only saw at church and no one knew about it. We were very discreet and I always tried to look like I didn't like her much in public. We often had lunch together or we'd sneak out in my van for a few stolen moments. Did

I love her? No, not really, but she filled a need I had for someone to tell me how great or how cute I was. This lasted a little over a year. I did all I could to keep my wife from finding out."

I looked at him wondering how a rather regular looking fellow like him could go over so well with so many women. I had only one other girlfriend besides my wife, before I got married and they were the only two women to ever seem to notice me. "So didn't you feel any guilt deceiving your wife and also having an affair while you were doing ministry for the Lord? Didn't you feel you were living a double life? A lie?"

"You know actually I felt nothing, no remorse, no guilt, and definitely no love for the woman. She was married and she had guilt feelings like that. She always told me she was going to break it off and that her husband would leave her and her daughter, if he found out. She also told me he'd kill me. That made me a little nervous, the threat of this guy killing me and all. But otherwise I slept great and did such a great job at the church that everyone was praising me and my natural ability to work with kids. They said I had a gift. I was able to come up with great programs and my pastor friend noticed this. He said to me, 'if I ever leave here; I'm taking you with me. I've just got to have you as my children's pastor.' I kind of believed him; but thought maybe this was just something nice to say to me. He didn't know I was leading a double life. I found out he was interviewing for a job in a rich community near San Francisco and that the church there really liked him. I had just brought a small house, in our little town, and did not really want to move. So my wife and I were kind of not really sure I'd follow him to his next assignment. But then one day all 'Hell' broke loose. My girlfriend got overwhelmed with guilt and told her husband everything. I didn't know this for a few days, since I had gone to a children's worship workshop with my wife. She and I had actually had a nice time together and I began to think I'd better figure out how to get rid of the girlfriend and give being faithful another try. But…..when we got back from the trip my pastor friend called me into his office. He told me to shut the door and sit down. I knew something was wrong. He told me my girlfriend's husband had told him everything about his wife and our relationship and that he wanted to hear from me if all this was true or not. The whole thing was quite emotional, since I could see how let down my friend was, and that he was highly concerned about his upcoming new job and his reputation as a pastor, by being associated with me. Even more than this, he was concerned for my soul. Also I had finally decided that I wanted to be fulltime in the ministry and thought that this was all rather bad timing. On top of this I thought my wife would find out and this would mess up my relationship with my kids and would blow the false front I'd been building, so carefully, all of those years. I also knew I was almost forty and that I didn't think I could start again. So I actually started to cry. Maybe I cried for the wrong reasons and I guess I cried because I got caught. I had been under a lot of pressure. But I really cried. I admitted the whole thing was true and that I had deceived everyone for a long time and begged him to not tell my wife. I could see he was torn. I had this great gift, he liked my wife and family like they were his family, and if this got out he'd never get that new job. So...he grabbed me by the shoulders and told me I was to never see my girlfriend again. He also told me that he would have to speak to my wife. But that he'd try and convince her to stay with me. On top of all this he told me either I joined him at his new church or he'd throw me to the lions. So much at one time! I was desperate. So I let him fix the situation. He spoke with my girlfriend and her husband and told them they could have the children's ministry position at our old church; but that he would make sure I never came near the wife again. This seemed to appease them; but he made them sign a statement that they'd never tell anyone what happened as long as I was alive. This made the husband angry; but he finally gave in when the pastor offered them one of the best salaries, ever, in a small church. He also made sure that the next pastor agreed to the same conditions. Then he called my wife and had her come into the office. I sat in the hallway for over an hour and you could hear my wife crying. She had the baby with her and he'd cry every once in awhile, and she'd try to comfort him and then she'd cry. It was the worst hour of my life. The pastor then called me in and we sat together staring forward, the baby was squirming and my wife kept crying. She kept saying she did not know why she wasn't enough for me and why I kept trying to find other women and how could she not have known about this affair. On and on. I became uncomfortable. Finally I said I would make every effort to be all that she wanted and that I was willing to move far away from the other woman and try and start again. My pastor encouraged her that this would be the best thing and that she should give me one last chance. He knew I could change. Well, that was what happened in the office... But when we got home there was quite a fight. Our two older kids locked themselves in their rooms and my older girl brought the baby with her. There was a lot of shouting and throwing things and even swearing. She took the kids with her and went to her mother's house for almost a month. I had to explain to people at church that she was visiting her mom before we moved. The pastor called me up front and told everyone what a great children's pastor I was and how he needed me in the San Francisco area church. He then introduced my ex-girlfriend and her husband as the new children's pastors. Now that was totally uncomfortable, but we all tried to play our parts. My wife decided to return after seeing I was really leaving, but she did not speak to me or let me touch her for almost a year. We couldn't sell the house and we had to get renters and this was a big financial strain for us. Also we had all of the moving expenses and start up costs that came with moving to a new place. So my wife had to take a job doing substitute teaching when we got to the new place and we had ladies from the church watch our youngest. In time my cousin, who lived nearby and attended the church, let the kids come to her house and she watched all of them. When they got older I got my cousin a job at the church. We were able to get a church owned home to rent and this cut down on the costs and we got back on our feet, financially, in a couple of years. It was at my three year mark, that I again began to feel my old wandering eye return. I approached a couple of women and one even reported it to the pastor; but since nothing had really happened, they dropped the issue. He told me I'd never be able to become a senior pastor, with my 'women' problem. He also said that I'd have to have another pastor 'over me', to be accountable to, as long as I was at the church. Now that really rubbed me the wrong way. The guy they put over me was one serious guy, who almost never laughed, except at people, and who judged me from day one. In public I tried to look like I liked the guy, but he really bugged me."

"You must mean Pastor Stan?" He nodded.

I was really getting into his story when I realized he had been speaking a long time, about an hour and a half. I looked at my watch only to discover that Mr. Stevens was going to be coming in, in fifteen minutes. I couldn't have Alex continue. So I said, "Excuse me, Alex, I need to cut this short." He seemed a bit miffed because he thought he was being open with me. But in reality I saw that this was a person, who used a lot of words. He was, however, absolutely disconnected from his feelings and from the affect his words and actions had on others. I pitied the man. He really could not see how cold and unfeeling he was. Anyway, I got up from my chair and shook his hand. "I'm so glad to have met you and I hope you will continue to come to see me. I've really learned a lot about you from this meeting." He seemed puzzled at this statement, thinking he hadn't said much; but in reality he said more than his words alone let on. I started to see his heart and it wasn't a pretty sight. But I thought that God could give me the wisdom to help this man, someday, come in touch with his real feelings. Perhaps he could learn to love his wife in the way she deserved. Of course I also hoped to help him and Rhoda heal their friendship. I led him into the hallway and he made his next appointment with my secretary. He seemed a bit leery of me, but resigned to trust me, since he thought he had been more open with me than he had been with anyone for years. In churches like his there is no trust, since people are expected to always tell the leadership everything, full discloser about yourself and about anything you know about others. Especially anything someone tells you in confidence. He would have to trust that I did not "swing" that way.

Chapter 5

Rhoda left a voice mail for me asking me if Alex had come in to see me and letting me know she'd made an appointment to see me the next Monday. She said she was just "dying" to know what Alex had said. Of course, I wouldn't be able to share anything with her, because of patient confidentiality issues; but I thought I'd explain all of that at our next meeting, instead of getting back to her by email or voice mail. I try not to chat with patients on the phone between meetings. I told my secretary about this, since I had a feeling Rhoda might call to see if I'd gotten her voice mail.

She was exactly on time the following Monday, at 10am sharp. I could tell she was all a brim with curiosity; but I cooled her down quite a bit when I told her about the patient confidentiality issue. I also reassured her it also went the other way that she might see the value of this rule, if she thought about her own situation and all she had told me. She agreed and then settled down enough for us to talk.

I asked her if she'd like a cup of tea. She shook her head, "No" and so we began to get into the real heart of her story. "The last time we spoke you had mentioned your not so pleasant relationship with Pastor Stan. Did you have more you wished to say about this?"

She looked down at Max, who was snuggled next to her ankle, and gave a wry smile. "Wow. You get right to the heart of the matter don't you? Pastor Stan had been someone I knew, before I knew Alex. He and his wife had come to our home for dinner a few times. I don't really know if I mentioned this. But he had the personality of a stone, so I actually had no desire to really get to know him or his wife, who was a nice enough lady from Finland, but a bit too phony to be my type. She wasn't too high, on my list of people I wanted to know better. I didn't really pursue getting to know either of them, as more than acquaintances, before this incident. But I still thought he'd be good to speak with in a counseling mode, since he also knew Alex. If I had known that Pastor Stan was such a legalistic a person to talk to, about an issue of this caliber, then I'd not have gone into his office for help in this matter. But once you talk to Stan about something on this subject, I'm speaking of sexual matters; he becomes like a Pit Bull with a bone. He can't just let it go, no way, no how."

I could see this subject was rather difficult for her to discuss, even more than what happened between her and Alex. "Rhoda, do you feel that Stan overstepped his bounds; if so how?"

"Honestly I fear he raped me spiritually. Let me give you an example. One day he made an appointment to see me to talk to me about not trying to reconcile with Alex. I came into the office about three minutes early. He had me sit in a conference room and said he'd be back. Next door I could hear him shouting at someone and realized it was Alex. I could not really make out the words, except for, "you'd better not do that!!! And "I told you so!!!!!!!!!!" Lots of shouting from Stan and Alex was crying. Then there was a lot of door slamming and running. Stan then entered into the conference room that I'd been waiting in all flushed and out of breath. Then he said, wagging his finger at me, 'as for you...' He told me that he could not believe that Alex would ever try to attack me, that he had asked him and seen innocence in his eyes. He said that I was lying; that I'd wanted to seduce Alex all along and that I was angry because Alex would not return my affection. I was shocked because I had spent all those hours in the past months telling him about what Alex had done, at the risk of ruining my friendship with Alex, and here this guy was accusing me. I asked him if Alex said that I'd done that and he said Alex hadn't; but that we all knew the truth. He said that I wasn't pretty enough for Alex to want and that I was not happy with my husband. Since my husband wasn't a Christian that I had tried to 'nab' Alex because he was a pastor. He then got in my face and started to shout, 'Confess, admit it. You are lying and you are the one who was trying to seduce Alex. Admit it.' Again and again he shouted at me and I started to cry and said that wasn't true; but he was unrelenting. I kept saying, 'I just want to talk to Alex and reconcile. He'll straighten this out.' He said, 'Alex is not going to talk to you, ever. You will never see him or speak to him again.' By this time he was beet red and he was banging his fist on the table. 'You're not leaving till you confess.' I kept saying, 'I cannot lie to make you happy.' He then threw me out of his office." She was wiping away a tear from her eye. "Wow, I had almost forgotten that scene. It was terrible. I left the office trembling and saw Alex in the hallway crying and looking like he wanted to speak. Stan came out and grabbed him by the arm and pulled him into the conference room. He slammed the door and continued to shout, but I could not hear the words. I went home and wept for about three hours."

"Rhoda, can I ask, where was your husband was during this time?"

"He was there; but I still had not told him the story, not wanting him to look down on the church and Alex. I thought I could handle this on my own. But after that appointment Stan called me into his office at least three or four times per week and each time he shouted at me trying to make me confess. One time he got really angry and asked another lady, whom he was training to be his assistant, to come in and speak to me to get me to confess. After only a few minutes she said, 'I'm on your side and Pastor Alex is obviously sorry for what he did. He still wants to be your friend.' She said she admired me for wanting to reconcile and that she had enjoyed our meeting. Two minutes later Stan storms in the room and reaches under the conference table to shut off a taping device. First, I did not know he was taping me and second, he was furious at the woman and told her to get out. She left not knowing what the problem was. He actually pushed her out the door and started yelling at me about how I was trying to get that woman on my side. But truly all I had done was tell her the truth. He then said that now he was going to have to be extra strong in restraining me. I was actually a bit angry and I told him I did not want him to "help" me anymore and he said it was not in my hands to tell him what to do anymore. I had to listen to him, since he was a pastor. If I did not listen to him he'd see that I never could speak to Alex again; he'd have him relocated. He also said he'd go and speak to my husband about how I wanted another man. That is when I decided I had better tell my husband the story before Stan got to him and caused me to have a divorce or something. Also this was finally getting to be too much for me to handle on my own. But I didn't know how to approach the subject." She was looking out the window, as if she was seeing the whole terrible scene being played out in front of her. "I think I'll take that cup of tea now. Mark do you know what Pastor Stan did right before leaving that session? He turned to me and said, 'If it wasn't illegal to kill you, I'd have done so already. I hate you.' Then he left."

To be honest I felt drawn to this story like someone who was watching a soap opera and I really wanted to hear the next part. My secretary buzzed me and said I needed to make a quick call to Mr. Johnson; he had some trouble with a recent medication I'd prescribed. So I excused myself and called him, hoping to give Rhoda time to gather her thoughts. When I returned she was holding Max on her lap and looking a bit more rested. "So how did you bring up this subject with your husband?" I tapped her arm to help her return to the room from wherever her mind had taken her.

"Well I tried a couple of times to speak to him and he was too busy and so I backed off. Then one afternoon he was soaking in the tub and I went in and sat on the floor next to him. I told him I needed to talk to him and asked if he'd noticed I'd been more emotional, of late. He said he had; but he wanted me to tell him what was going on and not force the issue. I told him the whole sad story: about Alex's attack, how Stan was abusing me, and even how Alex had half heartedly apologized. He was getting more agitated as the conversation wore on. He got dressed and said, 'I'm going over to that Church and I'm going to beat up Alex.' This caused me to jump up and block the door. I started to beg him not to beat Alex and told him I was sorry I even mentioned the whole thing. I started crying and he held me. He told me that he wanted me to quit and I said I was in the middle of a project and believing for Alex to repent and to have reconciliation. He was not happy with this; but soon saw that my only desire was for reconciliation, not romance, and so he calmed down. He said that he would sit down with Stan and see what Stan had to say on this subject. I wasn't keen on that; but I told him to go ahead since I had nothing to be ashamed of. I did tell him to be careful because Stan was a liar and would want to make me look bad. He went into the other room to make an appointment with Stan. I knew Stan would be licking his chops at the possibility of greater humiliation for me."

"Why would you have your husband speak to Stan when you knew how Stan felt about you?"

"Well, I thought if I told my husband he could not speak to Stan, he'd think I had something to hide. He met with Stan a couple of days later and Stan told him to divorce me and that I had wanted an affair with Alex. My husband, thankfully, could see Stan was not only a liar, but that I was not the woman that Stan described. My husband believed me. He told Stan where to go and that he was a liar. He warned me to watch out for Stan since Stan was an evil guy. Stan really got angry, when my husband didn't do as he said."

"Wow, you are a lucky lady. Many husbands would have believed Stan because he was a pastor and may well have divorced you. I hope I can meet your husband some day."

"Yeah he is a good guy. But he has had his moments of insecurity and has wondered out loud, if Stan might have been right, if we are in the midst of quarrelling about something. But deep down he knows I love him. Anyway, my husband told me he supported my desire to reconcile. The main reason was he felt that reconciliation was good is that this would stick it to Stan and his church. He really could have cared less about Alex. A couple of months later, I ran across a document, on my husband's desk, that listed everyone who had hurt him. He checked off if they were forgiven or not and under Alex's name was in huge red letters, "Forgiven." This caused me to love my husband more than ever. But he did say he did not want to get involved in this church mess that it was going to be up to me to fix it. That made me sad; but I accepted his limitations. I know that Stan was angry that my husband decided to stick by me. He tried to call my husband once and my husband said simply, 'I have decided to believe my wife,' and hung up on him. What a guy."

It was almost time for her to go. "So before you go, how long did you continue to work for Alex after this? This confession time with your husband was around March or so, right? (She nodded.) So when was the final cut off date for your job?"

"Well, in July, we were preparing for the Children's Bible Camp and the other summer programs and so he didn't let me go right away. He had me doing a few other office organizing things, along with those, to pave the way for his next assistant. I had been trying to pretend during that time following my March "confession to my husband", that everything would somehow work out and that I'd be his friend again, like before. But there was the constant spying, by Stan's associates, and the constant presence of our new office mate. We could not even speak to one another. There were times Alex and I would bump into each other in the hallway and just as we were about to speak, a spy would pop out and just stand there with crossed arms. There was constant taping of any attempts from either of us to call each other for reconciliation, and blocking of emails or stealing of letters from our postal boxes, anything speaking of reconciliation, was confiscated. We were called on the carpet about fifty times when they caught either of us trying to schedule a reconciliation meeting. There were constant harassing phone calls, made to my home, by the church, in which they'd make vague and not so vague threats on my life. On a regular basis people would come up to me, both inside and outside the church, and yell at me, on Stan's behalf. I was forced by Stan to attend Cleansing Stream classes (a Christian quasi-therapy series that has a person go back into their pasts and try to get healing for past hurts). The classes were taught by Stan, with his dark spin on the subject. Also I had to see a counselor, at a local Christian Church. While all of this was going on, I was also doing a huge Y2k project, for Alex and the church. I did a well documented report, but this did nothing to improve my reputation. On top of all this, I still would not change my story. Stan never let up and still had me come into his office, so he could yell at me for hours, a few times per week. This refusing to break and confess bothered Stan. On occasion

Alex's assistant was not able to come in and he'd have to speak to me about a job project. Stan would always come in to my office, at those moments, and stand there with folded arms, until Alex finished his instructions and left. Then you'd hear all of this yelling, out into the hallway, coming from Stan's office. He'd be screaming threats at Alex. It became more and more inconvenient and uncomfortable to work there. But I stayed hoping Alex would repent and that the church would still put me on staff. Crazy, huh? But on the first week of July I came to work and saw my office had been made a teachers' lounge for the Children's camp teachers. I just thought I was relocated; but Alex told me it was my last day. He started to cry and said that he was so sorry; but it had to be that way. He told me that I could no longer come to the Church except for worship and that we were not able to be friends anymore. We both started crying and I knew that he had pushed for reconciliation from his end as much as I had. But the bullies wouldn't allow it. I mean the other church leaders. I gathered my things, sobbing violently, and walked home. As I left he said sadly 'maybe someday we can be friends again'. I knew that was his hope; but that Stan would never allow it."

"What did your husband have to say about this? Was he angry or glad?" I gave her a tissue.

"He was glad I was out of the office, but mad that the church had used me and had even promised me a position and then just turned me out without any reason, just to cover their guy. Alex was still working there and I was on the street. They had just given me an impeccable review, before all of this started, and told me I was on my way to becoming a full-fledged employee, on staff yet. This review came from the head pastor who had not, as yet, been filled in by Stan. I later, that month, made the head pastor aware of the situation on my own. That is another story. Stan, knowing I was no longer a staff candidate, rushed to the head pastor telling him I was a liar. Though I had already told the pastor everything; he decided to believe Stan's version, so that whole humiliating process of going to the head pastor, got me nowhere. But though I no longer worked for Alex, I did do a few little odd jobs for others at the church, until Stan cut those things off, also. Other people had two responses: they either hated or shunned me or they tried to get 'brownie' points by stalking and harassing me. They'd then make full reports of their suspicions and usually, totally made up stories, to Stan. People even followed me into stores and restaurants to catch me doing something against the church. "

I shook my head; it was worse than most cases I had heard of. Stan was given total liberty to run rough shod over Rhoda and she did not have any voice or anyone to defend her. Alex had obviously made some sort of agreement with the church and she was hung out to dry. "Rhoda, I'm so sorry. You have been abused by those who should have protected you. Would it be okay if I prayed for you now? (She nodded and wiped a stray tear.) Father, your eye is on the sparrow. You see the beggar on the dung hill and hear the cry of the wounded heart. I pray that you will comfort and heal all the deep places that were injured, in my sister Rhoda, by ungodly and unscrupulous men who called themselves your servants. They were wolves in sheep's clothing. Forgive them and bring them to repentance and vindicate my dear sister, in Jesus name. Amen." Rhoda also said, "Amen." I then gave her a fatherly hug and lead her to the front desk. "Make the appointment for sometime at the end of the week, next week, will you; because I want to squeeze Alex in before seeing you again. Alright?"

"Ok," she said quietly. "Doc? Would you say, 'Hi' for me and tell him I miss him?"

"I will, Rhoda, I will," I gave her a pat on the arm and went back to my office to get ready for Tony Hansen, a preteen with authority issues.

Chapter 6

I knew I had basically just scratched the surface of this whole sad story with Rhoda and Alex and wondered how I could really help them, after this had all gone on for so long. Alex called my office on Wednesday and asked if he could see me on Thursday. That was short notice (I had thought I'd see him the following week). Thankfully I did have time open for him to come in between 10-12pm Thursday morning. So I told my secretary, Helen, to schedule him in then. I then had her call Rhoda to come in at 3pm, on the next day Friday, instead of the next week Friday; if she had the time. Helen told me both of them were fine with the times I suggested and so I took the rest of Wednesday to fill out insurance papers for the other patients and to plan how I was going to approach Alex, knowing what I now knew from Rhoda. I knew I'd have to be very sensitive, so as not to cause him to fear I knew too much and run away. I could see this avoidance of reality was something intrinsic in his character and I wanted to not give him his usual easy way out. I knew it would be a balancing act on my part. So as I wrote information for my other patients, on the pile of forms. As I wrote, I'd occasionally stop and make a verbal note into my little tape recording device. It was a bit old fashioned; but it sure helped me to sort my thoughts. I had boxes of the tiny tape cassettes.

I went home rather late and got in the door, just as my wife was leaving for her women's Bible Study class. She told me my dinner was in the oven, some sort of casserole dish, and that she'd be home by about ten and not to wait up for her. I think she saw how tired I was. Part of my demeanor was a bit down, because I was tired, since paperwork wears me out. The other part of my demeanor was feeling a bit of an burden about the things I'd have to discuss with Alex the next day. Therapists hear everything; but we are human too and an uncomfortable subject is an uncomfortable subject, even if you are a "professional". I gave her a big weary kiss and sent her off saying I'd be going to bed early. She tousled my hair as she grabbed her keys from the basket by the door and she was out of the driveway in a moment. She has a little mutt dog, Rusty, and he came up and sat on my lap, after I got my dinner out of the oven. I had decided to sit in the Lazy Boy and watch CNN, as I ate. Rusty was cuddled up on my left side and I ate in silence watching the latest bombing in the Mideast. I put down the dish on the little side table, on my right, and held little Rusty a bit too tightly. He wiggled out of my grasp and scampered off. That is the last thing I remembered until about 9pm when I woke, shut off the TV, and plodded my way to bed. I didn't even hear my wife come in. The alarm rang about 6am and I quickly shut it off. I took a few moments to rise, preferring to watch my wife sleep. She was in her early fifties; but still a good looking woman. I was so lucky to have her. She understands my crazy career and how it can be so emotionally draining, at times, and she still thinks I'm "Mr. Wonderful". I softly kissed her hair and began to get ready for the day.

After having a bit of oatmeal, I got into the car and headed to the Bart Station. I was surprised to find I was a bit early and took out my little tape recorder again, from my brief case, to go over things I'd have to bring up with Alex later that morning. I was deep in thought when the train appeared and I got in with the rest of the sleepy eyed passengers. We all sat in silence or slept till we got downtown and when the engineer called out, "Embarcadero" I was almost too cozy to get up. But I did, even though I knew it would be a chilly walk to the office from the station. I grabbed a lox and bagel from the street vendor near my office and a green tea chai. The oatmeal hadn't been filling enough. As I trudged up the stairs I saw that Helen was already in and she greeted me at the door and grabbed my raincoat, after I put down my breakfast. She had already got a nice fire going in the fireplace and the cheeriness of the warm flames made me feel less leery, of what I'd have to face in a few hours. I ate in silence starring into the flames.

Mrs. Phelps came in at about 8:30am and I listened to her tell me how her cat reminded her of her mother and this is why she didn't think she'd keep her cat and, to be honest, this went on and on for the whole hour she was there. I thought about her trivial trials and wanted to scream, but maintained a calm demeanor. I was so glad she finally wrapped things up for me. "Well, Doctor, looks like I've used up all my time." I nodded in a fatherly way and helped her to the door. She made an appointment for the next week, at the same time, and I waved her out the door. Helen looked at me knowingly and asked if I'd like another cup of tea. I smiled wryly and said I'd like her to give Alex and me a cup of the new hibiscus tea I'd purchased, when he came in. I normally tried to not make her do menial tasks like coffee and tea making; but today I was grateful she'd volunteered. I went into my office and closed the door and got on my knees with my elbows on the leather chair and the fire to my right. I prayed for wisdom and for Alex and then for Rhoda. This couple had for some reason really caught my attention and I didn't want to mess them up any more than they had already been messed up, by their church. I also prayed for their families and for a way to heal everyone in this sad scenario. The fire felt so good that I almost fell asleep again; but then I heard a knock on the door.

Helen was telling me Alex had just come in and that it was raining so she was trying to dry him off a bit. I told her to send him in and we could put another chair by the fire. He came in looking a bit like a rat terrier from the rain and because he had one of those kind of spiked hair styles. I handed him the afghan I keep on the couch and Helen brought in those two cups of tea with two of the biscotti I'd been saving for such a time as this. I threw a couple more logs into the fire and sparks jumped out of the fireplace causing Alex to back up a bit. I reassured him it was alright. We had not had any fires, yet. He seemed to settle into his chair a bit more and I put my hand on his shoulder for a moment before sitting down solidly into my chair.

"So Alex, how do you like the weather downtown? You guys over in the Bay Area have it a bit warmer than us city folks." He nodded and looked at me. I think he was trying to see what I knew and how safe I was. I cleared my throat and said, "Well Rhoda did fill me in on the main story line and now I'd like to hear your version. I totally trust and believe her; but I'm sure you have your own twist, to this sad twisted story. I'm only saying it is sad because I know this was not an easy experience for either of you. I'm not really putting a value judgment on you or Rhoda. I also want to reassure you that I will under no circumstances share what you tell me today with anyone and I mean anyone. This is totally between me and you. Rhoda will have to hear this from you because I won't ever share what you say with her. Do you understand me?" He nodded and stared into his cup. I had to make this doubly clear because of the kind of church he came from where, tattling on others made you more "spiritual".

"Rhoda came to our church with her daughter in 1997. She was always so cheerful and friendly when she'd drop her daughter off for children's time on Sundays. She'd greet me with a smile and pass a few moments with me exchanging polite pleasantries. Then after service she'd thank me for taking care of her daughter so well and tell me she was really enjoying coming to our church. That is how I first met her and her daughter. I knew she was married to an unbeliever and that he did not attend church with her and that she was a stay at home mother and had been part time teacher. Her little girl was about ten. She was a bit shy, but very polite. I could see Rhoda was a good mother. But that was all I knew about her. She only came on Sundays and to a women's bible study and would promptly leave to get back home. She mentioned her home was walking distance from the church. She had seemed to express an interest in some sort of volunteer work at the church and had even gone into the office to ask if she could help out for a few hours a week. Our over diligent secretary had told her to wait awhile to serve and for her to get more into women's ministry classes. This I heard through the grapevine at work and not from Rhoda herself." He seemed to be remembering something pleasant so I let him reminisce for a few moments.

"Alex, when did she begin to work for you, as your assistant?"

"Well about a year, after she began attending our church, she came into my office one day. I was literally going crazy. My last assistant had just left, my wife was working at a local Christian school, and was too busy with that and the kids to help me. I was literally surrounded by piles and piles of papers. I had so much to do and not enough hours in the day to do it all. I was working at the church till almost 11pm everyday and not seeing much of my family. This was beginning to get on my wife's nerves and she had recently started to complain about the lack of family time and about a few bills I'd run up. We got paid on a salary basis, so even if I worked overtime, no extra money came in. This also was ticking her off. We were constantly getting into little 'discussions' and yet I did not know how to fix this situation.

So one afternoon, while I was brooding about this, in walks Rhoda. She asked me if I needed any assistance, with my work, and tells me she has a few hours per week put aside for volunteer work. I almost started jumping, but pretended to be rather cool and said that I might have some work for her to do; but that we'd better pray about it. I told her to come back in a month and if she still felt it was God's will, we'd see what could be done. Actually I wanted her to start in two minutes; but I thought a waiting period was best. I had just lost one assistant and did not want to go through all that drama again. She seemed a bit dejected about waiting a month; but I wanted her to be really sure. Also I could see she was intelligent and I had a lot planned for her, if she did come on board. She had mentioned to me she was an elementary school teacher and that she loved working with kids. So.........I was thinking that she was a diamond in the rough.

It was almost a month to the day after that that she came hobbling into my office; she had some sort of leg injury. 'God told me to work with you,' she joyfully proclaimed. I wondered how He did that. I was glad, because I had peace about her helping out and I thought she'd be a good assistant. I was so overburdened I'd have taken almost anyone, to be honest. But I kind of felt like I knew her and was reasonably sure she was sane. We had a few women work for the church that seemed to have borderline mental problems; and it was a refreshing thing to have someone who was normal and even had had both office and teaching experience. She also lived only a few blocks away and I knew she would be able to come into work easily and even 'on call', if I needed her. So it seemed like a good deal for both of us. I guess I also liked that she seemed like a happy sort. I am someone who is easily depressed and I thought her enthusiasm might perk me up a bit. So I told her she could start anytime. I was highly impressed that she had crawled up the stairs to tell me she wanted the job. So I got another pastor's wife and we prayed for her new position in the office and for God to heal her injury."

I looked at him for a long time. He was smiling with a kind of wry half smile and I wondered how he had felt about her when he first hired her. So I asked him plainly, "How did you feel about her as a person when you first hired her? Any feelings other than 'pastorly' ones?"

"Oh I get it. She must have told you what happened later on. (I just looked at him, not giving him a nod.) Well, to be honest, I did not have any feelings for her but 'pastorly'. I hardly knew her and she was not my type, if you know what I mean. My wife is also a Jewish believer, but that is really the only thing they both have in common. They are like night and day. My wife is more serious minded and Rhoda is more, ah, bubbly. She was also different than the ladies I had affairs with. I usually chose slender blondes, who were rather quiet. So she did not interest me in any way. I just felt she was the right person for the job and this lack of interest made her safe. She seemed to be equally uninterested in me which was again refreshing since so many women at church seem to want to snag a pastor. I had had my fill of hero worship after my last affair was so messy. So I was keen on keeping a low profile and truly swamped with work."

"Well, were you correct; was Rhoda a good worker? Did she meet your expectations?" I wondered if anyone could meet his standards, he seemed to be a bit overly sure of himself. I did not pick up a person of real warmth, from even his few statements he had made to me.

He rubbed his chin in a thoughtful manner. "Remember that old rhyme that went, 'And when she was good she was very very good; but when she was bad she was horrid'? (I nodded.) She was a really hard worker and she had people skills. I used to use her to get volunteers for church and

49

(I never told her this) she got more volunteers than anyone ever. She also would work till all hours of the night at home to finish an assignment. She tried to please me with going the extra mile on projects and organized all of my piles of papers, making files and throwing out outdated materials. But she did mess up on the special Children's Seminar we have every year for all the churches. She did not ask questions, maybe I wasn't too available, and would try to figure things out on her own. But she figured a couple of things out the wrong way and this ticked me off. This was a big deal at our church and we ended up buying too much food and all the computer records were messed up. It was terrible. The money didn't match up at the end and my wife suggested she must have stolen it. I guess I believed this and this caused a misunderstanding. Sometimes she'd do things, that she didn't double check with me first. This would then mess up the whole thing like this poster we were supposed to do for the Children's program. It was the wrong size and I had to cut it down and it looked terrible. I did everything to perfection and she was a bit chaotic at times. So on the one hand she was great; but on the other hand she made me really mad at times. When I lost my temper she'd cry or get silent and sullen and it wasn't fun, believe me."

"Did you ever notice similar reactions from your wife or your previous assistants? Do you think you are an easy person to please?" I looked him in the eyes.

"Ok, ok, I do admit I had bad people skills then. I was less patient when I was younger and often too busy to take the time with people. But I was really patient when I began to teach Rhoda the computer. Her husband had mainly taught her to do email and use Yahoo, but I taught her basic Excel and more office software, which I'm sure she was grateful for. I didn't let her use our computers, on her own, at work because the last employee I had had screwed up the whole system. I vowed to never let another assistant near our computers. We had Window's 95 and I thought that was what she had at her home. So she'd do all of our computer work from home. But things got all screwed up when she did her job on Window's 97 and then tried to download the whole thing to our system for that Children's Seminar. What a mess. I didn't figure this out until about two months later;

but I never told her I was sorry for going off on her. I guess I should have. I never used to like to say 'I'm sorry', to anyone, not just her."

I looked at the clock and it was almost time for him to go since I had another client in a few minutes. "Well the time got away from us again. Two things I'd like to ask before you go. How were you and your wife doing at the time she was hired? And what did you think of Pastor Stan, were you friends?"

He thought for a bit before answering. "Well, my wife and I were having problems. Not because of other women, at that moment; but because I was buying a few large items and not checking with her first. She took care of our finances and I purchased a few things and did not write them in the check book. This bugged her. She thought I was being deceitful and I guess I was. I was trying to avoid a confrontation and I wanted what I wanted and didn't want to ask permission. I think I resented her being in charge of our money. I didn't see it then. But she was the most level headed of the two of us and I'd have no savings today, if she hadn't taken control. So we fought a lot about money and this is probably one of the reasons I didn't want to leave work earlier. I knew she'd be asleep by 11pm and if she wasn't she'd be too tired to really say anything. I guess folks at work might have noticed the tension, there was between us. Oh yeah, Pastor Stan. They put him in charge of me at the church and he was very controlling; but this was something they wanted him to be. He was supposed to keep me out of trouble, to control me. I had to report to him once per week and explain what I did during the week and he was quite critical. He didn't like that I hugged women at church meetings. He said I seemed to enjoy that too much and he felt I was too friendly. He didn't say anything when I was crabby in the office that was fine. But he didn't like me to make being a pastor seem like a 'light thing'. He thought I needed to be more somber. That was not my style and I liked that people liked me. So, no, we weren't friends. We had nothing in common. He was very stoic; and I liked having more fun. So we tolerated each other. I did fear him because he had the power to have me fired, if he did not like my reports or my actions from the previous week. So I tried to keep a low profile to please him and to keep my job. He never was someone you could go for coffee or a beer with."

I saw his heart even more clearly and shook my head. Here was the poster child for a "man pleaser", if ever there was one. But I also saw that maybe he had seen some of his faults over the last years and maybe God wasn't through with this man yet. So I didn't rush to judgment, though I was tempted to. "Okay, this gives me a better idea of where you were, mentally, at the time. Do you have anything you'd like to add?"

He looked at me unsure of what to say. Then he said quietly, "Are you referring to the situation between Rhoda and I? Well, there doesn't seem to be enough time today to go into it. Can we talk on the phone tomorrow, before you see Rhoda? I promise to be open with you and to let you delve into my psyche. This is not comfortable for me and being on the phone might help me to be less nervous."

"Normally I don't do this but I do need to know some things from you before I see Rhoda. So can you call me at, say, 7am? I know this is early; but I have to make notes before I see her. I really do want to hear your side and also know that tomorrow will be more of an overview we'll get more specific in the weeks to come. I promise to not make any judgments before I hear a lot more of this story. Alex do trust me. This is not like your church. I am a safe person."

Alex actually teared up when he heard those last words. But he didn't cry. He cleared his throat and said he'd call sharply at 7am the next day. I got out of my chair and shook his hand and lead him to the door. Although he was almost my age I got this fatherly feeling toward him too, just like I did for Rhoda. I wondered how his father fit into this story; and made a mental note to find out more about the one who taught him to have this set of values.

My wife and I went out to dinner, which was a bit strange for us, since it was a Thursday. But I just had to get out for awhile. She was glad to not have to cook. We went to a little Italian Restaurant in downtown San Francisco, in the Little Italy community, called Mona Lisa. The prices there are actually too cheap; but the food is better and more real Italian than any of the more high priced places anywhere in the city. Also they keep it really dark and my wife thinks that's romantic. We had a nice evening but I was distracted and my wife could tell. She put her hand on my arm and said, "Hard case, huh? Wish you could tell me more about it; but I understand. Hope God gives you what you need to take care of the problem." She and I decided at the beginning of our marriage to honor the client/therapist relationship and not discuss my cases in any detail. Mostly we did this because so many folks came from my church and she said she didn't want to prejudge anyone. So she doesn't even make an effort to pry information out of me. I think this was the best decision. All the same, knowing she stands with me is a great comfort, even if I'm sometimes bursting to tell her "the latest".

I was up wrestling with bringing up the c word or not with Alex. Or cult. After thinking over his and Rhoda's description of his church I began to wonder if I was dealing with a church that was a bit controlling or abusive or a full blown cult. I have known, from my past experiences with places like Alex's church, that even though this church may be part of an actual mainline denomination; it could very well be a cult. Just a few months prior to meeting Rhoda, I had had a client who attended a Baptist church and most folks see that denomination as solid and orthodox. But the pastor at that church had somehow convinced most of the members there that he and he alone knew the true gospel and that he had special revelations from God. He told the congregation that God had told him to relay to them that they were to sell their homes and give all the money to the church, in other words, him. Funny thing was that most of the people did as he asked. But my client had had questions about doing this and that was why he came to see me. He thought he had the wrong perspective. But during the last church service federal marshals came in while the pastor was preaching and arrested him. Seems he was also told by God to take the money and go to Jamaica. One family member had gotten inside information on the pastor's plans and reported him before he was able to catch his plane, that evening after the Sunday service. It also seemed he had revelations that some of the wives were also his and the whole thing got very messy. My client was glad that I had been so skeptical of the pastor's motives and that he had not sold his home. It took the others quite awhile to retrieve their money back from the sale of their homes and they had steep lawyer fees also. I used the word cult with my client and at first he balked;

but after a few sessions he came to see I was "right on the money". It was not easy to convince him and a few other members from his church that a Baptist church could be a cult. But some pastors make even denominational churches their little kingdoms and they rule over the people with an iron fist and somehow delude the people that they are hearing God's voice in a special way. Seemed to me that this was also the way things went at Alex's church. It was a more mainline charismatic church; but the pastors tended to do more of their own thing. This included keeping people from reconciling, even though the Bible clearly encourages people to do this. I was up until after 3am turning this over in my mind and I finally decided I'd wait a bit before confronting Alex with this. Once I made my decision I fell into a fitful sleep and was up at 5am before my alarm rang. I dragged myself out of bed, had a quick shower, and was off to Bart so I could get set up for Alex's call to my office at 7am. There was a food truck outside the Bart when I got to San Francisco and I grabbed a bagel with cream cheese and a coffee with an espresso shot.

Chapter 7

I had just begun to put a couple of logs on the fire when I looked at the clock and it was 6:50am. I started speeding up my process. I gave the cat his food and water, emptied his box, decided to make a "pit stop" myself, sat in my chair and opened my breakfast, and reached under my desk for my slippers. As soon as I put on my "work slippers" Alex called. I thought he had pretty good timing. Since my secretary wasn't in, I put the other phone lines on the answering machine so I could talk to him without interruption. Then I heard Alex whisper, "Good morning, Mark. Sorry I'm a couple of minutes late. My wife doesn't know I'm calling you and I'm in the garage. She sleeps in on Fridays and I don't want her to wake up. Long story."

"Hi Alex, are you trying to say that your wife doesn't know about our relationship? I always think it is best to let the spouses know if you are going to be doing any intensive work with me or any therapist, for that matter. Why haven't you told her yet?" I took a sip of my coffee and waited for him to tell me, though I could guess the reason.

"Well she knows the story about Rhoda and me; but she thinks I lost contact with Rhoda about fourteen years ago. I tried to tell her many times that we have never stopped our friendship. But I didn't really know how to do so without it looking weird, so I haven't really told her, in detail, to be honest, in about the last fourteen years."

I could see this was a problem, but didn't want to shut the door on Alex getting treatment. So I told him to put this problem on the shelf for a while and that we'd figure something out in the future. I told him it might be better if he waited, anyway, that then he could speak to her with a more healed frame of mind and perhaps this would be better for everyone. He sighed a sigh of relief and we got down to the main reason for his calling me.

I put Max on my lap, since he was trying to eat my sandwich, and I cleared my throat. "So Alex what do you remember that lead up to your 'situation with Rhoda' and the 'situation' itself? If you don't mind I will be nibbling on my breakfast as you speak. Feel free to take as long as you want; I don't have another client until 10am." Rhoda would be coming in at 3pm so I would have time to update my notes even with the two other appointments I had for the day. Normally folks only stayed the traditional 50min. But Rhoda and Alex had a special place in my heart and I saw that they really needed long overdue help; so I let them both take as much time as was needed. I was petting Max on the head, when Alex started to speak. I heard the sound of a car door shutting and figured he got into his car to speak more freely. I was glad he thought of this since I didn't want him to hold back anything, worrying that he'd be overheard.

"Well Mark, I don't have until ten I have to be at work by 9am. So don't worry I won't bend your ear too long. Let me think for a bit… Well we started becoming friends from the first day she came to work for me. Then as the days passed and we spoke about our dreams for the future and our past lives. Though we shared a lot of information, she never spoke about her marriage or asked about mine. I thought that was a healthy habit and so I didn't tell her that I'd been having trouble with my wife. We had been fighting quite a lot, mainly about money. But I guess this was mainly because my wife was also still upset with me because of my past indiscretions; not that I blamed her for that. But the money part was bugging me. I felt I worked really hard and I didn't want to ask her for permission, before buying things. For instance, I got this ham radio set. I had always wanted one as a kid and finally I saw the perfect model and purchased it on eBay. Well, that ticked her off. When I got it I didn't mention it, at first, (I had it set up in the garage, behind some boxes). The only way she found out about it was when I began to get flyers in the mail for a few of the ham radio clubs. I had just joined one and she saw the check stub for that. I mean what good is a ham radio without being in contact with other enthusiasts?" (I nodded, but could see how his wife could have been a bit ticked. I knew from another friend that that whole transaction, with the equipment and the club fees must have been at least a couple thousand dollars.) "Anyway, we argued a lot about that. I almost forget about that whole episode. But then Liz started calling me at work to continue her ranting. I guess others in the office overheard; but Rhoda never once asked about the conflict. This not being overly nosey and her cheerful demeanor made me feel more comfortable being with her than being yelled at by my wife. I saw my times with Rhoda as a time of rest from all of the tension. I could laugh again. I'd make stupid jokes and throw stuff at her and she'd laugh. Also she was always trying to encourage me to do more with my life and be a better person. Those kinds of things gave me a warm feeling towards her. I felt safe and admired. As my trials with my wife were going on, Pastor Stan, who was in charge of me kept getting more and more demanding. He wanted me to account for all my time and write an hour by hour schedule. I also was to write a detailed plan for how I was going to have more integrity. On and on, one demand after another. He constantly wanted to know how much time I spent with my wife and how our relationship was going. He even wanted to know my evaluation of my fathering skills. Guess my wife had confided in him. I suppose if he'd been a bit more bold he'd have asked for a detail report on our sex lives. But it was just too much pressure; so I enjoyed going to Rhoda's office and laughing for a few minutes with her. To top it off, there was that blasted Children's Seminar that I had to get done. Rhoda didn't realize she only had a small portion of the work. I was trying to do over 80% of it and on top of this I was supposed to give a class at the seminar, which meant I'd have to write all the material and learn how to present it, On top of this I had to do my regular Children's ministry work. I was in charge of the children's ministry, the volunteers, the Summer Camp, and even the maintenance workers. I had 26hrs of work every day. I had to try and get this done in 20hrs. Added to this, I had to try and be a dad, a husband, and even get some sleep. Even on Mondays when I had off, I worked nonstop from home. I stopped praying two years before I met Rhoda and kept resolving to try and squeeze some time in for that, during the day; but it never happened. I really was losing it. Rhoda was like a little oasis of joy in the midst of all this chaos, hard work, and utter fatigue."

I had finished my breakfast and had not interrupted him; but I could tell he needed a bit of a break. I asked him if I could speak for a moment. I wanted him to rest, for a moment, before going on to the meat of why I had him call. "So Alex, I'm surprised you didn't end up in the hospital, or the funny farm, with a schedule like that. I know I couldn't do it when I was a young man, let alone as a middle aged one. Why didn't you speak up to your head pastor? You two were friends right? I mean you didn't need just one part-time assistant, or volunteer; seems like you needed a full time secretary and even a few more part-time volunteers."

"Well, Mark, it was a bit complicated. The head pastor had just laid off two guys for not doing their share of the work and on top of that his wife had begun having some psychological issues. He had to send her to our church affiliated mental health facility in Denver. At that time, he often went to visit her for a few days. I felt that my stuff would be too much for him to handle at the time, so did the other pastors, about their stuff. We all tried to keep any problems from him and to solve them ourselves. We had five associate pastors to do the work of seven, because, as I just mentioned, he'd fired two of the pastors and had not rehired anyone yet. Also Stan was like a machine, I didn't care how much work you threw at him; he kept going. He not only got his work done; but he never seemed overwhelmed by it. I found out later he gave a lot of it to his wife; but at the time, I just thought he was so much more organized than me. His kids were all pretty much grown and out of the house. He had more time to just concentrate on his job. Anyway, I wanted the head pastor to think I was able to hold my own and I was feeling a bit insecure about my job. So I suffered in silence."

"Why were you feeling so insecure? You seem like you were working your backside off? Didn't you think they noticed or appreciated your all out efforts?"

He cleared his throat. "Well first of all I knew, the head pastor, was still ticked about my past experience, with that woman from our old church. Also there had recently been a few rumors floating around at church about me, and my recent 'relationships' at this new church. Then, lastly, I knew I had overspent my budget allowance for the second year in a row, right when the church was trying to cut down on expenses. This whole budget thing was why he hadn't hired the two new pastors, yet. So.......I thought I could end up as one more casualty, if I didn't keep more of a low profile. I guess these latter reasons, overshadowed the pastor's wife's difficulties."

"Okay so I am getting how much pressure you were feeling and how Rhoda seemed to be a bit of a pressure releaser for you. But when did you begin to cross the line in your mind from your being a friend to maybe wanting something more?" I put Max down and got my pen out to be sure not to miss anything he was about to say. I heard a long sigh and pause on the other end.

He was quiet for a time and then he got very raspy in his voice. "Well here goes: I don't really know how to say this nicely, okay? But this is the truth. My wife was so upset with me, during that time, that she didn't want to have sexual relations with me. So sometimes I'd, well, um, pleasure myself. And sometimes I'd think of Rhoda when I did this to kind of help me along, do you understand what I'm saying? Judge me if you will; but I'd think of her and I'd get to completion and then I'd go back to my work. I didn't tell this to her or anyone else. I did this in my office, in private. I'm not proud of this, it is just what I did. But because I did that and more or less 'used Rhoda', I began to get a sexual attachment to her. I knew it was wrong. She was/is a married woman and my wife should have been who I was thinking of, at those times. But with all the anger, I guess I focused on Rhoda. I tried to not let on to Rhoda. But it became more frequent, and after I'd give her her assignments for the day or went to her office to check on a report or how the seminar was proceeding, I'd hurry into my office and shut the lights and door, get 'release' and then go back to work. It worked for a time and no one was any the wiser. It might seem a bit twisted; but I did that and it was my secret."

It was more of an honest confession, than I had thought he was capable of. Men do think about sex more than women. It is a fact and as a therapist I have heard it all. But I knew this was really a breakthrough, for him, since he was always trying to appear to be perfect and here he actually admitted to being a human. A somewhat twisted human, but a human. "Wow, Alex, I know that was a lot for you to share with me. You were quite honest. But I have to bring you one step closer to the actual 'situation' with Rhoda. When did your 'fantasy love relationship', with her, drive you to try and bring your private thoughts to reality?"

I thought this moment of change was important for him to see. It is normal and natural to have "those types" of thoughts, whether or not a person crosses over into the sin category is between them and their God. I try not to judge what natural sexuality is, or what is sin, in those type of situations. Alex paused; he made a bit of an exasperated sound, and then proceeded. "Well I love the Christmas season above all the holidays and I was hoping I could get back into my wife's good graces. But, again, I made a few purchases for our kids that she was not thrilled with and I felt I got more kicked to the curb. I was frustrated in every area of my life: work, ministry, walk with God, marriage, sex; you name it. So I had a few times when I 'got off' even more than usual and when Rhoda and I were putting up the Christmas decorations I could hardly stand to be next to her. I wanted to tell her how I felt, but I didn't want to get graphic. The struggle inside was raging, as we finished our putting the last touches on the sanctuary. All of a sudden, in the middle of my musings, she jumps up and says she needs to get home and make dinner. I was so frustrated that I didn't know how to approach the subject with her, in a normal way. So I followed her out of the sanctuary, saying something mindless about her husband. Her daughter came running after us. I saw her daughter go off to play in another area of the parking lot, out of eye sight and earshot. Rhoda was smiling and trying to gather up her daughter and put all the papers she had for the project in her bag. I said, "Wait I didn't give you a Christmas hug." Rhoda was quite distracted with her daughter and all of her paperwork. She also at the same time, had a funny look on her face, which I couldn't read at the time, and a there was this lone tear going down her cheek. That was it for me. I grabbed her and pulled her in a tight hug. She immediately began trying to break free, for some reason, like in the movies. So I grabbed her harder and tried to kiss her and she turned her head away and got an even odder look on her face, like I was scaring her or something. I tried to pull at her bra in the back and she kept wrestling with me. That struggle increased my passion and got me more determined to conquer her. I guess I got a bit excited, which really seemed to scare her. To ease her fears, I told her that I loved her, hoping she'd see that I wasn't trying to hurt her. But she kept struggling and was crying. She said something and I let her go, afraid she might scream. (I really only wanted to kiss her and let her know how I felt.) She jumped back and grabbed her daughter and practically ran out of the parking lot. She seemed so scared and was crying so hard, that I thought she must have those feelings too, that they were just too much for her to handle. I was so happy she felt the same way that I did; I hugged myself for joy."

I was speechless for the first time in years. He saw her struggling as a sign she felt the same way towards him. He thought that this behavior showed she was excited about his loving her! He did not see the terror in her eyes or how she had totally rejected his advances. He saw her inner struggle her way to deal with the depth of her emotions towards him! Unbelievable. I paused, for a long time. "Now Alex why do you think her fighting you was a sign of her accepting your advances. I mean is it possible she might have been doing everything in her power to get away from you without screaming bloody murder and ruining your life? I mean you were right behind the church for anyone to see or hear. Weren't you afraid someone would see you struggling with her?" I was in amazement at his naivety and overly focused focus.

"Well, over the years I have pondered that moment and have come to see, it is possible, she did not want to know me, like I wanted to know her. I have thought she maybe actually did love her husband. Then again, this was just not the best way to have handled the whole thing."

"You think?" I was amazed, that even over all this time, he was still as muddle headed as ever.

61

"Well she was always happy to see me. That made me think she had feelings for me. Even when she returned to work after Christmas, after the whole incident, she seemed happy enough. Okay, I take that back, a bit, there were times when she would start crying, for no reason, and that did bug me. But I thought she just had to get used to the idea more. Some of the past ladies I had relationships with weren't 'on board' right away. They tried to seem like they loved their husbands; but in time they gave in. I just thought she needed a bit more time to get used to the idea. But instead she seemed to get more and more distant from me and even avoid me. I did try a few times to get her alone with me, during Christmas break; but she always had her daughter with her. But when Christmas break was over, I finally got another chance. I went downstairs to her office and there she was crying again. I figured she was missing me and went to hug her. But she just cried more and, yes, I got excited again; but this time she jumped back immediately and wiped her eyes. She said, 'No!' and I was shocked. I sat down to gather myself back to normal and she just stood staring at me, shaking her head. I told her to go and put out the chairs for the meeting and she just had this weird look on her face." Alex seemed truly surprised she didn't accept his advances. I was unable to believe his extreme blindness.

"Alex, since that was a clear second attempt on your part, and she did not behave as you expected, did you not see that maybe she just didn't want to go against her marriage vows?"

"Mark, do you know how many ladies have said those very words to me and ended up in my bed or the back of my van two minutes later? I thought she was playing hard to get. To be honest, it was working; because I was more interested than ever. With the other ladies, they usually came around after the second attempt. But she got even more distant from me and didn't even greet me in the hallway anymore. I could not figure her out. If she hated me that much, why didn't she quit? Or why didn't she tell her husband?"

"I am not trying to judge anyone here, Alex; but did you not know she had an offer to be on staff full time from the head pastor? Maybe she didn't want to screw up her chances for the position and maybe she even wanted to save your butt." I was starting to get a bit ticked and decided to back off. But I felt like reaching through the phone line and whacking him with the phone.

"Oh I didn't know about that job offer. I bet she was angry, when she didn't get it, huh? But I do know that about a week later she went into Pastor Stan's office and said someone had attacked her against her will. Didn't she know Pastor Stan was my accountability pastor and already against me? Why did she choose him to go to? Now that made me really mad! Of all the pastors, she chose Stan. She didn't come right out and say it was me, but Stan is not a stupid guy. He's hard and cold, but not stupid. He called me on the carpet ten minutes, after she left his office."

"Tell me a bit more about that interaction, I've been wondering how Pastor Stan's mind works, myself." I knew this would be interesting.

"Well, I got an intercom message to come to Stan's office immediately. He was as red as a tomato and I figured his wife had been giving him grief. So I was clueless, as to why I was there. Stan sat down behind his desk and had me sit in the interview chair. I started to figure out something was not good and I looked at Stan and said, 'So what's up?' He was twirling a pencil and concentrating on it, tapping the eraser on the intercom. He said, 'So how is Mrs. Du working out as an assistant? Any problems?' My mind was racing, 'No she is a bit clumsy, but otherwise alright.' 'Are you sure there is nothing more you have to say about her?' Now I learned how to make these 'doe eyes' to look more innocent in the past, when I was caught. 'I'm sure. I can't think of anything.' He looked at me long and hard and said, 'Just to let you know, Mrs. Du said someone from church tried to violate her. If I was that someone I'd be very careful and not say another thing about this incident to her or anyone and let it blow over. Otherwise a certain someone might lose their job.' I nodded and tried to get him off my scent by saying, 'I really have no idea what happened. You know she is a bit overweight; maybe she is trying to make some drama. Who'd want to attack someone with a weight problem? Ick. Hope you find out who it was, if it even was anyone.' I got up and left the office. He said, to my back, 'Let's talk again in a couple of days.' I turned and said, 'Sure Stan, no problem.' But he kept staring at me. When I got back to my office I shut the door and turned off the lights and I wanted to strangle her. She made an appointment to see me a few days later and would not stop crying. I was ticked. I said to myself, 'Why did she have to bring Stan into this?' I didn't want to hear her crying or see her pain filled face. I didn't know what to do, if I should just fire her or what? But the seminar was about to be launched and I couldn't lose her at that moment. The dilemma was settled for me. Stan hired a part-time assistant to be a go between or barrier. This way she would not have to interact with me. That position was the one I had been considering for Rhoda, not knowing the pastor had offered her another one. Anyway, we couldn't speak with this woman there all the time. Stan made sure she worked the same hours as Rhoda and I soon got frustrated; because after awhile I wasn't angry anymore and wanted to talk with Rhoda; but there was never time or a private moment. I also found that Stan had begun to track all my calls, confiscate emails and regular mail even in my home mailbox, and in general spy on me. I was constantly told I could not make things right with Rhoda. I guess she had the same treatment on her end. It was very very frustrating. I tried to reason with Stan that he had gone too far, that it all was a misunderstanding. But he just kept saying my job was in jeopardy and I had better back off. He'd bring Rhoda into his office for yelling sessions to break her down and make her confess that she lied. She would not say she lied, so he'd try and intimidate her. Meanwhile he also had me come to his office for yelling sessions for trying to speak to her, to apologize. I wanted to apologize even though I didn't feel like I did anything wrong. I just saw she was weeping all the time. But then she messed up the seminar and so I determined to let her go, in a few months, after I got her to do a bit more work for me. I told her to take a break. After a month off, I told her she could work for about another half a year. But she'd end up crying, every time she saw me. So, in July, I had to tell her she was no longer needed. I told her she was 'released'. I couldn't figure out why she had not taken this whole thing like the others had. The others had not wanted their husbands to find out. She told her husband in March or was it April, after the second attempt. I was actually glad that he stood by her, even when pastor Stan told him his wife had tried to seduce me. I wished I could have cleared things up with him for her. I could not figure either of them out." Out of nowhere he started to cry. I could not believe my eyes. He appeared to have real emotions, after seeming to be a bit heartless in what he had just shared. I wished I could put my hand on his shoulder. "I think I may have hurt her badly. But Mark I hurt too because I actually loved her. She was not like the others."

I wanted to say, "Duh?" like the teens do; but I held myself back and tried to understand his tears. "Alex, are you crying for her or for you?"

"Both of us I guess." With that we ended the phone session and I lead him in a short prayer. "Thanks, Mark. I have a lot to think about."

"Please call my secretary and make another appointment, for Wed. or Thurs. next week. I'll transfer you to her desk. Take heart, Alex, I see God working here." I hung up the phone and wept, not just for them, but for all the Christians caught in legalism.

Chapter 8

By the time Rhoda came in, at 3pm, I had seen two more clients and wrote up three session reports, including Alex's and I also made four new Plan of Attack forms. The second form is the one I made up myself, since I feel much of therapy is too loose, lacking direction. I like to name the "enemies" and make a definite plan on how to go about conquering "them". Many patients are kept in therapy for years and never really seem to get better. I'm much more proactive than this. The fourth plan was for Rhoda, I had forgotten to make one for her, after our last meeting. Speaking to Alex gave me better direction in making her plan, so I guess it was good that I waited. Therapy sessions are made to look, off the cuff. But actually we plan even the most relaxed sessions ahead of time. When you walk in the door of a classroom, you think the teacher just decided to stand up and teach, not realizing that every second is preplanned the week or, at times, the night before. Then I also did the rather tedious filling out of insurance forms for Alex and the other two clients. Rhoda's treatment was basically, "my treat" and actually the whole thing was so interesting to me that I'd have done it just for the experience. I decided to have her pay some nominal fee at the end, just so she would feel better. As a therapist, each case we do prepares us for something similar, in the future. We are always learning. I am someone who loves to learn and who is fascinated by my fellow humans. Anyway, by the time she came I was putting another log on the fire. I also had just made two cups of this new dark hot chocolate and put two raisin cookies out. I wanted Rhoda to feel more relaxed.

She came in, in a bit of a blue mood. I saw her eyes weren't dancing like usual and I was glad I had planned the little treat. She sighed and said, "Oh, hi, Doc. Thanks for putting out raisin cookies they're my favorite." I told her my wife had made a whole box of them and if she wanted more she could have as many as she wanted. She shook her head and said, "That's okay, thanks." She paused and looked at me for a moment, "Doc, do you mind if I talk about something I feel like bringing up today? I mean I know everything we speak of is good for me and all, but there is something that has been bothering me. I haven't ever been able to talk to anyone about it. It's still about the Alex stuff and all; but it is an 'uncharted area', so to speak. When I'm done you can bring up anything at all you want to chat about, I'm not bashful and don't want to spoil your 'lesson plan'." She gave me a wry smile and waited for me to tell her to proceed. How I wished all my patients were so polite. Some of them just plop in the chair and chatter for the whole session and hardly let me say anything. Then they wonder why nothing changes. I'm basically just their sounding board and not able to help them direct their thoughts; until they finally give me a chance to help.

I smiled a half smile and nodded for her to proceed. "Remember how I told you Pastor Stan was so controlling?" (I had a big piece of cookie in my mouth, but managed an, "Uhum" and nodded.) "Well, this ultra control lead to Alex and I devising a plan on how to get around his iron fist. At first we tried all the conventional ways. I wrote a few letters to the leadership and to him to ask for a reconciliation meeting. When those went unanswered I tried setting up an official appointment in his office. When the secretary told me to not ever call again; I tried emails. Then those were blocked. I even tried going down to his classroom on Sunday, when he taught Sunday school and asking to speak with him. Stan would push me away or have one of his 'servants' come and threaten me. Lastly, I tried having a friend or two speak to him for me, and they were told he didn't wish to contact me. Alex tried similar things from his end and he too was blocked by Stan. If we accidentally met in the hall at church or in our neighborhood he always wanted to talk to me. But his fear of Stan and Stan's spies, from the church, usually only allowed him to get out a sentence or two before he was so overcome by paranoia that he'd literally run away. So in other words, we never got to speak; even if we did meet for a moment. He never acted like he didn't want to talk, as Stan tried to lead me to believe. Over time I saw that Stan was the one making up the lie. Alex did want to speak to me. Alex just as much wanted to reconcile as I did. But it was obvious to me that Alex greatly feared Stan and the power that Stan had to get him fired."

While she collected her thoughts, I told her of a few church situations that I was in in the past. I went into greater detail on one of them. "Listen, Rhoda, I actually understand what you are saying. I have been in more legalistic or should I say abusive churches, myself, in the past, than I can count. I was even in leadership in a few of them. In one of those churches we did not want a man and woman to speak to each other, much like you and Alex. They seemed willing to forgive each other and to even try to be friends again. But we, the all knowing leaders, felt that the whole story of what they had been involved in, might come out and make our church look bad. So even though they actually wanted to talk to each other, we kept telling different folks to lie and tell each of them that the other person did not want to speak to them. We called in a few of her friends and told them to counsel the woman to not speak to the man because 'he didn't really want to speak to her anyway and that God wouldn't approve'. Then we had a few miscellaneous people from church mention to the man not to speak to the woman. We lied. After this, she had no desire to speak to him again. They ended up not speaking to each other for years, until he was lying in a hospital bed, dying from cancer, and then the whole thing blew up in our faces. They both knew they were lied to and the woman even tried to sue us. This is when I decided to leave that church and began to see how evil legalism was. So I told you that nothing you say would shock me. And now maybe you can see I really do understand you. Okay enough about me. Please continue...."

She looked at me for a few minutes and said, "Wow, you are really the first person who didn't say this was my imagination. Thanks, Doc. Well, anyway, because of this I began to write Alex a couple of emails with a fake address to try and get him to "accidentally" meet me at our local park. He actually answered those emails thinking I was a concerned friend writing on my behalf. He explained rather openly that he didn't think he could do that since he was constantly being followed and he implied he was afraid for his life. He also said he would find a way to communicate with me. I wondered what that would be and I even got a couple of anonymous emails with greetings from him. But that was it. Until I began to work for different companies in the area: a dentist, an auto shop, a financial planner and a couple of tutoring centers. He knew where I worked because he had been my old boss and the companies called him for a job reference, so he'd always know where I was working next. At each place I worked I'd receive at least one silent call per day. The managers said that the calls only came when I was scheduled to work and after I explained the situation they even forwarded the calls to my desk. The dentist office was the most interesting. My job was only to file folders and answer calls, after hours. So when I was all alone in the office; he'd call, with a silent call. I'd hear him crying silently and would sometimes either pray for him or read him a scripture. But we'd never talk to each other. Then I also began to get silent calls at home and blank emails, totally blank. At first I told my husband about them every day. Then one day my husband said that I should stop telling him and just handle the situation my own way. He didn't care. So when Alex would call or send a blank email, I'd send a one line email saying thank you for the call or email and telling him it was time to meet for reconciliation and that he could actually speak to me or write words. But he didn't ever get the courage to do so. Believe it or not this went on for more than fourteen years right up till the day I got the reconciliation call from him. Sometimes he'd attempt to contact me a couple of times per day and other times he'd stop for a few weeks and then resume. I only responded to him if he made the first move. I did contact him independent of a prior contact if my daughter or husband was sick and needed prayer, or if I was having surgery, or if on very limited occasions I felt I hadn't heard from him in a few weeks. I always sent only a one sentence response; something like: 'Thanks for your call, am having eye surgery on Monday, plz pray, lets finally reconcile, be blessed' or something similar. I might have written an actual three or four line note about ten times, still only on the theme of reconciliation. As I said we did this system of communication, for over fourteen years. I know this sounds like a lot of communication, but all I truly wanted was a reconciliation meeting. But he never gave me the meeting I asked for. It was frustrating and I am not really sure my husband knows that this communication went on for so long. I don't know if Alex's wife or his church knew. On occasion his church did catch him writing to me, in the early years, and he'd get reprimanded and I'd get threatening calls from his church. But neither of us ever stopped wanting reconciliation. Man! To be honest, if they'd have let us speak, at that time; we would not have tried so hard to keep communicating in such weird ways."

I had to admit this was unusual, to say the least; but I know how cultic places think. Alex was most probably told, "You are not to speak to or write letters to Rhoda; if you do you will be fired." So being a good legalist, he did everything they told him to exactly, to the letter of the law: he called silently, without speaking and he sent blank emails, without writing a letter. He did the actions surrounding the commands and still managed to not break the commands. He could show Rhoda he was thinking of her and yet not break his promise to the church. Clever way of living by the letter of the law and not by the spirit of the law. This probably would not have bode well with either of their spouses; but this was done because of the religious and utterly ridiculous commands he was given by his church. He could feel he was not breaking any promises to them and that he was also not technically going against his spouse. Rhoda, on the other hand, was so miffed at the church's unrighteous decrees that she felt every contact from Alex was a kick in Stan's "shin". She felt this was a way to spit at an evil church's control. She also truly believed God had commanded she and Alex should reconcile; so this was just a means of "helping God along with His promises." But she did feel guilty in not being totally upfront with her husband. Even though she wasn't responding to Alex's communications, to be romantic; she still was doing something a bit behind the scenes. One thing her husband didn't realize was because of his passivity, she felt like she had to act on this herself and do what seemed best to her. This actually caused her to not be as open with him, as she would have liked. Actually I wondered why he didn't jump into the picture and help his wife settle this whole thing, at the very beginning. Did he actually blame his wife for Alex's attack? I knew I'd have to speak to her husband in the future, about this issue.

I put my hot chocolate down and looked at her for a moment, "Rhoda, are you looking for my approval of this secret silent relationship? Don't get me wrong. I totally get how the whole thing got started. The church made all normal means of communication taboo. Both your spouses were frustrated that you two wanted to reconcile. His wife was leery of the reconciliation, knowing of his past women problems. Your husband felt threatened by another man wanting to make things right with his wife, wondering if this meant that Alex had feelings for you and if you had similar feelings back. Those were two normal responses on their part. But Alex had the cult mindset which made matters worse. In a cult or abusive type church, you believe that the leaders can see you at all times, even if there are not any spies around and you are totally alone. You still think somehow they know what you are doing every second, of everyday, and even what you are thinking. This mindset caused Alex to not be able to meet with you even in a town away from the town you both live in. He still felt somehow someone would know he was speaking to you. Can you understand this? He knew, with one part of his brain, that all you wished to do was reconcile with him and that God likes reconciliation. But with another part of his brain he feared the control of Pastor Stan and if someone who was over him told him not to speak to you he had to obey. Can you get this way of seeing? I know it is not easy for the normal mind to grasp."

She looked up at me and said, "Mark, I never told you this; but I was in a cult for over 12yrs, ten of those years in Illinois, and two in Los Angeles. I totally get you and I also get how Alex thinks. I was 'mind bended' in the cult; but I guess I never got as bad as Alex. I still could think for myself. I wasn't totally smart in cult situations; but I think I was more in touch with God and reality. But you do cause me to remember one instance in Assembly cult: They always made people go on diets. So one time, to be sure I lost weight, they sent me to take care of an extremely elderly lady, in a very small town in Illinois. She was to be sure I only ate diet foods, totaling about 500 calories per day. I had to stay with her all summer, 24hrs per day, and I had no car or money. I was isolated and my only fun was to go out for an hour per day and ride an old rickety bike to the downtown. I'd park the bike and walk about the little two block town. One day I got a letter from my mom with $20 and I took that with me to town. I had a great lunch and even bought a giant candy bar. I ate every bit of the food and used up my money. But as I did this, I was sure that the leaders who lived 300 miles away in Chicago could see everything I had done. I was afraid that I'd be found out and that they'd punish me in some way. I lived in fear for the rest of the summer and when I had not lost any weight upon my return, they accused me of cheating. I took that as a sign that they actually did see what I did. They kept shouting at me until I confessed. Then they said they knew it all the time. Of course they lied, but in my cult mindset I could not see that."

"Interesting so you really can understand Alex, huh? Rhoda, you never told me you were a cult survivor. This changes much of what I was originally thinking. The old saying, 'It takes one to know one', really applies here, huh?" (She nodded. But I could tell she did not want to open up that can of worms, concerning her cult involvement, at this time. So I let it drop.) Let's talk about that time in the other cult at a future date, okay? (She looked grateful and nodded. A stray tear trickled out of her right eye. Just one and she drank a couple of sips of her chocolate.) "What do you think about this silent relationship between you and Alex?"

"Well, Doc, there are a couple of things. First I have to admit when I think of how angry Pastor Stan would have been/be, if he knew he had not been able to control us, like he intended to, I get a little glow inside. I know it's a bit mean; but he was really, really controlling; I haven't told you anything about that yet. Also I feel I put one over on all his little assistants and spies. But I'm not happy about not totally discussing the whole thing with my husband, even though he told me to 'do what I felt was best'. Then I feel happy that Alex still wants to be my friend, albeit a weird friend or should I say unusual. I'd love to just be open and honest with all parties. Lastly, I feel God is still working and has been all of these years and this is why Alex was/is like a dog with a bone and can't let this go. I know I'm not that cute, Doc. No one could secretly or otherwise love me, without getting anything out of it, for all of those years. I show my husband everyday how I love him; but Alex gets a one sentence: "thank you for your call (or email); let's reconcile." How can that be any incentive for him to keep going "after me"? I think the whole thing is crazy, actually, and if we'd have spoken years ago, I think I'd probably no longer even have any desire to know him, in any way. I like sane folks and this doesn't seem sane. I know I'm sitting here in a therapist office, myself; but I still think I'm at least 90% sane. Anyway, I'm glad we are going to finally get this resolved. My mind can't handle this much longer. I want to be clear before all parties and not have any shadows in my life. I'm not ashamed of my continued push to reconcile, but I know others would think I have gone totally crazy, if they knew. No one from my new church knows about this whole scenario, I got so tired of being misunderstood I decided to keep this part of my life a secret, especially from my new pastor. Lately, though, I did let him in on a small portion of the story, mainly because I was getting a bit discouraged. I think I ended up confusing him because it was such a small slice of a big "cake." But not being totally one hundred percent open is something that goes against my nature. Alex was used to lying to his wife and others; I was not or am not, whatever. It's not technically lying; but it feels like it. I am not pursuing this for me, I really believe that God has wanted me to reconcile for all of these years. I have been willing and waiting; but now in the fourteenth year it is finally coming to birth. It is not something I could have put up with in the natural."

I was again holding and petting Max, thinking of what to say next. I decided to change the story line a bit. "Rhoda, let's put this topic on the shelf for a bit. I feel I need to bring this up with Alex and see how his mind was working during this silent time. I want to ask you a question that maybe you can answer now or maybe you will just have to dwell on it for a bit. Okay, here goes: How did you feel about Alex as a man? I mean did you have any sexual feelings for him?"

She smiled a half smile and shook her head and sighed, "I knew you'd ask this sooner or later. But here's how it was. When I first came to work for him I thought he was like a big kid. Really. He was always joking and throwing things at me: paper balls, socks, rubber bands. Just like a big kid and he always was jumping about. He'd come in with his roller blades, or his bike, or a football. He was the perfect children's pastor; because he was a big kid. So I could not see him as a sexual being; he was too childish. He made me laugh with his antics. He also had his dark side, he'd be grumpy and crabby and just not pleasant to be around. When he was like that I was patient and waited for his mood to pass. He also could be super critical or insensitive, but I tried to excuse that, thinking my job with him was only temporary anyway. I was looking to the future and being on staff and in charge of the Women's Ministry. Doing Children's Ministry was temporary, Women's Ministry, that was my ultimate goal. One time he actually told me that he had had many assistants, but they couldn't take his moodiness and they left. He said I was the most patient person who ever worked with him. I could only shake my head. But as time went on I saw he was a troubled man. He did not get along well with his wife, he didn't really have any friends, he didn't really like his kids and he had women with serious mental disorders, from church, continually following him around. I also saw he had a lot of pressure from work and didn't get much family time. So I kind of felt sorry for him and wanted to help him, so he could have a more normal life, with friends and family. Sounds a bit crazy, huh? He was the pastor but I felt sorry for him and wanted to help him. So I asked God to let me help him and to let me be his friend, since he didn't seem to have any. There was nothing sexual in that and I loved my husband almost as much then, as I do now. I love my husband more each year we are married. Anyway…He would tell me his dreams for ministry, at times, when we were working and I would share what I wanted to do for God. But I never, as I told you, would speak of my marriage, except to say how I loved my husband and how we really wished we had another child. I never shared anything negative, mainly because I was happy with my husband; but more importantly, because I thought that would make for a bad precedent, for us to start speaking about our spouses. I had read that doing that could cause folks to have an affair and I did not want to go there. A few times he tried to speak about his wife, in a negative manner, and I told him I didn't want to talk about anything like that and asked him about his kids instead. He didn't seem too thrilled about his kids and I felt sorry. My husband would have killed to have three kids and especially two boys. I used to be a bit jealous of his life. He was in the ministry, had a nice wife, and three kids, a nice house, and he was thin and athletic, what more could someone want? I had a nice husband and daughter and was thankful; but he had all of the things I had wanted, every last one. Yet he wasn't appreciative. That kind of bugged me. But I did see he was pretty much a loner, that he only had the shallow friendships that many pastors have and that he didn't have a wife who adored him. I adored my husband and loved my daughter beyond words. One day he told me that he was actually jealous of my life. He wanted his spouse to be less involved in his life and he felt that one child was more than enough. Can you believe it? But seriously, Mark, this is all I felt for him, compassion and a desire to be simply his friend. It was in the after math of the two attacks that I began to question that I might have feelings that I did not realize were there. I wrote in a couple of emails, to a girlfriend, how I didn't know if I loved Alex or not. The reason I wrote that was, another girlfriend had said to me, that men don't attack women out of the blue. She said I must have given him some message or hint, that that was what I wanted. She said I must have really loved him and didn't want to admit it, even to myself. So I told myself I'd give myself two weeks to have introspection to see if I loved him sexually or not. Weirdly, I prayed this would be clear and I saw I truly didn't have any love feelings, just friendship. But I did on occasion relive his attacking me, and thought that was a bit overwhelming, and I would think, "Why would a man love me, since I'm not gorgeous?' You know that kind of thing? But I put any idea of my loving him back out of my head, since I really really loved my husband. I was more or less angry, and yet flattered, that someone would feel that passionately about me. But to make a long story short, no, I did not love him or want him in a sexual manner. It really was all him. If I wasn't already in love with my husband or married I might have been able to care for him in that way. But not only was I married, but he was and I couldn't even consider that type of thing, if I were unattached. This is the honest truth, Mark. To be honest

I also would never want a man who could cheat on his wife. If he cheated on her he'd do it to me too. I liked my husband's whole character so much better, and I just simply love my husband."

I felt like there was a bit of conflict inside of her, but this is normal for most humans. If a sexy woman sat on my lap I am not sure I wouldn't think of doing something, for a moment at least; but I am like Rhoda in this; I simply love my wife. I patted Rhoda on, the arm and looked at my watch. "It's 5pm. I have to get home to watch a movie with my wife. I promised I'd watch a romantic one with her since she saw one of those car chasing karate ones with me a few days ago. Let's call it a day, Rhoda. Make an appointment on the way out for Friday, I've got the afternoon open. Take care." She left with a brighter mood than when she came in and I hurried to make the next Bart. I had a lot to think of, myself. First I thought about the human psyche. Often when someone sexually abuses someone there is a bit of an inner conflict that goes on. On one hand there is hurt and anger; but on the other hand sometimes there is a bit of an attraction that develops. It is like that Stockholm syndrome. On one hand the kidnapped victims hate their captor; but on the other hand they sometime develop; a feeling of dependency and even love for their captor. This is a bit like how the mind works with sexual abuse. Part of the mind is angry and hates what is done; but another part develops feelings for the person. This is just the way the mind works and the victim cannot do much about it. They have to wait for natural healing to take away those feelings and to clarify the person's thinking. I think Rhoda was probably just about healed; but she had a bit more to go. I also thought this whole thing was eventually going to set a whole lot of people free. Whatever God was cooking up, in this situation, was getting quite interesting.

I went into the outer office and told my secretary she could go home. Just as I finished telling her this a thought struck me, "You have got to find out about Rhoda's first cult that she attended before the cult she was in with Alex." (The church she had attended with Alex was definitely a cult in every aspect; but not technically classified as one.) But I just knew having her speak about her first cult would cast light on her experiences in her second. So before my secretary left for the weekend I said, "Just one question: Did anyone cancel for next week?" She said that in fact someone had cancelled for Monday morning and that I was open from 9-11am. I had her call Rhoda on her cell phone, before she left, to tell her I needed to speak to her on her first cult experience. I wanted to do this before I had my time with Alex and before her Friday appointment. I asked Helen to ask her if she could come in at 9am, on Monday. I knew it was short notice; but since this was all basically free help for Rhoda, I had a feeling she'd agree to come in. My secretary got back to me, wearing her raincoat and flexing her umbrella. She said Rhoda would be in my office at 9am sharp on Monday. I patted her shoulder and sent her out into the driving rain. Then I went into my office and prayed with Max on my lap for about ten minutes. I double fed him for the weekend and made sure he had enough water and bit extra kitty litter in the box, gave Max an extra snuggle and shut everything off and left. I just made the Bart and was home in time to watch a romantic movie with my wife. I think it was Casablanca. I had to admit it wasn't too bad. We puttered around the house for the weekend doing little projects and, to be honest, I missed church; but the time spent with my wife was so comfortable and warm. I didn't feel badly about missing the meeting, to bond more with her. I think they had a special speaker come out that week and I just wanted time to be with my "bride".

Chapter 9

On Monday morning I was running late and took a quickie shower, forgetting to shave, and practically jumped into my clothes. I think I had two different socks on, but waved that off. I hugged my wife who was finishing her toast and grabbed my briefcase and flew out the door. I did do a bit of speeding and got to the Bart at a few minutes to 8am, I grabbed my parking stub and skipped the escalator to run up the stairs jumping inside the Bart just as the doors closed on my coat. I had to stay by the door until the next stop to be released. Then I sat down in the closest seat to review my notes before I got to the office. I have one of those tablets and one reason I like it is I can make the font big and not have to wear my little grandpa reading glasses. I read through the notes and checked my emails. Rhoda wrote an email and said she was coming and would try and write down a few facts to remember about her time in the cult she was in in Chicago. She told me to be prepared for a wild story. I smiled thinking about all the wild stories I'd heard in my career. Being a therapist is not for the faint of heart or the delicate.

I ran up the stairs arriving at 9:04am and hoping Rhoda would forgive me. Luckily she was not pressed for time. I told my secretary to let me know when the next client was there, thinking this could give Rhoda a few more moments since clients were notoriously late. Now I knew how they felt. "Rhoda, I'm so sorry I was running a bit late. I guess I relaxed too much this weekend and couldn't get myself in gear. Forgive me?" I gave her a sheepish smile, that worked with my wife, and she said, "Oh I didn't notice; sure you're forgiven." I was glad she wasn't hard to deal with. I said, "Tell me you'll drink some hot cocoa with me. I get mine from the café next store they are the best," I said as I escorted her into my office. She smiled and nodded and I had my already-getting-into-her-raincoat-secretary get us some and told her to get whatever she wanted. She joked at how the steak and eggs looked great. I really didn't care what she got. I tossed Rhoda a quilt, my wife's aunt made, and told her to get comfy. I then quickly tossed and changed the cat's weekend business and gave him a bit of food and water. Then I put two big logs on the fire, lit it, and pulled off my wet shoes replacing them with my slippers. Rhoda was watching my performance and even clapped when I finally sat in my chair. I smiled and said, "Ta da", taking a little half bow from my chair.

"At last...Sorry Rhoda, but without doing what I just did we'd be smelling cat poop and shivering. This office is really cold without a fire. Okay, anyway... So it is about 9:15am; why not try and tell me your Chicago cult story, and I might butt in everyone once in awhile to clarify anything I'm confused about. When did you join this cult and what was its name?" The secretary tiptoed in and gave us our cocoas, she had a little paper bag in her pocket, so I guessed it wasn't steak and eggs. I whispered thanks as she backed out the door. Once it was shut Rhoda began to speak.

"Well, Doc, I was already saved and in a little house fellowship called, "The God Squad". We were a bunch of charismatic hippie high school kids who simply loved God and wanted to meet like the early church. At that time I had a girlfriend, who also went to a fellowship that was called "Open Door Ministries". Those kids were a bit older than us. We were all part of the Jesus Movement and very open to the move of God's Spirit. The "Open Door" kids lived in community and had everything in common and were a bit more hippie-ish than we were. I was looking for a community like that, but one that was more Bible oriented. They seemed to be more focused on their leaders' opinions and less on the actual Bible. I love my God Squad group; but wanted to go deeper. So one day on my college campus a couple of older students in their twenties, I was nineteen, invited me to a Bible Study on the campus. I decided to attend and it was so 'deep' I was immediately impressed. I got more and more involved in campus ministry and also began to go to the Bible studies they had at their private homes. A few months later, I also began to go to their worship meetings and prayer meetings. Oh yeah, the group was known as 'The Assembly' They had a brother's house and a sisters' house and shared all things in common. I liked that and they were connected like a family and this really got me. It was like the Home Church movement, that I had read about. I was soon totally involved there and my old group was concerned that I might be in a cult and so they came to see the meetings and to help me ask questions to be sure that the Assembly was totally Biblical. The meetings were boring to them, since they weren't charismatic; but they passed inspection. They were deemed Biblically correct. They had right teaching on who Jesus is/was, what He came to do, the Trinity, virgin birth, resurrection, His Coming, etc. etc. They passed all questions with flying colors. So my old group gave me their blessings; but no one from that group wanted to join with me (later two sisters did try, but could not meet the group's strict requirements). Anyway, after about a year the new group asked me to move into a sisters' apartment, they were just starting. I considered that a high honor. My parents were none too happy, since we had just moved into a new home in Berwyn, IL. My mom and I had decorated my room and I was in my second year of college, working on my Elementary Education degree. I had just switched from a Journalism degree, at a Junior College near my home and transferred to the University of Illinois, at Chicago. My parents gave me permission to move out, but said I'd have to pay my own way and this included for my own schooling. So it was quite a step of faith. The only possessions I had were $600 I had saved from a summer camp counselor job, the new bike I had just purchased, and my bed and dresser. Most of the six hundred went to my new rent (including first and last month's rent), food, and utilities. I got a part-time job at the local Sizzler and was able to get some student aid to help with the cost of my schooling. I would go to school fulltime, work 30hrs per week, do about 12hrs of chores and meal prep, attend two to three meetings per day, mentor people and be mentored, pray for at least an hour per day, and even do extra work projects for others in the group. We never stopped working and I would end up doing my homework into the wee hours of the morning. I slept less than two hours per day. We all had to have a schedule and mine was quite tight. Every half hour of my day was scheduled and we were constantly being checked to see if we were on schedule. The group had many layers of leaders. Layer one was the head steward layer. Each person in the house or apartment they lived in, got to take a turn at being the "stew" once per month. The "stew" would check to see if you were on schedule, give you permission to see family, tell you about extra work assignments, give and check your assigned chores, give punishments for any flaws, no matter how small, in your chores or if you had a bad attitude of any sort about anything, tell you what you needed to change in your life to be perfect, make sure you attended all meetings, and send you on to the next level of leader, if they did not know how to deal with you. The next level, if you were a sister, was the leading sisters (brothers were not subject to any leader from this level). This was not an official "office"; but if the leading sisters told you to do something for them or anyone else; you had to obey. They'd usually take you out for coffee or a walk and tell you how to improve yourself and give advice that had to be followed to the letter, this included diets, how to dress, and how to be a better servant. If you did not obey them or had an attitude problem you then went on to the next level of leader. This level was the leading brothers. These men were to be obeyed immediately and implicitly, no questions asked. They had the power to send you to other places where the Assembly had sister groups, to recommend you be excommunicated from the faith, to tell you who to see in regards to family or friends, and give permission for you to date, who they approved and eventually allow you to marry. Without their permission you would never be able to marry. The also told you what jobs you could do outside the group, what educational path you could follow, what career path to follow and gave long extended sessions of strict lectures to you if you strayed from their advice in any way. These sessions always included threats and shouting. Some groups had head leading brothers which were slightly above the rank of the regular leading brothers and some groups had elders. This elder level was the highest rank a man could hope to reach. They controlled everyone in their local assembly (there was about twenty-five assembly group in the US and around the world.), those in groups without elders, unruly individuals, had the final say on marriages, and sent out missionaries. But the ultimate top or head of all the Assembly was a man named Brother George Geftakys. He along with his wife Betty and two sons ruled the whole thing, from their home in Fullerton, CA. He had the ultimate say and would be who the elders went to for wisdom on who to excommunicate, from being a Christian and to damn them for all eternity. He would make a proclamation and it was law; he over rid all the other leaders and their decisions. Whatever decision he made did not ever change unless he changed it. Every movement you did, everyday, was tracked by all of those leaders and also the regular members were quick to tattle on you. This was especially true of those who wanted to be in the leadership someday. The common members who wished to lead, would be sure to try and find fault with you to gain favor with the leaders they served. Some leaders had little groups of followers that were kind of lackeys. They did whatever the leader wanted, including all of their chores. Another name for them would be: suck ups. Any leader could tell anyone to do their chores and other things for them, like errands, etc., at anytime of the day or night. There was to be no questioning or disobeying. Some brothers, like George Geftakys, took that to the extreme and made sisters they fancied have sex with them, as a way for them to please God. That was not known by most of the group until years later, when the group broke up. We were encouraged to not see family or friends outside the group and you could also be commanded, by a leading brother, to not see those people. Also you could not watch TV, listen to popular music, go out for fun, attend other churches, read books (other than recommended ones), date (unless you consented to go through a complex system of rules and regulations for engagement) and they usually had a recommended mate for you, and you had to wear your hair and dress in a proper Assembly manner. Sisters mostly wore longish skirts, long hair, and head coverings during meetings. You prayed in a set manner, outlined by George, for an hour each morning. You were to always be available for work details, on top of your regular work load. If you had a free moment, you could not relax, you had to be "productive" with it by: taking care of someone's children or doing their housework or remodeling. You never got to be alone, even in the bathroom. The doors were kept unlocked, when you were in the bathroom, at all times, so that others, of the same sex, could use the facilities with you. Never being able to sleep, never being alone, never being able to think, and never being able to rest, was our manner of life. In the midst of all of this, a great and overwhelming sense of loneliness would fill me and I was never able to stop weeping. I wept daily; because I, like most of the sisters, never had a man to love or children or any sense of stability. As I got older I wanted the normal things of life like have: a home, a family, a career, a ministry, friends, to see my family of origin, and to enjoy life. But this was not even in my realm of possibility. I had nothing and no one, only work and more work. There was also the constant evaluation by the leaders concerning everything about you. They told you: you were too fat, too stupid, too lazy, too whatever. You were never good enough and you just knew God thought the same way. We were not kind to each other. If you wanted to be a leader you would turn in people to get points with the leadership. Regular members were always watching you hoping to catch you doing something wrong and make themselves look good by turning you in and exposing some sin or wrong thought, according to Assembly standards, that is. No love, just constant unending criticism and punishments. I was subject to abuse, on a constant basis. I would even get taken down into the basement, at the sisters' house, and get yelled at for hours by the leading brothers, until I confessed to things I didn't do. Sometimes I'd eventually confess, just to get away from the yelling. Then there were punishments, from the head stewards, in which you'd be forced to do hours and hours of grunt work to for others, possibly for only saying something as bland as, "Why didn't you like my chore? What did I do wrong?" This would lead to being called rebellious and you'd get endless punishments for daring to question anyone over you; these were mostly hard labor of some sort. Once a leading sister did answer this question and she said, "You missed one corner of a picture frame. The whole room was spotless; but you missed that corner." She looked at me and asked me if Jesus would like that error when He returned. And I said to her if that was all I missed I didn't think Jesus would give a fig. Because of that statement, I then had to do a chore for each of the fourteen people in the sisters' house. I'd recently been transferred there from the sisters' apartment and was in extreme training, for what I had no idea. Yelling, put downs, rules, anger, scorn, and all manner of verbal abuse day after day for ten years. On year eight I was transferred to a sister Assembly in Champaign, IL., where the abuse was slightly less. I attended the University of Illinois at Champaign while there. Then I was transferred to Springfield, IL. to another sister Assembly because I had to finish my degree and so I attended the University of IL., at Springfield, and did a double major in Elementary Education and Social Services. There I met a man from Thailand and dated him briefly which caused me to become a 'leper' in that Assembly. I didn't really care for him that much and finally found the man who would become my husband a young man named Alex from Taiwan. He was very kind and by that time, with all the abuses I'd been through, I did not care if he was a believer, or not. He was better than any supposed Christian man I had known, in the Assembly. We married and moved to Fullerton, CA. which happened to be the headquarters of the Assembly. I rejoined the group for two more years. But this time I was less involved because we had our lovely daughter and my husband would not allow me to be as involved in the group. Also I was still labeled a rebel and pretty much shunned by the group. George did talk to me once to threaten me and then promptly forgot about me. The coldness of the group and a job transfer for my husband got me out of that area. Also I went to see a Christian psychologist and he told me I had been in a cult and tried to help me. But I left because we could not afford a psychologist. I began to have horrible nightmares and 'daymares' and would wake up in a sweat screaming, remembering the years of abuses and all of the mocking, yelling, and verbal abuse. Today this is known as PTSD or post traumatic stress disorder; but folks then only thought that happened to soldiers. I vowed to never enter another church or fellowship without my husband because: 1. I was afraid and 2. I didn't want any more religious abuse." She looked out the window and tears came down her face. "Doc, I wasted my whole life for nothing. They found out Brother George was a pervert and he just laughed, when they caught him red handed. All that suffering, all those years for nothing! I thought God hated me, I wasn't good enough and there was something defective in me that caused me to serve a pervert and his teachings."

I had dropped the notebook I was writing in a half hour before and I passed her a Kleenex, but I wasn't sure if she needed it or if I was going to need it. What a eschewed view of Christianity! She stayed because she thought to leave was to leave God's will for her life. Cult thinking is so twisted that the normal minded person always asks, "If it was so bad, why didn't you just leave?" But in the cult thinking this thought would have been too frightening. In a cult you are taught to slowly turn over your will, your normal mind, and you grow to accept the mind of the leadership and you soon view God as they do. A small hate filled God, who is waiting to punish you, at any moment. Leaving the cult is akin to leaving God.

I looked at her and saw a woman who was abused and battered and yet somehow survived. What did her husband think of Christianity after all of this and how had it affected her daughter? I had so much to ask; but I felt I knew enough to use this knowledge to see Alex and so I told her I'd think over what she told me and would ask her a few more questions on Friday, before getting back to the case at hand. I thought we could spend another three years on the effects of the Assembly. Also the same went for Alex. All the problems he had with women! We could spend years on that issue alone but I'd have to steer them back to the issue of Alex's attack and the response of his church. Maybe they'd both come see me on these other issues after we got the church mess mopped up. So I gave her a fatherly shoulder hug and told her I'd see her on Friday. So sad, most folks think that there aren't any cults today, that it was a hippie thing.

Chapter 10

I practically ran to my car and admit to speeding a bit, again, to get to the Bart Station on Wednesday. I was so curious what the meeting with Alex would uncover. But just as with Rhoda, I decided we needed to take a step back with Alex. We all just don't automatically appear on the scene, with our weaknesses. They all have their origin somewhere in our murky pasts. And that somewhere is usually our childhoods. I know it is rather cliché, but our relationships with our parents, unfortunately, do make us the adults we turn out to be. As teens and young adults we try desperately to separate ourselves from our parents; but ultimately much of our character is set by the time we are five. It takes a really severe life change to overcome this and even Christians are the products of their upbringings and influenced by them. This is the problem I have with some Christian dogma. They make change in our lives seem like it should be instantaneous, once we are saved. Yet, all I have seen over the years tells me change comes slowly, through a daily process. We can be stubborn and refuse to allow change; or, in some cases, we just don't see an area we are keeping from God. God has to chip away at our lives again and again, little by little until we can finally see our areas of need and how we need to allow Him to "make all things new", area by area. Just having someone touch you on the head at a meeting, is not going to help in these "stronghold areas". It is a submitting to God, at times a millimeter at a time, until he finally conquers or claims another part of our "land" or character. It requires a willingness to allow Him to work in these areas, not some religious determination on our part.

I mused on these and other things as I sat on the Bart. I often play with my laptop computer or notepad; but that day I was lost in thought. Therapy works when and only when people are honest and allow someone like me access into their "darkness". All of us do things or think things we would never want broadcast to others. With time we encapsulate these things and push them to the backs of our minds preferring to pretend they don't exist. Now I see this tendency even more so in men and Alex is an expert at this encapsulation process, kind of decompartalmentalizing of ones life. People, especially men, do this so they can avoid dealing with parts they don't want to look at. I vowed that somehow I'd crack open at least one of his "compartments", in my office, that chilly Wednesday morning.

I picked up a bagel, with a lox smear, and a spiced hot chai and went up the stairs into my office. It was a bit early, so my secretary was not yet in. I got three big hunks of wood and lit them in the fireplace. Then I cleaned up Max's litter box, fed him, and kissed him on his wet little nose. I put the electric tea kettle on and placed the quilt on the chair and then I sat down and ate my breakfast. I then made a "pit stop" and tidied up. Just as I was tidying my secretary arrived and asked if I needed anything. I told her I was fine and asked if she wanted some tea. She declined saying she just had some and I set out two cups one for me and one for Alex and put two bags in each cup and put out a plate of fresh made ginger snaps. I opened my brief case and took out my notes from the last session and flipped through them once again. I was deep in thought when I heard a soft knock on the door. Alex entered. I could tell he was cold. The folks in the Bay Area are wimps, next to us Downtowners.

"Alex, here is a nice cup of tea? Would you like sugar or honey? Gingersnap? Feel free to use that quilt on the chair. Don't worry I won't let anyone know you sat here wrapped in a quilt." I was over chattering and I could see Alex was not listening to me, but thinking about something.

"Oh, ah, hi, Mark. I'll take one teaspoon of honey and a couple of those gingersnaps. Homemade? Believe me; I am chilly enough to not care what anyone thinks about a guy wearing a quilt. Mark...um...my wife found out about these sessions. She got a hold of the insurance bill. So I had to come clean, with her. Man, did we have a fight! She is staying at her mom's for a week. She left fuming. But I told her I needed to heal and that our church had done everything it could to keep me from doing so. She is super loyal to the church and that statement really made her explode. But she really got ticked when she discovered I had not broken off my friendship with Rhoda, that it had continued on for over fourteen years after she thought it was over. She even threatened to go to the head pastor and rat on me. But I told her if she did that I'd divorce her. So she said she'd be staying at her mom's for a week. Her mom hates me and so I know that she'll probably come back divorcing me instead. Man!"

I shook my head and took a long sip of tea. "Alex I know that this seems bad to you right now, but I have got to tell you something, I've found to be true. Opening up to your wife in this area, though it has been messily done, is probably going to actually help your marriage. If you want you can either send her here to see me or have her call me. She works for the same church so your insurance should cover her too. Mention this option next time you two speak. I'll pray that this actually turns out to be a good thing, though, at this moment, it is uncomfortable. Tell you what? Let's leave this issue on the back burner for a bit, I think I can smooth things over if she speaks with me. I have to take you to an area that may be uncomfortable for you to discuss; but going there will provide the key for us, as to how we will proceed forward. Will you trust me in this area, we are about to enter?"

Alex nodded and had a curious look on his face, wondering where I was headed. "Well you're the expert, let her rip." I was surprised at what seemed like a moment of rare vulnerability.

The roaring fire and warmth from it had put both of us in a more relaxed state and Max was snoring at Alex's feet. "Well, I might as well just speak out. What type of man was your father? Was he your friend or more of an authoritarian sort?"

"He was strict and very distant from us. I have two sisters and a brother; none of us felt close to our dad. Our mom was kind of crabby, since he was tough on her also. We were not the Norman Rockwell type family. He got married when he was older and seemed like he always wished we hadn't been born, like we were a nuisance. So in short, he was not my friend."

I felt sorry for him since I was great friends with my dad and my dad was my mom's number one fan. "First of all Alex, no one's family is Norman Rockwell. Being in ministry we sometimes try to remake our childhoods to seem like they were picture perfect; but who are we kidding? Every family is flawed in one way or another. It is just how flawed that really counts. Okay?

Alex, did your dad believe in corporal punishment? Did he ever go beyond mere spankings?" I said "mere" on the spanking issue because in Alex's childhood days, most parents spanked their kids, even on "Leave it to Beaver."

"Yeah he hit us; it was mostly out of frustrations he was having, not for anything we actually did. It never got to the child abuse level, if this is what you are asking."

I was seeing another part of Alex that I'm sure he never shared with anyone at his church or in his community. That type of father, today, would be thought of as someone who was lower class, less educated, and Alex would want to appear as if he came from a higher class family. "Alex was your dad faithful to your mother, as far as you know? Did he ever have anyone on the side?"

He stirred in his chair, clearly uncomfortable with that question. "Well, my dad was a kind of a flirt. He'd always overdo it when he bumped into a woman, when he wasn't in my mom's presence. He'd say things like, 'Oh you're a lovely little thing or what a sweet face you have', or the like. The ladies would usually giggle and blush. My mom tried to ignore this behavior, when others would express concern. She was very lovely when she was young, but did put on weight as she got older. My dad, at around that time, began to stay out late and even did not come home a couple of times. They'd fight like cats and dogs and then he'd come home after work faithfully, for a few weeks. Then he'd be out with 'the boys' until the early hours of the morning. This was probably the source of my mom's dark or crabby moods. I tried to ignore this behavior, as a boy. So I'm guessing he had a few lady friends."

"Was your dad from another country? You sounded like you had a bit of an accent when you were copying him?"

"Actually no, Mark, my dad was from Washington State; he actually grew up on an Indian reservation; but he was not an Indian. He met my mom in Australia, in 1943, during the war and took her back home with him. So my mom had the accent. They were married in Sydney, Australia. They came and moved to San Leandro in the Bay Area, soon afterwards. He was in the Air Force in the war and became a commercial pilot over here. Anyway, though I loved my mom, I strove to have perfect English; but yes, a bit of accent does still come through. So my dad was colorful, but not really affectionate to his family.

"He wasn't too keen on you or your siblings, it seems; but how did you feel towards him? Sometimes kids like their parent, even when the parent is not too fond of them."

Alex looked like about five emotions were warring in him. "Well, first of all he died a couple of years ago. So I've actually been thinking about him a bit more, lately. As an adult I tolerated him pretty much and even tried to get to know him more. We did get closer, right before he passed. He seemed to get closer to God, too. When I was a little kid my dad was my hero, an airplane pilot. I don't know why, but I stuck to him like glue. Imagine this dashing (in my mind) pilot character dragging around this little blond skinny kid? I think now that he took me with him to give him more favor with the ladies, like bringing a puppy out when you go on a walk. As I got older I felt ashamed of his brashness and of the unrelenting over the top comments to the ladies. I just kind of stopped liking him when I was about eleven, I guess. I used to pretend I was from a traditional, 'Father Knows Best' family and I never invited my school mates to my house. I tried to have perfect speech and perfect manners to be different than my dad. It got worse as I went into my teen years. I left home rather early, after getting into trouble with the law for little petty crimes in my teens."

I could see that he did not have an ideal childhood. He learned how to relate to women by watching his father. I could see where he got his ability to turn on the charm, when he needed to, and how he had gotten a more twisted view of marriage. "Alex, do you see how your dad's behavior with 'the ladies' basically disrespected your mother? Here he had a lovely young wife and over time he began to give more attention to 'the ladies' He didn't give warm loving support to her or to her four children. Can you see this a bit clearer now? In his mind 'the wife' was mainly to be used to run the home, while he 'carried on' on the outside like he was still single. Can you see how he did this?"

He looked deep in thought, "You know I am seeing this, to some extent. To us it was just dad, being dad; but I was never comfortable with it. To the ladies and those on the outside of our home he was a fun charismatic pilot guy; but when he came home he was cold and distant. Yes, I can remember, now, that this did bug me at times. He never came to my school plays, or to parent teacher's night, and we never went to the park to play ball or just go for a walk. He used me as a prop to get the ladies' attention, but ignored me for the most part. In the home, life for us kids was rather regimented. It wasn't a hoot for my mom either. Hmmm."

"Alex, I'm going to go out on a limb and say that the disrespect your dad showed your mom was a deep influence on your life, as to how you were supposed to treat a wife. The affairs you had were just more ways of showing a lack of respect for your wife and her feelings. Also you thought it was your job to go 'chucking up' the ladies, with your need to be charming, at all times. Am I right? Can you see, a bit, that you were actually repeating some of your dad's behaviors?"

Alex looked a bit angry, "Maybe." He crossed his arms and got red behind the ears.

"You're looking a bit miffed. What is your problem with what I said?" I didn't want him to bolt. So I offered him another ginger cookie. Thankfully he took it and tapped it on his chair a few times, calming down with each tap.

He was a bit red in the face, "Well, I can't understand this at all. All my life I have tried to not be like my dad and you are telling me I'm not only kind of like him, but almost a clone. We may have had certain problems that overlapped, but I'm cultured and educated and on top of that I'm a Christian pastor. I'm not like him. I, I, I can't be."

I touched his arm slightly. "Look, sometimes it is hard to face certain weaknesses in ourselves. But when you finally acknowledge them, you can change and you don't have to end up like your dad, you can decide to change the course of your life and make things better. Comprendo?"

Alex, looked thoughtful and said, "I wonder if my kids don't like me? To be honest, Mark, I have had my moments when I have felt they were a burden. I only wanted two. The two seemed overwhelming to me. Then when we had the third it was more than I could stand. I started to feel choked. In order to make up for this feeling I used to take them on these wild summer vacations, kind of chaotic, no holds barred. Or I'd take them skiing. I did high adrenaline things with them to super charge them and make them think I was such a fun dad. But to be honest I was pretty crabby, the rest of the time. I wanted them to be perfect and to please me. So I was a bit militaristic. This kind of an attitude also kept them from getting too close to me. So maybe I am like my dad. My wife is my wife; but we are not really friends. She is excellent at her wifely tasks; but we just have never really clicked and I guess I have resented her for this, thinking it was her fault. Maybe I bear some responsibility."

"Can you see how this kind of thing, with your dad, has influenced your thinking and how this ties into your confusion with Rhoda and the other women in your life? Can I tell you something on the side, Alex (he nodded)? If your wish would have come true and you would have run off with Rhoda, do you realize you'd be 'chucking up the ladies' within a few months of your new relationship? You see it is not really the woman, who is married to you that is the problem; it is how you view the woman. No matter who you marry, there will always be the ghost of your dad's treatment of your mom, that will influence the way you see that woman, unless there is a fundamental change in you. You will repeat this behavior, the loving the ladies thing, until you get too old or someone's husband takes you out. Are you catching this?" I usually don't say so much, so bluntly. But I wanted to get a little breakthrough, so that we could get back on subject, at our next meeting. I pushed the limit and hoped I had not gone too far.

Alex was looking at Max and trying to avoid eye contact. "I would never have been so thoughtless to Rhoda; she's, she's such a sweet person. I...I..."; his voice was cracking a bit.

"Alex, I know you would never have done this consciously; but believe me you would have done it, none the less. Even the affairs you had. I don't think you actually sat down and said, 'Let's see, how I can disrespect my wife and use this woman as a tool to do so?' No. You actually may have thought you were in love (or lust) each time you strayed and that that supposed feeling, at the time, gave you permission to cheat. Am I right? Or if not that you were in love, that you simply wanted a woman sexually, and that this was going to happen no matter if it broke your marriage vows or not, no matter who got hurt. Right?" I looked him in the eyes, to show him I wasn't being judgmental just "straight up" with him.

He again avoided eye contact and he said, "You might be right. I never even thought of my wife at all, in any way, when I had the affairs. I just pursued what I wanted. I guess I was the same before I was married. I never felt really married, and so I just was the same, after marrying, as I was before marriage." He picked up his head and looked me in the eyes, this time, "I guess I'm kind of a creep, huh?" His neck got bright red and he looked out the window.

"Look, Alex, we are all 'kind of creeps" in one area or another. Maybe this is the beginning of your changing for the better. God is never done working on any of us." I patted him on the shoulder, like a father again. "Say can I ask you one question that is kind of off subject?"

"Sure, go ahead. I need to get off subject for awhile to sort my thoughts. I brought my bike so I think I'll go for a long bike ride after this. Shoot."

"Well, I'm not going to go into any details; but did Rhoda ever tell you she was in a cult before coming to your church? I'm curious because I think that maybe folks at your church would have treated her differently, if they'd have known her history."

He got a funny smirk on his face. "You don't know my church then. She mentioned the cult thing to me in passing. But she told Pastor Stan all about it and you know what he did? He tried to play mind games with her to make her submit to him, like she would have had to do in the cult. He even laughed, as he told me about how he'd made the experiences he put her through, scarier than any cult experience she ever went through. From what I know, he used this knowledge, of her cult experience, quite well and sadly he seemed to enjoy it. Why do you ask?"

I didn't want to tell him what Rhoda had shared so I just said, "Oh I was just curious. Don't worry about it. It has nothing to do with you. Pastor Stan sounds like quite a piece of work though, huh?"

"If you only knew…" He shook his head. I told him the time was up and that my next client would be pounding at the door in a moment.

"Could you ask the secretary what time you can meet, after Rhoda's next visit? I have forgotten exactly the day and time I'll be seeing her. Please make another appointment, even if this one was painful; I see God working. I will try to put us back on subject at the next meeting. After this church situation is settled I'd love to talk more with you on the women issue. Think about it. Maybe you could bring your wife, after a few sessions and we can get your marriage back on track. Let's see." I walked him to the door and the sun was actually out. I was glad we were able to broach this subject concerning his father's influence. I actually ran to the restroom to answer "the call", before Mrs. Morton arrived.

Chapter 11

I'm like the rest of the Nation. I love Fridays. In fact when Friday comes my heart starts to beat in anticipation of my being able to spend the entire weekend with my lovely wife. Even at church, on Sundays, we made a pact to only go to classes together, none of that men's or women's meeting thing for us. We go to couples classes and events at church because we can't stand to be apart. I guess some would say that was a bit too "sweetie", for folks our age. But since we both work all week and she does go to a Ladies Bible Study class one evening a week, we just feel there is too little time for us to be together. We weren't always that way; but after we turned fifty, we started to value one another more. Anyway, I woke up that particular Friday morning in a chipper mood, but wishing it were Friday evening. My wife and I have always had special meals together on Friday nights, even when our daughter was young, and I was thinking of a little ten table restaurant I had just discovered. I could even smell the wine. But I would have to proceed through my day before I could hear that cork pop.

Thankfully, today was Rhoda's day to see me. At least it would be an interesting day. The rest of the day I had a new client from my church, which'd be coming in the afternoon and tons of paperwork for me and the clients' insurances. So I was glad Rhoda made a morning appointment. I got to the office with my chai and bagel in hand, at about 8:30am, and went about tidying up the place and getting Max ready for the day. I don't know why, but I was extra chilly and decided to put a few extra logs on the fire. With fire it is the way you stack the logs that counts and I stacked them to make the most heat and hopefully to last through till lunch. I looked over my notes, from Rhoda's last visit, and I quickly ate my breakfast. I just put the electric kettle on when my secretary buzzed me to let me know Rhoda had arrived. I smiled as she walked in and said, "Morning, Rhoda. Tea or hot chocolate today?" I held up the containers and she pointed to the hot chocolate. "That is the best for a chilly day; I agree." When the kettle went off I handed her a cup after she finished getting settled with Max and the quilt. "So Rhoda, any new thoughts since last visit?"

Rhoda said, "So besides being a therapist you're also a psychic, right?" She gave me a half smile and said, "You know, Doc, you are the specialist; but before we into what you have planned for this meeting can I mention something that is bugging the heck out of me?" I nodded for her to plow ahead. "Well, first I think it was a good thing that we went over my first cult experience. I saw a lot of links, that corresponded to the time I spent at Alex's church, which you'd probably say was my second cult experience. I am tending to agree with that. But for some reason this random thought keeps coming into my mind and I don't really know why it has waited to rear its ugly head till now. So here it goes: "Back when Alex made his intentions known about how he felt towards me I was flattered, at first, after all he is a nice man and not bad looking. But then I found that three thoughts kept coming into my head, making me want to slap him a few times. The first thought that came into mind, at that time, was about gratefulness. Not that I was grateful; but sometimes when a woman is overweight men think she should be grateful that when they try to have sex with her. The thinking behind this is, 'Look, no one would want to 'jump someone's bones', who was fat like you; so for me to even try, was me doing you a favor.' (I started to jump in.) Wait, Doc, just let me finish my thoughts. The second thought that came to mind was anger, at the disrespect of the whole thing. I mean, after all, if some man jumped Alex's wife or daughter, he'd have punched his lights out. Yet he thought I'd gladly accept a man, who disrespected me. Like, if a guy whistled I'd follow. Like, I was desperate or something. And lastly, the third thought

I had at the time, was anger at Pastor Stan. You know what he said, Doc; besides all the other crud, he said? (I shook my head.) He said, 'Why would Alex pick you? Look at you. Why you're fat. If he was going to attack some woman, why didn't he pick my wife? My wife is at least an attractive woman. Why would he pick someone like, like you?' Look, Doc, I realize that I'm no Sophia Loren or something, but the gall of that Pastor Stan. Man! I only surmised what Alex was thinking, most of the time; but Stan just said what he thought right out. He was in charge of counseling women at that church! What a creep! I wondered if he went around, 'just being honest' with all those ladies?! But anyway there was this part of me, back when all this came down, that saw the whole thing as, as a devaluing of me. I did not see this as some sort of love on Alex's part and I never felt the love from Stan and the church. So what do you think, Doc, did I over thinking things or was I thinking in a mixed up manner?" Her cheeks were bright red, and along with her red hair, she was actually a lovely woman. She couldn't see this and with the way Alex, Stan, and the others treated her, I'd be surprised if she could. Also Pastor Stan's type of man always feels that they need to belittle a woman, to keep her in her place, under the sole of their shoe.

I thought for a few moments and then spoke, "You know, Rhoda, I was thinking, at first, that you were a bit too forgiving and loyal to Alex and that maybe you respected Pastor Stan a bit too much. But now I see that you have had your moments of…should I say, clarity? There is a confusion, out in the world today, that if you forgive someone you are basically saying that whatever they did was alright, not just forgiven, but rather: excused. But that is not real forgiveness and that is the primary reason people will not forgive. They think that by forgiving they say that the perpetrator is excused from their actions and that everything is all 'alright now'. No, this is not reality based forgiveness. Let me ask you a question before I go on. If a man rapes a woman, is that a minor offense (she shook her head and mouthed 'No'). Okay, then if the man is eventually forgiven by the woman, should the woman treat the man like that just never happened and keep spending time alone with him? Of course not! Though the man is forgiven, the rape did happen and she'd be wise to keep her distance and not let him have any access to her. She should, while she is at it, also report the rape to the police and prosecute. What if the man were to rape another person? Forgiveness doesn't take away from the facts of what happened."

"Okay, Doc, I get your point on that. But Alex didn't rape me; so where are you going with this?"

"Rhoda, I was hoping you could connect the dots yourself; but let me do some of that for you. We don't know if Alex thought you were the most beautiful woman on earth; we don't know what was going through his mind. But even if he thought that, it would still be wrong for him to attack you. I know you agree with this; but what all is involved in an attack? There are multiple factors: first there is just plain sexual desire, secondly there is power over a subordinate, and thirdly there is an element of violence—anger against women. Fourthly there is a wanting to keep someone from becoming your equal, to make them know their place in the pecking order. Of course there are lots of other smaller variables, depending on the person who is doing the attacking. There could also be something in you that triggered something in him, that no one else could trigger. So part of the reason Alex may have attacked you could certainly be a distain for women, maybe more so for overweight women. Maybe in that you reminded him of his mother or someone from his past or maybe he just has a prejudice, in the weight area. You are far from obese, Rhoda; but who knows what was in his past. So here he likes a woman, who is against his idea of perfection. Maybe this made him a bit angry and he decided to attack you to put you in your proper place, I don't know. Maybe also he saw you as a threat to him in the ministry and he subconsciously thought an affair would sideline your going forward. Maybe he had six things going on at once when he decided to cross the line. But regardless, he disrespected you because he decided to just 'take you'. He didn't ask your permission or care that you loved your husband or that you wanted to stay pure before God; he just pounced. Maybe he thought you'd just jump at the chance to have the privilege of having sex with him, that you were 'easy' as they used to say. I guess you and I will never know all the reasons. I don't even think he does. But it is disrespectful to treat any woman like that. To just take anyone without their consent or against their will demeans that woman and makes her into basically 'a slut', an object. So you were seeing clearly, in this. Sin is not pretty and the reasons behind it are not pretty. Sin has so many variables in the back ground, that even the sinner could never sort them all out. Comprendo? As far as that stupid set of statements by Pastor Stan, we can just say there are two reasons for his foolish words: one is just plain ignorance and prejudice and two is he was putting you down, to trash you, because you chose to come against him. He is an almighty Pastor and you were not to forget that. Pastors deserve respect, but he wanted adulation. It had nothing to do with you; it was all part of his twisted mind. Wow; would I love to see him in this office! Look, I hate to sound so dogmatic. But for you to pick up on the things you did, with those two fellows, was actually you seeing things clearly. You are further along in healing than I thought. I thought you might have a, 'the pastor can do no wrong' thinking, that can happen in cults. But knowing you could see beyond their titles is a good sign." I feared I had said too much and she might up and run like some do when they are touched by truth. But instead a silent tear rolled down her cheek.

She looked at me and gave a sigh of relief. It was like a huge weight came off of her shoulders. "Oh, Doc, I could hug you. That is the first time a feeling I have had has been validated and respected by someone. For so long whenever I have voiced a feeling, people have just waved it and me off, like what I said was insignificant. Also you were able to consolidate my random side thoughts into the picture and help me see that sin has so many hidden roots behind it. We do all sin; but the roots of why we do what we do are often a huge tangle of reasons from our very unique pasts. I guess, in part, this is why I eventually forgave Alex and Stan; because like Jesus said, 'Father, forgive them for they know not what they do.' Do any of us ever understand all the whys behind what we do or why we do horrible things to others? I know I don't know all my reasons for sinning. I feel like I made a good choice to forgive, and yet that doesn't mean what either guy did was alright. Gee...."

Both of us sat still for a moment, looking out the window. I was thinking about how God is the only one who really gets us. I stood up and got some brownies out of the box my wife had made up for me yesterday. It was almost ten and I wanted to speak to Rhoda for about an hour longer. "Here help yourself to a brownie or two. I always need a snack at this time of the day." She took a brownie and I offered to warm up her hot chocolate in my little mini micro.

"Thanks, Doc. Your wife is a good cook. I got to get to know her someday. Okay, so where did you want to take this meeting today? I know I kind of hijacked it, sorry."

"On the contrary, Rhoda, that was a very eye opening session for me and hopefully you. Okay…Before I explore some more of your and Alex's story, I had a couple more questions on your first cult. One is: exactly how did you actually leave the cult?" I thought that that was a bit blurry and wanted her to tell me how she got free.

"I think I told you; but I guess I was mainly free when I began to see my husband, the 'other' Alex. The leaders of the group in Springfield told me that I couldn't see my Alex and be part of the Assembly. So I chose my husband and after we got married, we moved to Fullerton, CA. I only went on Sunday mornings to the Assembly there. After we had our daughter, I got bulimia. When I saw that Christian psychologist, for the bulimia, and he told me I was in a cult. This kind of confirmed what I already knew inside. So one day I just left. I am sure I told you that last part."

"Yes you did; but how did you quit? Did you send in a letter of resignation or call the leaders or what? After quitting did they keep pursuing you, trying to get you back? I guess these two questions were not quite answered."

She thought for awhile and said, "It was so very long ago. But I did send some sort of letter to Brother George, who I said was the head of the 'church'. He and the other leaders were so sick of me flaunting myself, as they put it, at the meetings, that they were more than happy to see me go. Not one person, even good friends, called or wrote to me. It was kind of like the shunning done by the Amish. I was dead to them and considered an ultimate rebel; who knows maybe they even excommunicated me. So I never heard from them again. There had been some recent contact; but that is a whole other story for another time."

"So you didn't join or go to another church for almost, eight years, until Alex's church? How was your walk with God during that time?"

"You guessed the time pretty well, Doc. It was about eight years, until I set foot in a church once again. I think I visited a friend's church, in Texas, once; but fear of legalism kept me from ever going back. During that period, I had a daily quiet time with the Lord, read my Bible, did home Bible study courses, and watched TV evangelists, the good ones. I lead my daughter to Christ when she was seven. After that I tried very hard to mentor her in the faith and my husband always asked questions about the Lord, so I was his full time evangelist. But I really did not know or see another believer for those eight years, unless you count my daughter. We moved from Houston Texas to the Bay Area, when my daughter was nine. I felt the need for fellowship and wanted my daughter to get with Christian kids. When I first came into my new California home, I had heard a pastor on the radio and found out his church was three blocks from my home. So I ultimately decided to go to Alex's church, which was that pastor's home church. Alex was my daughter's Sunday school teacher and he headed up the Children's Ministry there at the church. I have never stopped walking with Jesus, except for the year when I met my husband. It has been an over a forty year experience for me."

As I looked at her I wondered if I would have chosen to be a believer, after all the crud she experienced. Out of her 40+ years as a believer, twelve were spent in the Assembly, four were spent at her friend Alex's church, and she alluded to having bad experiences at other churches. More than half of her church life was spent in abuse! That didn't speak too well for the state of the church. How was I to get her to see that there was more good than evil in the church? I wasn't sure if I could help her see that most pastors and leaders were godly loving men who were honorable and true servants of God. I myself got cynical about the state of the church, from time to time. Worse yet, I knew that there were Christians that would blame her for her choices and say she chose the places she did, because she was defective. But this is the farthest thing from the truth. Of course, she obviously had a prejudice in favor of more legalistic venues of worship; but on the other hand these type of legalistic cultic churches are sadly a dime a dozen in today's church. Frankly, it shouldn't have been so easy to find so many places of worship that abused God's people Many churches and Christian meeting places have some form of legalism and abusive behaviors; and this is a shame to the church.

"Thank you for sharing that. We'll spend more time on that at a later date. Ok? So Rhoda, try and give me a general overview of the progression of Pastor Stan's abuse. We will go into more specifics, in the following meetings. So it first began when you went to report the attack to Pastor Stan, hoping he'd help you get things cleared up with Alex. Is that right?"

"Yes, I told you how he tried in those first few meetings to make me into the one who seduced Alex. He wanted me to lie to please him and conform to his evil bunch of lies. Then I told you how he went and took every letter I sent Alex, blocked every email, and bugged every call, that I made requesting a reconciliation meeting and he did the same on Alex's side. Every week he had me come multiple times into his office and he'd scream at me for hours, trying to make me admit I'd lied about Alex. He took away all the ministries I ran and my church job, with Alex. He sent people to intimidate me in church, at my home and on the street. He told my Home Group and Bible Study Group that I was an adulteress and also told this to random people. He made sure to go around the church and tell a slimy story about me to different church gossips. He dirtied my name to all the pastors there, including the head pastor. He even told my husband to divorce me. He'd constantly harass me in the halls at church, being sure to yell at me so others heard. He even told any people that called the church, for a job reference, that I was accused of adultery and that I never worked for the church! He had lawyers call my home to harass me. He had different people from church make threatening calls to my home, at all hours of the day and night. He told my doctor, who went to the same church, that he could no longer treat me. He sent threatening letters and fake police with fake protection orders to my home. He spoke to pastors from other churches; I tried to attend, telling them about my 'adultery'. He had people from his church actually come to new churches and women's groups I joined to tell them I was trying to cause a married pastor to commit adultery. Basically he kept doing this for over twelve years. These last couple of years he finally stopped doing these things, outright, at least. Also he retired around the time the harassment stopped. But do you know what the worst thing was? (I shook my head and wondered what could be worse than the above list?) The worst thing was the false friend thing. He got a few ladies from the church to pretend they were my friends and get my confidence. After we would meet they'd go straight to his office with reports on my status. He wanted to know how his scare tactics were working and if I was ready to say I'd lied about Alex attacking me. I never did change my story and they tried everything to get me to lie. They also gave full reports on anything I said about the situation and if I had any contact with Alex. When I finally found out what they were doing, from others who were concerned, I stopped seeing those ladies. But the betrayal of those friendships was devastating. I truly trusted those women. Of course the other even worse thing was he kept me from speaking to my friend, Alex, for all of these years, even though Alex wanted to reconcile, as much as I did. Now that was demonic. Actually the whole episode was Satan's and not God's plan."

I sat in awe. I have met in my life very abusive pastors. But Pastor Stan seems to have won, in the number of years in which he pursued Rhoda and in the all encompassing relentlessness of his trying to crush and control both Rhoda and Alex. For Rhoda it was over twelve years of full time evil and for Alex the evil has continued on, for even more years; since he has remained under Stan, until his recent departure. Stan tried, night and day, to keep the two friends from any sort of reconciliation or contact, although they both wanted to make peace, so desperately. Alex mentioned to me, in passing, that Pastor Stan had finally quit working at the church, about two years ago; but until this day his law of no contact remains in effect, even though he is in a retirement home. He's even making sure he's being obeyed from his bed, in the nursing home. When the enemy comes out against a believer, he pulls no punches and is like a ravenous dog with a bone. Unless Alex can make a clear cut with Stan, he will never be free.

My time was sadly up with Rhoda and so I told her we could speak more on this subject at a later date. She left in the very thoughtful mood and said she'd call in to make her next appointment. After seeing my next client and finishing the pile of paperwork on my desk, my wife and I had a great time at what is now our favorite, hole-in-the-wall bistro. I really needed the weekend to recharge, after the drama of the day. I really felt sorry for Rhoda and other victims of spiritual abuse. I sat in the living, prayed, and even ended up crying for the state of the church, after my wife went to sleep. Some folks would make better Mafia henchmen or Nazi SS men, than pastors, and their missed callings were blight to the church.

Chapter 12

I was dusting around my office when my secretary, Helen, came in. "I just wanted to remind you, Mark, that Alex will be here in about fifteen minutes, you'd better stop dusting." She smiled and handed me my mail. She took my containers of Pledge and Windex with her and said, "Mind if I use these to tidy the front office a bit?" I gave her the roll of paper towels and she was out the door into her area. I know she thinks I'm a Felix Unger type, in other words: prissy.

I quickly put two more, larger, logs on the fire. I still couldn't shake the chill. Then I went to the coat rack and took down my favorite ratty sweater. I was finally getting more comfortable when I heard a knock on the door. "Come in," I said in a sing song fashion. In entered Alex shivering and asking if I had tea. "Don't I always? Sit down and I'll make us both a cup. Why not move that chair a bit closer to the fire? Would you like a quilt? (He nodded and I handed him one.) Oh, how about a piece of ginger bread? My wife gave me a piece to bring to work today. It's too big for just me." I handed him the steaming glass of tea and a piece of ginger bread on a napkin.

"Are we all settled now?" I asked, sounding rather grandfatherly.

"Yes, Mark. Man, can it get cold here! Anyway...My wife came home on Tuesday and she seems more okay with the whole thing. I was a bit worried. They really frown on pastors looking like there is any marital disharmony over at work. If she stayed away any longer I don't know what story I would have had to have made up. Sometimes it is hard to keep all the story lines going. Oh what a tangled web, we weave…etc. etc."

I shook my head. I could see he still thought having different "story lines" was the only way to make it as a pastor. Total transparency was a foreign concept to him. "Say, Alex I thought we'd get back more to the situation between you and Rhoda, this week. Or do you have anything you want to say that can't wait?"

"No, I guess I'm fine. Can you tell me how she is doing? Is she upset with me, since you have been reminding her of what a 'prince of a guy', I am? I know you can't go into details because of the doctor/patient stuff; but can you give me a hint, at least? We have not contacted each other since you recommended this would be best at this stage of our treatment."

I wondered what he actually meant by not contacting. Did he mean not actually speaking or no contact even of the silent kind? "You're right I can't divulge much, but I will tell you two things. She's still your friend and still thinks kindly towards you. Okay? Alex…When you say you haven't contacted her what exactly do you mean by that? Have you contacted her in anyways other than verbally? Maybe less conventional ways?"

He got two red patches on each side of his neck below his ears. "I think I am getting your meaning, Mark. Rhoda must have mentioned our communication 'game'. Okay, you don't have to tell me 'yea' or 'nay'. I did have a feeling she would have brought that up. You know, I am a bit ashamed of that whole thing. I'm not ashamed because that was bad. I'm ashamed because I had so little moral character that I could not do even the simplest act, without being paralyzed by fear. Stan used to ask me to come into his office, once per week, after the initial daily verbal abuse sessions were finally over. During that once per week meeting he would force me to give a full report (or so he thought), of my activities. He'd ask had I seen Rhoda, even accidentally, had I called her, written her, or had any other contact with her and had she tried to reach out to me? I would tell him, "No." Now at first Rhoda and I did bump into each other quite a lot since we are neighbors, that was when she lived in her old house. She would take morning walks down the same street I'd ride my bike on, on

the way to work. It was the main street near her home and went right by
the church; so I don't think she planned that. If I didn't bike, I'd roller
blade or drive my car to work and she'd wave to me. To be honest, I used
to try and time my leaving the house so I'd see her as often as possible and
maybe she did a bit of that on her end also. Actually that went on for about
thirteen years, but Stan only actually saw us, see each other, a few times.
He didn't realize it was almost daily. But I didn't say anything about that
since we never spoke and she'd just wave to me. I pretended not to see
her; but sometimes I would smile, I guess. So when he'd catch us passing
each other on the street, he'd yell at me for hours on end. Then I'd go to
work at a different time for a couple of months, until things blew over.
But I really started to miss her badly after that first year. She had started
to work for a dentist. I know that from the dentist calling my office for a
reference. Stan had told me to tell the dentist she was a mentally confused
person from my church, but she had never worked for me. I hated that,
but he stood over me as I spoke. Luckily she got the job anyway. Anyway,
I was very troubled in my soul. I wanted to see her, since I knew that Stan
was abusing her and give her comfort. But I was warned that if I had any
contact with her I'd be fired. I obeyed; yet I felt bad that she was abused
because of me and also I just wanted to hear her voice and see her smile.
They told me bluntly (they being Stan and the head pastor), that I could not
talk to her: on the phone, in person, by letter or by email. Stan said, 'No
words ever to her again! Swear to me.' So to keep my job I swore to never
say any words to her again. This got me very depressed and I decided to
speak without words. I devised a plan to 'speak' silently on the phone and
to 'write' her blank emails. I hoped she'd get they were from me. At first
she didn't get it was me and she'd ask if it was me and for me to give her a
sign. Then, the next day, I would drive up next to her with my car or skate
next to her and nod to let her know it was me. She would speak to me on
the phone when I called, begging me for reconciliation. Often she would
try and comfort me with scriptures and kind words, when she heard me
crying on my end. She'd read large portions of the Bible to me. She'd also
make sure to send a one line email to me, acknowledging either my calls
or my blank emails. She never really said anything, but thank you and that

she wanted to meet to reconcile. A couple of times, she sent me a paragraph telling me I was deceived and needed to leave my church. She'd say how she had found freedom. Things like that, but I didn't like the long emails since Stan always checked my inbox and seemed to gravitate to the larger emails. Stan caught her a few times and I had to pretend I didn't know what was going on. I'd lie and say I didn't know the emails were from her. She used to use made up names fearing Stan would be reading my emails. But sometimes Stan caught on. Sometimes he'd even block my account from receiving any mail. I kept sending those communications and calls to her for many years, right up till the day I spoke to her about reconciliation. To make a long story short, I haven't sent any communiqués like that, since we have been in treatment. I'm kind of ashamed at how juvenile that whole thing was. But I honestly did not know whatelse to do."

I looked at him and felt so sorry. He was a man trapped more in his own prison of the mind, than the one Pastor Stan had made for him. I also thought how ridiculous the religious mind thinks. When one is in religion or legalism, it is not the spirit of the law that is kept; it is the literal word or letter of the law. So it is okay in such a person's mind to call and not speak, to show you are with someone. But it is evil to use actual words, since they said you could not use any 'words' to communicate. So you could break the spirit of the command; without actually breaking the law. Not that the law was good in the first place; but the spirit of the law was not obeyed, only the letter. Rhoda was an enabler in this situation. She knew that he felt he was sinning, by speaking to her even without words and writing to her even without words; but she wanted to have a connection with him. So she let him do something that he'd feel guilty about, even though she knew there was no need to. Complicated, huh? Alex was right the only thing for him to feel guilty about was his lack of character that kept him from standing up to Stan and saying, "I will not obey this stupid command. I will talk to and reconcile with my friend, Rhoda. I don't care if I lose my job. My desire to reconcile is of God. You can take this job and put it where the sun don't shine." But alas, Alex was not able to make that stand. So he kept his promise, but always felt a bit guilty about his breaking the spirit of it, even though he knew Stan's commands were dead wrong.

This is the twisted thinking of a mind in a cult and makes sense to those who are in cults. It is ludicrous to outsiders. But I decided to keep these thoughts to myself since he would have to come to this revelation on his own, in God's good time. I was a bit frustrated with keeping quiet, but proceeded forward.

"Alex, let me ask you a side bar question. How did the head pastor get involved in this sad saga? Wasn't he, 'not wanting to hear about you having woman trouble again', after what happened at the previous church you two were in?"

He began to fidget in his chair and I could see he was uncomfortable. He took two bites of the ginger bread and I could see this was hard for him to answer. "Well, Mark, that's a good question. He and I had been good friends at the other church, until I got into the mess we have already spoken about. We were much less so after we started to work together at this new church, West Bay. His wife had started to have emotional problems. She was a rather large woman, nice as all get out, but not perfect like most of the ladies at our church. Just about everyone who is anyone there, in the women's groups, has had plastic surgery and has a toned and over dieted body. They look a bit overdone. The ladies never quite accepted her and she could feel the prejudice; it was very real, not her imagination. It got so bad that she ended up going to our church's center for psychological problems in Denver, where my daughter went for her anorexia. He was always busy going to see her and taking care of their teen children. Also I just think he never was too happy with my problem and wanted to distance himself from me. Pastor Stan saw how stressed he was and decided to keep the head pastor in the dark, as much as possible. This was more for his own job security than concern for the pastor's well being. If the church closed where would he find another position, at his age? Rhoda did not know this. She thought we had told him the whole story about her and my situation. So she made an appointment to see the head pastor and spoke to him as though he had all the facts. She wanted to complain about Stan's treatment of her and ask if he'd help her to reconcile with me. She had no idea about my past troubles and how the head pastor felt about those and how that was the first inkling he'd had of trouble. So the 'dung hit the fan', if you catch my drift. Stan and I were called into his office, as soon as she was out the door and wow was he mad. He said both of us should be fired and that this could make his ministry crash and that the payments to the church, for the new building project might be in jeopardy. He vented for half an hour. Stan, for some reason unknown to me, got between me and the head pastor and said that he was trying to spare him any additional stress and that he had total control of the situation. He reassured the head pastor that nothing had actually happened and that I was under twenty-four hour surveillance. Then I was kicked out of the room, while they spoke for another half an hour. When that was done the head pastor actually pushed me aside in the hall, as he left the room. Pastor Stan called me into the office. He told me he'd saved my job; but from now on I was on the 'dung list' and I'd better toe the line. He and the head pastor had decided to let Stan also handle the situation on Rhoda's end, and that she too would be watched, at all times. They wished she'd leave, at first; but then thought it was best that she stayed, at the church, so she wouldn't make what happened public. Also the building fund had several Christian millionaires donating to it and those men would not want to give more money, if there was any hint of scandal. The head pastor would not have time to take care of the new building, his wife, and the daily workings of the church, plus me. He only wanted to get a short monthly report from Stan, at the pastors' meetings. But that is how he came into the picture. I was really mad at Rhoda for awhile about this and did not contact her for a few weeks. She always did something to upset the applecart, as they say."

"Then I suppose the other pastors found out about the whole thing at the next pastors' meeting, am I right? (He nodded.) This had to be about a year after the incident, correct? (He again nodded and added a little sigh.) So you were kind of in the dog house with all of the leaders? (He said, 'Yeah' and shook his head.) So why not leave at that time?"

"Well to be honest I stayed because of a few reasons. 1. I was comfortable in this job and liked that fact that I could pretty much walk to work. 2. My kids were young and still in the local schools. 3. They pretty much told me I'd never get a recommendation from them, if I tried to go to a new church and get a job. Also my pastor's degree was just a two year degree from my denomination's Bible College. It would have been of no use in another denomination. I felt kind of stuck. So I decided to try and keep plodding forward, even though I started to see that the church was extremely legalistic and that I wasn't well liked by the other leaders, especially the head pastor. I think it was at that time that the head pastor's and my friendship was totally broken off. I think I was basically kept on because I was getting great comments from the parents on my Children's ministry program."

"Not many men are in Children's ministry. You had a problem with women. Tell me honestly, did you ever have a problem with..um.. children? Sometimes the two do go together."

I could see anger flash across his face. "No, Mark, I never had a thought that was immoral towards any child, okay? Don't ever ask me that again!" He crossed his arms and looked a bit angered by that type of a question. Then he looked down and said, "I never thought about kids in an unwholesome way; but Pastor Stan did ask the same thing. At least you look like you believe me. Pastor Stan made it clear he thought I was lying. I actually really liked kids. I liked other people's kid even more than my own; I'd never hurt a child.

"Alex you said, 'liked' kids. Are you no longer working with them?"

"Well Don, the head pastor who was my friend, left about four years ago. Before he left he had started to have me be trained to counsel women who had emotional problems. I know that sound weird. But they wanted to nip any rumors, in the bud, and if I was allowed to counsel women, then the church would look like it was standing with me. Then I couldn't be the rascal some were beginning to say I was. Right? Later the new pastor and his wife, at that time, let me continue in both roles, while I trained a woman, to take my place in the Children's ministry. They left about two years ago and we replaced them with a lesser known pastor, from our church. By all rights the position should have been mine; but I was skipped over because of my past problems. Pastor Stan decided he had to retire, around that time, since his wife was sick with cancer. He had stayed on longer so as not to lose control of me. So when he left, they put the woman I was training in charge of the children and they put me into Stan's job. I mainly do funerals, weddings, and hospital visitations and help plan larger events. I also am a bit of a 'floater' and help out where ever I'm needed. I'm going to be in a new position called Connections in a few months. This lighter schedule has given me more time to think, since I am tons less busy than I was. That is what gave me time to finally decide to get things right with Rhoda. I even started to pray again. Before I filled in my time with work to try and take my mind off the whole thing and to avoid the making a decision on the matter."

"How has it been since Stan left? Do you have more breathing room?"

He nodded and said, "Yeah, it is nice to be able to walk around church, without him or his cronies following me constantly. But before he left he spoke to the new head pastor and filled him in on the whole thing from his perspective, of course. I now have to meet every two weeks with the new head pastor. I decided to not tell him how I have kept in contact with Rhoda for these last almost fifteen years, especially because the contact has been so unconventional. I just never bring up that part of the story. I think the fact that Stan was mostly in the dark also helped; the new pastor is not that well informed. Stan didn't get into that part of the saga, too deeply, with the head pastor. So if this gets out I'm 'screwed', as they say. But Stan doesn't contact the church. He contacts me privately to check on me. He probably is living it up over at the church's retirement center in Arizona; unless his wife has had a relapse, that is. She was always so cheerful and so different from Stan. I don't know how she could stand being with him. They had three kids who all got married right out of high school to get away from their dad. Now, the poor woman, is stuck in a retirement center with him. I hope he leaves before I get there. Oh I didn't mean he had to die to leave, maybe he'll just transfer to another facility."

"It's getting a bit late; but I have to ask you this. Why did you not just go to Rhoda secretly and make things right with her? Why did you feel the need to keep some vow when you apparently weren't squeamish about breaking so many other vows? I mean, truth be told, you'd have gladly had a secret affair. So why was having a secret reconciliation so repulsive?"

He looked at me and then out the window. "Now this is where this gets complicated even for me, Mark. There were so many factors. I think

I should list them and then we can maybe speak of them at another session, how's that? (This time I nodded.) Well one thing we haven't spoken of is my wife's part in this. About two months into the whole matter with me attacking Rhoda and all, Stan had a secret meeting with my wife. By secret I mean he talked to her about me without me knowing, until a few weeks later. After this meeting she came to me and told me that I could divorce her, and marry or whatever Rhoda. Then she said that she would feel the need to get up and accuse me in front of the whole church of adultery, (surely a Stan idea). On top of this, that she would take my youngest son and never let me see him again. Then secondly, a few years later, my oldest daughter got anorexia and needed treatment, which I have already mentioned. She needed to stay at that live in facility (I also spoke of) and the church covered that 100%. I was thankful for this, as you can imagine, and I stayed out of a sense of gratitude. Over the years, I had different people from my family working for the church and collecting salaries. My daughter worked there for a time, my wife has had various positions, my cousin, and others came and worked there for a time. If I left, they'd all have lost their jobs. On top of all those reasons, there was the matter of my not being able to get a recommendation for any new ministry jobs or to get the level of salary that my church pays, at another church. The church has money and gives the best salaries in the area. They have a great health care plan, and that retirement home in Arizona. I owe a lot of money and need all the help I can get. All of this has taken on a life of its own. I am basically owned by the church, an indentured servant. I cannot see any way to free myself and still be able to afford my lifestyle and family. As I said before I'm stuck."

"Believe me I do understand. But don't you think God could make a way if you were to come clean and break free?"

"Theologically I do, of course, Mark. I don't have enough faith for that, at my age, in reality, however. I feel it is too late for me to start again." He seemed to be emptied of all his bravado and went kind of limp with despair.

I didn't want him to leave in this state. I decided to tell him my story of how I left my church, a few years back. Much of it was similar to his, sans the adultery part. I told him how God had provided for me. I was just two or three years younger than he was. I was a part-time pastor, while I was a full time therapist. I thought that when I left that church I'd never have any more Christian patients referred to me or be able to do any ministry again. But happily God kept my practice going and had even gotten me back into a ministry position, only about two years later. I lost some finances, true; but I gained inner dignity and freedom. I then prayed with him and he truly wept. He just said he was grateful for the prayer and he'd have to think the whole thing over. Then he got up handing me the quilt.

I took it back and held it as I walked him to the door. "Remember, Alex, I have only made a suggestion here. You have to decide what you should do before God. My office is not like your church. I do not command people to do anything. Whatever you decide is between you and God and I will respect you no matter what. Okay?"

He sincerely shook my hand and headed towards the door. "See if you can make an appointment for Friday afternoon. I want to see Rhoda before you come in next time. I think it will be time soon to have the two of you come in together. I think we're nearing that point."

"Oh that would be so nice. We haven't really spoken for years and years. Thanks, Mark." He made his appointment for Friday afternoon and walked out into something rare: sun shine.

Chapter 13

The next Monday I decided to drive into work, since I had to pick up some lumber for a deck I was planning to do off my second story bedroom. I had to leave the house about an hour earlier and so my wife was in the shower as I hurried to my car. I told her I'd bring home some take out for dinner, if she'd help me lug the wood into the garage. She shouted her agreement and went back to singing, "Heard it Through the Grapevine." My wife could get into old tunes from our high school days and wasn't too bad a singer, really. I, personally, like opera and that is not as easy to sing, even in the shower. I always get carried away, loose the soap, and make water splash everywhere. I got onto the expressway and was glad I left an hour early. The traffic was fierce, as usual. I, all of a sudden, remembered why I love to take Bart. Traffic stinks and napping and driving is frowned upon. I got to the office just in the nick of time, dashed up the stairs, cleaned the cat's box and fed him, got the tea on, and placed my notes on the table. I heard Helen come into the office and I told her to give me my schedule for the day. Then with big cow eyes I pleaded with her to get me a bagel with peanut butter from the shop downstairs. She told me she was actually headed there and asked if there was anything else. "Could you get two of their walnut raisin cookies? You know those big ones." She smiled and put on her sweater and puttered out.

The electric kettle was whistling as I was placing a few logs on the fire and turning on the gas starter. "Better shut that off, Doc; you're scaring Max." Max was hiding under the chair that Rhoda usually sat in. Rhoda had come in while my back was turned. "I hope you don't mind that I let myself in, the door was ajar and your secretary wasn't in her chair."

"Oh, Rhoda, that's fine. I drove to work today and actually just got here. How was your drive from the Bay Area? It was jammed packed from my house." I shut off the kettle. Got out some new chocolate tea and poured the steaming water into the mugs. Rhoda asked me for the quilt and I didn't blame her for being chilly, the logs were taking a bit longer to heat the room. Just as she got settled, Max jumped onto her lap. "Looks like Max has found a friend." She smiled.

Helen brought me my bagel and the two cookies and greeted Rhoda before returning to her receptionist desk in the outer office. I handed one of the cookies to Rhoda and put mine under my bagel. I opened the paper on the bagel and got comfortable.

"Well, it's taken a bit to get started, I'm sorry. But on the other hand it is good for you to collect your thoughts and feel more comfortable before we begin. You know Rhoda I am considering having you and Alex do joint sessions soon. It depends on how this goes today. If we make some headway, I'll see Alex alone one more time and then we can have you both come together for what would be your next session. If I still feel there is a bit more to bring out in you we'll make it the meeting after that. Are you on board with this?" She lit up like a firecracker.

"Doc, how could you even ask if I'm 'on board'? The only time I have spoken to Alex in the last fifteen years about anything real was for those few minutes, on the phone, when he asked to reconcile a few weeks ago. That was a short, but awkward, few moments, with lots of stuttering and uncomfortable pauses. I'd love to actually speak to him, in a normal manner, even if you have to be with us. I feel like that will be a dream come true. For years it has been labeled a sin for me t to speak to my friend. Glory be, you are going to not only let us talk; but you want us to talk. Ask me anything today, anything at all, so that I'll be ready to meet with him, next time around. Go right on ahead. Yes, Lord." I felt she would have loved to do a cheer for God, at that moment, if she didn't have Max on her lap, a cup of hot tea in her hand, and a giant crumbly cookie to deal with.

I laughed a bit and said, "Okay, it looks like you are on board. Now let me see…First I have a few general questions for my files. What kind of work does your husband do? What company does he work for? How is he doing with your coming here for these sessions? Also what does your daughter do and is she married? Does she still live at home? What's your relationship like with her?"

"Wow, that's a big list to remember. My husband is a computer analyst. He is into the data ware housing, data architect, and etl areas. Don't ask me what that all means, okay? He has his own company and he hires himself out to do contracts for various companies, right now he is working from home for Hewlett Packard. He wasn't too excited about me coming here, at first; but when he heard it was going to be pretty much free, he said it was good. He feels that I still am not totally healed from the whole thing. Do you know what Doc? My husband has said for years that God would have to bring this about. When Alex finally came to me, my husband said he could see God was in this. Neat, huh? As far as my daughter goes: she is not married; but she has a steady boyfriend; she is twenty-six. She graduated from college in Accounting, when she was twenty two, but ran away to LA, for a year. We were making plans to go and see her graduation, when she called and said she was not going to the ceremony, even more shockingly, that she had decided to run away to LA. She was out of contact with us for almost a year or so. Then she found herself broke and on the brink of ruin. One day out of the blue, she called us to rescue her. She had been living with us for the last two years. A few months ago she moved to Oakland and found she could live on her salary. She came back home with us for a couple of weeks and a couple of months ago she was given a job transfer to LA, by her company. We never hear from her. I try and call every two weeks, or so, and she speaks for two minutes and hangs up. Up until she was in high school she and I were inseparable and great friends. She started pulling away in high school which I felt was normal since we had been so close. I think I told you she had had a few bad church experiences along the way. I think she started to think I was the reason for this. She seems to have lumped me, Christianity, and church abuse into the same category. I don't blame her really. But truly I did not know how certain folks treated her, until long after the fact. One situation, I remember quite clearly, happened to her at school. Her classmate was Alex's niece and that young woman was going around saying I had had an affair with her uncle. Well, as you remember, my daughter was there during the attack. By the time Alex's niece started to spread the rumors, she was a bit older. My little darling, called her out in front of all their classmates and told the girl to take back what she said. She said she saw Alex attack me and that I had fought him off. She went on to say, her uncle was the weirdo. She must have done a great job, because no one bothered her after that at her school, even the niece believed her. I called Alex, as soon as I heard, and told him off, even though it was against the rules. I told him my daughter was off limits. She actually did try to help me confront Alex two more times. The first time he met with her in his office and told her his church would not let him speak to me. It was a command. The second time she tried to talk to him, he told her he could no longer speak to her and hung up abruptly. That second time, crushed her; because he had been her Sunday school teacher for years and she and he were friends. It was around that time, till now, that she has been a bit more distant towards me, than I would like. She even told me a year ago, she has never had any real admiration for me. She seems to be doing better lately. Maybe it is because she is a young adult now. But I do think this whole thing affected her."

"Hmmm. It's hard to say. She may be dealing with other things that you don't really know about. It might not be all your 'fault', as you are thinking. As far as you know, did Alex ever try to go out of bounds with her? Or did any other pastor act inappropriately towards her? I wonder if she was wounded in ways she has not mentioned to you."

"Thankfully, I know that Alex did not go out of bounds with her. But she was truly spiritually abused, by two pastors, from a Vineyard church I attended. They tried to turn her against me. They said I had had any affair with Alex and that I was a bad mother, because I had had an affair. Also some of the kids from Alex's church ended up at the same Vineyard church and they taunted her; the pastors saw them do this and joined in with the kids. I heard about these two things much later from another mother who was concerned about the way my daughter was being treated. Of course I don't know all she went through. But I can see why she grew to dislike church. She did try to come with me, last year, for a few weeks, to my new church. But she eventually felt it wasn't for her. Spiritual abuse can destroy whole families. I think this is another reason why my husband may be taking so long to come to the Lord. I can hardly blame him; after all, he has seen his wife and daughter go through great abuses, from pastors yet."

Unfortunately, I really understood her. Leaders in these abusive churches or cults think in their sick small minded minds, that they are playing some sort of one "upmanship" games with people. Their overwhelming pride makes them think that, through their superior "intelligence", they will eventually "win". Win what? Win the power game and put another mindless follower in their rightful place: below their feet. Problem is no one wins in these games. The abusers never get the help they need and they keep abusing one believer after another. They become serial abusers and get more and more proud of how they are able to fool others into thinking they're godly. They think they are getting away "scot free" with affairs and other crimes. They glory in the fact that they are believed over the victims, and how they never have to pay for their crimes. The victims also never receive healing or validation from others in the church; because the leaders, in these cultish groups, make them out to be sinners and rebels in the church. The victims' stories seem far too outrageous. Even if people do believe them, they fear to come to the victims' aid, fearing this move on their part, will ruin their own ministries. If they speak up for the victims, they know their days will be numbered in any position they hold in the church, no matter how small. So the victims are either ignored or made to seem delusional. No one ever validates their pain or acknowledges that they were truly abused. The victims learn to shut up and stumble on in life, being continually victimized for speaking out. They are told to forget about the past and move forward. No one ever says, "I will go with you to confront the leader who raped you or abused you." They say, "Just forgive, the leader or pastor, and move forward. You're holding on to a grudge." So not only is the victim continually re-victimized, but the abuse extends into the lives of the victim's children, spouse, and even into the community. The abuse never just destroys one person, in a vacuum, but all whom the victim has contact with are tainted. I hoped her daughter might one day be able to see that there are true Christians in the church, that not everyone in leadership is a two faced abuser. I had to snap myself back from my thoughts on this subject and focus on Rhoda again.

"Rhoda, what exactly are you doing at this time in your life? You said you were a teacher. Are you teaching? What are you doing?"

"Well, that's a good question. I did go to school to be a special education teacher. But I later graduated with a degree in Social Services and Elementary Education. When I was first married I, worked with Mentally Disabled Adults, in educational training centers. But then when we had our daughter, I chose to stay home with her. I did have an infant care center in our home, when she was very young. When she was in middle school and high school I did tutoring, out of my home. When she was in college I had official tutoring jobs, at tutoring centers, like Kumon and Score, out in the real world. I was a highly prized tutor. Everyone, of the center managers, begged me not to leave. For a time, I was a dental receptionist and worked for a financial counselor. But after working for Alex, I always wanted to do more church oriented work. But I couldn't really find another actual job, in that genre. I also volunteered at the various churches, I attended, after Alex's. I actually got turned off to working with children. My bad experience in Alex's church, gave me an aversion to that line of work. I have not enjoyed teaching, ever since, though had to tutor to make money. My heart was no longer in it and I eventually gave away all my tutoring materials. I tried to start various church groups, for adults, at different churches and did rather well with this. I started women's groups, singles groups, speaking groups, dinner for eight groups, etc. I had many people attend, but over time something would happen, usually along the lines of some sort of sabotage by other jealous women in the church. I even had one lady say to me directly, 'Who do you think you are starting a group? I stand against you. I'll see to it you fail.' The others were more subtle. I also did some teaching and speaking to small adult groups; but this was all volunteer work. I didn't mind that; but my husband wished I could bring in some money. I have been writing a book on my experiences, as a believer. I have chosen to use fiction to express things that I've been through. I tried to write a nonfiction book, but was told it was too honest and I'd be sued. I love to write and until recently I was also doing a blog every day on cults. But most significantly right now, my main job is remodeling my home. I got sick a few years ago, from some sort of chemical poisoning. I was unable to walk and got hundreds of serious poisoning reactions in my skin, hair, and other parts of my body. That episode of my life, lasted for more than two years and still has some residual effects today. During this time, my husband saw that I was getting depressed by the poisoning and decided to move us to another part of town. We didn't realize how much remodeling our new home would need and so I have been remodeling almost full time for the last two going on three years. Though I'm pretty much over my actual sickness, I have gotten much weaker because of it. I mostly only have time for daily remodeling tasks and my regular house work. I do feel the need to be a professional writer and a speaker. I have made Wednesday my official writing day and am almost done with my first book. I have two more in my mind, at this time. As far as speaking goes, I took Toastmaster's training and like I said I have spoken to small groups. But I can't seem to break into real Christian Speaking. Even my new pastor thinks this may be more my inflated evaluation of my ability than my calling. But he never heard me speak, so this is his 'guesstamation'. I'm sure this is God's call on my life."

"Listen Rhoda, I've heard you speak here in this office and I know you have a lot to say. Don't let even your pastor discourage you. Here is a business card from my friend, Dave. I think he can help you in the speaking area. I want to encourage you to finish writing the book and to continue doing the writing of books. Please also give me a copy and I'll tell others about it. Not only will you heal more, but I know you have a lot to share. You just have to start and determine to keep going, even if there are some who don't see your gifting, yet. You're an educated woman. You don't have to look or like a CEO to write or speak. You don't look like a country bumpkin or ignoramus, by any means. You just are not formal in your dress, like so many women in the church. To be honest I get a bit sick of the professionally done hair and the little church suits and church dresses, myself. I'd listen to anything you have to say, anytime."

She stared at me with her mouth a bit ajar. Tears filled her eyes. "Why, Mark, that is the kindest thing anyone has said to me in years, maybe ever. I get so many people saying, that I'm nice and all; but I just don't present myself like a writer or a speaker. Yet I have seen men speakers speak in suits, in jeans and t-shirts, and even in baggy shorts with Hawaiian shirts and flip flops. Not once did anyone put them down for not presenting themselves well. Yet women all supposed to dress in the standard church suit, with heels, and hair sprayed hair. Anything less and you are seen as deficient, less qualified. That bugs me and it is probably why I do all I can to dress the opposite of that. Even this look is not me. If anything I'm leaning more towards the New Age look in my style. I just can't afford to go as bohemian as I'd like to. But I'm not stupid; I just can't be churchy and formal. But thank you for seeing this. Many pastors get upset because I'm not a cookie cutter type person. I also don't fit in the grandma mode that many women my age are content to be in. I don't like the masculinization of the manly grandma clothes and the standard grandma cap haircut. Yuck. Anyway, funny thing is Alex isn't into the grandpa thing either. He still roller blades and bikes and dresses like a man twenty years younger. I've seen him on the street and I have felt like one of the reasons we get along is we still have an enthusiasm for life and hate being old stogies. I was like this, in the aging area, even more so before I got sick. I still love to be active and outdoorsy; maybe this is why I can't do the CEO/grandma dressing thing. I hate when people give up on life and let themselves get old, while they are still young."

She crossed her arms and looked at me. I smiled, "Rhoda, I wish more folks would feel free to be themselves. I can't do the grandpa thing either. Yet to be honest, I have spoken at Therapist Conventions and no has cared about my Hawaiian shirt or that I had a bit of a fuzz beard going on. I totally see your point. Now I have a more spiritual question for you and I want you to be more detailed than even your last couple of responses. Many people, I'm sure, have wondered why you want this reconciliation, at all, since you were actually attacked by Alex. I think you mentioned in passing that Pastor Stan could not understand why anyone who had been truly attacked by a man would ever wish to be that man's friend again. Maybe you could go into two areas on this topic. One why did you decide to reconcile with a man who hurt you? And two what did God say to you about this reconciliation? You have given little hints to me on these issues; but now I want you to feel free to delve more deeply into both questions. One reason is so that you might clarify for yourself why you are still believing for this to happen and a second reason is that you need to be able to tell Alex why, in clear words, you are so tenacious about reconciling. Also you should be able to explain this concept to others, so they won't think the reason is something more romantic, in nature, and not see the spiritual thing, you see it as. God has shown me, when I'm in prayer for you, that you truly see this as something from Him. So do you mind if I record this? I want to go over what you share, more deeply, a little at a time, and not distract you with my taking notes. Okay?"

She smiled and then got serious. "Pastor Stan recorded me, unbeknownst to me. I only found out later, accidentally. Also one day he dumped a box of tapes on the lecture room table at church and told me that those tapes had everything I ever said to him and others from church, on them, not just from the counseling sessions, either. He had also recorded my phone calls and discussions with people at church and even in restaurants in our community and who knows where else. I walked out of the lecture room, after that, and never had another session with him. But I should've taken those tapes with me and burned them. I could have knocked him over and just taken my tapes. Anyway... But since you have forewarned me, Mark, I'm cool with it. I see you have a little mini recorder like I have. I'm the one who should have taped the terrible things they said to me, at Alex's church, not them; I'm the victim in this. Funny, though, it never crossed my mind to be unethical. Anyway...Alex and I were great friends when I first came to the church. He was a demanding boss; but he could be a fun friend. When he was in the friend mode, he was always joking. But there were times, he could get serious and tell me things he wanted to do for God and his life goals. I had not had such a good friend, for quite a long time. He was never rude or crude and he always spoke about interesting topics. He also just knew how to be a friend. He'd often bring up a topic and he'd discuss the topic, back and forth in an equal and educated manner. I loved that. So few men would speak to me as an equal and even though he had the title of pastor he did not talk to me in a condescending way. We spoke about our life goals and neither of us poo pooed the other person's calling. We honored each other as people. I still treasure that. My husband is truly the only other person I have felt this camaraderie with for the last twenty seven years. It is a noble thing, friendship. So when he so unexpectedly went off the track and came on to me I was truly shocked. I did not expect that and to be honest I was spittin' mad. I wanted to slap him a million times and did not know what to do. How could I automatically hate someone who had up till the second of the attack, been a great friend and supporter to me? How do you just turn off and on feelings? I have heard that divorcees feel this way. They might get a divorce from a cheating spouse; but they find they still have feelings for the person. They can't just love the person one minute and then shut off that feeling the next. That was kind of where I was. People wanted me to automatically hate my friend, but I couldn't. Then as God helped me to really forgive him I began to see how he was a wounded soul who must have been abused by the church we were in, like me, and abuse in his former life. I didn't admire what he did to me, physically, and how he did not stand up for me afterwards; but I understood how it was to be both in a cult and to be abused. I didn't like what he did; but I did not feel he was purposely abusing me. He sinned and made a big mistake; but he never, except for the actual attack, came out to me in a violent or abusive manner like Pastor Stan. He had misplaced his love. What he needed was a friend; but he thought the way to be fulfilled in this desire for a friend was to 'claim me' sexually. Pastor Stan sought to destroy me and to wreck my good name, in the process; he did not love me in any way. This understanding came to me over time. That was one part of the equation. The second part of the equation was God. At the beginning, I tried to remain angry for a long time, almost a year. I thought that by being angry I could show Alex how he had come against my dignity as a person. I have quite a high sense of inner dignity and I felt this was violated. He invaded my space and tried to defile me. So I had a lot of anger towards him. I didn't see the thing as him trying to show he loved me; for me it was anything, but romantic. So I would go to God and rant or vent and tell God how mad I was at Alex and how degraded I felt. I did the same whenever Stan abused me or any of his little assistants at the church. But since I was not friends with Stan or any of his little 'demonettes', I did not seek to understand the 'why' of why they abused me, like I did with Alex. I honestly remained angry with Pastor Stan for at least four more years and that included his cast of little 'mini-mes'. But the more I prayed, the more I saw I had to forgive Alex. It seriously took almost a full year for total forgiveness to come into my heart. It was on Christmas day, almost one year to the day of the attack, that I was able to forgive him. He was reading a book to the children, up in front of church. It was a book about a little donkey. I realized the donkey, in the story, was me. He was reading the story to tell me how much he regretted abusing 'the little donkey'. At that moment I looked at him and forgiveness flooded my heart and I could literally see golden coins fall over us from Heaven. I saw it was the will of God for me to forgive my friend. Then a huge weight came off of my heart; I was free. But because of all the restrictions, I could not tell him. God then lead me to read many books on forgiveness, about 110, and while I was reading, I found a concept called reconciliation, in two of the books. I had never heard of reconciliation, in all my years of being a believer. One book that mentioned this concept was by a nonbeliever and the other was a book by Charles Stanley on forgiveness. Those two people changed my life. I asked God to show me more about this concept and He even gave me a seminar to write on this concept of forgiveness and reconciliation. I wrote it, but my pastor, at the time, said it was too honest and he would not let me do the seminar. During that time, I decided to do a survey and not one Christian I interviewed with, including pastors, knew what reconciliation was. Even the pastor I have now rarely mentions it. It is not his fault since this concept is basically never spoken of in the Church at large. After six years of study, on the concepts of forgiveness and reconciliation, God told me to preach and write on these subjects. He told if I did this to help others that my relationship with Alex would be healed and be a divine testimony.

He said He'd use from our situation, to illustrate clearly what reconciliation is. I began to pray about this, from the moment I heard about it, and tried to communicate this concept to Alex and to his church. Sadly, one day I tried to go to Pastor Stan and explain what reconciliation was, but he slapped me down to the floor and said, 'We don't believe in reconciliation, at this church.' I got up off the floor and never spoke to him again or returned to his church. But from that second on I knew I had a calling to tell the Church about reconciliation. After my years of study, I tried to speak on that topic at churches in my community. But no church wanted to hear a serious topic like that. One pastor said, 'People don't want to hear serious topics like that.' If I had said, 'Let's make birdhouses for Jesus,' I'd have gotten a better response. So I ended up sharing the concept, of reconciliation, only in small groups or when I mentored people. I also had numerous God dreams of angels and even God Himself telling me to do this ministry. These were not regular dreams or my dreams; they were God speaking to me in the night. It was not me making these things up for my glory. I also had numerous Christian leaders give me 'words' on this calling. And lastly I had an angelic visitation in which the angel came and showed me a vision of Alex and I both speaking on the subject. It was glorious and totally God. Alex also began to give sermons on the subject, at his church, which were not well received. I heard them on the internet. Believe it or not, over the years, I've had various Christians actually curse me, because I believe in forgiveness and reconciliation. I've been blasphemed and put down and told God would never have anyone reconcile with someone who hurt them or He'd never have anyone keep believing in this concept, for so many years. So the opposition and the angels and the 'words' from other believers and God, Himself, speaking to me, in my times with Him of prayer and study, all gave me a for sure 'I know that I know that I know' conviction, about His Calling on my life. Also I know that this 'foreign concept', reconciliation, is the definite call and plan of God for me to give to the Church. Even one step further than this, I knew that what God had promised would definitely happen for me and Alex. I have not had one drop of doubt in this area. Now I am able to see that in all my times of trial, God has been showing almost the same things to Alex.

This was why he came to me, because he too could not keep ignoring God's clear calling."

I got up and ran to Rhoda and said, "Can I shake your hand? I am stunned and overwhelmed with the power of God. He will finish what He has started. I can only say 'Glory!'. I know I'm a therapist; but for all the years I have been one, not one person has desired to go into the second stage, if you will, of forgiveness, namely reconciliation. It is an honor for me to speak with you and I know that when this time is over I'm going to be organizing speaking sessions for you to share this with my church and my patients. Do you realize Rhoda that the majority of people who come into my office are here because of an inability to forgive? But you truly have gone the second mile and gone into the realm of reconciliation. This is truly unheard of in the Church! Of course you and I know that some folks will never be healthy enough to reconcile. Forgiveness is done alone and can be done anywhere, even if someone is dead. But reconciliation means that two people have forgiven each other and now they want some semblance of their prior relationship. Sometimes that might mean with agreed upon restrictions by the parties or sometimes it is just going to be a willingness to make peace and heal from hurt. But to have a heart that is open to not only forgive, but to say I love you enough to grant you access to the friendship we once had, though maybe with some safeguards; this is none other than the very heart of God. I'm so sorry that most of the Church cannot see the importance of this. If they worked in this field, they'd see the importance and how only God could have brought you and Alex to this. It is not natural. I'm cautious about angels and I see that you did not get off into a freaky thing about their appearing to you. That too is God. He never wants us to get caught up with angels; but He only sends them when there is something super important He wants to convey. I believe each instance you have shared here. Maybe we can go into more detail on these things in the future. Wonderful. Rhoda I think you are more than ready to meet here with me and Alex for the next session. Just let me have one more private session with Alex and then I'll arrange a time for the three of us to get together. After that time is over, there may be few meetings with you two together, I'll make sure to have one or two sessions for the spouses and children. Alright? I'll fill Alex in at the next session. I'm so excited over this next step coming up."

Rhoda was quietly crying. She finally said, "Doc, in fifteen years and even in situations before this, no one ever has been on my side. Nor have they really cared about anything I've said. I'm really really touched. I hope your time goes well with Alex. Maybe God is ready to bring His promises to birth? Wow. Maybe I'll live to see them come to fruition." I think if she didn't leave at that moment, because she was late, I'd have ended up balling my eyes out. She was truly more on track than all her spiritual counselors, because she knew the Heart of God.

Chapter 14

I made sure to get to the office early on Friday. Alex was coming in the afternoon and I wanted to be able to totally focus on him and I had to decide whether or not he was ready to meet with Rhoda and I. She was ready; but I wasn't so sure about him. She had been totally transparent with me; but Alex liked to hide his real feelings to protect himself. This is normal behavior, for someone in a cult. I think a part of Alex knew he was in a cult; but another part of him didn't want to believe he was part of something so dark. Though he had his own personal demons, he had worked for the church for almost twenty years. This would mean that he stood with them, even if he himself did very little of the actual abuse. I could see he felt a bit removed, from that end of the "business". I thought that that particular day would be the perfect day to help him own up to how he was really just as culpable as the others, whom he saw as the more serious perpetrators of abuse, there at the church.

Alex came in about three minutes late looking a bit miffed. I asked him what the trouble was as I prepared our tea. I had moved his chair closer to the fire and put a foot stool in front of it to relax him. Max purred as Alex patted him on the head and then he lay down between Alex's chair and the fire. Alex said he had just gotten a letter from Stan, asking how he was and this bothered him, "I don't think he gave a fig how was feeling. I think he was trying to manipulate me again, even from Arizona. I have not wanted to see or hear from that man. He had made both my and Rhoda's life a living hell, for so many years. He said he wanted a full detailed letter of my comings and goings, this last year and a half. Then he said if I didn't send that along, he'd be sure to send a long note to the new head pastor that would say he'd had time to remember more things he needed to tell him. What an old creep!" You could tell Alex was really frustrated and in one of those damned if you do and damned if you don't situations. I always hate those, myself. Since he had not stood up to Stan in the past, he felt totally confused in how to handle this request. He thought you were supposed to obey everyone over you, even evil people. He did not see, yet, that this was cult thinking.

I told him, "Alex, I'm afraid you will have to break free of this man. Tell him, in no uncertain terms, that you want him to leave you alone and stay out of your life and that of those you care about. Then I think you should go to your head pastor and tell him that Stan is harassing you. Say you'd like it if he'd not let Stan communicate with him, you, or anyone else from your church. Tell him you don't wish to go into all the reasons why, at this time. Your pastor thinks you are coming here for marriage enrichment. So as your counselor, I can write up a note for you to give to your pastor from me. I can tell him how it would be detrimental to your therapy to have any contact with Stan or to have Stan have any further contact with the church concerning you. If he wants to, he can call me and I'll convince him Stan has some deep problems and that Stan needs help. He does so I won't be lying or exaggerating. I've had to do, this kind of thing, for many people in the past and I can convince him, I'm sure. I'll be glad to do this if and only if you break it off with Stan. He, not Rhoda, has been bad for your soul all of these years. Can I be blunt? It is like Stan is the older prisoner in a maximum security prison and when he saw your vulnerability; he claimed you as 'his girl'. You understand what I mean? I see Stan as having a fixation with you that may even be sexual in nature. It's like he didn't want Rhoda to take his place in your life. I don't know if you have seen this too; but unless you are bisexual, I don't think you want to be another man's 'Old Lady'; am I right?" I looked him right in the eyes with that sentence and he squirmed a bit in his chair and diverted his eyes.

"I have to be totally honest. I have always kind of sensed this; but his wife was so beautiful and he had three kids so I thought it was just my mind going 'off'. Yet I always felt he didn't just want to protect me from 'evil women' like Rhoda; but he wanted me and he wanted me to be in the subservient position. He wanted to be on top both figuratively and literally. That must be why I felt so dirty after being with him, for even a few minutes. The power he had over me at my job was like a kind of sexual dominance and truly always was full of tension. I'd try and move away from him and he'd keep pursuing me. Yuck. Now that I think about it, it was not how I wanted our relationship to be. I didn't want that type of thing with any man. He was so hard and cold; I actually would have done well to not know him, at all. So Rhoda was his rival. Wow. He'd swear up and down you were deceived, Mark; but I think you hit it on the head. On top of this, I always felt he got a kind of sexual high from abusing people, kind of sadistic. There was this one Chinese woman at church. Her husband was American and went to live in China. She liked Pastor Stan and he knew it. She hated China and wanted to live here in California. So she refused to join her husband. Pastor Stan told her God wanted her to divorce her husband and be 'under' him. She was emotionally unstable before this 'counseling' and that made her worse. Stan also told her she was full of demons and that only he could cast them out of her. He made her come alone to his office for hours of demon removal. He would keep casting these demons out, for months and months. He'd snap his fingers, loudly command the demons to come forth, and then she'd go all limp and fall at his feet. She'd shake and writhe on the floor and he'd scream at her. Then she'd throw up in his trash can. He' could be heard doing this for hours in his office. Most of this was done privately/ it was only when he'd cast them out in public and that I got to see his deviant methods. I always felt he had a thing for her or for the commanding the demons out thing. Over time she became totally delusional. Stan tired of her and her husband married another woman in China. The woman was left with nothing but a destroyed psyche. He had a number of people that he liked to shout at and make them seem delusional. He enjoyed getting off on his destruction of his victim's self esteem and their groveling at his feet. He also had at least two 'office women'. They'd just come and sit next to his desk, waiting for him to command them to do things for him. They spent their days either reading theological books he gave them or asking him theological questions that he could expound on. They were alone with him for hours. I'd get ticked because he didn't let me speak to Rhoda; but he had his little following of groupies. I'm not sure if he strayed or not, the door was always closed; but the women spoke in worshipable accolades about his many "glories". Yet no one thought this was weird. Now he seems like he was a bisexual to me. He wanted me and he wanted them. Again, he'd get really angry, if he knew we had said these things about him. Man."

I looked at Alex and thought that the stuff Stan did was bad, to be sure. But it was funny how Alex could see that clearly in Stan; but his own sins he hardly gave a moment's thought to, until recently that is. Interesting how our minds can excuse our own undesirable behavior; but how we can quickly jump to judgment on another person's faults. I cleared my throat and said, "Please Alex do as I suggested about Stan; break free from him and you will feel like a new man, a free man. He will feel like your ex-pimp. Let me know how this goes.

You actually, inadvertently, have opened a sag way, into what I wanted to talk to you about today. Do you have anything else you wish to explore before we proceed? (He shook his head, 'No'.) I was wondering how much you knew about the abuse Rhoda was receiving, from Stan and other members of your church? You did not defend her or claim any of the blame. What I mean is: did those who abused her at your church, discuss what they were going to do to her, first with you, to get your input? Or did they tell you what they did, afterwards? Did they suggest to you any specific ways to abuse her? How did that whole thing work?"

At the mention of this Alex became quite uncomfortable, seeming to show with his body movements how he was struggling on the inside. "Okay look, Mark, I don't know what Rhoda told you; but I do know she under-exaggerated what we all did to her. She probably wanted me to look like this good guy in the story. Sadly I'm not a 'good guy' and I was never a good guy in this story, okay? But one thing she has never known is how much they had me between a rock and a hard place. Let me explain:

Though my wife and I are more adjusted today, we never really clicked. It took me seven years to just like her, after we were married. I'm not talking about being 'crazy in love with her', but just to tolerate her. Something about her drove me crazy, in a bad way. I told you about that, but my kids were different. I told you I didn't like them, but that's not exactly true. I didn't like the responsibility of caring for them, true. But each kid touched my heart individually as beautiful people. I really liked them. I was a lousy parent; but I did try to be their friend. My wife knew this, and always used the threat of not letting me see them ever again, if we divorced. I actually would have liked it better, if she'd taken the kids to live at a different home nearby and we had gotten divorced. But she knew that wasn't enough punishment for me; she promised to take them and I'd never find them or see them again. Even for me, that was more than I could stand so I'd back down from the divorce, mainly because of that very real threat. One thing about her, she never makes an empty promise or an empty threat. Without any real love between us, the Church was all I had. After our first years of marriage, I eventually realized I'd eventually be too old to be a forest ranger, which is what I originally went to school for, and began to consider a career in the Church. The forest ranger life is a hard life and more suited to men in their twenties and thirties. So I decided to change careers and be a pastor. I spent a few years going to Bible school to become a pastor. Most of my pastoral life, I was a children's pastor. I don't have a teaching license and I started to feel too old to work with kids, these last few years. So for that reason and the ones I already mentioned, the church gave me a more custom designed position. The job I have now is a kind of a jack of all trades job. It's the kind they give to a pastor who will soon to be retiring. The head pastor and others in the church have already vowed to block any new job opportunities to other churches, because of the Rhoda incident. If I left I'd end up working for Costco, like another pastor who left here, and be without any recommendations. For many years, I had two kids in college and they have both since graduated. Now the young one is attending. My daughter had anorexia, which needed to be treated at an inpatient facility, which was quite expensive. The church paid for her bills. I have a huge pile of debt, a house that I can't sell in a nearby small town, sick parents (who only recently died), and a few legal troubles. The church knew all of this; that I couldn't leave if my life depended on it. They knew that there was no way out for me and that I had to stay on there, no matter what. But they also knew I was a good worker, doing the job of two or three people. They figured if they kept me on staff, I'd still be a money maker for them. That is why they made those threats to me, about firing me, if I contacted Rhoda. They knew someone else would have told them where to go, but I was locked in. I was scared of what they would do. I did not know what I would be faced with, if I was kicked out because of Rhoda. I have to say I really really liked, even loved, Rhoda; but not enough to sacrifice all I owned, my family, and my job. How could I give up all of that for a woman who told me clearly she still loved her husband? Everything was against me to a much greater degree than anything she might lose. So I decided to sacrifice her to the religious gods. It may sound foolish; but it was either: she goes down and loses a little or I go down and lose everything. I chose: the way of dishonor." He looked at the floor the rims of his eyes reddening, "I let Rhoda take the fall for my sin. She, basically, let me do this to her, because she cared more about my future than hers."

"Alex, why do you suppose she let you use her to cover your sins? What could have been her motive?" I asked this knowing the answer.

He picked up his head and looked me square in the eyes, "Love; pure deep love for a friend. I think of this often. I mean why didn't she have sex with me? Lots of women, who were sorry to say, more attractive than her jumped at the chance. I'm not Hercules, by any means; but women like that relatively nice looking caring type of man. The caring part, wins them over every time. Over time I was able to turn this feature on and off at will. Also there are always the pastor-camp-follower-types, who just want to belong to a pastor in an intimate way. Now that is a strange psychological problem, if there ever was one. But I often ask myself 'why didn't she do the nasty with me?' I would have kept all confidential and no one would have known. But the reason, I have come to see, is love, real love. Not love to just get sexual pleasure; but love that cares for another person more than you care for your own soul, kind of love. She loved me too much to defile me or my ministry, with a few moments of sexual pleasure. She loved my family and couldn't hurt them. I also ask myself, 'Why didn't she sue me or my church?' She had a real legal case, at the beginning. She could have gotten me on sexual harassment, with inappropriate touching. But again she loved me and even loved my screwed up church. Why? Because we were fellow believers. She couldn't see my career ruined and the name of our church besmirched. She also tried to make the whole getting right with me thing about reconciling, not about an endless rehashing of my sins. Again why? Love. Real love; not sex or immorality, but the true love of a sister in Christ for her brother and wanting his best, not to see him destroyed, even if by his own foolishness. When I finally saw these things, years into this whole mess, I wept for three days. No one has ever loved me this much, barring God, of course. She knew what a black heart I had and she still loved me."

"Alex, it took a real man to say what you said just now. You wear a lot of masks; but this showed me that there is a man with a heart, beneath all the crud you've accumulated, over all these years. Okay, we are getting somewhere. So did they do the abuses with or without your prior knowledge?"

"Well, as you know, there were so many instances (sadly), that it was a little of both. Sometimes Stan would come into the office rubbing his hands together and saying 'I think we will be rid of her this time' or words to that effect. Or sometimes he'd come in my office grinning and saying, 'We really smacked her down this time; she'll never recover.' Then there were the times they wanted me to play along. For instance, whenever anyone asked me about if I was having an affair with Rhoda, I was to give one of two answers only: 1. 'Rhoda is highly delusional and there is no truth to her story. In fact she has tried to seduce me and has stalked me and my family; I hardly know the woman'. 2. 'It is over now and we are never going to see each other again. She and I are no longer connected in any way.' If a possible employer was to speak to me, I was to tell them that she never worked for me and that all I knew about her was that she had had an affair at the church. I was supposed to answer all questions about her, in a way which implied, she had mental problems. I don't know all the details of what they did to her; but they wanted me to look like I was a man suffering unjustly, at the hands of a mentally unstable woman. I was Pastor Perfect and given glowing recommendations by other staff members for folks in the church to hear. I was made to look like a saint and Rhoda was painted as a delusional adulteress."

I was really angry, right then, at Alex for abandoning Rhoda and leaving her to the wolves; but I tried to keep that feeling inside and proceed as a professional. "Did this out and out lying make you feel any sense of guilt? Did you think about your friend sacrificing herself and her reputation for you? Did you at least want to come to her defense?"

"Actually, at first I was too into my own hurts. I kind of wanted to punish her. She had rejected me, the poster boy for masculinity, and hadn't given into my desires to have sex with her. This not only confused me, but made me angry. Who was she to reject me? Her husband was Oriental and okay looking. But I was athletic and strong, handsome, charming, and sexually attractive. Others thought she was just your run of the mill housewife, with little to be desired. She had a good personality; but what made her think she could say, 'No' to me? The great and wonderful me? Then when that stage was over, there was fear of what the church might do me and my other family troubles. I couldn't rock the boat; I had to stand back and watch. That nearly drove me crazy. Stan was always bringing her in to the church, for shouting sessions in his office, and you could hear her crying her eyes out and saying she wanted to 'just speak to her friend'. I'd find her weeping in vacant rooms, in our church school. She would sometimes rush out of a meeting to weep, where no one could see her. She lost weight, looked sickly and pale, was always at the doctor, and lost all of her friends over time. I finally felt she had suffered enough; but by then I had too much to lose, because I was given tenure and a raise. My wife told me I'd better not ruin this and better keep my nose clean. More than my increase in salary, my status kept growing. Finally I decided it was really too late for me to help her. She had long since begun her journey into other churches in the area. She wasn't our problem anymore." When he said that line, I was about ready to slap him; but I again gained control.

So with a slight trembling, which I was trying hard to suppress, I asked, "Can you give me a few examples of abuses you all did to her. You don't have to go in exact order just say them as they come to you. Don't go into great detail with each one and mention if you knew about it before hand or afterwards. Thanks." I was feeling protective of Rhoda because I knew her now and because I had been in circumstances that were very similar to Rhoda and Alex's at a few or the abusive churches, I attended. I had felt such a sense of helplessness while in them. Maybe the anger was at my own self and how I'd let this type of thing happen to myself.

Alex thought for awhile then he said, "Well Pastor Stan loved to do the 2am phone calls, where he'd threaten her with physical harm, if she said anything. He'd tell me all about the call the next day and then he'd laugh. He tried to disguise his voice or get someone else from the office to help him do these. Sometimes he'd tell me he was going to do one of those calls, beforehand. There were too many of those calls to count. Then there were the phone threats that were made to her when she started seeing the same doctor I saw. A couple of assistant pastors called and told her she could not see the same doctor, I was seeing, and if she continued to do so she'd be sorry. I knew about that abuse beforehand. Then there were the people the church had follow her, inside the church building. They'd curse her in loud voices, in front of others, to destroy her reputation. After she left our church and began attending others, these same people would go in teams to each pastor and each group of important sisters, in her new church, and tell them she was an adulteress. By doing this, her name was tarnished within a week or two of her arrival, making her doing any ministry, at those churches, mostly impossible. They'd even make calls to the pastors and women's groups she attended, sounding like concerned Christians who wanted to protect the churches and groups from a loose woman. These things I usually found out afterwards; Stan would fill me in on another victory for our side. People were put in charge of getting her phone records, sifting through her mail and then returning it to the mail box, recording things she said to others, and even hacking into her email sites. They used all forms of media to try and trap her. Stan had boxes of files and shoe boxes of tapes detailing her every move. There were women we assigned to be fake friends, so she'll tell them things in confidence, which we could use against her. We even had people who pretended to pray with her, who would later report to the church what was prayed. We sent letters to her home, even after she left our church, threatening her with legal action for wanting to reconcile or speak to me in any way. The church sent police officers to intimidate her at her home and a lawyer we kept on staff would make up false documents to scare her and would call her at all hours of the day and night. On top of telling lies to various groups, at the churches she attended, and we even got group members, to vow to report anything she said, about the situation, to our church. I usually knew they were planning to do those sort of things ahead of time. There was even a brother, from her home group, that we sent to intimidate her and to threaten her. We made him tell her that he'd be following and watching her closely and that he'd make her sorry if she said anything to anyone about what happened. I'm sure there was more; but I can't remember, any more, at this time. I was mostly told about these things, after they happened. But I would pretend to not care and to even support what they were doing. All the while she kept in contact with me and I kept in contact with her through our 'code' system. So we knew we were friends. But to my eternal shame, I let them do all of the above mentioned things and did not lift a hand to stop them. So I guess I wasn't that great of a friend, huh?"

"Having been in similar situations myself, Alex, I can tell you that the worst things are the constant curses from the pastors and your fellow members, the being made to look delusional, the being called evil, and lastly not just being able to just speak to your friend to get things straightened out."

Alex looked at me. "Mark, do you think I'm proud of my behavior, my impotence? No I'm not proud. I felt like dying when they denied her communion and made her sit in the last row with the sinners, when they told her she was going to be shunned and excommunicated, when they called her a liar and cursed her out at church, when they gossiped behind her back both at our church and into her new churches, when they treated her like a delusional nut case, and when they destroyed any hope she had

had for a ministry at our church and at future ones. Each time a pastor from a new church called for a recommendation to let her lead a ministry, we had to tell them she was a liar, delusional, an adulteress, and not to be trusted. I had to pretend that I thought this was all funny and not so serious. But it was her life, my friend's life."

"You saw all of this going on. Couldn't you at least have spoken to her quietly and told her that despite the lies going on you were on her side or told her how they were intimidating you? Alex are you not stunned that she still wishes to be your friend?"

"I am in wonder at this every day. We were only normal friends for a short time and yet she has been a loyal and true friend." He looked as though he might cry. So I jumped in before he had a chance.

I had to get a few loose ends put together before our next meeting. "Alex, please explain your code system once more and from beginning to the end. Thanks."

"When the church told me I could no longer speak to her or write to her I decided to do both, but without words. This was not easy because I did not know if she'd recognize the blank emails and silent calls from fictitious numbers were from me. She did have a hard time at first. But I decided to tie these calls and emails into events. Like if she saw me in the hall I'd send a blank email. If we went by each other on the street and she waved, I'd make a silent call to her. I called her at all of her jobs, when she was home, and I even called when her husband was home, remaining quiet on the phone, until he figured out it was me. I usually did a special click at the end of my call, so she'd get it was me. Sometimes I did this three times per day and sometimes I'd skip a week or two. I just wanted her to know I was thinking of her. She would then send me a one line note saying thank you and how she wanted to meet for reconciliation. She'd on occasion send longer notes, but this was more at the beginning. She would send them anonymously, trying to get me to finally speak to her. At first, I did cry on some of the calls; I wanted her to know I shared her pain. Sadly some of the first calls did cause me to think impure thoughts, etc. But over time I was just glad to hear her voice or know she knew I cared. I wanted to distance myself from my church and show her I, at least, had a heart. As much as she seemed to like my calls I could tell my lack of courage frustrated her. I'm also sure that over time I began to bug her husband. I wasn't able to keep everyone happy. I was just trying to keep myself safe basically. I accomplished that. The church still doesn't really know the extent of my contact with her. I'll never tell them either; it is none of their business."

I looked at him closely. I could see his inability to protect his friend had taken a toll on him. So I began to have compassion on him. "Alex can you see that by being silent you were just as guilty as your compatriots? The silence was also a form of abuse, to Rhoda. Can you see how you have to ask Rhoda for forgiveness, more for this issue, than the original attack? I hope you do confess to her. Do think you are now ready to meet with Rhoda and I? (He nodded.) If so, what would be a good day and time next week? Is Thursday morning good? Maybe around 10am?"

"I think 11am would be better for me. Is that okay? (I nodded.) As he was getting up to leave, instead he fell to his knees in front of the fire, almost hitting Max. He began to weep deeply. "Mark could you pray with me? I...I can't leave till I pray." I placed my hand on his shoulder and we prayed, he confessed his sin and how he had hurt his friend and we both cried. My secretary knocked at the door saying Mrs. Temple was there. I had to wash my face and get Alex out to make the appointment with Helen. So I told Alex we'd have to end things there. I also told him to call me if he wanted more prayer. I gave him a bro hug and went to wash my face. I kept thanking God for an apparent breakthrough, though I had no idea what set him off.

Chapter 15

When Tues of the following week came around I was feeling quite uneasy. I had had my secretary, Helen, call Rhoda and ask if Thursday at 11am was okay for her. Rhoda was very excited to finally be seeing her friend Alex. My secretary said she shouted, "For sure!!" and then got more composed and said she'd be there with "bells on". Why these two people were still friends, after all they went through, boggled my mind. Yet I, too, had had good and deep friendships, in the past; so I almost understood. Some people may ask, "How can two people be friends after one friend crosses decency boundaries and deeply hurts another friend?" That is a good question. In all my years of being a counselor I have actually seen this occure only a couple of times. Now I've had thousands of patients, over the years, and the percentage of those who deeply offend one another and then go back to being friends is very small. But it has happened and sometimes it has happened in spite of my own better judgment. I don't always agree with decisions my clients make; but they are adults and I cannot control them, nor do I wish to. I can only make suggestions. I'm always happy to see things work out better than my poor vision for folks' lives. The more I counsel others the more I find I don't have little pat answers. Each case is unique, what works for one client will not work for another, even if the cases are similar or appear to be so.

I asked my secretary if I had any clients for the next day, Wednesday. She said only Mr. Franklin and that he was flexible, if I needed to change my schedule. I asked if we could try to fit Mr. Franklin in at 4pm on Friday. Helen took care of it and even promised to bake him some cookies. He was more than willing to change his time slot. I had just finished seeing the only two patients for Tuesday and had already updated their files; it was only 11am. So I gave Helen the rest of the day off and asked her to come in and do a bit of paperwork for me and to man the phones. I told her that I'd be back at about 9am on Thursday. Just in time to get myself and the office ready for Alex and Rhoda's appointment. Though I was excited about this, I was also a bit nervous, wondering if they were truly ready to meet. I have a little fishing cabin on Morro Lake and I thought I needed to take a short retreat and time of prayer, to have wisdom in this important matter. If God had been so meticulous and careful with these two lives, all of these years, I didn't want to go charging into the situation like a proverbial "bull in a china shop". So I called my wife who was just going out on an errand and told her I would be going straight to the cabin, since I had a couple changes of clothes there, and I wouldn't be home till Thursday afternoon at dinner. I also said she didn't have to cook, on Thursday; I'd take her out to any restaurant she wanted to go to. She said she'd miss me, but that if I felt I needed time alone with God she'd not stop me.

So I got a few food supplies in Chinatown and headed out to the cabin. I wanted to pray, but I'm not much of a faster. I needed some good food to accompany me and I love Chinese. I arrived at the cabin a few hours later and tidied it up a bit, before I did anything else. I then made a large pot of coffee, poured a huge mug, and went to sit out on the porch, on a big Adirondack chair with a matching stool. Then I began to pray. Soon I was taken up into that special place with God and the whole area became one big Monet-ish blur, as I cried my heart out to God for wisdom. I prayed and read the Bible and sang a few choruses. But mainly I told God, "Why don't You just speak to me, Lord? I need to hear how You think and get direction from you." So I shut my eyes, quieted my spirit, and soon a still small voice began to speak to my heart. God was so passionate about

Rhoda and Alex's calling and how this reconciliation was going to be used to bring them and those they would minister to, closer to God. I spent the next day doing pretty much the same: seeking God, letting Him speak to me, napping, and making myself different simple Chinese recipes. On Thursday I was up at 3am and worshipping God. When dawn came I got into a little row boat we have and hoped I'd catch something for breakfast. I actually did catch a big fish and rowed back to shore as fast as I could and made myself a Japanese breakfast of raw fish, rice noodles, and green tea. I put the rest of the fish in the freezer, got dressed for work, and jumped into my car hoping to get to the office on time. I did arrive at 9:15am and I puttered about getting the office ready for the meeting with Rhoda and Alex. Then I cared for Max's needs, making sure to give him lots of hugs and kisses, too. I then put on the kettle, got out three cups and some rather top of the line hot chocolate. I also put out a nice dish of coconut macaroons from Whole Foods. I turned up the fire and put on my slippers just as Alex knocked on the door.

"Hi Mark, I'm a few minutes early, mind if I come in?" I waved him in and asked him to get comfortable. I told him I had to get my notes and I'd be right with him. I opened my briefcase and put my notes out in two neat piles, one for him and one for Rhoda. Then I sat in my chair, suddenly feeling very tired.

Alex said, "You look a bit wiped. You couldn't sleep, like me, last night, huh?"

"Actually Alex I slept like a baby; but I got up early and have been running ever since. I even managed to catch a fish this morning. I was staying at my fishing cabin, over by Morro Lake. I'm still having a bit of trouble adjusting to the two different worlds, the quietness of the lake and the bustle of city life. You know how that feels?"

He smiled slightly. "I am totally an outdoorsy kind of guy. I love the quiet, even the birds are too noisy for me. We, have a time share at Lake Tahoe and I always feel like I'm in a time warp, when I go from there back to the office. But seriously... I really could not sleep last night. Is Rhoda is still angry? She likes to say she is not angry; but Stan said that was a lie. He said that with all we did to her she had to be angry. He told me she only wanted to reconcile because she wanted to rehash things over, again and again. She wanted to smear my face in what I did to make me feel guilty and dirty. Since she wasn't allowed to communicate with me, I used to believe what Stan said. It was all I had to go on. What if seeing me makes her want to beat the 'crud' out of me? What if all this has been a ruse; so she could tell me off again, this time in front of you? I wouldn't blame her."

"Now Alex, I wouldn't worry about that. Also just put Stan's implanted thoughts out of your mind. You know what kind of a man he is. I wouldn't take much stock in anything he ever said to you. Rhoda's heart seems very much for you, though I don't know why, to be honest. I think she wants this time to be one of healing, like you do. Relax. I have spent a lot of time with her and I don't see that revengeful spirit in her." We both turned towards the door, which was ajar. "Hello, is that you Rhoda? Come on in. Don't worry we weren't discussing you. Alex just wasn't sure you'd be glad to see him." I barely got out that sentence when Rhoda flew across the room and gave him a hug around his neck and then slapped him on the top of his head, in mock offense.

"You are wondering if I would be glad to see you. You big dummy. (She slapped his head again.) What do you think I've been waiting for, for fifteen years? (She rolled her eyes.) Doc, I think you now know which one of us is nuts. It's him. Gee."

Alex actually laughed at her drama. He showed her to her chair by the fire and patted her shoulder. "You look good, Rhoda. I've never really seen you up close these last years. But you still look like you are in your 40's. It's I who has gotten pruney."

"Thanks for lying, Alex. This type of lying is totally permitted. You won't catch me complaining."

"Okay, you two, enough banter. (I knew they were both trying to act a bit like comics to cover the insecurity they felt.) We are here to work. Are you both ready to see this open sore healed? (They nodded in unison.) So when was the last time you saw Alex, Rhoda?""

"Alex, why did you see her about six years ago? What were you doing at the time?"

I have mainly seen him at grocery stores. The last time I had a real sighting was about six years ago. It was in the parking lot of a Lucky's Foods. I was just minding my own business and not expecting to see him. But then…Why don't you tell him about our momentary encounter, Alex?"

He smiled, "Well it was a weird day. I had just had an argument with my wife and to blow off steam I decided to drive to Lucky's. Normally I bike or roller blade. I was dressed in skate boarding clothes and even had my hair dyed blond at the tips; I was trying to look like a teen skateboarder. I went into the grocery and got a soda. Two lanes over I saw Rhoda joking with the cashier. She was finishing paying her bill and I walked out right behind her calling, 'Rhoda, Rhoda, Rhoda Du…' She looked around, not seeing me, and kept walking with her basket. I called again, 'Rhoda, Rhoda…' and finally she turns around looks like a truck just hit her. She is smiling, but can't move. I think she was in shock. She said, 'Can we talk, Alex?' She just left her car trunk wide open and her basket of food and jumped into the front seat of my car. 'Not right this second, Rhoda, later. I'll call you. Go and get your basket.' She retrieved it from the center of the parking lot lane and said, 'When, Alex, when can we talk?' I told her I didn't know and got back into my car and drove away with her waving. I got really scared and never contacted her until a few months ago. I'm sorry Rhoda. I was afraid my wife would want to leave me; if she found out I'd had contact with you. That was what we had been arguing about. She wanted me to never speak with you again and this command ticked me off. Then of course, I feared Stan and the church finding out; I'd just gotten another raise."

Rhoda looked out the window; one tear came silently down her cheek. "What you don't know is that my pastor, at the time, from Fiery Blaze church, had been giving me a hard time for believing you'd contact me, again. He thought I was delusional, for hoping to hear from you. There were also some ladies from the church that were spreading unkind rumors about me and saying I was crazy to want to reconcile. He was taking their side. So when you promised me we'd meet I was so excited that I was vindicated. I contacted him and told him how I'd met you in the parking lot and you said you'd call me. I was so sure that parking lot meeting was of God. He actually acted like maybe I wasn't crazy, like those women were implying. But when you never got back to me, he again began to see me as delusional and would not let me be in the church's ministry. I been leading at least three ministry groups, at the church; but after all of the drama of our meeting, he withdrew his support. He was intending to make me just stuff envelopes for the rest of my days, if I stayed on. So I had to leave the church, soon afterwards. I believed you and literally waited for two years for you to contact me, but you didn't. It was not easy for me to go through being misunderstood yet again."

Alex looked at me and then looked at her in the eyes. "Am I forgiven? I really, really did not mean to hurt you again. So very sorry, Rhoda." He put his head down and got bright red blotches behind his ears. She reached over and patted his arm.

"You know I did not really blame you. I have been mired in legalism. I knew how you had this mindset of checking out every blessed thing you did or thought with your church leaders. So I figured you went and asked them if we could meet and they said 'No' for the five hundredth time." She crossed her arms. "Alex, what did they have over you to keep you in such total submission? I believe they could have made you do anything at anytime, even kill for them. Am I over exaggerating or am I right? What the frick was wrong with those people? How were they able to abuse us so perfectly and why did you keep letting them? Why did I?"

Alex looked a bit shocked at her answer, especially the almost swear word. "You know, Rhoda, I have been wondering the same things, of late. In that instance, it was more a fear of my wife. But you are totally correct; the other leaders there had me over a 'barrel'. They did control everything I did and said, especially when it came to you. I did not have a backbone at the time to stand up to them, especially Pastor Stan. That relationship was so complicated that I had best save delving into that area for another session; if you still want to continue, that is."

Rhoda looked confused. "Of course I want to continue. I know what being in a cult is like. I was in a real honest to goodness one for twelve years. I really get why you felt you had to do certain things. It is just that

I was so frustrated. They were control freaks and you were a victim and your victimization made me a victim. On and on. But you didn't really know I was more angry with them for their abusing us, than at you for being afraid. We had best save this topic for another day. I really have to be going. I'm committed to our friendship and to seeing you free from 'The Them'." She was so very sincere and so wanting him to see this.

I stirred myself up and asked them a favor. "Please do me a favor. Can you both promise to not even have coffee, even with your spouses in tow, or call each other, until I think it is a good time for you to do so? I'm not trying to keep either of you apart from your friend or be controlling, but I want to make sure you are both more healed before you are face to face, without someone like me to referee. I don't want anything to undo the work we are doing here. Can you both promise to do this? I think you will see the wisdom in this request in the coming weeks. Oh yes, don't communicate by phone, either. By phone, I also mean email or any other media type of communication. Okay?"

Rhoda was the first to speak. "I promise, Doc. I have quite a busy schedule, anyway. Alex did you know we are remodeling our home? It is going on the third year now and we are almost done with phase one. Hopefully you and your wife can see it someday. I'd like that."

"I promise too. Rhoda, I hope we can come and see your home, sometime, you are within skating distance from my home. I have rolled by a few times. Another long story. But I'm busy too with my new ministry. I'll tell you about that sometime. I understand that we should let you decide, Mark, how we do this reconciliation thing. You have done this many times before. I'm trusting you know what you are doing. I sure have botched the whole thing, in my limited wisdom."

I stood up to escort them to the front desk. "Why not see what date you and Alex can come here together. As you know, my secretary, Helen, has the schedule book. I think we've made some headway here. Let's stay a bit longer next session, okay? Both of you take care and I'll see you next week." As I said this Mrs. Feingold entered the office and I motioned for her to take a seat in the waiting room, "I'll be right with you, Margaret. Did you have an appointment? Well, never mind, I happen to have time

147

to see you. Just give me a minute to tidy the office." I waved good-bye to the two friends and went to clean the office for my next patient. They went to Helen to make an appointment and did as they promised. They went directly to their cars, not stopping to talk in the parking lot. I saw them from my window. Rhoda did do a little wave and Alex nodded. Then my client, Mrs. Feingold, entered, who wanted to divorce her husband, for the third time in six months. I had a bottle of Advil ready, for when she was.

Chapter 16

*A*lex and Rhoda picked Wed. morning of the following week. I could see that both of them had determination written on their faces. This whole thing had gone on far too long. They had actually only worked together for about nine months. After that incident, they were told they could not communicate. Rhoda had stayed on another two years or so at the church, hoping to make things right, even enduring abuse to see her friend be free. She had also hoped to make peace with the church and get her reputation back. She had come to the church a year before working for Alex. She only knew him slightly before working with him. He was her daughter's Sunday school teacher and she would always thank him for teaching her daughter. Then she worked, as his Girl Friday or assistant, for nine months or so. So technically they had been friends for about seventeen years; but had spent almost fifteen of those years communicating by a secret code, they had developed. The church thought they had been separated after the incident; but they had developed their own means of overriding the control of Pastor Stan and his assistants. Most folks would have given up on the whole thing long ago; but they both saw this friendship was God ordained and this is why they continued. They knew the sin Alex tried to commit against Rhoda was wrong, of course. There was no confusion there. But they felt that the actual friendship was something God still wanted. The strain of this dual life was etched on their faces. As I was musing about this, they both had driven up at the same time and entered into the office in silence.

It had been drizzling again outside and both of them were damp. I asked them to pull the chairs closer in towards the fire and handed them both a quilt. I had just made a pot of chocolate tea and poured them and myself a cup. I had also just gotten some brownies from my secretary, Helen, and I offered each of them one. I took one and put the box on the side. Max didn't know who to sit with so he just stretched out in front of the fire. I was chilly, so I put on a huge sweater that my wife had gotten me from Germany. As soon as we were all cozy I spoke, "So... you both seem a bit somber to me, today; is anything wrong? Alex? Rhoda? Do you want to share anything right off the top?"

"All I know is that it is really hard to not communicate. You keep wondering if the other person is offended with you or if they are being abused or being threatened or what. Also your mind starts bringing up the past. Things you forgot and you feel vulnerable again," Rhoda shared this while looking at Alex out of the corner of her eye. "I was told that if I remembered this episode, I'd be made to relive it and thus become depressed. But that truly is not what is happening. What it has done is bring up long buried things I had forgotten about, some not even related to the incident. One of them being the death of my twin babies and how I tried to have more children and was unable."

Alex looked shocked. "Wow that is really wild! I experienced the exact same emotions. I also began to have memories of past smaller offenses I'd done to others and to Rhoda around that time period. I remembered little daily things that she'd done, that really bothered me. Problem with those memories is: I'm not sure what is a real memory or what is one that Stan implanted in my mind. Stan told me lots of things about you, that now I'm not sure you actually did. He'd also reevaluate things you did and give his spin on them. Rhoda, I find I have a million little issues to ask forgiveness for and the biggest one is just my believing Stan, over you."

I looked at both of them. "Know what's 'funnier' yet, you two? I thought today I'd let you both ask each other questions about various things that have bugged you for years. Reconciliation is an interesting part of forgiveness. In forgiveness we often do a blanket covering of others' wrongs. It's a, 'I forgive you for everything you ever did to me, type of thing.' But in reconciliation we have the time and the leisure, if you will, to pick apart the mass of material you forgave someone for and we can say, 'Why did you do such and such? What were you thinking?' Not only does this help bring about a fuller forgiveness; it clears up lies we have lived with and helps us to reestablish our friendship on a sounder foundation. Not one made of lies, but truth. Do I make myself clear? So we will have a ground rule here. Don't bring something up to smash down your friend and punish them. Bring up something that hurt you and ask them why they did this or that thing. Okay? (They both nodded.)"

Alex spoke first, "Rhoda, Stan told me that you were running around church telling every person you could about my attacking you. Is this true? If so what were you thinking?" I thought this was an excellent question. Many people, when they are hurt, want to hurt the abuser and to get back at that person, they try to discredit them to all who will listen.

Now this time Rhoda's face glowed red. I thought I saw fire come out of her eyes. "Alex the story is long and complex; may I take a few moments to speak openly? (He nodded.) When you first attacked me I told no one, not even my best friends. At that time I had about five ladies from the church who were my BFF's. I did not speak to them about this and more importantly I did not even tell my husband, who is not just my husband, but my number one and dearest friend. Also I, of course, could not speak to you, my second best friend, about you, and so I poured my heart out to God alone. But as time went on, I could not deal with this emotionally. So eventually I went to Stan to seek counsel. Instead of helping me and being a pastor to me; he right away started in on me telling me I was a liar and that I seduced you, on and on. I regretted, almost immediately, telling him anything; but it was too late. He was relentless in trying to abuse me verbally and mentally to make me repent of my statements I made to him. He tried to force me to lie. I was feeling so alone. So I told three of my five lady friends, at different times, with almost two or three months in between. I told them to keep this confidential and that I was in the process of forgiving you and that Stan was abusing me. Unbeknownst to me, they went and told others. I had sworn them to secrecy, and soon people came up to me with wild stories. What they made up was far more exciting than what really happened. I refuted those stories and said a true, but very simplified 'G-rated' version. Then I dropped it, hoping they would drop it too. But they didn't. Pastor Stan, on the other hand, went to everyone who knew you and I, and every group I was in or leading and told them our story. Those people knew nothing of our sad tale, as of yet. But the version he told was not true and he said that I had seduced you! Thing is that was the first time they had heard of the story; I had tried to put out the little fires I knew of. But he had gone to everyone and started a forest fire. Stan just figured I'd told everyone. He told the prayer teams and complete strangers from church and he went into great detail, albeit false detail, with those folks. He told them I seduced you and slandered you and was a liar. Soon most people I knew snubbed me thinking I was trying to wreck your marriage and falsely accuse you. But they all heard this fanciful tale from Stan's lips, not mine. Some came to me in righteous anger, defending you and your wife and chastising me. I didn't want to defend myself, because I was trying to protect your reputation. So I let mine get trashed, thinking God would defend me.

I let things go on this way for quite awhile, finding that not only did people believe Stan's lies, but God did not come to my defense. I originally had thought you were the one spreading the rumors. But a few good people came to me and told me what Stan had been doing. They told me what he had said to them and to even whole groups, at one time. Well, that made me hopping mad. But I thought that you had okayed this lying and were not standing up for me as a true friend should. So I got mad at you for thinking this was some kind of honorable behavior. Eventually when it got so bad that, people confronted me and called me a whore, etc. I finally told them the true story in a shortened more accurate G-version. I told them that Stan and you had lied. I was defending my character at least once per day, for more than a year and less often after that. Total strangers yelled at me, for trying to destroy your reputation. Thing is I didn't do any such thing. But after a couple of years of lying, from your church; I got fed up and spoke up for myself. It took me over four years to forgive Stan for this.

I forgave you much sooner because I finally saw you, too were a victim. I surmised that Stan had told you I was spreading rumors; but truly I did not do so. I merely defended myself, after more than a year of letting my reputation get thrashed. His lies ruined our lives. Because we could not talk; I could not tell you the truth or find out if you too were lying. I wept more about this, than what you did to me. This is the gospel truth, Alex. I tried to cover your sins, not expose them. I just knew you had fallen for Stan's lies and believed I had spread the rumors." She started to tremble and shake. It was the first time she was able to tell him what the truth was. She had lived under Stan's lies for so many years. I knew the feeling, from similar situations in my own life.

Alex was sitting with his mouth open. When he finally could speak and he said, "Man." He got tears in his eyes and his face was actually pure white devoid of color. "All these years I thought that you had been so evil, trying to destroy my reputation. To now see it was Stan who spread the rumors, and lied to me, pinning it all on you, makes me sick. But it gets worse, Rhoda. He and the church told me, clearly, to use two lies if anyone ever asked me about the situation. Lie one was: 'Yes, we had an affair; but it is over now. We no longer see each other.' Lie two was: 'She is trying to destroy my reputation and ruin my marriage. I hardly know the woman. She has mental problems and is delusional.' I was to pick the lie that seemed the most believable at that moment. I knew that Stan had told the home group, you were in, that you were having delusions about me loving you. They were to report you, if you said anything, at all, concerning me. But I did not get the full scope of the lies Stan told. He said to me, 'Sometimes it is alright to lie for Jesus.' I didn't really buy that; but I was so afraid of losing my job, that I acted like I agreed with him. Also he'd yell and scream at me every day, always reminding me to swear, to him, I'd lie and degrade you to others every chance I got. Rhoda, I'm so so sorry for not believing in you and for submitting to that madman. You tried to cover my sins and I helped Stan invent sins for you, to bash your character. This was all done to save my job and make me look good." He got down on his knees and begged for her forgiveness. This sudden realization of his part in the evil from his church surprised me.

Rhoda had the look of pity on her face, as she looked down at her wayward friend. "Alex, cults are so deceptive, that, believe me, you'd sell out your own mother, if they asked you to. It's over now. Please get up. I don't want to cry. I guess I thought you knew more than you did. I need to be forgiven for thinking so badly of you too." Rhoda really seemed to get his pain. Alex returned to his chair and looked out the window.

I just sat there wondering how, in the name of all that was holy, his church could let Stan have that much power and control. How could they let him lie and do nothing to stop this. Rhoda was sacrificed, for their new building. I hope, for their sakes, in light of eternity God sees their building as of greater value, than Rhoda's life. Her life and reputation were of no consequence to the leaders at that church.

Everyone just stared forward for a few moments. I got up and refilled the tea cups. A little liquid sometimes helps folks not to cry and to refocus. Then I said, "Wow this was a very big issue and I'm so very glad that it is now exposed. Both of you now have answers to something that was a major impediment in your relationship. Sorry, but we have to move on. Does anyone have anything more to say on this?

Rhoda did raise her hand, "Can I just ask Alex one more thing that kind of goes with what we just discussed?" I nodded. "Alex, why did you all continue to degrade my character, even after I left your bloody church? After I left no matter what church I went to there were always some little gossips from your church that either spoke to the leading sisters at my new church or the pastor. I felt that this was happening; but then I thought maybe I was paranoid. People would make snide remarks about my character even before I spoke to them or knew them in anyway. I began to get freaky whenever I went to a new meeting. But then one day a couple from the Philippines told me to be careful that Pastor Stan had told them and many others from church that I had tried to seduce you. On top of this when I was out of your church for over two years and joined a women's group, the leader of the women's group told me that someone kept calling her and telling her I was a slut. She had worked for your church and finally figured out it was Stan who was making the calls. She luckily knew my character and refused to believe him. But she told me to be careful this rumor was being passed around in the group, by women who were plants from your church. So my question is: why? Why couldn't you guys have just left me alone to start a new life? I mean you all destroyed my ministry at your church and ruined my reputation there. Why did you have to keep sending folks to the new places I went in an effort to keep destroying my reputation? What benefit was this behavior to any of you, even Stan?"

Alex was at a loss for words. "I truly did not know that Stan was doing this; but I believe you. He used to somehow know what you were doing at all times and ridicule your choices. He'd tell me, 'Oh she joined the Vineyard Church; can you believe she'd go there?' Or, 'I hear she is getting in close with the leader of that big women's group; who does she think she is?' Off comments like that, but I didn't know how he knew those things. Now I see it was from his spy/gossip network. Truly, Rhoda, I had nothing to do with that. That was all in his own twisted mind. During those days, I was simply missing you and wanting to speak to you again."

"Thank you, Alex. I now know, for sure, you were not trying to continue to hurt me or allowing Stan to do so."

Then I turned to Rhoda and said, "Rhoda, what types of things bothered you the most after the incident? Tell me a few things. Don't worry this doesn't have to be in chronological order. If either of you have a bitter memory or confusion and it comes to mind, during this exercise; just bring out it into the light."

Rhoda looked a bit pensive. "Well, Doc, (she turned to Alex's direction) Alex, there are so many things, I will have to prioritize them. Okay, I've got one. Why did you let them threaten me with a lawyer, on many occasions, and the police, on at least two? Do you have any idea what that kind of legal harassment is like? A lawyer, from your church, sent me a letter, saying it was a legal document, an order of protection, from you. It stated that I'd be sued if I ever spoke to you again. Since you kept contacting me I knew something was off. So I showed it to a lawyer, from the Vineyard church I was attending. He said that not only was the document false (a fake), but that you can't be sued for speaking to a friend about forgiveness or reconciliation. I lived in fear from that document for two years. Then there was the police incident. Did you know I was entertaining a missionary, at my home, when a police officer came to the door and told me I'd be arrested, if I ever spoke or contacted you again? I was at another church, at the time, and not even under the control of your leadership. The officer threatened me, as did the lawyer and that kept me from speaking to you for a couple of years, even though I had seen you on the street or in a shop. Maybe you would have agreed to meet if I could have spoken to you for a moment, like normal people do. What were you thinking regarding both these incidences? Did you give them your permission to send these false legal people after me? The lawyer was an elder at your church and the police man was your friend from church. How do you think I explained this to this mess to the missionary I was entertaining and to my husband?" She crossed her arms in front of her and stared at him.

He shook his head and did not know how to put what he wanted to say into words. "First of all the lawyer worked for our church for years and often did little side favors for us. The year before I came to the church the choir director had seduced a woman and they used him to intimidate her into not suing the church. He didn't want to give you that document, and even said you and I should talk; but then Stan said if he didn't do what the church told him to do that he (Stan) might tell the lawyer's wife, something that only Stan knew about. It was out and out bullying by Stan. For some reason the lawyer seemed quite nervous, after that threat; so he made up a false order of protection form. Stan said it looked real and that you were far too ignorant to be able to tell it was a fake. He met with you and Stan and me once. He made a few intimidation calls to you while your husband was at work, during the day. But you know what? He got so sick of the whole thing that he sold his home and moved to Arizona, or some other Southwestern state. He said he was tired of lying and he liked you. He said he couldn't treat you cruelly, for no reason, but saving my sorry butt. The police officer was a guy from the men's group, who heard I was having trouble, from Stan. He told me he could intimidate you if I wanted him to. I said no; but Stan was behind me listening to my conversations as he always did. He said we'd be glad to use his help. He didn't actually have my permission; but I also did not stop them from doing something that would normally be illegal. I knew that if I stood up for you, my job would be toast. Stan told me I had to follow along with anything, they came up with and that I had to like the plans. He that kind of lying was necessary for God's work. I chose to fall for that line of reasoning; because I had so many bills and needed my job. I guess I threw our friendship out the window, to save my butt. Again forgive me. Please. I only wanted to keep this stupid pastor job; I did not think of having any integrity. Now, I think I'd opt for integrity. But then I was more self-centered. Time and suffering changes us. How did you explain things to the missionary and to your husband?"

"Well, in the missionary's case I told her that there was confusion at church and that Pastor Stan was abusing me. I didn't mention you. She had been a missionary to China and had gotten breast cancer. Stan had been in charge of sending her aid for her mission field there. She wasn't feeling well because of the cancer and had come home for a rest. He felt she was exaggerating and said he could not help her anymore, unless she went back to China. He did not offer her any help with her cancer. She ended up going to see a doctor from church, which did cancer surgery in his office, for no charge. But she needed a place to rest and so Stan reluctantly found her a family to stay with. Problem was. before she got there he told the family she was in rebellion, for not being in China. He commanded them to make life uncomfortable for her, so she'd have to leave and return to China. They abused her and told Stan she didn't like the abuse and he got furious at her. He cut off all aid to her. She went back to China and lived in poverty for about another year. So she knew about and understood about Stan and she wasn't shocked, at all, about the police thing. Stan later spread rumors about her at church; so she now lives in Oregon. I told my husband about the police man and about the lawyer and his fake papers and he wanted to sue your church and even go to the newspaper. But I told him that that wouldn't help. I had gone to a lawyer and he said my case had too many holes and the church had more money. My husband said he knew Stan was a false Christian. I told him and others that Stan was definitely demonic and since that seemed totally rational to anyone who met him; my husband and others believed me. I wasn't happy exposing

Stan, but not one person was shocked. Everyone at church had a story of abuse, to tell me, about Stan, even when I didn't bring up his name in conversation. What a guy. Yet the church never fired or reprimanded him. He had ultimate power. Even the head pastor said, 'I don't do anything without asking Stan first.' Eek."

"Well Rhoda, I wasn't totally blameless. Most of the time, when he told me what his plans were for hurting you; I pretended to not be interested. If I ever showed the slightest interest, he'd make me sit for hours and hours in the conference room and yell at me, until I confessed whatever he wanted me to confess. Each time it was something different. He already knew after the first meeting I had with him, that I had indeed attached you. But he made me confess it over and over again. Then he said he would never give you the satisfaction of an apology from me or the church. He said he'd say until the day he died, you tried to seduce me. He said he'd keep trying to make you confess. Then when he finally broke you and you did, he'd bring you in front of the whole church and make you do a public humiliation and confession. He said that you made too much of a stink and eventually this would make the church look bad. He also said that no woman was going to besmirch our church's name or reputation. He said you were nothing but a stupid housewife and no one would listen to you. We were pastors they'd believe us. But I knew it was all a lie; I just did not have the guts to stand up for you."

Rhoda began to cry. "I feel like you let him and your other church cronies rape me, not just once but over and over. Alex, I chose to forgive you. But it wasn't so easy to do this because you said you were my friend. I was not only disrespected with your attack; but you didn't protect me. I guess I expected a good friend to love me so much that he'd even be willing to die for me. Why did your church sacrifice me like this? Why did they think I had no value? There is nothing Christian in any of this. The world isn't even this bad. Shame."

I hate to say it; but I was on Rhoda's side. Alex had sold her out for that "glorious" job of his. He thought that that was something worth fighting for. I decided to ask him more directly about this, so he might be able to see how he'd sold his soul for mere garbage. "So Alex, let me ask you; has all of this been worth it: the lying, the destruction of your friend, the secondary destruction of others (including your family), and all the additional crud that went with this sad story. Has all of this been worth it in light of your keeping your job? Has the job been that good that you were willing to not only sell your manhood, but also to sell your very soul? Are you proud of all you did? Could you even look yourself in the eyes, when gazing into a mirror? Did you/do you want that 'perk' of the retirement home in Arizona that badly, that you'd sacrifice a friend and your own honor? Can you flip God off and all that is holy, for some job at a church that is far from godly and basically evil? Tell me. Maybe I missed something here. Face what you did and tell me, tell us."

He jumped up out of his chair and began pacing. "Okay! Okay! I see I am the bad guy here. The blame falls on me. It's not fair; but I can't take all the blame for this. If only Rhoda had been stronger, had stood up for herself, and had not been so gullible. If only she had confronted Stan; if she had confronted me! But no, she acted like the Bible said; she trusted in God and in the leaders and did not stand up for her own rights. But no one came along and took her part and most importantly I left her high and dry, even when I knew Stan's plans. I left her naked and exposed. I let him abuse her. I wasn't a man at all; I was a wimp. It is all true and I can't run from it any longer, I just can't." He fell into a heap on the floor and wept like a baby. Rhoda and I stood back and let God do "surgery" on his heart. This was the cry of repentance. It was a good kind of cry. The blinders had fallen off, at last. Rhoda squeezed my arm, as we watched this scenario unfold. After about twenty minutes, he stopped crying and stood up a new man. Rhoda and I shook his hand. I told him how God was now ready to work.

I looked at my watch and was surprised to see two and a half hours had passed. I knew my next client was probably in the waiting room. I let Alex and Rhoda clean up in the restroom and I tidied up the office. I told Helen on the intercom to tell Mr. Rodriguez I'd be right with him. Both Alex and Rhoda came out looking presentable. I hugged them both and told them to stop at the desk and make another appointment. I had a client waiting. Mr. Rodriguez came in and began to tell me about his new job and the mean spirited boss he had. I wondered how he'd have liked to have Stan for a boss. But I pretended to be totally involved in the story of his crazy boss. Soon I was involved and I laid aside my thoughts of Rhoda and Alex.

When Mr. Rodriguez left, I sat gazing at the fire and I remembered a story I had seen on TV as a child: There was once an Ice Queen. She had great riches and there were two little poor children who found the entrance to her underground Ice Castle. They went down an old well into a dark world and soon they entered a room that was full of jewels, mostly diamonds. The little girl looked around and then she met the Ice Queen. The Ice Queen said that if the little girl served her she could have all the jewels there she wanted. But the little girl could tell the woman was cold hearted and cruel. So she refused and ran out of the Queen's dark underground castle. But the little boy wanted to remain and be rich. The little girl couldn't leave her friend so she gathered her courage and went back for her friend. She managed to fight for the little boy and rescued him. When they finally got back to the surface the little boy was so proud. He had stuffed his pockets with diamonds. The sun shone on the two as they began their journey home. The little boy pulled out the jewels and they began to melt. He saw all that he had wanted in that dark world was only ice, an illusion. There were no jewels; but he had been willing to sell his soul for only ice. This is what Alex did; he sold his soul for an illusion and now the ice jewels were melting. The sun showed what the boy's jewels were made of. Alex now knew what his precious job was made of; it was only so much "ice".

Chapter 17

$\mathcal{D}$uring the week that was in between my seeing Rhoda and Alex I thought long and hard about what area I wanted to delve into. I had already told them I didn't plan to go chronologically through their story. I had done that before, with many of my clients. Then they always would remember some out of sequence portions and we'd have to go back to those and this would throw the whole timeline off anyway. Instead I now went to the areas that either I or the clients deemed the most important, at the time of the appointment. At the meeting we were to have today, I thought I'd choose to focus on what seemed important to me and what might help develop more compassion on the part of both parties. So often we get into our own pain and cannot see the pain the other person is going through or has gone through. So since they were coming in at 11am I decided to make things a bit more lunch like. I had Helen get me three ham and Swiss bagel sandwiches, three lg. cookies, and some sparkling water. It wasn't as chilly out and I thought this would be the perfect light lunch. Also I have found that food keeps folks from becoming overly dramatic, so that they can listen more. It is like a pacifier and it calms people down. So I was glad that Helen got back about ten minutes before their arrival. I found people will eat the food I get, if it is already set up for them. But if I ask them if they want such and such, they always refuse. So I set up the food on a dish set my wife gave me for the office and I opened the windows to let some nice fresh air in. Max was sitting on the window sill sunning himself and I went and answered the call of nature, just before there was a quiet knock on my door. It was Helen and she said the "guests" had arrived. I went to the door and saw them sitting quietly on opposite sides of the waiting room with their heads down. I wondered what was going through their minds. I called over to them to come into my office and they both almost hopped over to the door. I could only think this excitement was that they were finally going to be able to speak to each other since I'd asked them not to speak alone, until I gave them the go ahead.

Rhoda spoke first to Alex. "Hi, my friend, I missed chatting with you this last week; how are you?" I could tell she was concerned since the last time we spoke to Alex, he did seem to feel he was the "bad guy". Although, in these kinds of scenarios, I have found that everyone shares some of the blame; he was indeed one of the bad guys. She then turned to me and said, "Hi, Mark. Your favorite duo is here." She smiled a bit, as she playfully punched my arm. "Oh what a nice little luncheon you have set up."

"I think you trying to use food to put us at ease. Is that right, Mark?" Alex was right on the money. I saw he asked that question because he really was nervous.

"Actually, I'm starving. I hoped you two would join me in little lunch, so my stomach wouldn't growl too loudly as we talked. I hope both of you are doing well today. Let me put you at ease. Today I'll pick the topic and I want you both to remember that no one here is the 'bad guy', at least not anymore, anyway. To be here in my office shows me that you are both people of character. God isn't finished working with any of us yet." After I said that little speech I took a bite of my sandwich and a sip of the water, to give them the permission to do so.

I put my sandwich down and said, "Today I want both of you to tell me, and each other, what the last fifteen years have been like. I know it is hard to condense fifteen years into two hours; but if you mainly focus on the bad parts, we can more look more at our accomplishments, at future meetings. How does this sound to you? (They both shook their heads in agreement.) Rhoda, I'd like to start with you. Try and be a bit chronological in this part of our therapy so that Alex can see how this whole thing has affected your life. Don't worry if you forget something you can mention it later. Also Alex if you have questions or comments I hope you'll raise your hand. The reason for this is: if I feel that Rhoda needs to really get something out, I want to make sure she can without interruption. If I see your hand up, I will tell you to wait until her full thought is out, before interrupting. The same 'rule' goes for you Rhoda during Alex's time. Okay, so let's begin."

Rhoda took a sip of her water and cleared her throat. "Well I'm not sure how much you, Alex, already know; but I'm going to act like you don't know anything. One reason is that you only were able to hear bits and pieces from others. The second is that most all that happened was filtered through Pastor Stan and this means you got his twisted version, rather than the truth. Ok? So....right after the time you jumped me or jumped on me. Sorry that is how I saw it. I was very afraid to tell anyone and kept everything quiet. But since I got more and more depressed, I decided to go to see someone who knew us both and I thought would bring us back together, with maybe a simple little office meeting. I have mentioned this, I know. But anyway, Stan was really mad at us both; but more so at me, the victim. I almost thought he wouldn't have minded, if we'd had a full blown affair, as long as I didn't tell him or rock the 'boat', at church, in any way. He told me I could no longer lead the groups I was leading and he went and told my home group to not let me pray about the issue, in anyway. I also had complete strangers come up to me, cursing me out on your behalf. I wasn't able, at first, to tell my husband, because I was embarrassed for you. I tried to not say anything to my girlfriends. I'd cry all the time, when I was at home, and my husband and daughter knew something was up. I couldn't tell any of my family, since they weren't Christians yet. I didn't want to mess up their view of the faith. So I was left to deal with the issue by myself. I would have told you, Alex, if you were not the perpetrator. People began to notice I was depressed all the time. Pastor Stan kept making me come into his office, calling me in, to curse me out. He would yell at me in the hallways and at the services and would say derogatory things about me whenever I was present in the room and behind my back. He also made me go to that seminar called, "Cleansing

Stream", where he pointed me out again and again to the class, telling everyone I needed to repent for being a seductress. He even had a woman shout at me to repent and keep yanking my eyelids and shaking me. It was horrible. I was still working for you; but we could never talk to each other. We had that one woman who always had to be our go between. I kept trying to talk to you and get things straightened out just between ourselves; but you kept avoiding me. Then we had those accusation meetings with the lawyer. Suddenly I was no longer working for the church. I could have left the church, at that time; but I was concerned for you. I had heard Stan yelling at you in his office and knew they were threatening you. I also hoped that my reputation would get cleared and people would see I was wrongly accused. I decided to stay on, hoping there'd be a resolution. I also hoped that the church would repent of their errors in judgment that they made concerning me. I told my husband of the situation and Pastor Stan told him to divorce me because I was in love with you. Can you believe that? Man! If I tried to talk with a girlfriend or get prayer for the situation, I was immediately reported. My phone was tapped, my mail confiscated (and then returned), my emails were intercepted, and some person from the church was always following me. I got threatening letters and phone calls from your church. Most of my girlfriends were 'bought' by the church, with promises of ministries and other perks. In exchange they were made to report to Stan, anything I said about our situation. I stayed on at your church for two and a half years and yet I could not make things right. The last day, I was part of your church; I went to make peace with Pastor Stan. I stuck out my hand to shake his and be reconciled. He then slapped me so hard that I fell on the floor, making his secretary run screaming into the parking lot. I got up and left your church for good, at that shameful moment. I then thought everything was over. I began to look for a new church and thought I'd found a good one over at Vineyard of the Valley." (At that moment Alex's hand shot up.)

Since it was a natural break in the thought process I let him speak. "Rhoda, if you only knew how I hated to watch all of that crud happen to you. But Pastor Stan had threatened me, saying he'd make my wife divorce me and the Head Pastor fire me. Later when the Head Pastor, Pastor Don, finally heard about the whole thing, I was made to swear I'd have nothing to do with you. They said if I called you or wrote you or tried to talk to you I'd be out on my backside and that no church would hire me, ever. Pastor Stan had me in his office every day, for years, to yell at me for hours on end. He wanted me to say you seduced me. I wouldn't do that and that had him boiling mad. I really felt terrible and even tried to take my life a few times, to be honest. I was glad you finally left our church; it was just too hard for me to watch. Pastor Stan said he'd keep making your life miserable, even if you left our church; because you had had the audacity to come against our church and most especially him." Alex looked miserable and despondent.

"I knew that; but it didn't make it any easier. I kept wishing you'd just tell them all to go to 'Blazes' and be free of them, so we could be friends again. If that had to be in a modified version, I was fine with that, too. Anyway a couple of good things did happen, at around that time. I started to go for long walks to ease my inner turmoil. At first I'd walk for twelve miles; it took that long for me to not be angry and to pray over the whole situation. Later, I cut the time down to walking 4x per week for 8miles and 1x per week I'd roller blade around the park. I began to heal, during those times, since on top of my regular time of prayer, I'd use the exercise time to discuss the whole matter with God, yet again. I'd even cry, as I walked; but by the end of the exercise time I could at least live in peace the rest of the day. I also tried to commit suicide a couple of times, just from the despair. I often saw you driving, biking, or roller blading to work, during my walks. Someone from you church said I was exercising on purpose, to bother you. But truly that was the best time for me to take the walks, as well as the best route. It was a bonus for me to see you and wave, even if you didn't always wave back. Secondly, I got so mad about the whole thing that I decided to finally learn how to drive. I hadn't needed to when I lived in Chicago. You had always put me down for not driving and so I decided to drive to show you I could. I also thought I'd have more chances to find jobs outside the church, if I could drive to them. I did find a few jobs and finally landed a job as a tutor for Score and Kumon. I discovered I was a great tutor and had a nice little career tutoring kids for a few years both at tutoring centers and in my home. So those were good things that came out of the sadness.

Oh yes, and I found out more about what forgiveness was and about what reconciliation was. I read over 110 books on the subject, plus saw various videos and heard hundreds of teachings on these subjects. After a period of time, I also went to Toastmasters, to learn to give speeches on forgiveness issues and even did a few videos. These were well received. I wrote many articles on forgiveness, including a seven class seminar on the subject. Those things were all good coming out of bad. But truly the bad was, at times, so bad that I wanted to die. I wanted to call you and get things all straightened out; but your church kept threatening me, night and day I'd get calls and letters from your church lawyer and a policeman, from your church, even came to my house to threaten me. It was Hell. But the worst to me was the continuous harassment at all the new churches I ended up going to. For example: when I went to the Vineyard church the pastor there was really favorable towards me and he let me help out around the church almost immediately. I went to his office and told him what Pastor Stan did to me and sadly what you had done to start it all. He started to cry and wanting to go and speak to Pastor Don. As a matter of fact both he and his assistant were both on my side and were ready to defend me. But then they went to a luncheon in which Pastor Don was seated next to them. He told them I had seduced you; then they both were against me. They didn't let me work at the church, in any capacity. I also was no longer the receptionist for the Healing Rooms ministry that we had. Soon they distanced themselves from me. Two women from your church even came to my church and stood in front of me for hours with their arms crossed to intimidate me. They looked like they were going to beat me up for Pastor Stan. So my pastor made me hide with him in a back office. In the meantime they went to all the ladies and spread rumors about me. They told the pastor I was trouble. I soon was forced to leave that church, the gossip was overwhelming. I then went to a large non-charismatic church were again the pastor liked me and had me serve at the church. But when Pastor Stan found out where I was he again sent spies to the church and told the leadership I was an adulterous woman. I again went to another church were the Pastor there said he had not heard anything bad about me. He said he would pray to be able to talk to you; but that he was afraid of your church. A group of women from your church came and told the women of my church I seduced you and they in turn made rude comments about me to the Pastor there. He told me he could not stand up to them, they were main contributors to his church. I ran about three ministries at his church. I was then told to stop the various ministries I was a leader of. I was also told I wouldn't ever be able to speak in the church, because this would offend the leading sisters. A couple of women there actually threatened my life and told me that they hated me. I went to another two churches and the pastors there said that since I did not have pastoral support from my previous churches, that they also could not allow me to serve in their churches. Finally now, I think I have found a good church; but I tried to be open with the pastor there about this and he did not think my wanting to reconcile with you was healthy. He is a great man of God, but he sees this whole reconciling with you as confusion. I couldn't explain all we have been through and what God has told me in one little office meeting. There are a couple of sisters, even at this new church who went to Alex's church and believed rumors from the past. One is well known and another attends every Sunday; I have kept a low profile around them so the past wouldn't get stirred up. I chose not to serve at my new church, for the first couple of years, because of all my bad experiences from the past. But lately I have been expressing interest in having a home church or small group meeting, associated with the church. I have very few friends, at the church or in the community now. Most of my friends live in other states. This is mainly because I have had to rid myself of false friends who worked, unbeknownst to me, for Pastor Stan or where influenced by him. They eventually left me when I wouldn't confess that I'd seduced you or repent for going against your church. I have strangers still come up to me, on the street, who must know Alex, and curse me. My daughter was harassed both at school and in church youth groups, so much so that she hates to even be called a Christian. I missed out on jobs because your church said I never worked there and said I was untrustworthy. I found this out when potential bosses told me what your church told them, when they called for references. I also have had my husband wonder if I secretly really loved you. The list goes on and on and yet God has told me to write a book on forgiveness and reconciliation and to speak on the subject. I just don't know how this speaking thing will happen, since I can't get my foot in any door. Oh yeah, I even had people from your church tell me I could not see my doctor, because he was an elder at your church. The same people actually called a woman's group I attended warning them I was a husband stealer. The list could go on and on; but this along with all of the mocking and threats over the years made it not so easy remain your friend. If I didn't believe this whole thing was somehow of God I'd have dumped you long ago. I have believed in spite of all of this that God wants me to befriend and to reconcile with you for His glory. This is why I let you silently call me and send me blank emails and why I didn't just blow you off. I know in spite of all this torture, this has been God's will. It was not God's will for you to hurt me or break your marriage vows, of course. But He wants to use a very terrible thing to give him glory. He still wants us to reconcile and share what He has taught us, through all of this. I can see that all of this suffering has deepened my walk with God, my understanding for others, and given me wisdom I never could have gotten any other way. What the Enemy meant for bad God truly turned into Good. This long story is a general rundown of my last fifteen years. I know this is Mark's second time hearing these things."

I spoke up at that moment and said, "First one small question: What was that pulling of the eyelids thing? Second question: You know that you could have sued Alex and his church any time during that period for sexual harassment, stalking, and slander, right?"

"Well, a few times I did contact lawyers to sue the church, not Alex. (This was at my husband's prompting.) But the lawyers told me that we'd never win and that the church had more money than me. They said there would be no way for that to work. Later on, they also said that the case was over seven years and could no longer be prosecuted, statute of limitations and all. But mostly I actually believe the Bible when it says that we aren't to sue our brothers in Christ since these 'things' should be handled in the church. I believed that most of the time during this issue. This mystified

Pastor Stan. He was sure I'd want to sue. (He'd tell me Alex did nothing in one breath and then ask why I didn't sue since Alex sexually harassed me.) He couldn't keep all his lies straight. But I was not looking for vengeance; all I wanted to do was speak to Alex. I tried every way I could think of to reconnect, even sending go betweens; but nothing seemed to work. I did not want to ruin any hope of reconciliation and on top of all this, I felt he was just as much, if not more a victim, like me. God helped me care for your soul, Alex. People mocked me for trying to make things right." She looked at him in the eyes. "I really am your friend, you know."

"Oh and Mark, the woman pulled my eyes because she said to close your eyes in prayer was evil and that I was to look into her eyes during prayer. Stan trained her to be a counselor for Cleansing Stream, Stan version. She was so evil; I could not look at her eyes. Also when she yelled at me, during prayer; I'd close my eyes to pray to my God."

Alex looked down at his new running shoes. "I wish I could say I didn't know any of this. To be honest I knew most of the parts you have shared and the behind the scenes parts. I got to hear the planning sessions both Stan and the head pastor made to cut you down. I always knew you had a gift for serving the Lord and it hurt me to see everyone of your attempts shot down, mostly through planned rumors and public mocking. I was trying so hard to save my marriage, help my daughter with her anorexia treatments, and keep my career that frankly I did not care what they did to you as long, as I was not involved or I could appear to be disinterested. Yet God told me that I must reconcile with you and that I was supposed to defend you. But it took me fifteen years to finally reconcile and I still am not sure if I'll ever have the guts to stand up to your enemies and defend you. I'm not sure how much I want to lose and if I'll have any semblance of a career if I try to help you at this stage in the game. I'm still honestly debating this. I've lied and been passive for so long." He began to cry again and I went and put an arm around his shoulder like a father.

I spoke, "I think Rhoda is not really looking for you to go and ruin your life to make things right. I think that this reconciliation with you might be all she needs at this time. How are you thinking about this Rhoda?" I looked her in the eyes and saw they were welling with tears.

"To be honest I'd love to have Alex tell the truth to all of my enemies and defend my honor. But I have no desire to ruin his life, hurt his marriage and family, and bring him down in anyway. So, Alex, do not let this thought plague you. I am your friend as I have always been. No change in this and I think you can only go as far as you can. I can't make you go any further. You just walk with God in this and let Him speak to you. I have no demands on you. I gave up any need for justice to God years ago." She wiped away a few tears and folded her hands in her lap looking at him with a mixture of pity and love, the love of a real friend.

Alex took a drink of his water and said he'd try and speak for a short time on how his time was spent the last fifteen years and maybe he'd have to continue the process the next session. I said that this was fine and for him not to rush things.

"Well as hard as things admittedly were for you; they were harder in some ways for me. You have to remember one thing: I had fallen in love with you. I mean I really fell hard. It is funny I never had a problem finding women and sometimes I had an over abundance of them both before and after marriage. But honestly, usually I only cared to know them sexually and even my wife and I married more because we were in lust than in love. So I have cared for my wife; but never with the passion she deserved. I think she always felt this. I regret how I have treated her, now more than ever. I see that I never gave her enough of myself and that this in turn caused her to have less passion towards me. It was a vicious cycle. I guess when I met Rhoda I saw how exciting really loving someone could be. I knew we were both married; but this feeling seemed to go beyond that technicality. I guess I just somehow hoped she'd feel the same way. I never counted that she loved her husband or wanted to be a good Christian. I know she really liked me; but I thought maybe just maybe she also loved me. So when I attached her I hoped she'd do like they did in the movies. They say no and then they submit and I hoped you'd see me as your dream man. But instead you got nervous and afraid. I tried again to make you admit you loved me too and you still claimed you loved your husband. So I didn't know what to do. I always thought I was really handsome and that any woman I showed interest in would crumble in my arms. I didn't think her husband was as great a guy as me and that if she compared us, I'd come out the winner. It was so easy for me to get other women to submit and she was resistant and some of the others were cuter in some respects. So I just didn't get it. She should have been easy to 'conquer'. Admittedly I didn't know what I'd do with her once I got her. I wasn't sure how her husband would take me seducing his wife and then what I planned to do with my marriage. I knew that my affair with Rhoda would be the straw that broke the camel's back, in my wife's mind. But I hadn't considered divorce. Also I loved my younger son and my wife said if we divorced she'd never let me see or speak to him again. My wife was from a rich family and if she wanted to disappear they'd help her. I'd never see my children, especially the young one, again. So that was a bit of a dilemma and then my career would be in the toilet. Many folks don't like divorced pastors, especially those who commit adultery in order to divorce. So these things were up in the air. I thought maybe if Rhoda and I just went to Hawaii for a few weeks I'd get tired of Rhoda, then I could crawl back to my wife and eventually find someone else to get to know. I was a bit confused at the time and thought maybe there'd be some way out of all this, after I had a fling with Rhoda. But her desire to stay true to her husband and God actually made me love her deeper and so I tried very hard to deal with all the new feelings I was having. Stan knew I was the one who had tried to seduce Rhoda and he also knew that I loved her. During our times when he'd yell at me, I'd admitted as much to him. He felt a loyalty to the church and to the head pastor, whose wife was sick at the time. So he tried to make Rhoda say she had seduced me, more for the church's reputation than mine. Also even after the head pastor's wife got better, he developed a weird kind of obsession with wanting to destroy Rhoda. He kept after her for almost fourteen of the fifteen years we were apart. Even in his retirement, he told the different head pastors to not let me ever reconcile with Rhoda. He made each new pastor swear to this and even would call and threaten me from the pastors' retirement home, over in Arizona. As much as I hated the whole thing, I felt I had to listen to him, like he was put over me by God. I knew Stan was evil; but I could not shake this blind obedience. For the first few years, when

Rhoda left, I still had to go into Stan's office once per day for my 'yelling sessions'. He'd yell at me for hours, at times, and tell me that just because she was no longer part of the church, that did not mean we could contact each other. They had my phone and cell records, my mail, my email, and I, too, was followed everywhere. Rhoda was not being paranoid; this is how we took care of trouble makers my 'church'. There were a couple of times I tried to speak to Rhoda, at church, and someone always saw this. I was reported each time and thus had more yelling sessions. Stan even called my wife and told her he was concerned about me, more than a few times. Home was a place of sheer misery and work was misery. To dull the pain, I ended up having sex with a few women at the church; but each time I did that I felt I had betrayed Rhoda, not my wife, but her. Even weirder, if I had sex with my wife, I also thought I was betraying Rhoda. I ended up having affairs, less and less. I tried to send Rhoda blank emails and silent calls hoping she'd see my heart was still hers; but I never could tell if they pleased her or not. Most of the time, she hung up on the calls. If she did talk it was only to plead with me to reconcile.

When I sent blank emails, she would send a small one liner email begging to meet for reconciliation. Believe me, I wanted to do that reconciliation a million times; but each time Stan would find out my intentions or just put so much fear into me, that I'd stop the process. It was like he always knew what I was intending to do. Also over the years Stan would find Rhoda's one liners, when I forgot or was slow to delete them. Then he'd say I was in 'big trouble'. I'd get feeling it was safer to stop contacting her for a time, then I'd restart the process. I know she often thought I'd lost interest, when I was pulling back on contact; but actually my interest was greater at those times. I knew she was right we had to reconcile; it was God's command, for us. Rumors about me went around the church. People began to say I was a womanizer (which was actually true) and that I had actually had an affair with Rhoda (which was a lie). To my shame I never defended her honor. Years passed. I never got a promotion. I never could look for another job and my wife and I were more or less estranged. My kids didn't respect me very much; they began to believe the rumors, too. My older son and daughter thought I was a creep, for the way I'd treated their mother, and they were right. My older son moved out as soon as he could. My daughter had that eating disorder and other psychological problems because of my character. She sensed the anger between me and my wife. My younger son grew up in a cold home, that was full of suppressed anger. I'm not sure how much he really knew. Many of the times I bumped into Rhoda, right after the incident; he was with me. He'd say things like, 'Dad there's that lady again.' He knew something was special about her, just not exactly what that was.

I always knew there were those at the church and in the community that took Rhoda's side and thought I was a scum bag. They'd give me those looks. Though they'd pretend to defend me, I could tell they thought I had possibly abused Rhoda or had even raped her. Rhoda was such a nice person that most folks, even the church kiss-ups, could not bring themselves to truly hate her. Even my wife said that Rhoda had tried on numerous occasions to reconcile with her and make her understand she loved her as a sister in Christ. She had reiterated again and again that she would never do anything to hurt Liz or our marriage. She even gave my wife a couple of gifts and told her how sorry she was that I was such a scoundrel. My wife admired her for that and almost could have been her friend, if the circumstances were different. So I knew that many people thought I was a bastard and that I'd mistreated Rhoda. Over time other affairs I had had began to come to the surface. Pastor Stan seemed to get immense pleasure out of telling others how weak I was in the sexual arena and he also seemed to have an obsession with abusing me. Sometimes I thought he actually got pleasure from finding out what wrong things I had done and then being able to yell at me and threaten me about them. I felt like his 'prison wife' at times and still wonder if he had a 'thing' for me. But the worst thing was every time I saw Rhoda, she always smiled and waved and she always wanted to just get things right. She never tried to get back at me. I was in awe of this and admired her. Stan would tell me that she passed around rumors about me and that she never wanted to see me again. I wasn't sure at the time, if that was true; but I knew she cared. She was not being caring to 'get sex', but just because she was my friend. This undeserved friendship thing, blew my mind and caused me hours of weeping. I had never known full forgiveness or unconditional love. I never had it in my family or in any church I had ever attended. I saw Jesus in that kind of love." He stopped and looked at me and Rhoda. "I wish I'd have come to my senses much earlier and understood what a true friend is. Rhoda please, please forgive me and forgive my insensitivity."

"You old fool, of course I forgive you. I have forgiven you many times over. I have simply wanted reconciliation. That church acted like I was a harlot and an idiot, for wanting something so outrageous. That was the hardest thing for me, to be mocked for so many years." She looked at her watch. "Oh pooh, I have to leave. It is really late and I have to get home to make my husband a special birthday dinner. Doc, I really have to run." She stood up and got her purse. Alex and I stood, as gentlemen do.

I said, "To be honest we went abit overtime. Can you take up from here, next time I see you both, Alex? I will open up the time for both to speak on whatever you want, after Alex finishes his line of though, okay?"

They both agreed as I bundled them towards the door and then the appointment desk. "Also be sure to ask questions on the things you have shared today at the next meeting. Better write them down today before next session. A week is a long time." They made their appointment and were down the stairs and out the door in a matter of minutes. Again they refrained from speaking to each other, as I had requested; but they did both wave good-bye.

Chapter 18

$\mathcal{B}$eing a therapist can become like other jobs over the years—a bit boring. Rhoda and Alex were the shot in the arm my career needed. In their case I felt like I was really helping two people. That it wasn't just an exercise in futility. Sadly, so many of my clients come to me for attention or companionship, having nothing really wrong with them. Or they come to just talk to me about what they should have been speaking to a best friend about. They are lonely and haven't any real friends. They are willing to pay me to be their friend for a couple of hours per month. They don't really want to deal with the core issues, like why they have no friends or how they need God; they only want to chat. So for the most part, I let them, and when it seems that they are rehashing the same issues over and over and that no suggestions I make are being heeded; I politely tell them I don't want to see them for a few months. I hope that when they return, they will finally feel like working on some real issues. So the night before my next meeting with Alex and Rhoda, I could hardly sleep. I was like a kid waiting for Christmas morning. I wondered where we'd go, psychologically, and how God would speak. Since I was wide awake I decided to pray for them and the whole situation again and for wisdom for myself, in counseling them. Don't get me wrong I love being a therapist; but those two put the fire in my belly back. I am forever grateful to them.

They were coming bright and early for a 9am appointment. I really had to rush to get downtown, since I was taking the Bart. Bart isn't the fastest way to get anywhere in the city; it is just the most convenient. Parking is expensive and not always easy to find. I also can review my notes or nap during the ride; it fits my needs perfectly. I chose to review my notes; because I was intending to try to bring Alex to a clearer understanding of what he actually did to Rhoda. I could see he still felt that somehow he was a victim, in the same league as his friend. But what he did not see clearly enough, yet, was that he was a victim because of choices he made and because he chose to stay in that church's system. He couldn't trust that God would give him a way out to something better. That is a different 'league of victim' than being a woman who chose to serve God and who then got abused by her spiritual leaders. He'd been with those people for years and knew how they treated anyone who crossed them. She'd simply been serving God and trying to be his friend. Through no fault of her own, she'd unwittingly fallen into the hands of evil men. He chose the salary, perks, and retirement home over hearing God. She chose to listen to God, run from evil, and leave. Both were victims; but not in the same ways. He kept his career and sacrificed his integrity and she lost her career and found her dignity. I thought on the differences of their choices. The world and those in his church saw Alex as a successful pastor. They saw her as a failure, someone who couldn't do anything of value; but be a housewife. I wondered which choice God was more pleased with. They were both sincere believers and good people, for the most part. But I thought Rhoda chose the better part. I try not to take sides; but this situation seemed like it showed the hearts, of the two people involved, quite clearly.

It was really raining hard, as I practically ran from the Bart Station to my office. I got inside and up the stairs and saw that Rhoda was sitting quietly on one side of the room and Alex on the other side and both were soaked, like me. My secretary had voluntarily gone next door to get three chais and three hot pastrami bagel sandwiches. They both told me, she was going to be back in a minute. I excused myself to go into my office and clean the cat's box, light the fire, and use the facilities. I did all of these things, in about two minutes. I then went out into the waiting room, as my secretary was coming up the stairs. I asked Alex and Rhoda to come into my inner office and give me their wet coats and shoes and put these in front of the fire, while they took their quilts and settled into their chairs. I opened my desk drawer and handed them two pairs of wool socks. I told them to push their chairs as close to the fire, as they felt comfortable. My secretary knocked and handed out the chais and the bagels and took her food items. She went into the front office, closing the door behind her.

It was then that I realized I was cold and I went and got my sweater and slippers. (I felt like Mr. Rogers from that kid's show.) "Well, now that we are all set up...how are you two doing? Alex?"

"Well, Mark, I have been having a hard week at work. Not everyone is thrilled with my being the Pastoral Care Pastor; some think I'm not solemn enough. A couple of those, who believe the rumors, are not sure I should be alone with vulnerable women, in my office. Some of the rumors of my past behavior are now being more openly discussed around the church; this is not the best thing, for my reputation. I've been feeling less popular. I'm the one who was always the popular pastor; so this experience is new for me. Then to top it off, my wife and I took a couple of friends to the Medieval Festival, where I mentioned that the little serving wench was cute. My wife overheard me and she hasn't spoken to me for a week. She said she felt 'disrespected' in front of our friends. I was out of line; but she was a cute girl."

"I'm sorry to hear that, Alex. I guess it isn't easy to escape our pasts, huh? We'll get back to you in a minute. So how are you Rhoda? Also do you have any questions for me or Alex before we start?"

"Hi, Doc, ah Mark; I'm doing okay, I guess. I've just been having a bit of stress with my daughter. I think I told you she graduated about three years ago from college and ran off to LA to become an accountant to movie stars. Unfortunately she became poor instead, living in a ghetto area and working for a coffee shop, instead of being an accountant. My husband and I had to go down to LA to rescue her and help her out of a few financial jams. She has been living with us for the last two years or so. Recently, after paying off all her debts, she went back to LA. Well, she never contacts us and if we call her she only speaks for two minutes and hangs up, sometimes while you are talking. This frustrates me and I find myself worrying if she'll have financial and other problems again, seeing her attitude hasn't really changed. Besides this, I'm fine. Ugh. But I do have questions; I have compiled a list for Alex. I know that some of the things may fall out of sequence; but I have wanted to know about these things for years. Since we could never speak I could never get them answered. Can I ask the questions now or should I wait for him to finish his thoughts from last week?"

I really wondered what these questions were going to be; but I thought it was best to ask Alex what he preferred. "Alex what would you prefer: to finish your thoughts from last week or to answer Rhoda's list of questions?"

"You know, Rhoda, you've got my curiosity peeked; so let them rip. Let's do one at a time and I'll keep my answers as short as possible. Okay?"

Rhoda smiled, "At last I'll know what the heck you were thinking. Yeah. Okay, this is a two- parter: One day after the attack, while things were still relatively normal at work, I bumped into you in the hallway and you said, 'you know, you are not like the rest of those I've cared about. You're different.' And then you said that you had something you wanted to give me and something you wanted to tell me. What were you talking about? Who were 'the rest'? What did you want to give me and say to me? You left me 'hanging' for fifteen years on both of those phrases."

"Okay, I'll tell you the 'shocking answers'. First of all, I did have other affairs. They were with the more airheaded women; you know the kind that hung around the office all the time? (She nodded like she understood his example.) They'd hang around clinging to my every utterance and they wanted to have flings. Maybe they were lonely and maybe they didn't get attention from their husbands. But I had short sexual encounters with many of these willing candidates. I do not remember their names or even their faces. I never even knew some of them for any length of time. You are the first person who tried to befriend me and did not let me have sex with you. This not submitting, intrigued me,; you got under my skin, like none of them ever did. As far as the second question (s), I think I had a bracelet for you, at that time; but I ended up giving it to my wife when she found it. I told her it was a surprise for her. I was going to open up to you about my unhappy marriage hoping you'd have sympathy on me and I guess, I thought that this would make you more receptive to my advances. But when all the trouble began, a few days later with Stan and all, I decided to not open up to you. I thought I should lay low and stop any intense pursuing. Did that answer those questions?"

Rhoda looked down shaking her head. "I kind of always thought that you'd say something along those lines. I just hoped not. I'm sorry, Alex. Another question: "One day I was on my morning walk and saw you walking down the street about a quarter of a block behind Pastor Stan. He was carrying a huge Bible and chanting some sort of prayers, out loud. You were quickly walking behind him with a giant yellow umbrella opened up, all the way. Strangely, it was a sunny day and not hot. You were chanting back to him. Please tell me what you were doing; it really looked bizarre."

Alex looked a bit embarrassed at this question and squirmed around in his chair. "Okay that was bizarre, I admit. Stan said that He was going to pray prayer curses against you and curse any influence you had over me. He said you had put hexes on me and our church and that you might have put some on the street we were walking on. He said you might have been a witch and that we had to use black magic back against you. So he read curses from that big book. That wasn't a Bible, it was a Satanic book of curses. He picked it up in a New Age bookstore. He'd say one and I'd have to shout, 'Amen, let it come!' The umbrella was to keep the curses from falling on me. He told me we had to do this, to protect me. He said you were evil and demons only understood demons. I let him do that at the time because he threatened to fire me, if I even questioned that strange evil practice. Forgive me."

"Wow. I told the people, at the Vineyard Church I went to, about that. They and I felt God was telling us, this was what you guys were doing. We just didn't know about the book of curses. Don't worry; we prayed for protection for me and that Stan's curses would return to him. But 'eek' is all I can say." She sat shaking for a few minutes and then continued. "Okay remember that day I was walking down the street, for my morning walk, and you rode your bike up to me jumped off and started a long one way conversation? (He nodded.) There were two things you didn't know. I had just had a vision that you were going to do this, literally two minutes before. You ended up doing exactly what I saw in the vision I had just had; now that blew me away. Secondly I was so stunned I couldn't remove my earphones and I did not hear one word you said. I wished you would have snapped me out of it and told me what you had to say, without loud Christian rock music blaring. I did not hear one word. So now tell me what you said and why you said it. Please."

I stepped in at this moment. "Alex before you answer her question… Rhoda would you please tell us what your vision entailed? We'd like to know. Go ahead."

"Well, I was walking past my favorite new little city part and looking at a tree in the center of it. It somehow reminded me of Moses' burning bush and I stopped for a moment to offer up a prayer for Alex. Instantly while I was awake, walking on the street, I was transported to Heaven. All the angels were joyful and actually jumping. They were all crowding around something on the floor and peering into it. I was too short and couldn't see. I pushed my way to the front, only to see a portal that looked like a TV. It was focused on me taking my morning walk on the sidewalk. I could hear me praying and clearly see me. One angel shouted, 'Oh look, here comes her friend. He's going to talk to her.' Another said, 'I'm so excited they are finally going to meet.' Everyone was holding their breath and then you came around the curve, jumped off your bike, and spoke to me. All of Heaven was shouting and clapping. Then I was back on the ground and you came around the curve, jumped off your bike, and spoke to me, just like in the vision! This is why I could not speak to you, or remove my earphones, when you came up to me. I was in shock and awe."

He looked at her in wonder. "That's right, come to think of it; you didn't answer me. I remember that now. I thought you were so angry, that you were incredulous that I was speaking to you. All of this time I thought you actually heard me and rejected all I said. This would have been hysterical, if it wasn't so sad. What I had said was, 'Rhoda, I know that you have wanted to meet with me for reconciliation. I want to. They won't let me. They said I'd be fired and my wife said she'd divorce me. I have to obey both parties. I want you to know how sorry I am for hurting you, in the past, and how I wish we could meet and reconcile. I want to reconcile with you right now.' I kept shouting, 'Do you hear me, do you hear me?' I thought you were ignoring me. I didn't know you couldn't hear me. I spoke to you because I had had a dream the night before, where God told me to go to you and make things right. I took a chance that one odd morning, but thought you had rejected me. Did you know that Pastor Stan drove by, at just that moment, and so did my wife? Wow, did I get two giant lectures that day, or what? All of that crud happened to me afterwards. Wild how you never even heard me. I am in awe of the vision God gave you. Too bad both of us messed up that day. Wow."

"Well here's one more thing I bet you didn't know. My girlfriend from church was parked across the street eating breakfast, in her car, at that same moment. She said both you and I were beautiful: smiling and weeping and totally radiant. She went and told a bunch of people, without my permission and Stan got wind of it. I didn't know until later, so very sorry.

Do you remember that community prayer meeting, we had at that church downtown? (He nodded.) Remember how you entered the row backwards, for some reason. You ended up sitting right next to me. (He nodded.) Remember how Stan was sitting right in back of my chair? When you did that, I could hear his teeth grinding. Remember how we sang every song standing together and how people from my church introduced you to me? (He nodded again.) That was awkward, huh? But why didn't you speak to me when we bumped into each other after the service in the parking lot? Why did I get a letter from the church lawyer two days later saying I stalked you? I was just sitting with my friends, at the meeting, and you sat next to me? Both of those things happened within a few days of each other."

"Actually, Rhoda, I did know about your friend, who was eating breakfast. She came and told me how happy she was about my trying to reconcile with you. I got mad and told her to not mention this to anyone. I told her if she did she'd loose her dancing ministry. (Rhoda crossed her arms.) I had to do this; Stan made some big threats after you and I sat together at that church meeting. I even got a decrease in my pay. Pastor Stan did not like this double dose of contact we had had. He told me we had to scare you, so you wouldn't get the wrong idea. This is why we had the church's lawyer send a threatening letter to your home. To make it all more frightening we also sent that police man. You knew the letter was a fake didn't you? Stan said you'd be too stupid and that we'd scare you so good that you'd never contact me again. That was ten years ago. Little did he know we'd be in contact for over 15yrs. He also didn't know you'd take that letter to a lawyer and find out we tried to frighten you, intentionally."

"I have dozens more questions, but I'll just ask two more, okay? Why would you contact me sometimes two or three times per day, by phone and by email, silent calls and blank emails, and then sometimes not contact me for months? What was that about? Were you trying to confuse me? Wait till I ask the second question, then answer them both, okay? Lastly, remember about five years ago we met in the Lucky's Grocery parking lot, accidentally? You wanted to speak to me and then told me you'd call me back in a day or so to make an appointment. You never did. What was that all about? I waited for you to keep your promise. Why did you lie?" Rhoda looked like a little girl and her lower lip was quivering. You could tell she'd been hurt and hurt badly. Her friend had not followed through on his intentions to make the situation right; she felt abandoned and betrayed.

Alex could see her pain. He kept clearing his throat and finally accepted my glass of water for him. "First of all, I felt like a creep contacting you in an 'almost' fashion. Here I was a grown man and I felt I had to resort to stupid games. I sent multiple blank emails and silent calls when I was depressed and I was depressed a lot. I missed you every day, all fifteen years; but some days were worse than others. On those days I would send you a blank email or a silent call. I'd do this whenever I wanted to scream and race over to your house and just bloody reconcile, not caring who saw me. But Stan was ever present. He threatened me every day for fourteen years of the fifteen years. Do you know how hellish that was? You know how terribly he treated you, right? But that was just for about four years of you life. Okay, he actually kept at it, in your case, for almost fourteen years. It was just not full time, up close and personal, like in my case. When you were at the church you only had four years of the daily, in person, yell secessions. I had fourteen years of, face to face, daily torture: yell sessions

182

and other forms of torture. When I was on vacation, had a day off, and even during my sabbatical; he'd call me constantly, to check on me. He was unrelenting day after day. During those fourteen years, sometimes I'd break down and confess I'd been corresponding with you, however silently. This would make him irate. He'd copy all of my files and seize all of my phone records, for all of my phones. Then he'd tell me I'd better not connect with you again, or else. So I'd hold back for a few weeks or months; then I'd reconnect with you.

Also in the spirit of being totally open, I did have a few flings during that time. I would discover I couldn't take care of my wife and family, you and a girlfriend, so I'd stop talking to you. I'd finally realize the, mistress of the minute, was dull and then I would break up with another nameless woman. No one compared to you. I'd try and enjoy my wife and family; after a few days I'd be wishing I could talk to you. I'd keep reconnecting and disconnecting. But I always came back; because I simply missed you. Your little one line sentences you sent were so kind and no one in my life was kind to me. I wanted to speak to you. Yes, lastly, that time I saw you at Lucky's parking lot was so special. You had grown your hair and it was the same color as your suede jacket. I was walking behind you with a soda. I had just been rollerblading and I had gotten into my car to go and grab a coke. We only have health food at home. I kept calling your name and you kept ignoring me. I finally got your attention. You smiled so sincerely at me and asked if you could talk to me. I said that would be fine; so you tried to get into the passenger seat of my car. I knew someone from church would see that. You left all your groceries in the middle of the isle; that was a little scattered. So I told you that I'd get back to you. I was right about someone seeing us. Pastor Stan's spy system was large and complex. One of his spies saw us talk and I was called into his office the next morning. I got yelled at, for about three hours, and actually broke down and told him we'd been communicating for over ten years almost nonstop. I don't know why I said that. But...the church lawyer called me. He warned me that if I spoke to you; I'd be fired. He said you'd sue me and that they would not be able to help me. Also my daughter was sick again with her anorexia, so I had to drop it; there was no way out. I wished I could have at least explained; but they forbid that…I knew you would think I was a liar. But I was having a very hard time."

I decided the session had gone on long enough, "Alex before we leave maybe you can explain to Rhoda and I why you didn't just leave. I know you liked your job, the perks especially the medical care, and you were aiming for that retirement home; but all in all was/is being in that dark system worth it? Was it worth hurting your friend, Rhoda, and your family? If you would have left, anytime during that ordeal; do you think God would have just abandoned you?"

"I guess my faith was/is very small. I have always hated change. That is probably why I never divorced my wife, even though I had so many affairs. I could not see anything better than my church and being a pastor there. I…I just don't know what kept me there and I still don't know." He sat with his head down and shoulders hunched looking at the floor, totally dejected.

I stood up and put my hand on his shoulder. "We all have something like that in our lives, Alex. But I'd like you to pray about this. Maybe you are supposed to leave there, even at this late hour. It is not for me to tell you. Ask God. We will not judge you, whatever you choose. I guess it is time to leave. Alex we will let you finish your thoughts, from last week, and ask Rhoda some questions, on our next session. So God be with you both; my next client will be here in a minute. Please make the appointment and see you next week. Take care."

They left silently and went into the outer office to make their appointment.

Chapter 19

$\mathcal{M}$y wife and I took a nice trip to Lake Tahoe, for about four days; but we couldn't swim because the water was too cold. We ended up having a nice time, anyway. We went for walks and spent time grilling nice fresh seafood on our little Japanese Hibachi and drinking some better wines. We walked along the water's edge, arm in arm, and got reconnected. We always try to do this every three months or so. I find it keeps our marriage fresh and we don't miss out on much of what the other is going through. When we were younger we only did this once or twice a year and then the other person always felt ignored, in some way, or that they were going through too much stuff alone. I try to recommend this to my clients too. I found myself thinking that if Alex did this with his wife, maybe he'd not be so prone to stray. I think he strays because both of them got so consumed by the ministry and raising the kids that they disconnected with each other. They basically forgot what they loved about one another, in the first place. Of course in his case there are so many other mitigating factors; but I sense this is a pretty big one. Rhoda and her husband seem to be more friends, with each other; but I sense there are a few holes in their relationship too. I haven't really gotten into either one of their marital relationships with their spouses, yet. So far I've only just brushed the surface. Anyway... my wife and I had such a lovely time that she had to actually push me into the car to drive back home. When I retire it will have to be somewhere near the water; I just love the serenity of being on the water and just soaking in the sun and the sound of the surf. But I'd have to make sure we won't be in a flood plain, because my next home will be my "right before going to the glory" home. We drove back at a slower pace; stopping at all the little towns we passed, on the way out. We even took the time to stop at historical markers. We had lunch in a little town at an outdoor deli, which also sold crabs. It was such a nice break. I felt more in love with my wife, than when we were newlyweds. When you are young and not married you sometimes think that once you're married that's it. But I have happily found there are deeper dimensions of love that you can enter into with your spouse, if you just take the time. We arrived home late Tuesday night.

The next morning was a Wednesday and Rhoda and Alex were my first clients. My wife and I had gotten some new tea and a bit too much fudge on the trip so I brought some of the fudge to give a piece to Rhoda and Alex with their usual cup of tea. I set up the tea, and some apple slices, along with the fudge, about twenty minutes before they arrived. Then I tidied the office. Helen, my secretary had taken care of Max for me while I was gone and he was really glad to see me. I got him his food and water and gave him a cat snack we had purchased for him on the trip. Then I went and put fresh wood on the fire, changed into my "work slippers and sweater" (I felt like Mr. Rogers again and even started to sing, "It's a Beautiful Day in the Neighborhood." That is a sure sign of senility setting in.) As I was buttoning the last button on my sweater there was a knock at the door and in came both Rhoda and Alex. They had arrived at the same time, accidentally. I greeted them and handed both of them a steaming cup of gingerbread tea and offered the fudge. Both things were gladly received and we all took our usual chairs. "Seems like a long time, huh? I just got back from Tahoe and it was great; just too cold to swim. Anyway Alex I think you were going to finish were you left off two weeks ago and then ask Rhoda some questions. Is this still the plan?"

Alex popped his last bite of fudge before answering. "Well, Mark, I was thinking that I actually got out pretty much of what I was going to say two weeks ago. Rhoda asked me some really good questions last time I was here. I really did sit down and think, and yes pray, about whether I should leave the church and I'm still thinking about this. My new head pastor recently called me into his office; his name is Pastor Nick Sty, have you heard of him? (Both Rhoda and I shook our heads.) He's a nice unassuming sort and frankly how he became the head pastor I still have no idea. He wasn't even on the staff for that long. He certainly is mild mannered, to say the least. But he wasn't mild mannered when he called me into his office. As a matter of fact, he was a bit, for lack of a better word, ticked. He told me that certain rumors had been trickling in about past affairs and other conflicts I had had. Pastor Stan, actually, had recently called him to give him a heads up report on me too. So…To make a long story short, I was told my days were numbered being the Pastoral Care pastor; because that was 'too visible' a position. He said that I had been a good worker all of these years, but that he had to consider the church's reputation. If only you two knew the things I knew about the type of things others on the staff have done. You'd be surprised that the whole group of us wasn't fired. But anyway…He gave me a choice, he said I could leave and have no endorsement from him or anyone else on the present or previous staff. Or I could work in the new Connections and Membership department, while he decided if I should still officially be a pastor or not. He said I could keep my same salary, but there wouldn't be any raises coming for a long time. He also said that he'd try to see if I could still have access to the retirement home. He's looking into this, since it is mainly for pastors, in good standing. I was stunned and yet saw the hand of God. Since I'm hesitating, about deciding to stay or leave, He's trying to help me see what a load of crud the place really is full of. Maybe I somehow have not really gotten this yet. I will go into this new role soon, after I train my successor. People will be told that I needed to spend more quality time with my family and work less hours. Pastoral Care pastors have to attend Weddings, Funerals, and visit the sick, among other duties. This is on top of regular office time. So it will look like a viable reason for me to leave. The new position is straight office work with some extra time doing activities with new members and helping members find their ministry mainly in a class on Sundays. Anyway…Enough about my miserable life. Rhoda, I do have those questions, that have been bugging me, that I want to ask you. May I be really blunt with you and will you promise to answer me honestly and not leave anything out?"

Rhoda nodded her head and also said, "Alex, I think my answers will free the both of us, so don't hold anything back with me, either. I want to be free, don't you? And by the way, I'm really sorry about the job change. Maybe God is going to lead you into something better. Actually I know He will. Let 'er rip."

"Okay. Now you said that your friend, Mindy, had mentioned to you that I needed an assistant and that is why you chose to help me, is that right? (She nodded.) It took awhile for me to want to have you work with me. Do you know the real reason for that? (She shook her head, 'No'.) Well, I was afraid to hire you. I thought you were really nice. You and I always bantered in a fun way when you came to get your daughter from Sunday school. I enjoyed those little chats and I was afraid I could really like you. I didn't yet; but I just was so warmed by your sunny disposition. I didn't know you were married, since I never saw your husband. Your daughter was so sweet, too. I guess I just thought how refreshing you both were. Our church is so super rich and people have rather plastic personalities. But finally I relented; I let you come and work for me. I was determined to see you as only a coworker. But now here is my question, 'Why did you say in the first chat we had, when you started to work for me: 'Pastor I'm here to do anything for you; I mean anything. I want you to know that I'm glad to serve you in whatever way I can.'? Why did you say something like that to a man, if you were not interested?"

Rhoda looked confused. "Whoa...First of all: I have hardly remembered saying those things. I'm starting to now because you have mentioned these things. But Alex, I did not mean what you thought, not by a long shot. I was in that cult, The Assembly. Remember? (He nodded.) We were always taught that that was how a servant was supposed to speak, to the one they wanted to serve. It had no sexual connotations. We always went to a brother we wanted to serve and said those lines. We then added, 'I'm doing this so that you will be free to do your ministry, without any obstacles in the way. Let me take care of your small stuff, so you can serve

God more fully.' That was how the cult leader's wife trained us to speak, to someone who we wanted to serve in ministry. But now I see, how you could have taken those words the wrong way and I'm sorry. Wow."

Alex looked at her and thought a bit, "Okay, I'll take that; though I still wonder. Why did you decide to stay on and serve in Children's ministry with me, when Pastor Juan told you to go and find another job? Why did you dig your heals in and defy his command? I thought it was because you liked me, with more than average liking."

"Well, first of all God had not told me to leave that job, yet. Secondly I did like you, but only as a friend and colleague. Also he was just being an 'ass'. I would've hit him, if I could've and remained a lady. I don't like anyone forcing me to do what they want, even a pastor."

Alex chuckled. "Remember I shook your hand after that one? He was being an 'ass'. I admired your boldness. I just wasn't sure, why you were so adamant. Okay, let's bring this to something more real. Remember when you wrote that article about your sexuality for that woman's magazine? (By the way did it ever get published? She shook her head.) It actually wasn't too bad. Why did you give that to me to read? Can you not see that I'd take that as you coming on to me? It was all about women's sexual issues."

"Actually, I gave that article to you, when I sensed you might like me more than as a friend. If you remember, I tried to address this problem, the problem of one person in a male/female friendship liking someone more than as a friend, in the article. I was hoping that you'd see yourself and get your thinking straight. It was meant to be a piece that explored, why some men and women can't be friends. I felt too embarrassed to discuss that type of subject with you. I decided to try and write an article, for a women's magazine, that tackled this issue. I told you I wanted you to edit it for me, hoping it would speak to you. Instead you saw it as an article about my sexuality. I guess that plan back fired. Ugh."

Alex looked a bit perplexed and then seemed to think over the article in hindsight and he said, "I guess that could have been what you were trying to do. At the time, I thought you were trying to make me think of our relationship in a more sexual way. Guess I misread that one, huh?" (She nodded and said, "Duh.") He continued on, seeming to find this whole time a revelation. "Now this is one that has been bugging me for years: Remember we were fixing the chairs so they wouldn't mark up the walls? (She nodded.) Well, I started in on a little test to see where your emotions were at. I said, 'You know, if I ever found the right woman I'd leave this job and go off with her to Hawaii and just forget everything.' Then you got all angry and said, 'You better not. You have the nicest wife. If you even think of doing that, with some woman, I'm going to tell her!' Now how could you not have known I was making a hint regarding you? How dense were you? What did you think I meant? Would you have come with me, if I'd have asked more forthrightly?"

"Am I glad you finally asked this? If you remember, you and I were just doing our work and laughing about stuff that happened around the office. Out of the blue, you asked that weird question. How was I supposed to know it was about me? You and I never spoke of anything like that before. All of our conversations were about office stuff. I know I had never made you think I wanted to run off to Hawaii. I loved my husband and that would've been crazy. I thought you were talking about one of those 'camp followers' of yours. There were always different women trying to work 'one on one' with you. They always seemed to have other motives; no one wants to file papers that badly. I thought one of them had broken through into your 'end zone'. You and your wife always seemed to be fighting. I thought you had found that 'one who was going to make everything alright'. While I was yelling at you, I finally got a revelation and thought, 'What if he's talking about me?' Then I dismissed that thought. Why would someone with a really pretty wife, want an overweight Plain Jane like me? I excused myself and went downstairs to work on some other chairs. Later you joined me and seemed to be acting normally again. Why didn't you at least explain yourself, at the time? That conversation was before the attack. All of that mess could been avoided. If we could have talked, I would have said I was flattered; but loved my husband. That would have been the end of that. Right?"

Alex shook his head and said, "I cannot believe we were so out of sync. I was testing the waters; but was way too obscure and that confused you. I'm so sorry. At that time I wanted you and no little statement about your love for your husband would have deterred me. If anything, I might have tried even harder. But can I tell you something? First of all, those other women who did the 'camp follower thing' seemed like pure air heads to me. Even women that I had had affairs with and didn't even care for, had to have some substance. I could not stand women who were foolish and silly. Those were mainly the type that used to seek me and the other pastors out, by the way. The ones I sought out, were always people who were real and more down to earth. I never liked any of them enough to think of leaving my wife, for them, however. But you were different; you made me seriously consider leaving her. Can you please speak more highly of yourself? Where did you get the idea that you were a Plain Jane? You are and were a vivacious woman with a unique and interesting character and look. Your humor and kindness stand out when people meet you. I think you are pretty. Your weight issues, which you mentioned, by the way, never even mattered to me. I don't think others focused on that aspect of you, when they met you. It was/is the whole package that everyone, especially me, finds so charming."

Rhoda blushed and looked out the window. "Well not everyone found me charming, Stan, for instance. But can I tell you something honest, Alex? When you told me about the running away to Hawaii thing, I really got what you meant, about two days later. I cried my eyes out. My whole goal in life, at that time, was to see you go further in the Lord's Work. To hear you say that to me, discouraged me. But beyond that, when I pondered, the whole situation, I got a bit more angry with you. Let me tell you why. By the way you asked, me that question, I could see a couple of things: 1. you weren't proposing marriage. It was a fling you wanted and nothing more. I had no security in that type of arrangement. Yet you wanted me to leave all I knew and loved: my husband, daughter, and ministry, to run wild with you on the beach. That would go on until your money ran out or your grew tired of me. 2. I could see you'd never leave your wife. You loved your kids way too much, especially your youngest son. You could never risk not seeing him again. I also had an inkling that you'd been this way before and had crawled back to your wife. I thought 'whatever happened to those all those cast off women'? 3. I actually loved (love) my husband and daughter. I was not going to throw my marriage away or my relationship with my daughter, for a few cheap, short lived, thrills. Also I was trying to lead my husband to Christ. If I was unfaithful; that would never happen. 4. Lastly I thought that you must have thought I was some cheap 'ho'. You thought I'd just drop all of my moral standards and run off for a few weeks of sex in Hawaii. You thought I wouldn't even care if you really loved me and wanted to commit. I thought you must have thought, I thought pretty shabbily about myself, like I hadn't any real worth. Over time, I actually didn't see that whole conversation, as a good thing, or a flattering thing, that you wanted to run away with me. I saw it as degrading. I didn't get how you refused to see how much I loved my husband."

"Hmmm. I can see how you think. But I wasn't trying to degrade you; at least not consciously. You are right on one thing; I wasn't ready to commit. I thought we could go to Hawaii and I'd see if you were the right one for me. If so, I'd let myself commit more; if not I'd go back to my wife. She did take me back in the past and I knew, for the sake of the kids; she'd do it again. So you did have me pegged on that one. You do have to remember, that up until that time I had not heard much from you, as far as how you felt about me. I didn't want to get too involved, until I saw more enthusiasm from your side. I guess I thought, sex would be an indicator of your feelings. I think we can pick up a lot, about how a person feels about us emotionally, during sex. That is where they show their passion or lack thereof. I guess, you wouldn't have felt comfortable having sex, for fun alone, after coming this far in life. I guess, you do have Christian standards. I just hoped, you'd put them aside for me. Don't you hate being bound up by moral codes? Where is the joy in life?"

"Joy can be found in not living a life you'll regret. Don't you see, Alex? If I had gone off with you; I'd have lost everything. I had/have a loving husband, a dear daughter and had a reputation that was unmarked in anyway. I also was hoping to have a ministry and was trying to be a follower of Jesus in my heart, not just outwardly. I would have never been comfortable sinning, like that. To be part of your destroying your family and hurting so many people, especially your wife, was something I could never have lived with." She started to cry, because of all the confusion of all the years, which had gone by. "To me, my faith is real, not just something I do for show. I really believe in pleasing God; I love Him. How could I spit in his face like that?" She wept onto the arm of the chair.

"Rhoda, I'm so very sorry. I have been pretending to walk with God, for so long, that I guess I have forgotten, what actual wanting to be holy and being a true follower, was like. I guess I thought you were like me. I started to think that most Christians were only faking it. But, correct me if I'm wrong, weren't you and your husband having a hard time together? You seemed to have some big disagreements with him. Also he is a non-believer and a foreigner. Wouldn't you have found me more 'easy' to be with? Don't you think I'm more handsome than he is and more fun? Other women have told me I'm fun and handsome."

Rhoda looked him in the eye, "Alex, you are nice looking, in your way. My husband is nice looking in his. I actually like his beauty style more; it is my preference. He is a cute little old guy today. He is fun, too; just in a different way than you. I thought you were loads of fun at work. I'm sure you still are. A woman in love, doesn't leave the person she cares about, just because someone else is fun and attractive. If I was shallow like that I'd be falling for every guy, I ever befriended. Marriage is about more than cuteness or fun. I have a deep 'heart commitment' to my husband. He loves me more than anyone I have ever met. Why would I want to exchange that for some 'maybe' situation? How could I hurt my husband? How could I leave someone I loved? Sure there were times he and I disagreed. I never shared any real issues with you, since I tried to stay away from speaking about both my marriage and yours. I heard that doing that could cause an affair. I might have told you how my husband I disagreed, in the past, on homeschooling or whether I should be more involved at church or something of little importance, like that. But my husband and I were friends, from day one of our relationship, and are even better friends today. I never was anywhere near as dissatisfied with my marriage, as it was obvious you were/are. I'm sorry if I ever gave you that impression. He is my best friend on every level. You may have read more into what I shared with you, about just the little things of life."

Alex looked out the window this time not knowing what to say. He asked for another cup of tea. I handed it to him. "Okay, let's get to the day of the 'attack', as you called it. I admit I wasn't smooth in my seduction. I was rough and I just came at you with no warning. For that I'm sorry. I'm sure I frightened you, huh? I wasn't trying to; I just had so much emotion, bubbling inside of me, that I jumped on you, literally. Moving on...We were struggling I tried to kiss you and you wouldn't let me. You were like a deer, in the headlights, and full of fear. I could see this; but I had hope that you would eventually breakdown and embrace me. So I said to you, 'I love you Rhoda, I love you Rhoda.' I noticed you looked more terrified and I was thinking you were about to break. You said to me, 'I love you too,' in baby talk. I said, 'Really?' You said, 'Yes, yes I do.' I thought you were now mine and I released you. I was hoping to be able to take you downstairs, to the church's bridal room, and have relations with you. But instead you grabbed your daughter and ran. As you ran I told you that I hoped to see you on Monday. You looked at me incredulously and didn't respond. You continued to run, right past me. Now here is my question: If you didn't care for me why did you say that you loved me too? What was the purpose in saying that, if you didn't enjoy the attack?"

Rhoda began to cry, "You jerk. You stupid jerk. I said that out of fear and confusion, just to get you off of me. I had been praying for a way to get you to release me, from the second you grabbed me. Did I look like I was enjoying the whole thing? How could I have thought rationally in a situation like that? I was having fifty emotions run through me all at once and I didn't know what to think or do. You almost raped me."

"Well, I don't see why you wouldn't have enjoyed the encounter. There was lots of passion and I really wanted, to know you. I thought you feared the actual act and that after it was over you'd actually want more. I've been told I'm a good lover. I thought I was being romantic."

Rhoda looked at him, "Romantic?!! Unbelievable!! Why would I want someone to just take me, like a cave man? Even if I wanted to cheat on my husband, I'd want some wooing first, a bit of wining and dining. I felt, that you thought I was a cheap date. I actually value myself and I'd never to give myself to someone cheaply. If I had had a chance, to digest the whole thing I might have had a different thought, at the time. But we will never know. But to just be taken, and to be expected to be enjoying that kind of violence, that was way over the top. Look Alex, I was, am, and will be your friend; but I'd never have swung that way. I'm friendly, but not wanton. I honestly have a very deep feeling of friendship for you, even after this misunderstanding. But if I ever have an affair, it will be something I'm interested in, not just the man. I am able to be your friend and not even consider going into any other relationship realm. Are you able to do so?"

Alex began to cry and shake. "I am now; but I wasn't then. Then it was, 'I want her and I will have her'. No one ever said, 'No', to me, in that type of thing. They all eventually just caved in, when I came on to them. I can be your friend. As you know I have been your friend, for all of these years. I could have come to your home, at anytime, especially when your husband worked out of town, and gave it another try. But after that second attempt, I respected your decision. I knew that your mind was made up."

I looked over at Alex and thought that this was the most real conversation he had probably ever had, in his whole life. I admired him for putting himself out there. Rhoda was quite open also. By them doing this interaction, they were finally on the launching pad to true healing. They might have seemed disappointed and even a bit angry; but those were normal emotions, kept bottled up for years. I turned to Alex and said, 'do you have any other questions for her'?"

I thought he'd say he didn't, but he said, "Just two little ones. 1. Sometimes you wrote me notes that seemed a bit extra personal with phrases like: I miss you, I care about you, I love you, etc. So did you mean any of that or what? 2. One time I called your house and thought you were drunk and you began to tell me how you cared for me and went on and on and then you said, 'I love you' and hung up the phone. What was that about?"

"Okay, I know what you are talking about. Let's back up a little. At first I sent you angry letters and cards, whenever you called I'd yell at you. Remember? I wouldn't talk to you in the halls at church or at any church doings. I was pissed. Then I forgave you, a year after the incident and started to read about forgiveness and reconciliation. I read over 110 books and studied other materials. Each of these books, etc. gave advice on how to win back a friend. I tried all of their advice, multiple times. Then I got counseling from different people. I tried all of their advice. So people said to make sure the person knows how much you love him and if you remember I always said, 'I love you as my friend and brother', to clarify. I tried everything everyone suggested, Christian and not Christian, and not one thing worked. I tried long letters, short letters, calls, and even having a couple of people go to you as my representatives. So I can see how you got confused. I never wrote you anything 'sweetie' without you being sure the statement was directed to you as a brother and/or a friend. I tried to follow everyone's advice. Some folks liked you, some hated you, and some were indifferent. Each time they gave me advice I'd pray about it and give it a try. Over the years I saw that you liked only a one line emails that asked for reconciliation. You did not want any long letters or sweet talk. The second question I'm rather embarrassed about. I could not sleep for a long time, when I got sick from that poisoning. I tried drinking and doing whatever it took to make myself sleep. I got so frustrated that I went to my doctor and told him I needed sleeping pills. I took a pill called Lunestra and if you know anything about that drug it has weird side effects. One night I went into the kitchen, sleep walking and ate three pounds of raw pig liver. The next morning I awoke covered in blood and couldn't find the pig liver. Do I eat pig liver raw? No. Another time I drove down the wrong highway ramp going the other way. I never do that either. I found items in my car that I had no memory of buying and used to have hallucinations, one of them being about a little ballerina in a red tutu. Ugh. My doctor said I'd get over those reactions and then one night, you must have called after I took one of those pills and dozed off. I woke up with the phone in my hand, saying I loved you. I then realized it was you, because the phone was silent and yet I knew there was someone on it. I freaked out and hung up. So, no, I did not mean whatever I said. Please don't tell me what I said, I'm embarrassed enough. Ugh."

This time I started to laugh, because patients do get weird reactions from Lunestra and I knew she was not exaggerating. I told Alex how that last statement was totally true. Yet I did wondered if maybe she felt that way deep down and didn't want to acknowledge it.

I then asked if either of them had any more questions, for each other. "I think that is enough for today and I think you both have gotten to some core issues, though you went more through the back door, when confronting these things. I was going to ask some of these things more, out in front; but I think this way ended up being better. Okay I have a homework assignment for you both. I want you to think of how God spoke to you during this time you and your friend were apart. I guess I'll start with Rhoda first; but if we have time, I might ask Alex a few questions. I want to know about your personal prayer times, your Words from other believers, your godly lessons you learned from books and other sources, your Bible verses, yes, and even visions and dreams God gave you. I want you both to see clearly like I'm beginning to how this was all born of God, even your mistakes are for a reason. You can even jot them down. Fifteen years is a long time and it is almost a sure thing that you will have to cut some of the lesser instances out or we'll be here till Christmas, of next year. I will comment on these things and let your friend question you or comment. So this may go into two more sessions. I think that we may be nearing the end; we'll see. On your next to last meeting I do want to have you bring in your spouses and perhaps we'll bring in the next generation on our last session. So if any of your family are complaining, tell them to save their complaints and they can 'lay them on me' during the last meeting (s). Okay?" I went towards the door to escort them into the waiting room and they made their appointment. I then went into the office and cut off a wedge of fudge for each of them and told them to share it with their spouses. Both of them seemed to have a huge weight lifted off of their shoulders. I felt a bit chipper, myself, and cut two more wedges of fudge for me and Helen. Then I went into my office and picked up Max and had a little nap in front of the fire, before my three o'clock.

Chapter 20

When the next Wednesday rolled around I was full of anticipation, so much so that I was on autopilot, when my wife was speaking to me at breakfast. I, like other men, heard a lot of buzzing and murmuring in the background, while I was shoveling in my oatmeal. Between bites I occasionally would answer, "Yes, dear, mhhhmmm" while my mind was really thinking about all the day had in store. I finally snapped out of it when my wife said, "then I told him I was too old to sleep with him. I was old enough to be his mother…" "Huh? Say what? What are you talking about?" I said scratching my head. She laughed and said, "I knew that line would get your attention. You must have some case today. Is it the mysterious case of Rhoda and Alex again? You know I'm dying to know what that is all about; I sometimes hate the confidentially thing. Maybe you can tell me, in a couple of years, what this story is all about. I'm bursting with curiosity. (I grabbed her hand and kissed it.) Now that I have your attention I have to call the plumber, the sink isn't working right. Are you okay with this?" I started to chuckle and said, "I'm sorry, Honey, this whole thing is really very thrilling. It really is in need of being kept confidential, more than anything I have been involved with, so far, in my glorious career. I will be sure to tell you, with a few modifications to protect the innocent, in maybe four years or so. Who knows maybe I'll even write a book or something. But as for the sink, use your own judgment, this and my other cases have me too busy to be able to try and fix it myself. Thanks for the oatmeal. I have to leave early; I'm planning on praying when I get to the office. They chose the first appointment slot again. Speaking of which…I have to run. Can I have about ten of those chocolate pinwheel cookies you made last night? (She got a baggie and handed them to me. She then kissed me with exaggerated passion, winked, and sat down to drink another cup of coffee.) Thanks, Honey, we'll have to remember to start from where that kiss left off when I get home tonight." I took the cookies and put them in my briefcase, grabbed my raincoat, slipped on my loafers and was out the door. As I drove to the Bart I pondered about what a great wife I had and how blessed I was. When I got on the Bart, it wasn't as crowded as usual and I found a nice window seat. I took out the notes from the previous week and went over them. I wondered if they'd done their "homework" like I'd requested. Sometimes the clients are all prepared, like for a quiz at school. Sometimes they come in like they just tumbled out of bed, with a case of amnesia. They have no memory of how I'd asked them to prepare. The prepared ones always get so much more out of the sessions. I bounded up the stairs, key in hand knowing that my secretary Helen wouldn't be there yet. Outside my office door in the hall we have a little bench that we put there for early bird patients and for those patients who sometimes have to wait for a ride. To my surprise there was Rhoda sitting on the bench dabbing her eyes with a rolled up Kleenex and sniffling. I went over and tapped her on the shoulder, "Rhoda? Are you okay?"

She kind of smiled, in the midst of crying, "Oh, this? (She pointed to her swollen face.) It's not as bad as it looks. My husband wants me to do a few errands around the city, so I took the car here today. While driving I started to think about more examples of God's direct intervention, in light of our homework, and I am actually crying out of gratitude. Don't worry I'm not planning to jump out the window of your office or off the Golden Gate Bridge or something. I just got here before your office opened and was having a lovely time thanking God. Doc, now that you are here and Alex isn't can I mention something? (I nodded.) Well, I've noticed that I'm more healed and in my right mind than Alex. Have you noticed this, too?

I mean he doesn't seem to really get about the church being a cult. I think he's beginning to see it, but he's still not totally convinced."

I had been thinking about the very same thing earlier and I told her, "Whenever I do reconciliation meetings no two people are ever exactly on the same page. Often one person wants to go more all the way, no holds barred, into the reconciliation, while the other only wishes to enter into the situation, on a more limited basis. Or in a case like yours: one person sees the whole picture more clearly and objectively and repents for their role they played in the problem, no matter how small. While the other person only can see a part of the picture and is still unable to claim full responsibility, for their part. This can happen, even if they are the one who caused most of the problem. But you know what I learned a long time ago? (She shook her head.) Just start with people where they are and only take what they can give. As the old saying goes, 'You can't squeeze blood out of a turnip." The person who has the least insight might in time catch up to the other person or even exceed the other person someday. Some people have their epiphany one or two years down the line. Be patient, God won't forget to work on Alex. Just the fact that he is coming to these sessions is a miracle, considering where Alex has come from. He couldn't have done this even a year ago. God had to really work on him. You were ready to begin work on this, after the first year. It took him fourteen years to get where you were then. By the way I do think you have a gift in this area, counseling, have you ever considered looking into being one."

She said, "I actually have wanted to be one. I even did a co-undergraduate major with Social Work and Elementary Ed. I never used the Social Word part of my degree, because you need at least a Masters to do anything real in Social Work. I actually like Social Work and Sociology better than education. I was not sure how now, at my age, that I'd be able to find a position, especially since I have to be to the university first to get my Masters. Social service, of any sort, requires an internship, so you'd have to actually be on a campus at least some of the time and then you'd also have to go out into the field for the interning portion. I think it's too late for me."

"Hey don't let age stop you. If, when we are finished with these sessions, you want to know more about this profession, let me know. I can give you a few connections and maybe some direction." Rhoda asked if she could use the restroom, before Alex came, and I showed her where it was down the hall. In the meantime, I went into my office and turned off the answering machine and turned on all the computers. Then I took care of Max, put on the tea, and put out the cups and cookies. I asked Rhoda, who just returned from the restroom to make herself comfortable in the waiting room. Helen arrived and they began to chat. I waved to Helen and went into the office and shut the door. Then I fixed us all a nice fire and put on my sweater and slippers, I knelt down by my chair for about three minutes of prayer. Then Helen, who had just come in, announced over the intercom that Rhoda and Alex were waiting. So I got up and opened the door. I glanced over at Helen who was surrounded by files and looked quite busy. Rhoda and Alex entered my office. I could feel that this meeting was going to be more super charged than the rest.

I looked at Rhoda and she had tidied up quite nicely. Alex looked like he was ready for his first day of first grade, for some reason. He had his hair slicked to the side and had on a tidy white shirt and a tie. He explained that the new pastor, who was being trained to take over his pastoral care position, was on a vacation and that he had to stand in for him and preach at a funeral, after our session. Rhoda laughed a little and said, "You look a little too perfect. Maybe Mark can mess your hair a bit." It was a funny comment, in a strange sort of way. I was a bit perplexed; but then I decided we needed to get into the session and let it slide.

"So did we both think about what I mentioned at the end of the last session? I do hope so because I truly believe today will be the beginning of a huge breakthrough, for both of you. Rhoda, what did God say to you right after the attack scenario or maybe how did you approach Him? Give us a little taste of that time in your life."

Rhoda pondered for a moment, as if she was trying to peer through a mist into the past. "Well I have to go back a few weeks, before the attack. I was in one of the most happy and productive times in my life. My husband and I were planning on having an invitro baby, I had a really good friend (Alex), I was in charge of two ministries at the church, I was working on the Seminar for the church, the children's ministry office work was

201

interesting, I was taking computer classes in Excel and Web Design, and the head pastor was considering me for a real, on staff, job for the women's ministry position. I had a great relationship with my husband and was having great fun with my daughter. On top of it all it was the holiday season. How could life be better? I finally felt God was restoring me, after the years I wasted in the cult. I was happy and I was walking with God. All was as it should be. This was true right up until Christmas Eve 1998. When Alex attacked me, I went from being so happy and content to be totally destroyed and without hope, all in the matter of seconds. Right after the attack I ran home and fell asleep for hours, there was no Christmas Eve dinner, or family time. I told my husband I wasn't feeling well when he came into our room to check on me. But at about 2am I woke up and began weeping and trying to pray. For the first few days all I could do was cry. I was unable to pray. Whenever my husband wasn't in the room, I'd weep. I'd weep even on the toilet and in the shower, everywhere. I continued to work at the church and what was once my before work time of prayer, became my before work time of weeping and asking God why. Work was the hardest time. I'd cry before work, during work, along with the crying I'd try to pray. I pray for strength, to forgive, to keep being in the ministry, to fix things, for protection from Pastor Stan and his agents, for direction on what to do next, for healing, etc, etc. I also cried and prayed to be normal again and to be a good wife and mother again. I prayed to not want to commit suicide and for God to straighten out the whole bloody mess. I prayed for my reputation and to still be used by God. So many heart-felt prayers and long sessions of reading the Word of God and having God comfort me. After a few months I went and got prayers from friends, from other pastors, from the church prayer team, from TV preachers, from anyone who'd pray with me. Many of the ones I prayed with, had prophetic words for my life from God. Each speaker who came to the church, and later at other churches I began to attend, had specific messages from God about how He wanted me to first forgive and then later to reconcile. Over the years I had hundreds of prophecies though I never really said anything about what happened. All the prophets said the same thing. Whenever I got counseling, they all said the same thing, and all the prophetic words said the same thing. When I studied the Bible on an individual basis he kept saying the same thing: forgive and reconcile. All of the books I read and all of the pastors' sermons, kept saying, 'Forgive him and then reconcile with him.' Later I found out that some people had different ideas about what forgiveness was and what reconciliation was then I did. But God was speaking to me and not concerned with the vessels delivering the message and their personal idiosyncrasies or doctrinal variations. God never stopped saying the same message. The one exception was Pastor Stan who kept telling me that his church didn't believe in forgiveness and reconciliation. I knew that was wrong. I'd spend hours praying in my home and on long two hour prayer walks. God kept telling me the same thing, day after day and year after year. The message remained the same and did not change for over fifteen years. Some people, even pastors, told me to not forgive or reconcile; but most people who humbly followed God were on my side and glad I chose to forgive someone, who others cast aside, as worthless."

I was very impressed and Alex sat like stone in his chair. It was hard to tell his emotions. He was outwardly blank. I pressed her further, "So were there any what you might call supernatural occurrences? Any signs and wonders type things?"

"Yes there were hundreds. Over the fifteen years, I'd pray and God would sometimes answer only a moment or two later. For instance, I'd miss Alex and want to reconcile with him. But as you know any kind of communication was taboo. So I'd sit and pray and tell God my pain and then only a moment later sometimes as I was saying, "Amen." The phone would ring and it would be Alex. It was always right after I'd pray or tell God how sad I was. The same thing would happen on those two hour prayer walks; even if I varied my schedule Alex would roller blade by me on the street or ride his bike past me. It was truly God because I'd pray and there he'd be. I'd pray to see him at grocery stores and other community locations and there he'd be. Both he and I'd feel so glad to see each other that even other people would remark at our joy, as we past each other; but neither of us had the courage to go against Stan's orders.

There were also some super over the top miraculous things. One day I was doing a lot of laundry, piles and piles and so I decided to pray while

I worked. As I prayed I began to weep and could not stop weeping. I kept folding the clothes and praying for God to rescue me. I was kneeling beside my bed and folding the clothes. To my left was a mirrored closet. All of a sudden it started to glow. I turned towards the closet and there over the closet were velvet green drapes. That was weird enough, but as I looked at the drapes I saw a lovely person about seven feet tall, that was where the glow was coming from. The person said, 'I am here to show you what will happen in the future.' But the person said it to my mind. He then said, 'Get up and stand behind me.' I almost fainted; but I obeyed and stood behind the Angel. He reached over and pulled aside the curtain, now mind you I was totally awake, and he said, 'Look'. I looked from behind him into the mirror and saw a large theater. I was on the stage talking about this whole ordeal and even telling a few jokes. People were listening to me and as I finished, I called for Alex to come out and everyone clapped. He told his side of the story and how God had not let him forget what had happened. He knew he needed to reconcile. He then told the audience how God brought him to that place of reconciliation with me and how he had finally reconciled. The theater erupted in joyful applause. We hugged, and the place exploded. The Angel turned to me and told me to remember what I saw there because God would surely keep his promises. Then the Angel left and I wept to God in Thanksgiving. There were hundreds of Angelic dreams with Angels coming and telling me that God heard my prayers. I remember the morning prayer walk, I mentioned it in an earlier session. The vision about the angels and the portal, remember?. I saw from that all of Heaven was pulling for us to reconcile. God did things like that, at other times, and it was only through prayer and the goodness of God, that I continued to believe. But sadly, even with all of that; we still did not reconcile. However, God always, always showed me that He heard my prayers. During the last year or so before our starting to reconcile, the evidence of this was less. But God still confirmed His promises. I think, as time went on, God was seeing if I'd believe without the big obvious miraculous signs. I did and my new church has had many people believe with me. This year, with our reconciliation in full swing, God has finally vindicated me. He has shown me that I actually did hear Him and He does speak to someone who is not an official some or prophet.

Alex, one thing I'm sure of: God spoke to you just as much as he spoke to me; but I think sometimes you chose to ignore His promptings. When you tried to connect, even silently, with me; it was the Spirit. Even though it was unbeknownst to you, I'd been praying at that very moment, you decided to make that connection. The thought, in your mind, to do so was from Him, because of my pitiful prayers. God has always been in this. This is why I never have or will give up on you."

With those words, Alex fell into a lump on the floor and began to weep uncontrollably. Rhoda and I were shocked and then saw the Spirit was convicting him. Both I and Rhoda went and placed our hands on his shoulders. We could feel him retching and trembling. Rhoda went and got a rag, from my rest room, and cleaned up the vomit and wiped his face. It was like the crashing of a dark ceiling of black glass. We prayed for total deliverance and literally saw him shake and then he seemed to faint. We realized it was a "sleighing in the Spirit" experience. He stayed "out" for about twenty minutes and we, Rhoda and I, continued in prayer. We then saw clearly that Pastor Stan had, somehow, put a demonic spirit on him. God showed us its name was Fear. After the time of prayer and calling out the demon Fear was over, I swear the room smelt like roses. We all could feel the overwhelming presence of God. Alex was free from demonic possession. Rhoda was out from under the influence of that "thing" from the pit. (Some Christians don't believe Christians can be possessed; but sadly I have seen it.) We all hugged and I helped Alex out to his car. I made sure he was alright, before driving. Rhoda promised to follow behind him, in her car, until they got nearer to their town. She still had to do her husband's errands. We were both nervous about Alex on the highway, in that spiritually heightened state of mind. They called in, later in the week, to make another appointment. Though Rhoda had much more to share, we decided that next meeting, Alex should tell what God showed him, during his time of deliverance. Glory!

Chapter 21

The next appointment for Rhoda and Alex came after the Men's Retreat, at my church, on a Tuesday afternoon. The retreat had been so good and refreshing. During that time, I saw how the sadness from their horrible experience, had brought my soul down. It happened a little at a time; so I hadn't really noticed this. I was glad to get a fresh perspective and a renewed connection with the Lord, at the retreat. Since I'm a secular therapist, I often have to leave my faith out of the conversation. This sometimes leads to my getting a bit depressed; but this was more like oppression than depression. I wondered if Alex and Rhoda felt it, too. When we helped deliver Alex, the previous week, from demonic or Satanic possession; I'm sure we made the devil angry. Thus this oppressive feeling was Satan's way of getting back at us. When things like this happen (depression or oppression) I try to face the feelings head on and not just offer a litany of pious platitudes. Have you ever been around Christians, who can't talk or think in "normal terms?" Everything is some mish mash of scripture, with nothing real ever being said; I have. The person, trying to help, is like a spiritual quote dispensing machine. There is no wisdom or actual concrete advice given. A person has a real need and they go to the spiritual quote dispenser and say, "My husband left me today." The dispenser says, "Just trust God, sister. Glory. Amen." Then the dispenser walks away to deliver another empty phrase to another bleeding soul. No wonder so many folks don't want to be Christian; they can be shallow and lost on their own, they don't need Jesus to help them be more nebulous. Since there is always spiritual warfare, after someone is delivered from demons, I thought if they too were having feelings of oppression; we could have a time of prayer for protection and to get rid of the enemy's hold on us. You sometimes have to remain in prayer for a time to break the hold of the evil one.

Anyway, I really wanted to hear what Alex had to say about the spiritual things God had shown him. I knew that two things were likely to color Alex's revelations: 1. He still is in the grip of some sin, not having fully repented of his past "wanderings" or he still wasn't free of the cult's influence; and 2. Being a man, he would be less likely to get really descriptive about his experiences. If Rhoda had the chance, to speak on a deliverance experience; she could have gone on for five days non-stop. Most men like to keep things short and to the point. That is just how the majority of men's emotional makeup is; I'm not sure if it is totally based on sex, this my anecdotal observation. I ate lunch right before they arrived and so I decided to keep the snacks light. I put out tea, tangerines, and some shortbread cookies. Max jumped into my lap as Helen buzzed me that the two friends were in the waiting room and I told her to let them in. Max was nestled in my arms when they entered and this caused a little grin on both their faces. "Hello, friends! My two favorite clients are here! How are you, both?" I must have been extra chipper because they both just nodded, they were fine.

Alex spoke first. "First I want to thank you for that prayer of deliverance last week. I truly felt something come out of me. The thing's talons were sunk into my heart. Thank you, I know it wasn't pretty to watch." I jumped in before he could continue.

"Alex, before you continue on. Have either of you felt an oppression in your spirits, this last week? I have and I wondered if it had anything to do with Alex's deliverance. When the enemy gets angry; he often uses extreme depression or oppression to get back at those who come against him or his kingdom. We can stop everything now and have a time of prayer if you like."

Alex spoke, "I don't know about you, Rhoda; but I did not have a lot of warfare, this last week. I felt so free, after my deliverance; I was walking on cloud 9, as they say. Rhoda, do you need some time for prayer. (She shook her head, motioning for him to continue. I just dropped the idea and also motioned for Alex to continue.) I have things to share about this topic of what God said to me during the time of formation, as we have labeled those long years of Rhoda and I waiting to reconcile. I am bursting to do so. I feel that the 'God component', in this whole thing, is why she and I are still here, wanting to reconcile, after all of these years. I mean what other friends could remain so loyal, to each other, with so little incentive? I mean look at this clearly. I only knew her, in reality, for a little over a year and a half. Most of this time was in a regular work environment, where we actually worked. So we had very little actual friendship time. Yet we have been trying to reconcile for over 15yrs! There is no marriage, affair, or kinship keeping us together. When all is said and done; she goes back to her husband and I go back to my wife. I don't 'get the girl', like in the movies, and she doesn't 'get the boy'. Most likely our spouses won't let us be cozy cuddly friends. Where are the benefits or incentives for either of us, to remain friends? If this wasn't a God thing, we'd be truly crazy. We already are a bit wacky, as you know. So to leave out the 'God component' in this would be an even wackier proposition." He turned to Rhoda and smiled, "I mean, Rhoda, you're cute and all; but not cute enough to keep me, or anyone, going through all this pain, for all these years. You understand where I'm coming from? No woman is that charming; but God kept the connection vital and kept stoking my care for you, in a good way. (Rhoda teared up and nodded, in total agreement.) God won't let us forget our unique connection; how this whole reconciliation thing is to bring Him glory."

I sat in amazement and stared at Alex. This was the most real and profound thing he had said, since coming to my office. I was thinking that maybe God hadn't given up on this guy, yet. Somewhere, deep inside, still beat the heart of a committed servant of God. That someone existed before all of the mess with women, and the lies and deception of his church. I was so entranced by what he shared, that I almost forgot how I was going to conduct the session. So I shook myself a bit and cleared my throat. "Wow, Alex that was so insightful and right on the money, as they say. Thank you, friend. Before we go any further, do either of you have any questions for the other? They can be little unconnected questions or big lines of connected thoughts. I just don't want things, to get swept under the rug. As a matter of fact, we might just establish a question time, each time we meet, from now until the end. How's that sound?" Both of them said, "Sounds good."

Rhoda had a few I could tell and she began right in. "Alex, remember the time I asked you to pray for my husband's digestion? Okay, that was weird, I know; but he had really been sick for a few weeks. As we were talking, a lady who was about ten years older than you and I came up to you and began to pick lint off of your suit, straighten your tie, fix your hair with her fingers and straighten your collar. The whole think creeped me out. Your wife had just come by to see you and she hadn't doted on you, like that. Here this lady was grooming you, like she was your wife. Remember; what was with that? (He squirmed in his chair and nodded.) Well, did you ever have an affair with her? The whole thing seemed just too sensual. Oh yeah and, in light of this, remember that one very emotionally fragile woman, from the Children's ministry, I think her name was Tamera, or something like that. She had a meltdown, in the hallway, after you let her go from the ministry. Was she another one on the list? I have been wondering. Okay, might as well get it all out in the open: Did you ever do anything impure with that woman who was put between us at work, to keep us apart? How about the woman downstairs, in the supply room? I just didn't feel right about these women; they seemed to know you a bit too well. I tried to ignore the uncomfortable feelings, but they came up each time I saw you with them. I wasn't jealous; I was really hoping it was my imagination. Sorry, I have been wondering for years."

Alex got very red in the face and said, "Yes I have known each of them on an intimate basis, except the assistant placed between us at church. I actually did try to get her to succumb to my advances; but she was hopelessly in love with her husband, so it was a no go. The lady from supplies was a very big girl, around 300 lbs; but I did have limited experiences with her. I thought she'd be grateful and do what I wanted and to some extent, this was true. But the first woman, you mentioned, and I had a long affair of about five months. She broke it off because she felt she was too old for me and I'd eventually tire of her. She was right, actually. I had just wanted to try an older woman. Tamera and I had about a one month affair; but she was unable to make a clean break from me. To be honest no one caught my heart like you did. I had little flings and affairs, before and after knowing you; but they were purely sexual in nature. The ones you mentioned, were before you and I knew each other. To be honest I did have a couple of one night stands after you; but they ended there, since there was no substance to these women. After knowing you I had a hard time wanting to be with anyone else. Remember how women would come downstairs, to look for me? They'd tell me they wanted to do anything they could for me. Well, sadly a few did. I even was with that woman who was borderline mentally disabled, who said she wanted to make signs for the children's ministry. She really just wanted to be with me, so badly. So there I am totally open before you and Mark and God. I was a jerk and I am not proud of it. God forgive me; I was a wanton man who cared only for what made me feel good. I did not give a moment's care or thought to any of those women."

"Lastly, for today: What were you thinking when you saw my husband and I making out, against the telephone pole, in the deep fog, across the street from your church? It was really foggy. You truly couldn't see your hand in front of your face. This made my husband get amorous and he was kissing me, thinking we were invisible. While we were doing this, out of nowhere, you rollerbladed up to us, stopping only an inch from our kisses. What were you thinking? What did you mean when you said to him that you just 'wanted to be sure she was happy'? Oh yeah, in this same vein, remember when you and my husband went to the park together? (He nodded.) My husband said you actually asked him, if you could have me, like I was a sheep or some other piece of property? Both of those things came off as a bit weird to me." Rhoda's forehead was deeply furrowed, as she stared at her friend and waited for an answer. She even folded her arms and tapped her foot.

Alex was a bit flustered at the memory of those two events. I think he'd tried to forget them and here they were staring him in the face. "Well the fog thing was an accident. I knew you went for a walk at that time of the day, but I didn't think you'd be out with your husband. In the fog all I could see was the pole and since the fog was so thick and I was on rollerblades, I thought I hold on to the pole and rest until there was a break in the fog. I didn't know if it was safe to cross the street. To my shock there you were, on the pole, wildly kissing your husband, and I was basically staring him in the eyes. Awkward. So I decided to ignore you and speak to him. I asked how you were doing, with all of the abuse and all. I told him how I cared so much about you. It may not have been the best choice of words. He stopped kissing you and said you were doing well. It was hard for me to see you so passionate about your husband.

The second experience with your husband was weirder still; that was before things got really messed up at church. You were trying to make him and me friends; so that you and I could, in turn be friends; then you, me, him, and my wife could eventually be couple friends. That too was… awkward. He did not know yet that I tried to seduce you and you were still in shock from the whole thing, maybe you still hadn't processed the situation fully yet. But what you didn't know, was that I was thinking for a long time about how to have you and not sin at the same time. So I thought, if I asked your husband's permission and he gave me you, then I'd not really be sinning. Everyone would be happy. I even wondered if he'd maybe take my wife as an exchange, but thankfully, I never asked. Okay, okay, that was a weird thought. Believe me it was only in my mind, for a few days. I started to see the wackiness of that idea. Also my wife would have killed me. Trouble was I had actually verbalized the part about you, to your husband. I'm surprised he didn't beat me to a pulp right then and there. But he just stared at me, with his eyes opened as wide as they could be. Then guess what? We continued on with our walk and neither of us mentioned this. I guess he asked you about this when he got home, huh? (She nodded and said, "Hmmhmm.") I guess that is one reason he never wanted to become buddies, huh? (She said, "Duh".) Well, I thought it was worth a try."

211

"For cry in' out loud, Alex, ugh." She looked close to slugging him.

I stepped in, "Okay, Alex, before she beats you, or I do. Why not tell us what God said to you, now that that is out of the way." I shook my head and would have laughed, if this were Saturday Night Live or something. But it was real life, in all of its sad insanity.

"Finally, I have a chance to speak on something more uplifting. (Rhoda and I gave each other a quick glance, because of the drama of that phrase.) After all the stuff happened, meaning my trying to seduce, Rhoda and all. I began to have a hard time. The situation looked impossible. Pastor Stan was on my back night and day, shouting, shouting, shouting about what a filthy sinner I was and how I was going to go to Hell for cheating on my wife. Okay, I have to interject something. My church and Pastor Stan had to protect me in order to protect themselves and their donations. So they knew I was guilty; but to Rhoda's face Pastor Stan would call her a liar and tell her she was delusional, about my trying to seduce her. But he actually believed every word she told him; but, for the church's sake, he treated her like she was a moron. He did this both to her face and in front of those who would enquire about her accusations, in public. But in private, he came down on me like a line backer: screaming, shouting, and yelling scriptures. The whole office could hear our 'private' conversations. They mainly heard me crying. Stan could always make me cry, even if I hadn't done anything. His wild screaming and threats echoed throughout the whole building, but the office had grown used to these outbursts of his. I am sure that the others in the office thought I was a degenerate. I am one, I guess. But he even hit me a couple of times; he was so mad. At first I was just angry. Angry at myself for falling off the morality wagon again, angry at Stan for his feeling he was better than me, and angry at Rhoda for rejecting me and then going to the most legalistic guy on staff for advice. Rhoda, what were you thinking? That guy hasn't smiled, except with an evil glower, since 1960. How could you, even think, he'd be empathetic? Anyway…with all Hell literally breaking loose and my wife ready to leave me, I finally prayed. At first they were just prayers of, 'Lord get me out of this mess with Pastor Stan and Pastor Don.' But in time I actually began to connect with God again. I'd pray prayers like, "Lord just let me see

Rhoda on the street; let me see she is okay." Or, "Lord, let Rhoda say kind words to me on the phone, so I'll know she is still my friend." Etc, etc. But sometimes I'd get little notes, that were about four lines and not her usual one liner emails, from Rhoda, saying, "Last night I had a vision and an angel spoke to me about you and said, '…..' The funny thing was usually I would have had a similar dream that same night and heard the same message. Sometimes our dreams were identical. Thing is I wasn't allowed to speak to her to tell her, so I'd silently call or send blank emails, hoping she'd get I was trying to tell her I had those dreams also. She usually did and she'd write me back saying she got it.

But my favorite times were when I'd call and she'd say, 'I was just praying for you.' I'd get this nudging from the Spirit for about a half hour before hand saying, 'Call Rhoda, call Rhoda…' Finally I'd break down and call and she'd always explain how she was praying for me at that same time. I felt a Divine connection.

There was one dream that she and I had that was awesome. She dreamed that she and I were two little kids, a brother and a little sister. In the dream my mom (God) told me to watch my little sister. But being a boy I left her on the road by herself and went off to play with the big boys. It wasn't until much later, that I remembered my little sister and went back and got her. God showed me that I had left Rhoda on the road, so to speak, and abandoned her. I needed to go back and rescue her; because it was getting dark and she was afraid. That was over ten years ago; but I am slow to obey the Lord, I guess. But to be honest in most dreams I had, she was trying to rescue me.

I also had at least two angelic visitations; they both said I was to reconcile with my sister. I saw myself speak with her, in front of a large group, about forgiveness and reconciliation. I never had the courage to obey the angels. I did preach at least three distinct messages about forgiveness and reconciliation. I was put on punishment after each one because the church thought some people might remember what I needed to be forgiven for. They thought others might believe I needed to reconcile and our church did not believe in reconciliation. But God told me to preach what I preached and so I did.

Random people from church would come up and give me words from God on this subject; so would guest speakers and other church leaders. They did not know the story; but I kept being told to reconcile with a friend. I did try on several occasions, approach her. Each time either Rhoda seemed afraid of me or someone from church was watching and I had to give up. But whether from any outside Word or my own personal time in the Word, the message stayed the same: Forgive and Reconcile.

Remember that time at church, about two years after everything started, when I came up to you and started weeping? You were with a girlfriend and I didn't care; I just wanted to make things right. Well, Stan saw us talking and after that he had someone following me almost constantly. The only time we almost got together, it seems, was at grocery stores. Remember? Once I was praying about you when I was at the Safeway, by your house, and a few moments later you were there, wearing a little red jacket. My youngest son was with me and you just kept looking at me in the eyes and not speaking. My son kept saying, 'Dad, isn't that that lady?", and tugging on my sleeve. I saw that was not going to be a good time to speak; so I just kept staring back. Another time you were with a rather large and noisy friend, Mindy, she shouted out my name as loud as she could at Costco. You dropped your ice cream bar and ran up to me asking to speak to me. I was just about to, but another pastor, from church, came up behind you and I had to run. Two times you were in the checkout line when I was behind you and I couldn't get to you. We already spoke about the Lucky incident. Before each of these grocery encounters, I had prayed to see you and to speak to you. God brought you right to where I was. But something always stopped me from doing His will and speaking to you.

If I didn't call or write you; I'd get sick. God kept telling me to connect with you and I couldn't rest until I contacted you, at least silently. God never let me alone or let me forget you were waiting for me to act. I had dreams, visions, Words, and constant revelations from God. The more Stan came after me, the more I knew for sure this was of God. Every time Stan came against you; you never gave up on me and always remained a loyal friend, even after you left our church. You never gave up believing, in not only reconciliation; but that I was a worthwhile human. God used you to tell me I had value so many times and I always heard positive things from you when I felt like giving up. So yes I always knew God was in this and is in this."

I looked at him and said, "So tell me, what was it like, right before you finally spoke in a definite way to Rhoda about reconciliation."

"Glad you asked that question. For about two weeks I kept having dreams about reconciling with her. Each dream was a different scenario; but in each one I did the same thing. I saw her, prayed for strength and wisdom, approached her, apologized for taking so long to reconcile, put my hand on her arm and asked her to forgive me; then I asked her to reconcile with me, and took her out for coffee. Every day for two weeks this went on. But funny thing was I had not actually seen her for about two months, not on the street or in any shops; she was nowhere to be found. I saw her at a coffee shop, but did not approach her. I decided to call her and I did."

I asked, "Can I ask why your amount of calls and notes lessened with time? I mean Rhoda said to me at first you'd call sometimes two or three times per day and also sent multiple blank emails. What made your pursuit lessen?"

"Well, one thing I noticed, the more I called or wrote, the more she'd think the chances for us to have a face to face conference were increasing. I didn't want to give her false hope. So I'd pull back, hoping she'd cool down her expectations. I knew she didn't want to do anything immoral; but at the same time I was so carefully watched, there was no way for me to connect with her face to face, like she hoped for."

I looked at him and said, "Okay, last question for the day. Why did you let Stan and others molest Rhoda and not stick up for her? Every church she went to harassed her, thinking they were doing God's work. Her husband and daughter, as well as others, had their faiths destroyed by the things that your church, or agents from your church did. Didn't this bother you?"

"Yes, it bothered me; but every time I stepped out and tried to make amends, my church put me on punishment. They told me I was rebellious and a possible candidate for removal. They weren't kidding. At least five pastors were kicked out, while I was on staff, and nothing they did was anywhere as terrible as my infraction. To top it off one pastor, who helped Rhoda, was fired immediately, because he recommended her for Bible College. So I was totally afraid; I knew they could do whatever they threatened. But now when I look back and see all the destruction; I admit I was wrong for fearing evil men. I was younger then and could have found a job at another church, somehow."

Rhoda looked at him, "You do know my daughter has totally left God, right? She said your church caused her to question whether Christianity was real and whether she could be a part of such a two faced system. She saw how you guys preached forgiveness and reconciliation; but whenever I tried to do this in real time, you guys came after me and said you didn't believe in those concepts. She said that church was all 'crap' and that the pastors were liars and deviants. Kind of sad to be so bitter so young, but that is what she saw and to be honest, that was totally true in the situations, she was exposed to. She saw how Stan hated me and how you did not stand up for me, to protect me, like a true friend would. So this is still a sorrow for me. There also were all of the people that were forced to lie and to abuse me and who believed your church's lies. She saw all of those good Christians come against her mother. That was a terrible horrible thing and was not a joke like Stan made it out to be. I have met some of these people, your church used, today and most of them hate God. Are you guys proud of yourselves? My daughter may never be recovered. This kills me. How dare your church play with people's lives, with my life. I have value and that smashed my face in the mud."

Alex looked down, "Rhoda, of course, you are right. I'm not proud of that. Also I know that leaders will be judged more harshly, when Jesus returns. He's going to have a lot to say about the leadership at my church and the controlling influence we had over the people in our church and even over other churches and pastors. It is like a fast spreading cancer; and you and the others were sacrificed. This was all so that I could keep my job and the church could keep its reputation. Both are equal to dog dung, as far as I can see. Stan is proud of his work to this day. He says he won. But what did he win? How can he even hold up his head? I can't."

Though the things said were a shame to the Church, as a whole, and to Alex, I was glad to finally hear Alex say them. This would be the beginning of his total deliverance, from his cult and from his sin. I was glad I had the privilege to be there, to watch God deliver a man who others might just have just tossed aside and said had no value. They'd brand him a sleaze ball and throw him away. But God saw his value and God still had plans for his life and for Rhoda's. Amazing.

I stood up and said, "Well, I think God has had a breakthrough here and I am hoping to see more and more deliverance, in the last final weeks. Next weeks' homework will be to think on how you would done things differently and on how you should have seen the situation."

They both got up and shook my hand and each other's hand and went into the waiting room to make the appointment for the following week. "Don't forget to write down any questions you have for each other or me; so we can handle those at the beginning of the next session." They both waved and were out the door.

Chapter 22

I was so glad about the breakthrough Alex had had the week before. I began to think about how I could help things along a bit and I decided it would be good to really delve into what a cult is and to get Alex and Rhoda really free. Of course I also wanted to go through their questions and the homework assignment I had given them. So I thought this might turn into a longer session. I made sure that Helen didn't book anyone after them, just in case. They were coming in for a 2 o'clock appointment and so that worked out just fine.

I hoped that, during the week, they both had had some time to think over what they shared about how God had come through for them, during their time of separation. And how He had and was still working in their lives. They both arrived exactly on time and were covered in a fine drizzle that was happening outside at the moment. So I quickly took their rain coats and offered the usual quilts and mugs of tea, with a few raisin cookies, made by my sweet wife. While they got settled I put two huge logs, on top of the others, and stoked the fire. When we were all ready I decided to speak. "You both know that I mentioned to bring along questions you had and to do the homework assignment from last week. But before we begin I wanted to clarify something. Both of you have, semi-mentioned, about how you know that the church you attended was a cult and this is good. Now how much you really see this is something only you and

God know. I have worked with many ex-cult members and even was in one myself, plus a few abusive churches. It usually takes me quite a long time to convince victims that they were in a cult, even if they have been physically out of the cult for many years. Why this is I can only speculate. Many times a person is out of a cult; but the cult is not out of the person. I think much of the problem might be blamed on the pure Satanic nature of a cult. Cults offer a substitute for the real God and His Church. They are so well orchestrated that they can fool the wisest of men and women. I can see how this whole cult thing can get under your skin and become deeply imbedded in your soul. Both of you seem to, on some level, see the horror of the cult system. Rhoda you have been in at least two cults, along with a few cultic or controlling churches and I do think you have learned from those experiences. Yet maybe you don't quite understand what the underlying need or wrong thinking in you has been, that causes you to keep choosing such places. Alex, I'm not too clear on your past places of worship; but you have been at the cult/church, you are at now, for over twenty years. You've seen the evil in it and yet have continued to stay on. There are so many past issues in both of your lives that have caused you both to choose a "bent" place of worship and the accompanying "bent god" that goes with it. While such places are evil, a cult can also be a comfortable place to choose to be. It takes the control of our lives out of our hands, with all of its decisions and failures, and puts them into the hands of others. Others tell us what to decide, how to live, what is godly and not godly, how to do everything in life, including how to follow God. The responsibility for our lives is no longer ours. Along with this, others get "off" on controlling us and others. They are ready and right there waiting for us to relinquish our ownership of our lives. They are only too glad to step in and take over the lives that we abdicate to them. This feeds their need to have power.

They take you money and your 'free slave service' to advance their kingdom (not God's), and they get more converts to follow their idea of god. The cult God is a fake, a counterfeit and he needs worshippers. Satan loves this whole deal because he can get people (believers and unbelievers) off track, kill you and your desire to be of service to the real God. The process is painful. You have to give up your freedom of choice to evil men (and women) and do things that are against your will. You are often given punishments and made to feel like trash; yet you still choose to be in the cult because you don't have to grow up and take responsibility for your life choices. In the back of your mind, you also have the hope that you, too, will someday have power over others. You envision becoming someone big inside the cult system. So you let others tell you to do things that you'd never do and you hide behind the cult's fake wall of protection. This is very complex; but I think you both can see how you have done this over the years. You have abdicated your power, your will, to the servants of the Evil One, out of fear but also out of a hope for future power. Am I right? (They just stared at me with eyes as round as saucers.) When the leaders in these groups told you what they wanted you to do, couldn't you feel the demonic talons squeezing your mind? Didn't you have a sense that what you were being told was somehow off? But yet you stayed. Rhoda left earlier and has been trying to get free for years. Alex, I think you are beginning to see the depths of the evil in your own life and in the church you still choose to be part of. But I have to tell you both that there is still a long way to go. Rhoda I suggest you come to my office for some additional therapy later on. We'll see what it was in your past that made you so easily swayed to join that many cultic groups. Alex, I think you are going to need extra therapy for your sexual addiction and for your addiction to a place that emasculated you and robbed you of your life and calling. Both of you still have time to do your destinies; but you need a bit more healing in these areas, and perhaps others."

Both Alex and Rhoda just sat rather stunned at my words. Rhoda spoke first and said, "Mark, I really get where you are coming from and I'd be more than glad to work on this area of my life, once we are done here. I know my husband will gladly pay for that kind of therapy. He'd like to have me be all I can be as a person and in my destiny with God. I promise to continue on with you for a few months to a year, when we are finished. I have done a lot of study on cults and abusive churches and I want to be able teach others about this. The more healed I am the better for my students." I was so very glad to hear a person who was open and speaking so humbly.

220

Alex shifted around in his chair. "This all makes sense and I'm sure I have abdicated my power for 'their' power. It is just more complicated. I have one son in college, the older one is independent and doing well, and one daughter who is on again/off again sick with her anorexia. That disease requires expensive treatment, you know. I also have a wife who likes to spend and keep up with the Joneses, house and car payments, medical bills, and all the other expenses of daily life, plus tons of debts. I have no real skills in the secular world and the church won't give me a recommendation to another church. I'm almost 60 and for me to start over, is pretty much out of the question. On top of this I had planned to retire to the pastors' home in Arizona and so I really didn't save much toward my retirement. It seems foolish for me to leave this job for total uncertainty. My wife and my cousin also work for the church and if I left they'd be fired and lose their ministries and salaries. I know the place is evil and that I'm selling my soul; but I frankly don't know what to do. They'd toss me out, on my ear; if they knew I'd been doing this. I chose to go against them; but I also chose to just not tell them. I would like to find a way out; but I can't see it and I'm trapped. It was easier for Rhoda in some ways. I'm stuck in a dark demonic world."

"Wait a minute," Rhoda started to tremble. "Easier? My husband almost divorced me, because he believed Stan's crap, albeit for a short time. Even though he told Stan off, there was a part of him that didn't think a pastor could out and out lie. He found out later he was wrong. Every church I went to, except the one I'm at now, has had someone from your bloody cult go to my pastor and tell my pastor I was a seductress and rebel. This crud pile of lies has kept me from any productive ministry. I have had slander and out and out lies about me spread to every church and to as many secular people, in my community as possible. I have had your people lie to potential bosses who asked if I worked at you church and thus been kept from jobs. (I only found this out later.) I had friends leave me and enemies harass me on the phone, through letters, and on the street. I had my daughter question her mother's integrity, when she was told by pastors at other churches her mother was a whore. I could go on for hours, Buddy. I'm not sure I had it easier. I also, on top of all this, was not able to see or talk to you in a normal manner, though you and I were friends, and I had forgiven you. Who are those dictators at your church who thought they could tell me who I could and could not associate with? Is this Russia or something? I missed you and wasn't allowed to be a normal friend and just speak with you, if I so chose to. Easy, no it wasn't easy. You had a hard time, sure; but you did not have to suffer slander and mockery from supposed leaders of the church. Who the Hell did they think they were? Excuse my French. Man!"

Alex, "Okay, okay. We both had a hard time. My hard time was on a different level than yours; it was pastor to pastor, supposedly equals. You, like or not, had to be in the subordinate role: first you are a woman and second you are not a pastor. It was horrible, but some church leaders think they can boss and abuse subordinates, I was supposed to be their equal. My head pastor, who was once my friend, lost all faith in me. Pastor Stan had his hand up my backside, for years, squeezing my brain from the inside. He controlled my every thought and movement (although I did get around him at times both with you and with those flings). I had people talk behind my back and distrust me both in the office and in the congregation. Yes, I too was kept from talking to you, my best friend. I was made into a man who was too impotent to control his own life. I know you thought I was a wimp. I was and I still am." With that he started blinking away tears and she was doing the same.

I cleared my throat and spoke, "All I can say is, 'wow'. God is working here. I really get both of you, really I do. As I said we need to work on these cult issues in future sessions. These are not easy resolved and are too deep to deal with at this time. Alex you do have a dilemma. If we were not Christians; I'd be feeling the hopelessness you feel. But let me tell you something I have learned, realtime. If we honor God; He really, really will honor us. Putting this plainly, if you quit and cut all cords with that evil sham of a church, God will take care of you and all of your issues. As you spoke just now I thought that you would have a great future career in speaking on issues like this in churches. Your life could save many from legalism and cults. I'm not saying you have to speak with Rhoda. I think you might have your own call for speaking on this topic. I could just see you doing this. If you let me, I'll get you in touch with a speaker, on similar subjects, I know and maybe you might see some hope, in this whole thing. Okay? Alright... I guess we had better go on with our usual session. It has been about an hour now, but I think that was worth it. Agreed? (They silently nodded their heads.) Rhoda do you have any questions for Alex?"

"Doc, could I have some more tea, please? (I poured her some more and she took a couple of sips before continuing to speak.) Alex, remember when you came to me and said that you decided that we should be together? Those weren't the exact words you used; but that was the general drift. Remember? (He nodded.) Well, I thought of your pretty little wife. She really is the prettiest woman at your church, even today. The rest of those ladies have had everything imaginable lifted and stretched and they look like mannequins. But your wife is naturally pretty. At that time she was small and petite. I know her weight fluctuates like mine; but she is still lovely. I was forty pounds heavier when I knew you, than I am today. I felt huge next to her. I thought you were nuts. Here you had a woman who was pretty, who took your crap (excuse the French, again), who worked at a part-time job, worked for you at church, and on top of those things took care of your three children, and she even loved you. You could see it in the way she looked at you. I used to think, 'Why would this guy want me when he had that perfect mate?' But what I said to you was, 'What? Look at me. I'm overweight, I have glasses, and I'm just not as lovely as your wife. Why would you want someone like me?' Of course the unsaid thing was, 'Oh yeah, and I'm married, and by the way, you're married. Duh?' But then you said to me, 'Oh, I already thought about all that and it's okay with me.' Say, what?! I still wonder what were you thinking and trying to say to me? Were you thinking a fat girl should jump at the chance to be with a 'hunk' like you and leave everything (husband included) and go with you into a dark and uncertain future? What were you thinking? Marriage? What?"

"Man this question took me by surprise! To be honest, at the time of the attack, I had not thought that far. In the past sessions you mentioned that I'd probably use you and then go back to my wife. Well, I wasn't thinking so much like that. I mean, I truly don't think my wife would have taken me back, after another slap in the face, like you and me going to Hawaii. Even she would have seen that as the last straw. But honestly, I wasn't sure about the marriage thing either. I knew your body wasn't like a super model's and that really wasn't my concern. I have had women of every shape and size; I mean every. But I wondered if we would be compatible, over the long haul; since there were times you made me spitting mad. I thought I might find you bugged me, after we got to know each other better. So I was going to use the trip to Hawaii as a test, of sorts. If it didn't work out, I figured I could always find someone else. Maybe that seems hard hearted, but that was really what I felt, at that time. I guess I was a kind of a shallow guy and a bit mean spirited. But I loved you. I just wasn't ready to commit to you."

Rhoda crossed her arms over her chest. "Well that was just great. I was supposed to leave a loving husband, a sweet daughter, all I knew and my walk with God, to boot, and go off with you to Hawaii, for a test. What kind of a woman did you think I was? A cheap, babe, huh? Man!"

Alex got squirmier in his chair. "Rhoda, I never saw you as cheap. Of all the women I cared about, besides my wife, I felt that you had the best qualities to be a long time partner. You also were the only one who ever said no to me. That told me you respected yourself. I just was unsure of marriage and I knew how my temper didn't allow you to be yourself. I wasn't sure how long you could stand, my going off, at the drop of a hat. I wondered if my dark side would be set off by your little quirks or if I could adjust. The problem was more with me and my character, than you. I have always thought you were great, maybe too great for someone like me. But I wanted to give it a try. By the way I'm glad you lost those forty pounds and don't have to wear glasses. You look much younger. But I loved you no matter how you looked, even on your bad hair days."

I looked over at Alex and said, "Did you have any questions?"

Alex thought for a time, "Since your early letters were so angry, when did you actually forgive me? I noticed a change; but I never knew what the catalyst was."

"Didn't I ever tell you? I thought I did. Oh I guess I told Mark; I never told you. Mark should I share this with him? (I nodded. It is good for people to know how and when we forgave them.) Almost exactly one year after you and I had our first sad encounter on Christmas Eve, a year later on Christmas Day, you got up in front of church and you read a book to the children about a little donkey, remember? I listened to the story as you spoke and I realized the story was about me. That like the little boy missed his donkey friend, you missed me. At that moment God said to me, 'Can you forgive this man with your whole heart?' At first I said I could never forgive you and He reminded me of how He said that in order for me to be forgiven I had to forgive. I took about fifteen minutes of arguing with God. Then I said, 'Yes, Lord. I can forgive him.' Do you know what happened next? I had a vision of gold coins falling out of Heaven onto you and me. It was like Heaven's confetti. All of Heaven rejoiced that I forgave you. I kept seeing gold coins fall on you until you left the stage. At that moment I totally forgave you from the depths of my heart. It was soon after this that I read that 110 books about forgiveness and reconciliation. Reconciliation was a new concept; I never heard this concept preached in any church, before that moment or after it. From the moment, I understood the concept, I wanted to reconcile with you. God again spoke to me and told me you and I were to reconcile for His glory. This is why I never gave up. I still believe this."

"How lovely, what a God we have and what a friend you are, wow." Alex wiped away two stray tears. "My next question is, 'After the attack, were you afraid of me? Sometimes you'd back up from me at different church functions like I was going to hurt you physically or something."

"To be honest I went back and forth on how I felt, at first. There was anger, fear, and just plain confusion on my part. I didn't know how to be around you. I wanted to be like before, when we were just simple friends. We'd smile, give each other a friendly hug and then we'd just talk about work or your kids. But after that incident and my reporting it, I felt you were probably mad at me and that you might even hit me. Okay, yes, I did fear you." Rhoda looked down at the floor for awhile. "I just didn't know how to take you after that; I lost my trust in you."

"I am so sorry. Maybe someday it will be restored. Lastly, remember the time I started to talk to you in the closet at work? Remember that black woman who came in and interrupted me? You knew I was trying to speak openly to you and ask why you went to Stan, right? That was a real example of me trying to reach out to you, to understand. But you saw her and got afraid she'd tell Stan, since she worked for him. So you ran out. You see, I did try. There were a few other occasions I tried to speak to you. But you usually were afraid or someone usually reported us. I usually got into major trouble with Stan afterwards. Well that woman did go to Stan and mentioned how I was giving you a hard time in the closet. Did you tell her that?"

"First of all she was Pastor Stan's pet and was totally controlled by him. She was not my friend; I didn't tell her anything. I knew she was untrustworthy. She must have seen our faces and felt Stan needed to know about the situation. She surely wanted brownie points with her leader. I actually think that Stan may have sent her down to spy on us; don't you? Stan never trusted you with me. I didn't know that woman, until about a year later; she was my daughter's friend's mom. Remember the time when you came into my office and there were no chairs? So you got down on your knees to talk to me? Remember how Stan appeared in the room, just two seconds later, and stood there with his arms crossed, until you finished giving me the instructions for my project. He was having smoke come out of his ears and he tapped his foot behind you to speed you up. You do know one of his spies had seen you come into my office and get on your knees, right? The place was full of spies and we both were followed all the time. I even had people follow me in church bathroom, in my neighborhood and when I went shopping at the mall. So, no, I didn't talk to that woman."

Alex shook his head, "I wish I had known some of these things earlier. I had a lot of things against you and now I see most of them were Stan's doing, he pinned them on you, you weren't involved. He also would tell me stories about you and I never thought to check if they were lies or not. Man! "

"I knew you blamed me for things Stan did. You thought that I told people about what you did, that I gossiped about you and the church, and that I said things I never said. But all the time it was Stan. He would tell you I said and did things; he actually did. But you know what made me mad? I was ticked with Stan, of course; but I thought if you were really my friend that you wouldn't believe the things he said and secondly that you'd at least ask me if they were true or not? But you seemed to just believe anything he told you. That is what made me mad. You should have asked me."

Alex looked concerned, "Yes, Rhoda, I did you a disservice and I was wrong. Forgive me for that. Will you? I guess I let Stan tell me what to think, because he was over me. Not because he was godly. I'll bet he was the main person, who gossiped to everyone at church about us. Forgive me."

"You are right about Stan and I do forgive you. It is hard to believe a pastor could be so evil, I know. I no longer put anyone on a pedestal, just because they have a title. I have to see the good fruit like the Bible speaks of, before I trust anyone."

"Okay, our time is almost up. But I do want to ask you both the two questions I gave you for homework. 1. How would I (you) have done things differently? 2. How should I (you) have seen the situation? I think you both have skimmed the edge of these two questions during our time together; but now I'd like a more definite answer. I have to start with Rhoda, since she, though she was the victim, was actually the one who started the whole forgiveness ball rolling. In the past, your ladies, Alex, kept these types of things silent, pretty much, and didn't rock the boat. But Rhoda rocked the boat, because she was innocent. Okay, so Rhoda, today what would you do differently, if the same situation happened?"

Rhoda looked out the window and thought for a moment. "Hmmm. Well today, I'd be more aggressive and would have smacked and maybe even punched Alex, even if this would mean getting fired. Before I feared pastors, too much, and I feared I'd lose my job. Today I would have slapped him and told him to not ever touch me inappropriately again, or I'd report him. If he didn't fire me; I'd be a lot more distant. I'd be more removed emotionally from him, not be so kind or friendly. If he tried it again, I'd have told him, clearly, I was then going to go to the head pastor. I would not go to a man, like Stan, whom I already knew was legalistic. If they wouldn't take me seriously I'd report them to the main governing office and then leave the church. I might even sue. I stayed on, thinking God would make things right and rescue me. He'd change everyone's heart, so I was passive. But today I'd take the bull by the horns and deal with it all right away, like a grown up. When a line has been crossed; I now think it is best to quit. I'd also tell my husband, as soon as the crime happened. I'd forgive and maybe have a limited reconciliation, when I felt healed enough to do so.

"As for the second question, 'How do you think you should have seen the situation'?" I wondered what she'd say to this, since she seemed to be a bit stronger than she was when it all happened years ago.

"Well, first of all, I would have seen what Alex did for what it was—a pass. I would have seen that Alex had some problems, that it wasn't me or my fault. I also would have seen that Stan should never have been allowed to abuse me, as he did. At the first sign of abuse from Stan; I'd have called him on it and gone to the head pastor. If that didn't work I'd have gone before the church and exposed them all and left. I did not deserve Stan treating me as he did. I might have forgiven Alex; but I would have decided not be friends. I would have seen that by what he did; he did not know how to be a friend. I think God came to me where I was and used the situation to bring about reconciliation, to teach me and those in the church what this concept is."

"Sounds like we would have not been friends today; if you hadn't been so naïve. I guess I should be glad you were more naïve then. I thought you knew more about the world than you did. Forgive me for destroying your simple trust. As for me: I would have first spoken to Rhoda openly and told her how I felt about her. Just attacking her out of the blue was not the way to show her I loved her, or thought I did. I would have then started to try and woo her. If that worked, I'd have begun asking her out for coffee and such, winning her heart a little at a time. If she had rejected me, then I'd have had her transferred to another department at church and would have distanced myself from her. I probably wouldn't have kept working with her side by side, because my feelings were too great. I'd have tried to get closer to my wife, maybe even get some therapy. Also I'd have tried to reconcile with Rhoda, much sooner and thus spared us both the pain of this whole episode. I would have tried to keep Stan out of the picture, in the first place. He didn't need to know about my feeling for Rhoda. He wouldn't have, if I would have made things right, right away. If Stan did step in to the picture; I'd have tried to go to the head pastor and gotten him to see how I needed to make things right with Rhoda so she and I could move on. The second question is hard to answer. Maybe I should have seen that I was having a crush, because I was having a difficult time with my wife, at that moment, and that I really wasn't in love with Rhoda. I just needed to be close to someone and that someone should have been my wife. She was being distant, at the time, and so I put all of the responsibility for my emotional stability, on Rhoda. I made her the object of my affection. I'd faced the truth and seen clearly that she loved her husband and only wished to be my friend. I was blinded by lust and I'd have called myself out on this and taken it to God. Again I would have gone to a real counselor, like you, outside my church."

"Wow, can you both see your progress?! To me this is all God and I give Him the glory. I do hope you both see that you have come really far in just a few weeks. I'm so happy. I hope you both see this is a good step forward today. Anyway...For next week's assignment I'd like you to tell me what positive things you both have gained from this experience and from just being friends with each other. Also think of more questions to ask each other. I think we are nearing the end of our time together. Thank you both so much for being so willing to change and to hear God. I am in awe of all He is showing you both. I know that when you are not here in this office that you both are seeking God's wisdom and that He is downloading it to you guys."

With that Rhoda and Alex stood up and handed me their quilts. Rhoda reached down and gave Max a big kiss and squeezed him. Alex patted Max on the head, while Rhoda held him and they both smiled. "We want to thank you Doc for helping us cast out our demons. Thanks."

"Helen is still here, so please make your appointment for next week. I can't wait." Then I walked them to the door still holding the quilts in one hand and Max in the other. I left them on the other side of the door and went back into my office to pray about all that had just transpired.

Chapter 23

S ince I live in the Bay Area, I decided to take advantage of the warmer weather and go out for a jog. We have walking trails near my home. I left my still sleeping wife and headed outdoors. The air was balmy and as I jogged I thought on my two favorite clients, Rhoda and Alex. I was more on Rhoda's "side", than Alex's; I had to admit. Part of me felt that it was Alex's own choices that got him in this predicament, whereas Rhoda truly was a hapless victim. Had she done everything right in this religious mess, no? But she had remained friends with a guy who more or less destroyed her life or at least the life she had intended to live. I wasn't sure Alex actually deserved such loyalty or forgiveness; but I had to admire it. I did feel sorry for Alex in one aspect, he had fallen in love with Rhoda and he didn't know how to stop loving her. I know he said at our sessions that he didn't love her anymore; but I was almost sure that he still had her on his heart. Because it was, what it was, he would just have to go forward, there was no other choice left for him that would be sane. I know that isn't an easy thing to do, to stop loving someone. Rhoda, I think, could easily have fallen in love with him, had the situation been different. However, she was truly in love with her husband and trying to obey God. So whatever she could have done, "in the natural"; she had to prevent herself from going down that road. To her there was no other choice, I really do think she had managed to keep herself pure. I did not have much hope for their friendship continuing in a normal fashion, once this reconciliation was completed. I was not too sure how their spouses would react to their keeping a connection, of any sort. But I had to remind myself that my job was to help complete the actual reconciliation. They'd have to take it from there when all of the "hoopla" was over. Contrary to the way their old church thought, I knew that they were adults and those decisions were theirs to make not mine to impose. I wondered how my wife would feel about me having a close female friend. I must have jogged about five miles or so when I realized it was getting late and I would have to shower, before I got on the Bart and met Rhoda and Alex in the office, at 1pm. I really do like the flexible schedule that being a therapist allows me to have. Some days I have clients from 9am–6pm and other days I see only one or two people. I am doing what I love and paid handsomely; so I have no complaints. On occasion, I can choose to have a few clients who don't really pay the actual price, for my services, Rhoda's bill would have been in the thousands by now. I am glad I chose this field, instead of computer programming, like my family wanted me to pursue. I ran in the door grabbed a bagel and some bacon, gave my wife a kiss, and bounded upstairs to the shower. I was totally ready in fifteen minutes and told my wife to make reservations at her favorite Italian place that night and ran out the door with my briefcase in tow. I jumped in the car, drove for a few minutes, found a parking spot at the Bart station, put my money in the slot, and got on the escalator. As I got to the top of the platform, my train pulled in. Since it was around 11am there was no one on board and I picked a nice sunny seat and pulled out my I-pad. When I arrived at the office Helen, my secretary, was at lunch and so I tidied my office, fed and cleaned up after Max, and took out some dark chocolate hot chocolate, that I'd wanted to try. I put it in the tea pot and got out three giant sugar cookies and the cups and saucers. I then went through my pile of mail on my desk, tossed most of it in the trash, and answered the call of nature. Helen arrived as I was washing my hands and peeked into the office, asking if I needed anything. I said I couldn't think of anything and as we were speaking Alex and Rhoda came up the stairs. I asked them to come in and stoked the fire a bit as they got comfortable. I handed them a cup of the hot chocolate and sat down in my chair. "Tell me, if it is chilly in here, okay? How are you both doing today? I hope you had a chance to do your homework and that you both found something positive, in all of this sorrow. Before we begin are there any questions you have for each other? (I looked at Rhoda, who was shaking.) Rhoda, are you chilly?" (She nodded and I put two more logs on the fire.)

Alex spoke up first, as my back was still turned, "Well, I had a couple. The first one is: when this whole situation got started you were in one home group and they used to meet out in the countryside near your home. But after you and I were more entrenched in this struggle, with Stan and the rest of the church, why did you go and join the group that my cousin held in her house? Didn't you know that I sometimes went there? Why would you choose that group when you already had one and when you knew it would put my cousin in a weird predicament? That really bugged me."

"Bugged you?! Do you know why I left my original group? Pastor Stan personally went to the group one day, before I arrived, having called them at to a pre-meeting meeting, to tell them I was a loose woman who wanted to make a pastor, you, love me. He told them that you and your wife had had enough with me pursuing you and stalking you. He also told them I had mental problems and to treat me like crap, to get me to see the error of my ways. You know how I know this? A couple from the Philippines, that attended the group, came and told me. They told me to watch out because Stan was trying to destroy me. They said they knew me and respected me and were leaving the church, because of Stan's lies. They thought they should come and tell me, before they left; so I might confront Stan. I got sick to my stomach that that man had resorted to out and out lies, telling everyone in my home group, basically, I was a whore. Then I heard, from a friend, you had stopped attending your cousin's meeting. So I decided to go since it was the nearest group to my house. Also, since I knew I was innocent; I had nothing to fear. Once I got there, I could see Stan had again spoken to the group. They had a very rude attitude towards me, from the moment I entered the room. After about three meetings, I went to your cousin, in a respectful manner, and asked her if she might help me talk to you to, get all of the mess cleaned up. She then told me off. She said she didn't like me and that because of me you could no longer come to the group. She didn't want me to come back.

Alex looked surprised, "That is not what Stan told me. He told me that you were disruptive to the group and threatened my cousin. He said you told her you were at the meeting to confront me in front of the others. Man, can that guy lie or what? I'm so sorry Rhoda. I'm betting about 90% or more of what he said about you, was one big fat lie. Forgive me for believing him. I knew you were my friend. I guess I didn't think that a fellow pastor could be such an outrageous liar. Man! Okay, I want to ask a second question. A few times we met in groceries and on the street and you had perfect chances, to speak to me; but you didn't say anything. Why was that? I was under a ban, to not speak. You didn't have that ban, once you left the church, so why didn't you just speak up? Why didn't you just come to my house or try harder to reach me? Your attempts seemed kind of half hearted at times."

"Well now, what was I supposed to do? As far as talking goes, the hurt was so deep and the attitude you had was, so rude that I couldn't find the words to say. I tried to utter, even a phrase, and sound would not come out. Whenever I did muster up the courage to speak, you kept looking around, like you were going to get killed by Stan. I felt all of this pressure to say whatever I had to say as shortly and concisely as possible; before you ran away or saw one of "them". I couldn't gather my thoughts quick enough. Most of the time, I also had just prayed and asked God to let me speak to you and 'boink!'; there you were. I was overwhelmed and speechless. But as far as me trying 'half heartedly', to reach out to you, I think you are crazy. When everything first happened I sent letters, cards, emails, and called you. I had so much to say and I tried to tell you how I felt, but you just never responded. I only got those silent calls and blank emails and I never really could tell if you sent them because you agreed with me or were trying to reassure me, or were trying to warn me. I had to make up, in my head, what they meant. Over time, I felt that maybe I was guilty of overkill. I concluded that I would just send one sentence replies to you to basically thank you for the silent calls or blank emails and to remind you that I still wished to reconcile. I kept up this 'game' with you for fifteen years, almost daily; I don't really feel it was a half hearted attempt. Also did you know that Stan continued to send me threatening letters, phone calls, emails and 'threat messengers' both civilian and police to scare me into not contacting you? Also they hired a security guard, on your church property, to keep me from coming to your office. Did you know all of this was going full steam, up until just four years ago? Stan threatened me on a continuous basis, though to a lesser degree, up until last year. Anything I did, in open and standard fashion, to contact you was always intercepted by him either before or after you saw it. So I had to contact you with our code system. Anytime I contacted you I actually risked being sued. Did you realize this?"

"Actually I knew very little of what went on between you and Stan and the church. They kept most of what they said or did to you from me. I only knew what they did, on my side, and when it actually involved me; or Stan wished to share his triumphs with me. They also, always found anything I tried to send out to you. Whatever got to you, I tell you, was only a small part of what I sent. I did try to call you and speak. They had bugged the phone and so any attempt had to stop. They said they'd sue me, for harassing you in the church's name. I wasn't harassing you and you wanted to hear from me; but in order to scare me they told me that anything I did would be a violation of a written policy I'd signed. The stupid thing is, I fell for signing that original document when I had put it in front of me after beating me down. I just wanted to get over with the abuse. That's why I developed the silent calls and blank email underground message system, with you. I was under legal constraint, because in a moment of weakness I signed a document to stop Stan's constant verbal and sometimes physical abuse. Stan would sometimes twist my arm behind me, till it almost popped the socket and subjected me to other other forms of torture. I'm glad he didn't do anything physical to you. Mostly I sent the silent calls and emails to "tell" you I agreed with your one liner notes or something you say to me on the phone, and to reassure you of my continued friendship. Believe me I was always grateful for your kind words. I was glad that you seemed to get what I was trying to say to you, even if it was done silently."

Rhoda shook her head, "What kind of demonic monsters did you and I submit to? I also believed most of their threats. Stan was always so dark and he would say 'lovely things' like: he was going to tell my husband I was a cheating whore and that he'd be believed because he was a pastor and I was a mere woman, etc. Some pastor! Okay here is one thing I've been wondering. How come the various jobs, I applied for, after leaving your service, were told that I never worked for you? Why would you do that? Why not just give them a perfunctory quick statement saying how I was a good worker and send me out into another career? Why lie about me working for you? Why did you also not stand up for me when folks from your church lied and just say some perfunctory statement like, 'Rhoda is a nice person; I'm not going to have you speak ill about her,' and leave it at that? Why lie and say, 'She is delusional or the affair is over,'? All you had to do was make a simple statement and not lie. Why lie?"

"Rhoda, both Stan and the head pastor told me to say three things: '1. She never worked for me. 2. The affair is over now, or 3. Rhoda is delusional and thinks she is in love with me.' That was all I was allowed to say to inquiries about you. Oh, yes, I could also say, 'That is very interesting; let me talk it over with those who are in charge of me.' I was constantly watched and evaluated. If I ever went off script, they said I would be fired, perhaps sued. They warned I would lose all of my benefits and never ever be a pastor again, at any church. I did tell one more lie. When people would ask me to reconcile with you and make things right, I usually said, 'I don't know where you got the idea I wanted to reconcile or speak in any way to Rhoda. I hardly know her and I have no wish to speak to her.' That one I made up and they approved of it. Our whole goal was to make you look crazy. First, we wanted folks to think I didn't know you, or hardly did; then we wanted people to think you were in love with me, stalking me, and that I had no clue, as to why. I was supposed to appear concerned for you; but when folks told me lies about you or asked questions I was just supposed to have a concerned look on my face, like you would with any crazy person. I never told anyone, who lied about you, to stop or called them out on their lie. I never acknowledged that we were friends or that I had continued to know you, for all of these years. If I had done anything differently; I'd no longer have this job and might even be in jail. Stan vowed, on his own life, to keep us apart and he was committed to doing this or to die trying."

Rhoda's face was red and she had her fist curled. "Man, I'd love to smack those guys. Why did they treat me like that? I am their sister in Jesus. Alex how did you sleep at night knowing I was in so much pain and that Stan and others in leadership were abusing me? Why didn't you try and come to me secretly and at least tell me your predicament. I'd have been stronger if I knew you were on my side; but couldn't do anything to change the situation. Just that alone would have helped a lot. Instead, I was left on the side of the road to rot. I was a nice lady and at the time, a mommy. So it was okay to sacrifice me. I meant nothing and no one would notice or care. Is that how it worked?"

"Well actually, yes; that is how it worked. When we looked at the whole situation, it made sense; you were only a woman, a mommy, who was once a teacher. You had no worth in our eyes; you did not have a theological degree. Who were you to any one important, in our little limited world? The answer was: no one. We could not sacrifice the church's reputation or my job, since I was such a good children's pastor. To top it off, your husband was strangely silent on the whole issue, and you had no real position in the church or community. You were expendable. We chose to sacrifice you for everyone else's better good. Also, as you know, we were collecting money, for the big building project, the multi-purpose facility. We could not risk a single dollar not coming in, because of some scandal. It was over two million dollars and we wanted to have all the money, before the project even started. We didn't want to have any debt. We thought the people would think this type of thinking would mean God was in the whole building project and we wanted to look good. So you were like a little fly in the ointment and we knew you did not count in the entire scheme of things. You just did not matter. I say this now with a knife in my heart. Rhoda, if I had any sin in this; it was the sin of just letting them 'rape' you. I stood by and watched the whole process, without helping you. I am party to a gang rape, committed by the pastors at my church, and lead by Pastor Stan. Other than the attack, that is my greatest sin."

Rhoda started to cry as hard as I had ever heard anyone cry. It turned into a loud gut wrenching wale that came from the depths of her soul. Alex had expressed what she had sensed, all along; but was unable to articulate. I got up and put my arm around her shoulders and she cried onto my sweater, until she could cry no more. Her whole face was swollen and she was trembling. "I do have worth; I do have worth. I am at least equal in worth to any of the sons of bitches, don't pardon my French, that had the gall to call themselves pastors, at your church. Alex, why did you let them do this to me, why? I forgive you; but I have to tell you I always stood for you and never told people anything negative about you. Even if I told a couple of best girlfriends what you did; I told them I'd forgiven you. I told them I knew you cared about me and had made a misjudgment. I always made you look better than the truth. Why just throw me to the dogs, and let them have their way with me?" She laid her head on her arm and wept some more. I was going to stop the session; but I thought this would not be the way to have them leave. I decided to continue on with the session as I had originally planned it.

I got up and gave Rhoda a cup of soda from the fridge and a kleenex. She gladly drank it to get her composure back and wiped her nose and eyes. I told her, "Rhoda, don't be ashamed of your tears. Believe me they are the expression of the deep pain, you have felt all of these years; maybe it is good that Alex sees how they made you feel. Alex, do you get the reason, why, her sorrow is so deep? First of all, the pastors, mainly Stan, treated her as less than human. Secondly she felt betrayed by you, her best friend. What would you like to say to her about those atrocities?"

Alex got off of his chair and knelt in front of Rhoda. He also began to cry; his cry was more of a moan from the depths of his soul. When he finally could speak he said, "Forgive me, precious, friend. My passivity was just as cruel as Stan's verbal blows to your soul. I let them take you and rub your face in the muck and mire; I turned my head away. I wanted to save my precious position and my place of authority and privilege. I was a monster. I ask now, at this late date, for you to forgive my sin." He began to cry on her forearm, she patted his shoulder, and said, "I do forgive you and I am still your friend. Your seeing how this hurt me, has given me a glimmer of hope for your soul. I do now see you are truly repentant. It is alright now." She even wiped his tears with her sweater sleeve, like a mother to her child. He returned to his chair.

I cleared my throat and said, "I don't want to seem insensitive; but I do need to ask you both, how you feel you have benefitted from this whole experience. What good lessons did you learn through all of this suffering? Was all of this worth it?"

Rhoda had calmed down enough to be able to proceed with the session and to answer this question. "Before all of this happened I was a believer. I became a Christian when I was 15 going on 16. Almost 30 years later, at 44; I got into this strange situation with Alex and his church. I was a normal believer, with the ups and downs of life that everyone goes through; except for the time I was in my first cult, that is. I had times of great joy like when I got married and had my daughter. And times of great sorrow, like when I lost my twin babies. That experience and other life experiences caused a certain amount of growth in my life. All and all, I was a naturally happy person with a positive outlook on life, even when I was in the first cult, in the midst of all that suffering; I was basically still sunny in my outlook. When I lost the twin babies, it took two years before I could laugh again. But in time, I was happy go lucky me again. Even my previous cult experiences didn't dampen my enthusiasm for life. But this thing, this thing, came out of the blue and took all the wind out of my sails. I had never been betrayed, by a good friend, nor had I ever seen such out and out cruelty by leadership, even in my first cult. Nor had I ever had a situation that didn't seem to get fixed or worked out, in some way, eventually. Yet, in this thing, God also never spoke so clearly to me, or was with me so palatably, or made such glorious promises to me. I was devastated and literally destroyed, by this whole thing. But I came out of it knowing God better, deeper, and stronger than I ever had. I learned to hear God speak and saw actual visions and miracles right before my eyes, on a sometimes daily basis. Beyond this, I learned about forgiveness and reconciliation in much deeper ways than I ever had before. These words went from mere concepts to actual realities, that transformed my life. I also learned what true friendship was and how to tell real Christianity from fake and real servants of God from imposters. I had learned this from my first cult experience, to some degree. This was on a much deeper level. I learned to have faith in God and how He loved me. I also learned the depth of my husband's care and love for me. So this is what I learned in a general nutshell. I have individual examples of all of these things; but I think I don't need to go into those right now."

I sat speechless for a moment and then turned to Alex and asked him the same question. He said, "I have finally seen myself for what I am, in the clearest light, I ever could have. Yes, Mark, I'm still going to come back here with my wife; but this is what I have gotten so far: 1. I have used women all my life to try and fix a broken place inside me and I never loved any of them as I should have, even my wife. 2. I have been passive in most of my interactions, mostly out of fear. But also hoping things would somehow take care of themselves and, you know, they never do. 3. I have not known how to be a real friend; until Rhoda taught me. 4. I have been faking my service and love to God, only wanting to be respected by others, but not out of a real passion or heart for Him. 5. I have put my values on the wrong things and given my allegiance to things that were not of value to God. Namely I stayed in this church for my glory, even when I knew it was a evil dark place that destroyed believers. I see the negative things, I put my hope in; but I also now see the more positive things: 1. How to love women purely, as friends, and how to respect and honor my wife. 2. How it is a good thing to stand for the truth and protect others, to not be passive. 3. How to value a friendship. 4. How to love God, serve Him from the heart and not care what others think. 5. How to value what is good and true and not what looks good. I'm sure I've learned more, including how lying destroys lives and walking honestly before God and others build people up. I'm certain I'll learn even more when my wife and I come back for counseling for our issues. But, Rhoda, Mark, I'm grateful to you both. Really I am. I can now be real and genuine, no more acting holy or trying to please others, for me."

I shook my head, to snap me out of my state of shock. "I am so in awe right now. Do you know how elated I feel? God is so good and so kind; isn't He? I will meet with you both next week. I think we might have that as our last meeting, with just the three of us; before we introduce your spouses into the mix. Alright? Oh Alex I have two questions. The first one is: Just what have you been telling your church, about why you come to see me? I got a note from your office wanting a detailed reason for your treatment. Knowing cults I decided to come to you first. I am planning on saying you are here to get a better and deeper love for your wife. How does that sound? Is this close to what you are telling them? Secondly: What is happening with your retirement home issues and are you planning on remaining in this church? Are you still a pastor?"

"Well I did say I was coming here for marital counseling; which they highly approved of. Usually, they frown on pastors admitting they need help. Since they know some of my past troubles with women and how I had a few rumors going around about me, they actually are encouraging this. I told you, most of the people who were in the office when Rhoda was there, are no longer at the church, didn't I? So most everyone knows there is trouble with me and my wife; but no specifics. So I would appreciate it if you focused more on my relationship with my wife, when you communicate with them. Thanks for waiting to respond to them. Secondly: they said I most likely will not be able to go to the pastors' retirement home. I'm not exactly, a pastor in good standing, anymore; but nothing official has been done on this issue, no formal removing of my title. I am thinking of leaving the church; but don't know where to go yet, so I've not given them my resignation papers. Do pray for me; it isn't easy for me to do this for loads of reasons. My wife is not happy about this, at all, and maybe I can have her call you and talk more about it. This is all I can tell you at this time. I'm proceeding, just slowly."

I stood up and shook Alex's hand. "I am so proud of you for your steps in the right direction. Wonderful! Glory to God! Rhoda, please search your heart to be sure you keep forgiving all of this that you faced today. You know forgiveness is the best way to be free and you have already forgiven so much." I gave her a slight hug and helped her on with her jacket. The three of us walked to the door and they went and made their appointments. I went back into my office and got on my knees and prayed for about an hour. I wanted to tell my wife everything that evening at the Italian restaurant. Instead I asked her about her week. Glory!

Chapter 24

The evening before Rhoda and Alex's appointment, I sat in my study thinking about the whole situation. I could see that both Rhoda and Alex were near the end of working on this issue, but I still felt there were loose ends that needed to be shored up. It is one thing to clearly see our problems and name them and another thing to conquer them and to learn to live in a different manner. I also know that many Christians out there think forgiveness and reconciliation are the same thing basically. One pastor even said, to me, "Reconciliation is just a 'fancy-smansy' word for forgiveness." He could not have been more wrong. Rhoda and Alex had totally forgiven each other, before they entered my office. These last few months they had begun to walk through the process of reconciliation; and it is a process. Things had gone so easily and quickly; because they had walked through much of it before even coming into my office. The sessions, I shared with you, might have seemed, too cut and dry. But you must remember, they had already gone through fifteen years of being taught and molded by God, in these areas. Most of the work was done, before they ever thought of coming to see me for help. I was just the one who facilitated bringing all the loose ends together in a neat reconciliation package.

There is a type of reconciliation, that I call 'limited reconciliation', in which the individuals agree to give up resentment and anger, try and clarify some of their motives and some of the things they did to the other person. But when that process is over, the people basically shake hands and walk away in peace. This is usually the type that is done with individuals who were involved in something immoral or violent. If Alex had actually gotten more carried away and actually raped Rhoda; I'd have definitely suggested the limited reconciliation process. Because with a crime like rape or murder or some other extreme violence, you must do all to keep the victim safe. But if a person, who was a friend, loses control for a moment or two, and yet does not fully act out on animal urges, I leave the decision totally up to the clients. Who among us has not fantasized about a friend or a colleague being our mate, even just for a brief moment? If we are honest, just about all of us have; even if the thought was not a sexually explicit. But if you are a relatively civilized person, you usually just move on to more constructive thoughts and feelings. Now Alex did act on his fantasies, this is true; but on the other hand he still was able to keep himself from going 'all out' and actually raping Rhoda. Was what he did right? No. Could they learn to be real friends and not cross over any borders? Yes, I think they could. The only snag I could foresee, in this was: could their spouses accept their friendship and might their friendship, even if they stayed pure, somehow hurt their respective marriages? This again only the clients could decide and of course their spouses. I never recommend going forward in even a reconciled relationship, if the spouses are not comfortable; marriage is sacred and not even a God ordained friendship, should stand in the way of that. I do sometimes have the people sit down with their spouses and map out a plan for how they would like the friendship to proceed. This can go anywhere from ending the relationship totally, to having the spouses put specific limits on the friendship. One such group came up with the decision that the friends could email each other, once every two weeks and on holidays, and that they could be invited to attend doings at each of the couple's homes; but there should be no other contact. If an emergency came up and there had to be a phone call then the spouse was to be informed, before the call was made or told the moment the spouse could be contacted, if it was something that could not wait. This was acceptable to the two reconciled friends and everyone was happy with this arrangement. So, too, I knew that Rhoda and Alex would have to either totally end their friendship or have a similar setup, to the one I just gave as an example, with a tweak here and there, perhaps. I wondered how the spouses would choose to see the friendship play out.

I scratched my nighttime beard and got up to shut the light and go to bed. My wife was already snoring lightly and I kissed her gently on the forehead. I then prayed for about twenty minutes for the Lord's direction for the session, in the morning, and watched some CNN news. I went to sleep forgetting to shut off the set. I awoke at 5am the next morning, shut off the TV, and went out into the back yard to use our hot tub. The warm water felt good, I napped for another half hour and had a short time of prayer in the tub as the sun was coming up. I put on my terry robe and went into the kitchen and whipped up an asparagus frittata for my wife and I and made a pot of that chocolate tea and put out some fresh muffins, from the bakery. My wife awoke when the muffins began to warm in the oven. We put everything on a tray and went and sat in our garden. I have to confess, my wife is most beautiful, to me, when she first gets up. She looks about ten years younger than when she gets all made up for the day. She doesn't have any makeup on, her freckles are all over her face, and her hair is usually gathered up in a top of the head ponytail. I never really was a fan of the 'perfect little church woman' look. I make sure she normally doesn't wear the church lady suits and tailored clothes; I like her more casual. She is most comfy in jeans, a sweater and blouse and that is how I prefer her too. But the just awakened look is my favorite. Anyway, she asked how my work was going and if I was going to be seeing my favorite clients? I told her I was and that in two years, instead of four like I told her before, I could tell her most of the story, with changed names and places, of course. She laughed and said, "Well, looks like I have to stay married to you for at least two more years then." I distractedly said, "Yes…hey wait a minute." I threw a crumb at her and she laughed and stuck out her tongue and ran into the house. I cleared the table and ran up the stairs to get ready for work. When I came down, she was washing the dishes and I playfully smacked her backside with my brief case as I headed out the door. I was a bit too relaxed on the Bart and slept all the way to the Embarcadero station.

I opened my eyes just in time to jump on to the platform and bumped right into Alex who must have been in the train car next to mine.

"Good morning, Alex. You are a bit early aren't you? Notice how chilly it is? It is literally only warm here about ten days per year here. Oh…I'll stop blathering. You look troubled. What is it, my friend? Want to grab a chai with me? There is a coffee/chai shop downstairs from my office. Would that be okay?"

Alex put his hands in his pockets and said, "I'd really appreciate that, Mark; I do need to talk to someone and it isn't always comfortable in front of Rhoda. You catch my drift?"

"Sure," with that I grabbed his elbow and lead him to the shop. "Alex, let's get chais for us now and grab three more and three cookies on the way out. Okay?" He nodded. I made the order and claimed two of those big cozy chairs, that are always full, but weren't on that day, and sat down.

"Okay, let me get right to it, Mark… I…I just don't love my wife. Even without Rhoda, anywhere in my future, I just don't think I can ever muster up a feeling I never really had. I had the feeling of real love, to be honest, maybe twice in my life. Once was with a girl I loved when I was about eighteen and the second time was with Rhoda. The rest of the time was more or less sexual feelings only. I want to do the right thing and make up for all of my sins against her and God; but I don't know if I can pretend to love her, until I die. Rhoda made her choice and it was her husband. My wife wants to try again and I have even started to look for new pastor positions in our area. So it looks like things are coming together, in some areas; but I don't feel satisfied. I feel like a phony. I was a phony for years both in my marriage and at church; don't get me wrong, but now I actually feel the phoniness and I hate that feeling." He wiped away a stray tear and gazed into his chai. He took a sip and said, "I never had this stuff; it's not too bad. But, Mark, what should I do?"

I could see how this was a dilemma for him and one I would not want to have. "You know Alex, I'm going to say something to you that I usually don't say to any of my clients, or friends for that matter. When we are done, with this group of sessions, with you and Rhoda, which should be in a couple of weeks, then let's start right away with special counseling sessions, for you and your wife. Divorce is a big step and can impact many lives, so jumping into that would not be feasible. Whatever you decide remember it will affect, all of your family, for years to come. If when we finish the sessions with you and your wife and you still feel the same, then let's have a talk with your wife and try to have, what they call in the media: an amicable divorce. Sure everyone still gets hurt even in an amicable divorce; but I can at least help soften the blow and show you two how to muddle through something like that. What do you say? Promise you won't go out and find a solution in another woman and that you will give me and God time to work? Promise?"

Alex stuck out his hand and shook my extended hand. "I promise and I want to thank you; if this was my church, they'd have threatened me into complying; and it would have been against my will. In this case, I am totally choosing to try your way. Say didn't Rhoda just walk by the window? I think that was her. We'd better get those cookies and chais. We should get the black and white cookies; they are Rhoda's favorites." We put our cups in the trash and finished our order. We then went out into the chilly dampness and up the stairs to my office. Rhoda was speaking to Helen and they were laughing, as Alex and I entered the outer office. She turned as we entered.

"So were you two plotting against me, huh? You guys probably made plans on how to ask and answer today's questions. Hmmmm. Two against one, I should be offended." Rhoda did a fake pout and winked at Helen. We all entered my inner office and while they got settled I took care of both the fire and Max's needs. By the time that was done, everyone was cozy and each of us had our chai and cookie in front of us.

"Actually, Rhoda, I bumped into Alex at the train station and we went for a pre-chai chai and spoke about an issue that didn't concern you, alright? Just to be clear... I do hope that you both have a question or two for each other. In the reconciliation process questions keep coming to the surface. This is the nature of the beast. People say that forgiveness is like an onion and if you peel away one layer and forgive that that there is always another. Now that's true; but to me reconciliation is even more so. You forgive someone and even go through a few of the onion layers of forgiveness. Then you decide to reconcile and find that there are seemingly unending layers of questions about motives and actions taken, during the situation. Some things need to be exposed to be truly forgiven or reconciled. I remember one pastor who said that a client, who was seeing me, only needed at the most two reconciliation meetings and that that should be plenty enough. The client and perpetrator ended up spending a year and a half talking through everything. Last time I saw her, she said that even now, three years later, they still speak about certain unclear motives from their situation, when they go for coffee. They find that when they face the questions and don't avoid them, that their friendship only increases and that little unhealed areas get healed, as they speak. So don't be surprised if this sort of thing happens in your relationship too."

Alex spoke up, "You know it is funny, in a sad way. But Pastor Stan actually told Rhoda, he and some other pastors had reconciled, for us, and that we were done. We didn't need to speak one on one, to each other. That is like getting married to a person for someone else. That can't be done. No wonder Rhoda looked at him like he was an escapee from an institution for the criminally insane. That statement was insane. He was a pastor according to his degree, yet he could not in any way feel for humans or understand basic human emotions. Sad. So sorry Rhoda, that that way of thinking, was forced on you. Any way I did wonder did you go to Life College to become a pastor? Whatever happened to that whole thing? Wasn't there something strange with the youth pastor? Did you graduate? I was too busy being abused, at that moment, to know what was happening to you."

Rhoda looked surprised, "Alex I really thought you were a much better 'stalker'. It seems like you weren't 'up to par' on your game. Well, I knew that the youth pastor was, out of the loop, with the rest of the older pastors. He didn't hang out with all old timer pastors. I thought maybe he did not know what I was going through, with the church. When Pastor Stan said to me that all I was good for was 'being a housewife or babysitting at church', instead of smacking him in the head; I decided to go to school and maybe take his job someday. So I enrolled at Life Bible College because it was part of your church's system. I took the maximum load in order to graduate in two years. I was then going to decide, if I wanted to go for my Master's of Divinity degree, once I became a pastor. Believe it or not, I got all A's, maybe one B+, and the school asked me to not do my work so well, because I went beyond the knowledge of the pastors who were my professors. As I was set to do my second year, God said to me, 'Do you want to be a pastor just to get back at Pastor Stan or to serve Me?' I saw I was just trying to stick it to Stan and so I dropped out. I felt vindicated that I could have easily done his job; but I wasn't happy with my motives. Oh yes, the youth pastor got fired; because he recommended me to the Bible College and he, unknowingly, went against Pastor Stan. He saw that I was a godly woman; but he didn't know Pastor Stan had a vendetta against me. I still feel sorry for him. Later he told me I should have told him Stan hated me."

"So sorry, Rhoda. I wish you would have finished. I always said you were smart. You just made a couple of errors, when you were my assistant that drove me crazy, at the time. I do want to apologize for three things. I apologize for yelling at you about that poster. I admit I never told you any specifics and I just thought you would have known. Unless you read minds; you never could have known what I wanted. I apologize for thinking you stole money from the seminar and that you purposely messed up the computer work. I did not know you had a different Windows program system at home. You were Window's 97 and we were Window's 95. That was not your fault; I blocked access to our church computers, so the problem was never caught. Lastly, I apologize for not standing up for you more with Stan and others at church. I have never really said I was sorry for those things and I am so very sorry." Rhoda put out her hand and placed it on his arm.

Rhoda spoke next, "Okay this question is more serious. I have wanted to ask it for a couple of weeks. Are you more computer savvy than you have let on to others? I mean are you a hacker and do you have the ability to do video and sound bites, on me, through my computer? I won't have you arrested; I just need to know. You see some things were just too, coincidental' and though I believe that God hears prayer, I still think you may have hacked my computer a few times and possibly heard some of

my prayers for you, maybe through some audible type hacking. You can-
-come clean; we won't look down on you, though I again feel vulnerable
and exposed. Were you hearing my prayers through an audible or visual
hacking device or some sort? My husband and I have a camera on our
computer for Skpe; they see it can be used for that. Tell me."

Alex got red and started to squirm in his chair, much like Rhoda
described went on in the session with the lawyer at their church. He
said, "Well yes and no. I mean I am fully capable of computer hacking.
I do this for a hobby, even though it is illegal. But you did find me out,
it seems,; so I'm not as smooth at it as I thought. You used to have these
long sessions of prayer for me that were almost any hour long, in front of
your computer terminal. I usually got bored after a few minutes, or so; but
sometimes I did hear the whole prayers. I'd get guilty that I was listening
in on your prayers to God and I'd shut the hacking devise off. I only had
audio equipment, no visual. Then I'd contact you, when I figured you
were done. I did hack into your emails, Facebook, and even My Space, at
the beginning, but I stopped that after a couple of months. I read articles
you wrote that were for the public, like your Facebook statuses and your
forum articles and your blogs. I didn't have the ability to listen in on phone
calls. I did this only when I was bored or wondering what you were up
to. Actually, as much as you write, I'm sure I only scratched the surface.
Much of your early stuff was about me and I'd hack in to see what you were
telling others. You did discuss me with many people on those sites, even
though you never mentioned me by name. I got a bit mad about that. But
if I told anyone, they'd know I'd hacked your computer. I could have gone
to jail for that; so I basically kept the information to myself. I noticed you
stopped praying for me in front of your screen and so I disconnected my
listening device. That was all I used it for. After all I and the others did to
you I really couldn't blame you for discussing the whole thing with others.
There, I've confessed. I want to apologize and to thank you for all of your
prayers. Do you still pray for me? I know I was wrong; but they wouldn't
let me speak with you and that is how I stayed connected."

"So most of the time you contacted me was because you heard me
through the computer and it wasn't a God thing?! Wow, that rocks my

world. But I suppose you needed to hear those prayers. You sometimes followed me around town too, didn't you? (He nodded.) Is that how you knew where to call me? (He nodded again.) But how did you get away from work to do those things? I worked strange part-time hours; yet you always knew when I was in my different offices, at the various jobs I had."

"Sometimes I just found out from folks, who knew you, when and where you were working and sometimes I did 'stalk' you. I'd look around town for your car. When I was at work I used to make an excuse like, I needed to pick up something for the Children's Ministry. No one ever questioned me. Stan thought he had me totally tracked on my phones and computer, but I had alternate phones and computer sites. I guess I could have spoken or written to you on the sly; but I was afraid to trust you. I had made a promise to not speak to or contact you. Which I broke on one level; but I kept on another. Complex, huh? Looking back, how I kept that all up for so many years, I'll never know. Part of me was also always trying to stick it to Stan, like you." Alex was totally exposed and this transparency was a new thing for him. He had been so used to lying.

All Rhoda could manage to say, to all of that honesty, was, "Wow."

After their questions for each other, were done, I saw that I had very little to ask them about. I think that they had figured out much of the aspects, of how to do their own healing; but I wanted them to get the full benefit of the session; so I decided to press them a bit more.

"Both of you have been more than honest. I have two questions for you both. Where are you with this whole thing, in your relationship to God, today and what direction would you like to see this friendship take after the final meetings are accomplished?" I wanted to see how realistic they both were, at that time in their relationship. We all want different things when a relationship first ends, than when we do a few years down the road. This was more than a few years; it was over fifteen and I knew both of them had changed, considerably, in what they wanted.

Alex raised his hand, "May I share first? When I first had my feelings for Rhoda and tried to share them with her and she rejected me, I was angry. I told myself she had lead me on. I thought, she thought, she was too good for me. I thought that I was actually better than her. I also

249

thought she was trying to destroy my life, by telling everyone. But when the anger subsided I missed her. I missed her terribly. She worked for me for awhile, after the incident; but we could no longer talk because of the woman that Stan placed in our office and church's spies. Also Rhoda was no longer as trusting and so she pulled back from speaking with me. But in my demented mind, I thought she'd come to her senses. That she'd beg me to forgive her, to want her again. I thought she'd leave her husband and run away with me. I thought she'd see how I was the better man. I prayed she'd see that; that was how I was praying. I actually prayed for her to commit adultery with me. Odd, huh? She chose her husband. I had a hard time facing this. I thought she'd come around eventually. She didn't. So I began to pray for me to change my feelings, After about five years, I think I finally got it that she was another man's wife and I was wrong to try to take her advantage, like that. Today I pray for her best and that she'd be blest and that somehow, on some level, we could be friends. I'm willing to accept whatever her husband is comfortable with; but I hope I don't have to totally cut off relations. I want to be able to contact her, but this time in a healthy way, with words, be they words on the phone or in an email. I would love if she'd occasionally come to my church (if I stay), with her husband and perhaps some social situations, again with her husband, of course. But I have finally accepted we can never be alone again or have a close friendship again. That is where I am at."

"Rhoda." Rhoda was smiling because she seemed to have a similar plan in mind and she was happy he sounded logical.

"Well, Doc, I am really kind where he is at today. I never wanted him to leave his wife for me. In fact, I kept trying to get him to know and love her more. I wanted him to see her value and what a great woman she was and is. I truly used to wish, at the beginning, that we could be in the ministry together, whether in Children's Ministry or in a new ministry. This desire changed as time went on. Then I came to hope, he'd preach about reconciliation with me and that we would speak to huge crowds about our story. I wanted to be his partner, in that type of ministry, and serve him as his assistant, again. I used to pray for this for years. But then, these last eight years, God said to me that the ministry was to be my own and that he was not to be a part of it. I did have a couple of visions on how he might be a guest speaker, on rare occasions; but I have stopped wanting to have any co-ministry with him. He has a ministry of his own to fulfill, whatever that is. I'm not in control of his life. I now pray for him to increase in his love for his wife and kids, to be free from the cult, and to follow the Lord with a pure heart and not go after any more women. I pray that God will honor him for choosing to leave the cult and to choose honesty and godliness, over power and corruption. I see him as a friend and am willing to follow both his wife's and my husband's friendship boundaries, whatever they feel comfortable with. To be honest, I also can accept, if they totally cut off our friendship. I mainly have wanted to see this reconciliation and with this happening, I'm content, either way. I truly am your friend Alex; but I also truly am madly in love with my husband. I want him to be pleased with our friendship and not insecure about how I feel about you. I don't want him to always wonder."

I thought they both skipped the part about where they were with God now, when answering my questions. I did feel I had to ask this, that it was important. "I didn't get where both of you were with God in this situation? Could you clarify that a bit more for me?"

Rhoda spoke first, "Well, as I shared I went through various stages and at first I really believed His promises were for Alex and I to be in the ministry. I was so sure the God wanted one thing and then I saw that He wants to do another. At the beginning of this journey, I'd have gotten freaked out that God had somehow lied or changed His mind. But now I feel that God must have redirected His promises, maybe this was because of weaknesses in Alex and myself. I think He will still do His promises, just in a bit of a tweaked version. God can not lie. So God and I are cool. He has a purpose for my life and for Alex's and we shouldn't let any naysayers block us.

Alex then said, "Rhoda, I admire your being willing to let God redirect you. I thought that God had brought you into my life, to be in a work with me, also. I even thanked Him for that. But I left out two important people, our spouses. I was mad at God for awhile that you weren't willing to go with what I thought was God's plan for us. But over

251

time I have come to see God would never destroy two homes so that two people could marry and have a ministry. I see that that way of thinking was mine and not God's. I truly have gotten this and I now am "cool" with God like you. I am thankful that you kept me from sinning with you, too. I'm not sure I ever told you that." He sighed and looked at the floor.

I rubbed my hands together and wanted to dance, but decided that would look a bit weird. So I said, "This has been a great experience for me! I cannot contain my joy at seeing the powerful hand of God. Wow! Changing modes for a moment… Okay let me tell you the plan here. Next week will be our final session with you two and me. Your homework is to tell me what your future plans are, both for your callings and your marriages and your current relationships with your children. After that meeting, we will make arrangements to have your spouses join us for the next session. Then we will have a final session which will be a two parter. Part one will be a meeting with your children and part two we will have a meeting with all the cast of characters. We want to make sure that everyone is clear with each other, no going away with a grudge. I will also have a catered dinner party, for all of you, here in the office right after that mega session. Nothing fancy, but something where you all can have a chance to relax and even get to know all of the 'cast members' as people. So this makes three more meetings. If, after that time, either of you or your families wish to see me, independently, about these things, we can arrange that. Then I'm hoping to have both of you back for the separate issues, we mentioned. Alex will be meeting me with his wife and Rhoda will be meeting me about her Assembly experiences, for the most part. Then, Rhoda, maybe we can have a few meetings with your husband, at the end of that time, to help him deal with any anger issues or confusions. Alright? I just want to make sure we are all on the same page. Any questions?"

Alex stood up and shook my hand, "Sounds good, Mark." Rhoda got up and gave me a little hug, "Doc, this has been fantastic; better than I could have imagined or hoped for."

"Hey, you two, don't act like this is the farewell meeting. These next three sessions are going to knock our socks off, I think. They are all going to be such wild cards. Also, I will be glad to be a friend, to both of you;

after your second set of sessions are done. I might even invite you guys, with your spouses to my house for dinners, if this is acceptable to everyone. I actually feel like we've all become friends, not just business associates. Let's leave this all in God's hands. Shall we?"

They went and made their appointments and I went back into my office and began to praise God and I even did a little dance. Max loved the dance part.

Chapter 25

When I woke up on Thursday morning I knew something wasn't right. My arm was lying under me, but facing the wrong direction and I was in great pain. I almost cried, but didn't want to freak out my wife. So I said in a trembly, calm voice, "Honey, we have to go to the emergency room. I am in a lot of pain. Don't worry it's not my heart; but I seem to have popped my arm out of its socket. I don't think I can change my clothes. Just get me to the emergency room. I may pass out in a second." She jumped out of bed and put on a jogging outfit and quick combed her hair and brushed her teeth, a two minute job. But to me it seemed like hours. I began to get wobbly and she grabbed my good arm to steady me. She got a wool neck scarf and secured my hanging arm to my chest which helped in one way and hurt like "heck" in another way. Then she put on my slippers and put a shawl over my shoulders and we were out the door. I fainted in the hallway at the hospital, on the way to the ER, and woke up in a sunny room. A cheery little nurse told me that a doctor would be right in to see me.

"Hi Mark, Dr. Wong, here. You really did pull that out. I would have thought that the pain would have woken you up, and yet you only noticed it when you woke up. You can sure endure a lot of pain."

"Well I occasionally take a prescribed sleeping pill and that puts me out like a rock. I have a meeting at my work today and I am so excited about it; I couldn't sleep. So....Well, can I go to work at 3pm today? Can I take the pain medication after my meeiing? I really need to go."

Dr. Wong rubbed his mustache. "Well normally I ask patients to rest; but you seem so determined to go...alright; but someone else will have to drive you. You can't drive maybe for a week or so. Do you have a driver? (I nodded.) Do you promise to rest before and after your meeting? (I nodded again and realized that they hadn't given me anything for the pain, which was building to a crescendo as I spoke to him. A small scream came out involuntarily from my mouth.) "I'll give you a shot for pain in your arm muscle and it will numb the shoulder. Here is a prescription for the pain meds. I think you will be okay, until after your meeting; but then you are really going to feel this. So don't forget to take these, okay?" He handed me the prescription and then he and the little nurse sat me up and she held me down while the doctor popped my arm back into the socket. I think I screamed quite loudly; because my wife came running in from the waiting area, which was about half a block away. When she came in I was smiling and weeping at the same time. It was back in the socket, but that really hurt and the muscle was really sore.

"I thought they killed a water buffalo." My wife can make a joke about anything.

"I sounded that bad, huh? Sorry. Dr. Wong said that you will need to drive me to that meeting today. I wouldn't make you do this; but I have to be there. Besides then you can at least meet my mystery clients; but they won't be able to tell you their names. Is it a deal?"

"Oh, okay. I haven't been to the city in almost a year. So it will be fun. We could go to that deli Molenari's over in Italian town, on the way home. Okay?" She took the prescription from me and waited as the doctor took my pajamas off my bad arm and tapped my arm to my body. Then my wife covered me with the shawl and drove me home. She gave me a little shallow bath, which would have been romantic, under other circumstances, and helped me brush my teeth and comb my hair. She tried to not make me scream as she dressed me in some jogging clothes, letting one arm go empty. She told me to rest on the couch, while she made lunch. After lunch she got herself all made up, for a day in the city, and put on my sneakers and socks for me. She then drove me to my office on the crazy midday freeway. Helen was there and they shared a couple of jokes over 'their klutzy guy'. I was starting to feel my arm coming awake as Rhoda entered.

"Oh, Doc, you look terrible. How are you doing? Poor guy. What happened?" She looked at Helen and then at my wife. "Is he okay; should we make it another day?"

I grabbed her arm and said, "We have to do this now while I'm still alive." They all laughed, but I actually meant it. "Rhoda this is my wife, Anne. Honey, Rhoda. I can't tell you her last name. I guess her first name is out of the bag. Ugh. And here comes her partner in crime. This is my wife Anne." Everyone started to shake hands. Alex was a bit slow; it was only after five minutes he said, "Hey Mark did you hurt yourself?" I rolled my eyes, "No this one arm thing is a new fashion statement. Ugh. I pulled it out of the socket. It's a long story."

The clock showed it was time to get into the meeting. My wife gave me a careful hug and said she'd return in about three and a half hours. She whispered in my ear, "Such a cute couple." She sauntered down the stairs and on to her shopping extravaganza. We all sat down and Rhoda made the tea and got out some coconut macaroons and put them on the plate. She then checked Max's area and fed and tidied up. While she did that Alex put a couple of logs on the fire and got out the quilts and even put my feet up on the stool. Rhoda put on my comfy slippers and everything was ready to go. I could see they both had servants' hearts and this encouraged me. I did start to feel the pain returning; but they made me so comfortable that it wasn't as bad as it was earlier.

"Well, well, well, I can't believe that this is our last real session together. You both heard my wife, she said she'd be back in three and a half hours; so if you want to, feel free to go the entire time. I'm snug here. Are you two excited? I am. I think now both of you will really be used in a powerful way for His Kingdom and I'm not just saying that. This Word will be even more so after we finish the second set of sessions, on your personal difficulties. So do either of you have questions for each other? If so, this is still the time to ask.

Rhoda raised her hand and then realized she didn't have to. "Alex, can you fly a plane? I mean one of those small little private planes? I know this may sound crazy, but every once in awhile someone flies one over my house and buzzes me. I keep imagining you in the plane. So be honest do you fly?"

Alex kind of shifted in his chair again. "Well, to be honest. I do know how to fly. I started doing this when a guy from church said he could teach me and help me get my license for almost nothing. I do buzz you on occasion and I always hoped you'd noticed; but I didn't think you did. Does that bother you?"

"No, but I just wanted to see if my hunch was right. Know how it is to think maybe your imagining things? Okay here's my second question: A woman, who is the wife of a millionaire, used to go to your church but left right before I started attending. She started a local women's group and became my good friend. She said that right before you came to work for the church that the choir director had run off with a woman from the choir. She said she tried to help this choir member. When she tried to step in, she was put on the church's black list. She also said that around this time, you came to be a pastor at the church. She told me that there was a rumor about an issue concerning you and another woman at church. She said that because of the bad press concerning the choir director that your issue was quickly swept under the rug. Did you have an affair, at church, before trying to have one with me? What happened to this poor woman and were you still seeing her when you tried to get to know me? I have always felt funny about this possibility. I fetl that that possibility makes the whole thing even cheaper, than it was. Also is this why the leadership came down on me and you much harder than they would have normally? I always wondered this."

"Yes, sadly, I did have an affair; but it was only for a couple of weeks. I didn't think anyone ever knew about it. The head pastor asked me about it and I denied it and the issue just 'went away'. He was still dealing with the choir director, I think. No one ever came up to me about it, again."

Lastly Rhoda said, "Not what I wanted to hear. Okay...moving forward...There is a woman at my new church, who knew you through the Children's ministry. Because she was originally from your church I asked her if she knew you and how you were doing. I told her we were friends, and then she said something strange. She said, 'I know Alex. I am fully aware of all his weaknesses and problems. If I were you, I'd give up on ever trying to be his friend.' Then she promptly prayed for me to be delivered from having any desire to be your friend and she acted like you were famous over at church. Do you have any idea what that was about?"

"No, not really, a few ladies from my church attend your now. I am not sure who she is."

"Okay, Alex, I'll just drop that question. Don't worry I don't feel intimidated by her."

Alex thought a bit, "Okay, well, I had one question, maybe two. Why did you send me and your husband out together for that fall walk? I had nothing in common with him and here I found that you have made a date for me to spend the afternoon, at a wilderness park, with your husband. I, at least, thought you were coming with. That was awkward. What were you thinking?"

"Okay, that is simple to explain. I read in several books that if a woman is married and wants to be friends with a man, she needs to have him be friends with her husband. Also if the man is married, she should be friends with the wife. That was going to be my step two, which we never really got to. I guess I wasn't as keen on your wife, as a friend and you weren't as keen on my husband, as a friend; as I'd hoped we'd be. That is the walk where you had that weird talk with him about that permission thing wasn't it? Ugh."

"Well, yes I believe it was. To be honest, I didn't feel he loved you enough or was right for you. I kept looking for ways to be with you, not with him. I was not comfortable being his friend, sorry."

"Okay, last question. Remember the Thanksgiving before I had the 'encounter' with you? (Rhoda nodded.) Why did you invite me and my family to your home? I thought by that time you might have noticed I liked you. The whole thing seemed awkward. I wondered if your true intent was actually to get me to your house for the holidays. What were you thinking there?"

Rhoda looked a bit miffed. "I was thinking two things: 1. I needed to see you with your family to get it in my head that you were actually married. You never acted married and 2. I wanted to get to know your wife better; since she seemed a bit cool towards me at work. You always sent me home when she'd come to work. I never had a chance to befriend her. But she was rather cool at my house, too; so that strategy didn't work. I thought maybe she'd be more relaxed, if I made a coffee date with her later on. I also wanted you to see how happy my married life was. I wasn't trying to get you into my house. Geez. Your little son hated the food I made and was quite verbal about it, cute as that was, and I realized I had failed in my socialization attempt and my cooking attempt. So sorry on both accounts."

Alex seemed to get her motives. "I'm sorry I made it all about me, again. It was a nice time and the food wasn't too bad; just a little undercooked. Your home was so cozy. Honestly I did get sad when I saw how happy you appeared."

I told them I needed to know a few more things, at the meeting. "I'm going to ask the following question, rather 'rotely', if you don't mind. These things are necessary, since next week we meet the silent partners, in this relationship.

Rhoda, what are you doing now? What do you plan to do in the near future? What is (are) your long term goal or goals? Also tell me about your husband's career and goals if you would."

"Well, Doc, I love this topic. May I start with my husband first? He is a computer contractor and is working for HP, out of our home, as of this meeting. But this changes with his different contracts. He loves working from home. He wants to start his own business and has for years. But he just can't come up with a business that will guarantee he'll make enough money to keep us, in the style we have become accustomed to, and he is getting a bit frustrated. I have told him I'd be his assistant, but not his partner and he gets me. He knows I have my own calling. He ultimately would like us to retire to a small farm and grow herbs or maybe llamas or some such creature. I actually like this plan, as long as he will put in a pottery station for me, with a good kiln.

259

But all of that is for our golden years. Now, he and I are remodeling a home we purchased that is actually quite close to Alex's home. I literally do remodeling, whenever I'm not cleaning. The place is a bit big for me to handle, to be honest. We bought it with hopes of our daughter living with us again. She only lived here two years and is now out on her own. So now the 'castle', is all mine. I also do all the gardening and take care of our two cats. It all adds up to a more than full time job. Some people have asked why we live near Alex's home. First we always loved this neighborhood, even before meeting Alex. Since moving in we truly only saw him one time, in our actual neighborhood, when he was out skating. I saw him a couple of times, at the grocery and Costco, but truly that was it. When I have seen him at those places; it was usually from across the room, no interaction, except the two times I mentioned. We have different friends and time schedules; so my husband and I have never seen this as a problem. But they think that the proximity reminds me of the bad things that happened. Actually the only thing I have ever thought of, when I have seen him, was this reconciliation. If I saw Stan then that would be a nightmare. But he is at that Pastors' home in Arizona, I think. God has healed my memories and is healing them even more with this whole experience.

But as for me and my calling... I used to be an elementary school teacher and did tutoring after I got married, until we moved to this new home. Now I'm writing a book on cults and abusive churches and trying to get into doing speaking sessions, on these and other subjects. I don't really have support, in this, from my church. Maybe it is because, I don't look the part. I don't dress churchy or act too church ladyish. But God has told me I am to write and speak and so I am not really affected by this perception. It is nice to be supported and I wish I were. But if you aren't, you have to go with God call, above men's opinions. I like my pastor and am blessed by his preaching. When I'm done with the book, then I'll begin to write speeches and other books. I've been doing a daily blog on cults and abusive churches for two years; but decided to stop this blog recently. I still try to help those who were once involved in cults, but now it is more on an individual basis. I also try to have a dinner or a movie night, once a month for friends. I don't want to be involved in typical women's ministry;

it isn't my style and so I haven't found my niche at church yet. Honestly I'd be more comfortable in men's ministry, not because of the men; but because of the deeper teaching they get. I'm also thinking of mentoring young women.

My hobbies are: conventional medicine, alternative medicine, and nutrition. I try and do needle crafts, when I have the time. I fully intend to take up pottery in a couple of years, because I can see myself doing it. I also love to work with plants and garden.

About 4 years ago I got very sick, I mentioned this earlier. We think it was some sort of chemical poisoning, from Bayer Rose Fertilizer and Bug Repellent. I haven't been the same since. I'm better now, but not the same. I used to go for long eight walks, roller blade, and ride my bike, until getting poisoned. But after I got sick I lost the use some of my muscles, my hair changed, and I find I have very little energy. I haven't been as active, not because I don't want to; but because I can't. It also makes the remodeling go slower. I hate being slowed down. I never want to become a lazy old lady. If I hadn't had nerve damage and damage to other parts of my body, I'd probably be running marathons. I love to exercise and be active. Now I'm limited.

I don't have the close friends, like I had when I was younger. Alex knew how to be a friend. My husband is pretty much my only best friend today. Other friends are either far away or I've had to let them do because I was more their therapist, than a friend. So right now I'm trying to make new friends."

"Well, Rhoda, it seems like you have covered it all. By the way you seem friendly enough; I'm surprised you have so few friends. I think you might have many associates; but you are careful not to call anyone a friend unless you can feel a deep connection. I understand this. Now can you tell me a little about your daughter? What is she like and what does she do? Where does she live now?"

Rhoda looked more serious than usual. "My daughter has always been a bit different. I'm not sure if it was the way we raised her or if she was just felt different from the start. She's a great girl, but never seemed to really bond to me or my husband. She has never been very family oriented.

When she was younger she and I were inseparable. We'd go to the Mall, movies, roller blade, swim, and ride bikes. Then we'd also do girly things like bake and go for coffee. I so loved those times. I guess I was more her friend than her mother and I thought we'd grow closer as she grew up. It was during her high school days that she began to drift away from me. She is very pretty and very talented. She always got mainly A's in school and did excellently at anything she tried, be it martial arts, horseback riding, music, you name it. She plays piano and was really good at acting, but she isn't doing these things, at this time.

She was interested in making movies, for many years, and got more and more involved in media type things, as she got older. However, she finally settled on majoring in Accounting; kind of different than film, huh? She got her degree and promptly ran away to Los Angeles where she wasted her life in 'riotous living' and her dad and I had to rescue her. She stayed with us for two years and recently finished paying off all of her debts, including college loans and then got an accounting job in LA. She wants to one day be an accountant to movie stars. She wants nothing to do with the Lord, at this time, though she was saved as a young girl and even wanted to be a pastor, at one time. And lastly, she says she doesn't think she'll ever marry or have children. She is seeing a young man, but won't tell us anything about him. Since she doesn't feel that close to her dad and I; she rarely contacts us. I always hoped for one of those close mother and daughter relationships; but even if she lived nearby, I don't think it would happen. This is hard for me, but I still love her very much."

I looked at Rhoda and saw that she was lonely. She hadn't any real friends and even her daughter wasn't her buddy. I felt sorry for her, but was glad she was at least friends with her husband. "I wish I had had the opportunity to meet with her when she lived here. I have a feeling there is more to her story. It may not even be anything connected to you and your husband. I still think that the episode with you and Alex and the abuse from the different churches, you both attended, has really affected her. She just has repressed these things and is taking it out on you and your husband and even God. Hopefully she'll try to heal in these areas, as she gets older... All of this gives me more to go on in how to bring these sessions to a good conclusion for all of you. Now Alex though we know pretty much of your story, please feel free to follow a similar pattern to Rhoda's, in telling me about you and your family. Thanks."

Alex looked at a loss for words, at first. I think this was because he had so much to say. "First of all I am so glad that you let me peek in on Rhoda's life. I have only heard bits and pieces over the years and these have been from various sources, some reliable and some not. Thanks for this. I do want to admit, here and now, that much of her loneliness is my church's fault. We spread rumors about her to all the churches she attended. We also planted spies in her life that posed as friends. This helped make her less likely to trust people and to form any solid relationships, I'm sure. I apologize for Pastor Stan and the others, who worked with him, against you. I should have seen how we were destroying all parts of your life and spoke up. I was too impotent at the time, to do anything, or at least I thought I was. So sorry, Rhoda.

Well, as you know, I work for a large mega church, near Rhoda's and my home, West Bay. I have worked there for about 20yrs. I was the children's pastor for many years and received many awards for the work I did, because, honestly, I am talented. I also did side things like maintenance, children's choir, plays, Summer Camp, organizing volunteers, and helping put together different special events. Folks say I'm artistic and creative. I guess I had to be, with all of the things they put me in charge of. It was be creative or bust. I occasionally give talks, at other places of worship. I have organized various seminars and even taught at them. But because of various wrong decisions with women and things shifting at church, like different head pastors; I was put in charge of compassion ministries a couple of years ago. I had to plan weddings and funerals and such. I didn't like it as much as doing the children's programs; but I wanted to keep working at this church, so I took the transfer to the Compassion Services Department. For various afore mentioned reasons, I could not go to any other church. But rumors, and maybe lack of interest on my part, caused the church to consider relocating me again, recently. Now I'm in charge of Connections ministry and help people find their fit at church. I still do the compassion ministry; but we are training others to take my place soon. This is not what I enjoy doing, either; but again I do this to keep my job. I am no longer a pastor in good standing; but most people still think I am. We let them think I am, not wanting to do any formal ceremony to clarify this. This is again for various reasons, mostly the woman problem I have had. I was counting my days till retirement, to go to that pastors' retirement home, and now that may have fallen through; they're still deciding. So, I am, secretly putting out resumes and trying to see, if there is a place for me at another church, perhaps in another state. I'm doing this secretly, so as not to let them in on my decision, until I pretty much have a new job.

In the future I'd love to go to Hawaii or some other state near the ocean, to retire. I could also do the desert. It just depends what my wife and I finally settle on and can afford. We have a lot of debts to pay off. Now that that retirement home may be off limits, we will have to live very simply.

I love sports. I love to swim, to roller blade, to jog, to bike, to be as active as possible, as much as possible. I enjoy water sports and skiing and will do anything that has a high degree of risk and adventure. I went on a long bike trek across the US with my daughter, a few years ago. I keep thinking of new areas to conquer. I had some back trouble over the years, but nothing that has kept me down for long. I'm lucky. I hope to keep going this till I'm quite old, since my dad lived to be in his nineties. I have other hobbies: I like to do ham radio and to join various biking clubs. I'm like Rhoda, I don't want to get the Grandpa mentality, even though I'm going to have a grandchild soon. I love to ride my unicycle around church and dress young. Old is a bad word for me. I guess I liked that Rhoda also had this way of thinking. Sorry she is not feeling well, at this time.

I, myself, have been healthy, on the whole. I did get sick, for awhile after the troubles with Rhoda; but I'm better now. I guess it was stress related. I also do not have any really good friends. Most of my relationships are church based and, to be honest, rather shallow. My wife isn't really my friend, like Rhoda is with her husband, so I basically end up going to coffee with different church people or just doing more solitary sports. I do garden, not out of love for plants; but because I have to. I do chores around the house. I'm still renting, so I don't do too much work on the place. I actually replaced the whole roof, myself, a few years back.

I have three kids. I really don't want to tell you much about their lives. I'll let you ask them if you wish. I already feel I've gotten them into more messes than they should have ever been part of.

They all finished college and are doing their various careers. I don't see my older son too much, so I get Rhoda's pain. I think the kids are closer to their mother, than me. That is probably my fault for not being around enough when they were young.

My daughter was always my favorite. But she ended up having the most troubles. She is super intelligent and did well in school. She went to a really good school and was doing well; but then she started to become anorexic and we ended up having to withdraw her and have her at home, for a time. She eventually got so bad we had to send her to an eating disorders clinic and it took quite a long time for her to get normal. She sometimes slips a bit; but she's been doing better. She is in a very caring relationship and I'm happy for her. She worked with horses for awhile and that seemed to help her heal. She is social, but still very attached to her family. We think she was influenced by her second cousin, who works with me at the church, who also has an eating disorder. She frequently babysat her when she was younger and my daughter was told, all the time, she was too big. She is not overweight and is very active. She's beautiful, but I think that thought, just stuck with her; it made her dislike herself. I also think my dalliances might have been part of the cause of her anorexia. It is a complex disease and it is hard to know all the root causes.

My wife used to teach part time at a Christian school, in the area; but when the trouble with Rhoda got into full swing, the Church made her come in and do office work. Over the years she has had different positions. She likes women's ministry and will probably end up doing something in that area in the future. Though she enjoys working at the church, she is not as actively involved, as I am; it not her whole life. She gets her main enjoyment from gardening and doing special work projects, at the church, not so much from the church. She was and is a very involved mother and spends a great deal of time with our daughter. She and I are trying to spend more time together. The kids are finally grown; we have more time. She is a patient woman and has put up with a lot from me. I think she sees herself as doing gardening and reading books in her retirement. Me, I hope to remain active in sports, until they bury me. I'm not really thinking of a second career or anything work related. But I don't see retirement as slowing down; I see it as a time to do more of the activities I love.

So that is my family and my story. I hope when my wife and I have private meetings with you, we will learn to enjoy each others' company more, as we age. There must be a reason we are still together. I also hope to be one of those fun grandpas, who remains young at heart and is considered 'cool' by his grandkids."

I thanked both of them for their information. I also thought these questions would show each of them, the person their friend turned out to be. Their knowledge about each other seemed to have basically stopped at the time of their 'episode'. Rhoda seemed to have more future work ambitions and Alex seemed to be thinking more of scaling work related things down. I hoped this might help Alex, especially; see how both of their lives were taking entirely different paths. They had less in common, than they once thought. Sometimes we intersect with someone, when we have more in common; only to find out that a few years later we and the other person want totally different things out of life. Rhoda was looking forward to beginning many new business things with her husband and her own writing and speaking career. Alex was looking forward to simplifying his life, except in the area of sports.

Rhoda spoke a bit timidly, which was out of character for her. "Alex, I have a question for you. When we are finished with this process, would you do me a big favor? (He nodded.) I need you to help me go to a few people, who have come against me over the years, to help me straighten things out. I need you to help me explain that I was not delusional. Don't worry it won't be everyone, just a few key people. Also I'd like you to come with me to speak with my current pastor. I want him to know I am a rational being who could be trusted to do some speaking and maybe take a more active role in his church. Would you be willing to do this, accompanied by my husband, of course? Various people, starting from Pastor Stan on down to all his little cronies, have gone around lying about me. This has ruined my reputation. Again, would you help me fix things with the worst of these folks? Maybe we might even have something said publically at your church; it would have to be negative; it might just be you and I saying we have finally reconciled and leave it at that. This would help me immensely. Please, friend."

Alex said, "Well this is against my nature; but I guess it is the least I can do. I started this whole thing. When this is done, I'll contact your husband and see if he is on board with this plan. Let's do a couple of emails, back and forth, about this (approved, of course) and I'll mull it all over. I'm not against you, Rhoda. I'm so sorry for all of the damage that was done to you. But we all know that often things like this cannot be healed or fixed on this earth. If I need you to do this for me will you?"

"Of course, if I get permission from my husband. I'm here to help you, too. We'll have to see where your wife is on this subject and she'll have to accompany us. Let's pray about this. Sadly some folks have either died or are no longer cognizant."

I was so happy to see this willing attitude, in both of them. "Alright friends, we have been here a long time. Do go and make an appointment with Helen. I hope to see you both here, with your spouses, next week. If you both need special times, to accommodate everyone's schedules, just let Helen know. Thanks so very much. Be sure to give your kids a heads up about coming the following week. It isn't going to be easy getting everyone together." I really felt intense pain and started to shake. Alex went into the front office and was mentioning this to Helen when Anne came in. She had my pills and gave me both of them. Alex helped bring me to the car. Rhoda was on the cell phone with her husband and Helen was shaking her head. Helen followed us all out to the car and leaned in. She said she'd come in to get Max taken care of, the next day, and then would work from home, the rest of the day. She also had rescheduled the other clients for me. I told her to close up shop and go home for the day. Then I thanked her as I shut the car door and immediately fell into a deep sleep. Even in my pain, I was glad for all God was doing.

Chapter 26

I don't usually wear a full suit to the office. I like my tweed jacket and brown slacks of various materials or jeans. But since I was meeting the spouses of Rhoda and Alex, for the first time, I thought I'd better dress up a bit. I have a more relaxed suit that I sometimes wear when I speak at church and a dark colored shirt with a matching tie. I wanted to look professional, but not nerdy. I checked the weather report for downtown San Francisco and of course they said it was going to rain on and off all day. So I got out my "Sunday" raincoat and big black umbrella, that I'd picked up in London, a few years before. My wife walked me to the door and gave me a big kiss and told me I was a bit too dapper today. She warned me that the women on Bart would be fighting over who could sit next to me. She then gave me a playful swat on my backside. Anne has a great sense of humor and I think this is one of the main reasons our marriage has lasted so long. You'd be surprised how many therapists are divorced.

By my house I was a bit warm in all of those clothes; but as we got nearer to the city I got more and more comfortable. Helen was already busy at her desk when I came in at 9am. She handed me a lox bagel with everything, like I like it, and a large Chai. She said, "Morning, Mark. I went to the bagel place and picked these up for you since today is a special day for you. I know that you are excited and nervous at the same time, eh? Don't forget the group will be here at 11:00. I made sure to tell them to mark off about four hours for the whole session. I know you aren't sure how long it will all take, but better to be safe than sorry." She took my wet coat and hung it up for me. "Let me see is there anything else I have to tell you? Oh, yes I finished the three patient reports, including insurance information, from yesterday's appointments. They're on your desk for you to check through. Just buzz me and I'll come in to file the charts and send off the information to the insurances. See you later." With that she shut the door and went back out to work on our yearly reports for my taxes and for the insurances. I thought how blessed I was to have such an efficient secretary, who always did more than was expected of her. She was the one who kept me in business.

It took me almost an hour to go through the files Helen put on my desk. I buzzed her and told her to let the two couples right into my office. I didn't want any scenes in the waiting room. You never know how spouses in situations like this will act. If I'm present, there is less of a chance there will be any outbursts. Max wanted to sit on my lap; but I had to refuse him since I didn't want to be full of cat fur when I met everyone. I pulled out my notes from previous sessions and looked them over. Funny, clients tend to get offended, if you forget a few of their stories; but I am seeing about 40 clients, on a regular basis, and then maybe another group of thirty or so short term people come through every month. So I always have to look at my notes prior to the clients coming in. About fifteen minutes before everyone showed up I got out the tea cups, Chamomile tea, and special French cookies I purchased the day before. (Chamomile seems to calm people and I thought these folks might need extra calming.) Then I turned on the tea pot. I put extra large logs on the fire, to warm up the place and take the chill out of the air. When the pot whistled I got up to put it on simmer and at that exact moment there was a knock on my door. Helen popped her head in, "Alex and his wife are here." She ushered them into the room. "Mark, Rhoda and her husband are coming up the stairs now." She turned, "Right this way folks. Make yourselves comfortable." She gave a nod and a smile to everyone and went back to her reports, gently closing the door behind her.

I took everyone's rain coats and hung them next to mine on the rack. Then I shook each hand (everyone had sweaty palms) and introduced myself. Then I said, "I have been waiting a long time to meet the two people that are lucky enough to be married to Rhoda and Alex. I know you all have questions for me; but we can get to those at the end of the meeting, if they aren't addressed, during the course of the session. I also know that both of you (I looked at Alex's wife and Rhoda's husband), must have felt these sessions went on way too long. I get that. But by the end of this meeting I assure you that you both will want to have more meetings on this subject with me. If you feel the need for this, I can meet with either of you couples, individually, before we all come together next week. Do let my secretary, Helen, know and make an appointment. Also to make things more clear, next week is mainly for the children to get healed, or at least begin their healing journey. Do try and work with me, today, on your issues. Like I said, we can work some more at another time, if you like, just do make it before the meeting with the kids. Okay? Okay, let's get started." Before I could say anything more Rhoda's husband, whose name is also Alex, (we'll call him Alex D. for identification purposes) raised his hand.

"I'd like to speak directly to Alex. (He turned toward Alex, who was shaking a bit.) You are a pastor. What were you thinking when you attacked my wife? What kind of pastor are you anyway? Besides the fact that you attacked her; you left my wife high and dry and let her get abused by your church. You never came to her defense. And what about me? You never took the time to come and apologize to me and you made my wife go through years of suffering. I should come over there and beat the crud out of you! You are a lying little coward! I'm not a Christian; but I never tried to seduce anybody's wife. The women I knew, before I married, wanted to be with me. I didn't have to jump on them in the parking lot. I could slap the crap out of you." Rhoda grabbed his arm and whispered to him to calm down. "Calm down, calm down... Alex, do you know how angry I've been at you and your so called, church all of these years? I should have sued the whole lot of you. If Rhoda hadn't have stopped me I'd have beat you to a pulp and sued your whole church." Alex D. was clenching his fists and red in the face. "I let her work for you and your damn church and the thanks I got was you trying to force yourself on her. No one from your church has ever apologized to me either, especially that Pastor Stan. He knew the whole story; yet he lied and told me to divorce my wife. Where do you guys get off having sex with other people's wives, or trying to? Then to add insult to injury you not only lie about the attack; but make everyone think my wife seduced you! You bag of crap!!! And what gave you the right to constantly send her blank emails and make silent calls? Have you no respect for our marriage or my feelings?!!!! Have you no shame? What kind of twisted bastards did you work with at your church? They made our lives, Hell. Christians, ha; I'm sick of the whole lot of you. " He looked like he wanted to rise out of his chair and beat the tar out of Alex.

I decided to let him get some of how he'd been feeling off of his chest. This situation would be hard enough on a believer; but I could see how an unbeliever could be filled with rage and not know what to do with the anger. Over the years it grew and grew under the surface. On the other hand I had to protect Alex, just like judges have to protect defendants. You might not like what a person did; but they have the right to be respected and heard. So I said, placing my hand on Alex D.'s arm, "Believe me, Alex D., I get where you are coming from. You have every right to be angry; but if you let me move this in a slightly different direction, you just might see that Alex has changed. Here take a little more tea and be patient. I promise you can ask more questions of anyone in this room, at the end. Ok?" When Alex D. saw I respected him and so did all of the rest of us in the room, he sat down and calmed himself. People are afraid that no one will hear them and that they will have their dignity trampled on, as it was in the past. His outburst was totally understandable. Here was a pastor, a Christian, and his church, doing more evil than most people, who didn't know the Lord. He felt betrayed on many levels. "Alex, you understand how he feels don't you? You'd act the same way, if another man did this to your wife, wouldn't you?" Alex was glassy eyed and all he could do was nod. His wife's demeanor changed and she crossed her arms.

I turned to her, "Liz, are you alright? Looks like you're angrier than when you came in. Want to share with us, for a moment before we go further?"

Hot tears came down her face and she turned to Alex D., "First of all, I'm not sure my husband would stand up for me, like you have for your wife. I, for one, really understand you. Even if your wife was violated, as she says; I feel you and I have gotten the shaft in this whole thing. I see your wife's side of the story; I've seen that side of the story more times than I can count with the 'other women'. I think that now, perhaps, Alex thinks he has found a true soul mate, not like my husband's usual bunch of disposable women. But it is how this whole thing came about that bothers me. Your wife was a hard little worker, for my husband, and she admired him. I was doing occasional substitute teaching, volunteer work at the church, and raising three kids, at the time, this all happened. I didn't have time to spend hours with my husband and I was too busy and too tired to admire him. He frankly was not very 'admirable', at the time, either. She came in and unknowingly took my place and she became his fun partner, the Work wife. I became his angry demanding Home wife. Why wouldn't he gravitate towards her? Your wife is a nice woman and attractive; but I'm no slouch. Even your wife told me I was the prettiest lady at church, at that time. Alex was never home. He worked over fourteen hours a day, sometimes, for the church. He had three jobs there, and when he was home he was always doing paperwork or chores. He had no time for me, the kids, or for any kind of family time. I felt like a single parent. If he had any free time, he'd ride his bike or roller blade. He also spent money like it was this unlimited supply, forgetting we had debts to pay off, three kids to send to college, and a retirement to save for. So with a situation like that I admit I was angry and over tired. When he came home raving about how great your wife was: I was ready to beat him. Here I was slaving away for our future and here he was having an exciting career, exercising, and having a woman at work admire him. I'm sure I helped drive him to your wife. I was breaking my back for him and our family and he was totally unappreciative. The last straw came when the church tried to tell me that my husband had tried to seduce your wife. He had promised me att that time, his chasing women days, were over and that he was going to be a faithful husband. There he was trying to make you wife go to Hawaii with him. Where was my trip to Hawaii; we didn't even go to Oakland?

Anyway, Alex D., you and I got lost in the shuffle in all of this. The church focused on keeping them apart, punishing them, counseling them, and you and I were left out of the loop. Why didn't the church force them to apologize to us and honor how we felt? We were totally ignored, as the church tried to fix their relationship. Where was the blasted church when my husband and I were struggling? Did anyone ever come to your door and try and make things right with you? (Alex D. shook his head.) Who comforted me when I was trying to do my job, my housework, take care of the kids, and help Alex? I had to act, as though, my husband was normal and be a good little pastor's wife. All the while he was off trying to find my replacement. So I really catch why you're mad. Even this counseling was all about them. I have a lot of things I'd like to work on, regarding this issue. Thankfully we are going to come for special meetings for this and other issues, in a couple of weeks. But I do feel like we were forgotten, like we weren't that important, like we were an afterthought. I really get you, Alex D." After this both spouses sat with their arms crossed, looking none to happy.

I sat there and looked at Alex and Rhoda's spouses. When people have affairs, they focus on the one they wish to have the affair with and totally forget about the people they are hurting. Even Rhoda, didn't really think how her wanting to reconcile would make her husband feel. How maybe her husband didn't see the glorious plan of God in letting his wife go back to being friends with her attacker. Maybe he saw the desire for reconciliation as Rhoda's wanting to be reconnected to a man who loved her and maybe she loved. Maybe Liz felt the same way about her husband pining over reconciliation with Rhoda. These things aren't seen by people who are focusing on how, they feel and their own needs. They can't see the pain in their partner's eyes and heart. I shook myself from my thoughts and said, "Well, I can see we are going down a slightly different path than I intended; but I think it is good. I think that both Alex D. and Liz really got down to the main issues. They needed, to be truly seen. by their partners, and they needed to feel they were loved and appreciated, not some component that could be replaced. Can all of you see how much of the blame, in this, falls on that church?

That church mishandled this thing from the get go. Alex, I hate to say this, but by protecting and coddling you; they didn't help you. They did what so many parents do when they protect their kids from the consequences of their sin; they don't let them feel the pain of poor choices. Therefore they never learn the lessons they need to learn. These lessons are only learned by facing their sins head on and learning to accept the consequences, when they blow it. But you, like some spoiled rich kid, with 'affluenza', were made to feel invincible like you could do anything, at anytime, to and with anyone. You felt like you never had to look at your sin, head on, and never had to suffer, even a hint of a consequence. And as for you, Rhoda, they made you feel invisible. You came to them for help and they did not see you or help you in anyway. Instead they mocked you, falsely accused you, and destroyed your soul and your reputation. They weren't being your pastors, instead of protecting you from the wolves; they let the wolves feast on you and they, themselves, were the wolves.

They took the name and honor of Jesus, spat on it, and did it with impunity. If that church cared about Alex, it would have given him his full consequence. I believe your organization has a three year dismissal period, from being a pastor, in types of sin like you were involved in. Am I right? Don't you also have to prove you are totally healed of the sin, before you are restored? (Alex nodded.) It might have been good for you, to be a greeter over at Costco or sell shoes, while you waited to be restored to your position. Because now the position you are in, is based on a lie; this can't be sitting right with you. From the person I have come to know, these last few months, I don't think you have been comfortable, with living a two faced liar life. Have you? (Alex nodded.) Rhoda, as far as you are concerned, what happened at that church destroyed your life and has kept you from fulfilling your calling to be both a pastor and to be involved more deeply in God's work, am I right? (Rhoda nodded.) You have such passion and desire to teach God's people; yet because of all this, each church you went to was intimidated into not letting you serve and teach. Is this correct? (Rhoda nodded again and started to cry.) Rhoda, do you want to say something?"

"You all know I've forgiven Alex, his evil church, and, sad to say, evil fellow pastors. But what you all don't see is I have wanted to enter into serving God, since I was saved at 16. At first I was too young to do all I wanted, then I got into that blasted cult, called the Assembly, and then I ended up at Alex's church. I finally felt I was starting to serve the Lord, in full time ministry, when I worked for Alex. I was finally happy and feeling I was in my 'sweet spot' in life. After the mess at the church, I was kept from serving, at a higher level, at each church I was at. I'd start to do a ministry and then someone from Alex's church or Pastor Stan would spread a rumor or speak to the leadership and I'd be pushed back down again. Imagine getting slapped down for no reason; but your desire to serve God for forty years!!! No one ever gets over this pain and disappointment, though with God I finally have healed more than I thought possible. Alex kept serving, even the moment after I reported he attacked me. He kept getting accolades and honors and I only got lies, mocking, and rumors. God has told me, what I am supposed to do and every demon in Hell has come into different churches and blocked me. Many of these demons had their home at West Bay, Alex's church. This was not 'my perspective'; it really happened. Alex has served everyday of his life, even in the middle of adultery and lies. It seems so unfair." With that she broke down. Liz went over to her and put an arm around her shoulder. It was like Liz finally saw Rhoda as a person, not just Alex's "almost substitute" for her. It was a great moment of breakthrough.

Alex just sat transfixed, watching the scene of his wife comforting a woman, who would have been his mistress. I decided to seize the moment, "Alex, hearing all the pain you caused these and other people what thoughts do you have?"

Tears rolled down Alex's face and he struggled to compose himself to speak. "First of all I'd like to say one thing, 'Seeing my wife comfort Rhoda is so utterly remarkable, that today I have grown much deeper in my admiration for my wife.' Honey, this moment, I now see your beautiful soul much more clearly. Over the years we have had so many issues, mostly mine, that I lost sight of the tenderness in your spirit that drew me to you, so many years ago. But let me go in order in this, alright? Alex D. I want to sincerely apologize to you for trying to take your treasure, your wife, Rhoda. She is a treasure. I hope you can see what a great woman you have and how much she loves you. I want to reassure you, she never ever once gave me any reason, to want to have an affair with her. It really was all me. Maybe her kindness met an empty place in my life and she is attractive. But she was 100% faithful to you and you should be glad that you have a faithful wife. I, unfortunately, have known many wives, who do not love and respect their husbands. They followed me around at church, all the time, and I let myself have affairs with them from time to time. I didn't have affairs with all of them and the blame is not theirs, but mine. But the fact is, that there were many women, who were more than ready to get to know me, because I was a pastor, or they thought I was more appealing than their husbands. Remembering those other women, shows me how faithful your wife was and is to you. So you should bless her, for her deep love for you. Rhoda I admire you. This all would have been far worse, if you didn't want to please God and show love and honor to your husband. Thank you for not having an affair with me. I will give you my help in anyway both going back and helping you be vindicated, with certain people or in your future career endeavors; I will finally help you as I should have. Lastly, my dear Liz, you have put up with so much crap and nonsense over the years and I was oblivious to your pain. I just didn't care about you and your needs or your feelings. I just wanted, what I wanted, and nothing and no one, was going to stand in my way to keep me from getting it. If I wanted sex, I wanted it now and I wanted it with anyone who was willing and available to give it, anyone. The list is long and tedious; I will go into greater detail when we have our private meetings with Mark, next month. But mostly I have lived a lie. I have said I wanted to be a pastor and serve God, but I have committed adultery again and again. The Church didn't stop me or punish me for that. They punished me for ruining their reputation, for opening them up to the possibility of lawsuits and for less donations. But they didn't help me with the core issue—my immorality. It comes down to that. I am an immoral man and I have never really repented. But I now see that I must repent to each of you here, to others I have hurt over the years, and I must stand before the church and make a public confession. I will allow the church to decide what my fate is after that.

But to be honest, I think I have lied long enough. Maybe I should stop pastoring. I have been putting out resumes for a couple of months and was offered a teaching job, for comparable pay, in Oakland. I guess it is larger salary because of the risky neighborhood. I have decided I'm going to take that job and resign from being a pastor or worker in the church. But before I do, I will make a clean breast of things to those I have hurt personally and to the church. I won't hide this sin, or series of sins, any longer. I want to be right with each of you and right with God." The moment he said that, he went over to Alex D.'s chair and started to weep. He wept as though he would break into a million pieces and said, "Alex D. I beg you to forgive me. I do not want you to not come to Christ, because of the mess I've made of being a pastor and the way I have presented Jesus to you. I beg you to consider Jesus and to forgive me and even those men who were in my church who called themselves pastors. Forgive us. My life is in your hands. What can I do to make this better? I will do what you want."

Alex D. had never seen a person express true repentance, in his whole life. He had never seen this genuine expression of sorrow for sin and never had anyone ask for his forgiveness with such brokenness of spirit. He tried to not cry; but for the first time in his life he found himself crying, not just the couple of stray tears that men usually wipe away, but really crying. He knew that he had to forgive. He saw Alex's humanity and his true sorrow and he put his hand on Alex's shoulder and looked him in the eyes and said, "I forgive you and this is the most real expression of Christianity I have ever seen. I am very close to coming to Jesus because now I can see He is real." He got up from his chair and went to his wife and knelt down and said, "Rhoda, forgive me for ever doubting you were faithful and for ever doubting that God has wanted this reconciliation. I can now see that He has wanted it and it is for His purpose, even though it has been the most difficult thing in my life and our marriage. I love you and I thank you for honoring me and loving me. I see that Alex loved, maybe still loves you, and I see you care for him, as a friend. But you have chosen to love me

277

and not go after what might have been more exciting for you. I love you. Thank you, Honey."

Rhoda stood up and knelt down next to her husband. "This whole time I have never stopped loving you. I never ever wanted to have an affair and this is not just a matter of duty for me. I truly love you. Alex is a friend and nothing more." She kissed her husband on his cheek and went over to Liz. She knelt before her, "Liz, you feel like you are forgotten and not valued. But you have more capacity to love than most people. You took Alex back every time he strayed and you forgave him and tried to make your marriage work. I know you love him. I saw you cry that day at the camp registration after the incident and that kind of crying is only possible for a woman who loves a man to do. I admire you and I want to ask forgiveness for anything I have ever done to make you feel insecure or devalued. Forgive me, if I ever gave the impression of wanting to have your husband, as more than a friend and an employer. I want you to know I'm so sorry for all your times of loneliness and feelings of not being wanted. Liz, I want to be your sister and friend, if you'll have me. I understand if you don't wish to be my friend. Forgive your husband. I think this is finally a time of sincere repentance, on his part. I think you will not be sorry, if you'll just give him one more chance. He loves you and I think he's finally getting how he hurt you. I love and value you, Liz." Liz didn't speak she just hugged Rhoda and wept on her shoulder.

I sat and watched as the Holy Spirit fell on these four people and saw it was Him doing the work. I was glad my agenda got thrown out the window. I got on my knees and thanked God that He took over this session. After about an hour more of prayer, with each person, I stood up and said, "We have seen the Spirit of God at work in this room and we need to not go out of here and act like we once did. We need to let the 'heart' work done here last. Can we make a vow to not forget what we all agreed on today? Please sit down, for a moment, to tie up a few loose ends from today. We want to have total closure. Okay? Question number one: Rhoda and Alex do both of you now feel that you are finally reconciled?"

Rhoda, "Yes, this is true reconciliation. I have only dreamed and prayed for this day, for fifteen years."

Alex, "Yes I am finally reconciled to Rhoda and her husband, Alex D. and hopefully my wife; though she and I have a bit more work to do on our marriage.

"Question number two: What type of relationship will you, Alex D. and you, Liz, allow these two to have after this meeting? Will you let them still be friends?"

Alex D. spoke, "I am for them being friends; but don't ever think they should be alone together. If they see each other, in person, at least one of the other spouses, preferably both, should be with them. My idea is that they can send an email no more than twice per month, which should then be read by their spouse. They should only call in case of some emergency or some appointment that might need confirmation immediately, like a meeting etc. But if there is a call there should be notification to the spouse that a call is going to be made and full disclosure as to what the call is for. I think this is fair, overly fair. All must be approved by the spouse, no secrets of any kind."

Liz said, "Those sound like good boundaries. I also think if they break these boundaries, they should not be able to communicate for two months, as a consequence. If this happens more than once then the friendship should be cut off. Agree?"

Everyone said, "Agreed."

Rhoda and Alex hugged their partners and the other spouses. Alex said, "You both have been more than generous and we accept these limits as good and fair. Thank you."

Rhoda said, "I second what he said."

Then I said, "Lastly, Alex will you help Rhoda go and make things right with people from the past, maybe pick a new group once per month, until this is done, accompanied by at least one of your spouses?" I wondered how the spouses would go for this.

Alex D. spoke first, "This will be okay with me, as long as I get to go with. I also would like Alex to help Rhoda with getting her book out there and with being able to speak on the subjects of forgiveness and reconciliation. These things he can do on his own without contacting Rhoda. If some sort of meeting must take place, I want to be there. Liz can come, too; I just want to be sure to attend any meeting that they are involved in, be it church or business. Also I hope that Rhoda and I can attend Alex's public confession, over at his church. We want to stand with Alex and show our support for him. Could you arrange this? Maybe you could also make some sort of public statement of Rhoda's innocence at that time? See what you can do Alex."

Alex answered, "I think that those are fair requests; since I have destroyed so much of Rhoda's life. It is the least I can do."

"Alright, I have to end this time; since I do have a client coming in at 4:30pm. I have never seen such an out pouring of His Spirit, outside of my church. I know there are more issues; but I will work on those, when I see each of you couples for your individual issue sessions." I stood up and gave each of them a hug and moved everyone towards the door. "Please don't go for dinner together; wait until after next week's session. Be blessed and drive safely." They all went to the desk to make the last appointment, for them and their children. The presence of God was so strong in my office, that I wept a prayer of gratitude and then had to compose myself, before seeing my next client.

Chapter 27

I'm sure some of you, who are reading this account, might be scratching your head about what exactly "went down" at the last session I had with Rhoda and Alex and their spouses. Where were the confrontations? Where were the endless questions and revelations about things Rhoda and Alex were thinking, during that time, or what they really did, etc.? Let me tell you a bit of back ground on that session. Being trained as a psychotherapist in a secular school; we are always taught to bring our clients to closure. So I had a list of questions for both of my clients and their spouses that I hoped would cause everyone to finally put all their cards on the table, in kind of a giant truth service. I hoped that Alex would tell everyone how he continued to contact Rhoda for fifteen years, how he had done this secretly for fear of the church, and how Rhoda had contacted him back and continued to be on him to reconcile. I also hoped that the spouses would totally open up about how whatever contact, they were told about, made them angry and how the whole incident still angered them. I also hoped that there'd be more discussion on the request of Rhoda and Alex to have a continued friendship, even though it would be a limited one. I had it all planned, on exactly how I was going to get everyone to open up.

Then secondly, I had also been trained in rather legalistic churches, in my past, and knew how the leaders from those churches would have relished having four people under their control, how they would be able to make them do, by force of will, whatever they wanted. Pastors and leaders in legalistic churches, are like a dog with a bone, in situations like this. If they know something about someone or have knowledge of secret information, they will not be stopped until everyone knows everything, no matter what the cost. For instance if they knew that you said or did something that would cause your spouse to divorce you, if they shared it, or if they said it in a certain way, that this would cause trouble in a client's marriage; they'd be sure to say it anyway. They'd say that all had to come to light for the sake of honesty and damn the consequences. But God knew what things needed to be said and what things didn't need to come out. God is not out to totally annihilate people and make more destruction to their lives. So when the Holy Spirit took over the meeting, He let get out the things that would heal and not destroy. Legalistic churches actually use a sadistic form of honesty to break up a person's marriage and destroy lives. This makes leaders from these churches feel more superior and holy and makes those under their direction feel more worthless and vile. The legalistic leaders can then feel righteous and like God's avenging angels. Pastor Stan did this with Rhoda when he told her husband to divorce her; because she was in love with Alex. I, contrary to Stan's philosophy, didn't feel it was my place to totally expose Alex and Rhoda. I got no sick pleasure out of seeing people and marriages destroyed, like their Pastor Stan did. Even if they didn't do anything wrong, I could have said things in such a way as to cause their spouses to feel betrayed and sinned against. Then I'd have looked like some mighty avenger, a holy sinless Christian counselor. I could have walked away looking ultra holy, but leaving their lives and relationships in shambles. I could have done either or both of the above. But God had other plans...

Right when I was going to go into my set questions and going to lead everyone to my ideal conclusion, the Holy Spirit showed up. This is what changed the meeting from the angry hurt tone Rhoda's husband Alex D. had had, to the repentant and merciful tone it eventually took on. Instead of me leading my clients and their spouses to what I thought they should say and how I hoped they'd feel, the Holy Spirit showed them what areas of repentance and forgiveness were to be focused on. They did the things

I'd hoped they'd do and more so without any prompting from me. On top of this the emphasis was not on confessing each individual sin or mistake or bit of anger; the emphasis was on the larger picture. They didn't get bogged down in silent phone calls or blank emails; they took responsibility for their actual sins and their need to forgive one another. My church teaching, from the past, would have told me not rest until everything was exposed, down to the smallest minutia. This extreme honesty would have been the goal, even if this would have irrevocably hurt the other party and would not have helped the situation. It is kind of like when you get married to someone. Does it really help going into exact detail about your relationship with a former boyfriend or girlfriend? In most cases I counsel couples to not be specific, so as to not permanently scar your spouse with indelible memories of what you did with someone else, before you met them. Most people say that they can handle such information; but it usually sticks in your future spouse's mind forever and it isn't helpful for anyone. So too for Alex and Rhoda to go into descriptions of things that might upset their spouses, beyond repair, really would not have been necessary or useful. I was not planning on being legalistic, like my former churches. Yet I think the Holy Spirit knew how even the most innocuous thing I might have said could have been misread and done damage. So He took over. I was glad to see that the greatest Psychotherapist ever, the Holy Spirit, had come into the situation and did the therapy session His way. I walked in awe literally all week following that "jam session". Glory!

I woke up feeling a bit melancholy on the morning of my last meeting with Rhoda and Alex. I knew I'd be still seeing them when they would be coming in, with their spouses, for their for their individual marriage sessions. But it wouldn't be the same; they'd be different because they'd be with their spouses and not playing off of each other. There'd be a totally different dynamic. I did see why they liked each other. They were much alike in many ways, personality wise. Their goals and activity levels were different. But they both were in committed loving relationships, (though Alex and Liz still had some issues in that area). Their soul mate thing, would have to be laid aside, and they'd have to put all their "eggs" in their own marriage basket. The restrictions their spouses put on their relationship, seemed more than fair. They'd have to settle for a limited reconciliation of their relationship.

What most people don't get is that forgiveness has basically three parts: 1. Forgiveness, which can be done anywhere and anytime, with or without the other party and with or without the opposing party's repentance. 2. Reconciliation, which is a mending of the actual relationship. The parties aren't just forgiven; but they are determined to heal the rift and resume the caring. This can be limited in cases where it is unsafe, as in actual rape or some other violent crime. The parties can be at peace, but no longer be friends or spend any time together. But in most cases the parties determine the extent of contact like in Rhoda and Alex's case; in which they left the friendship boundaries up to their spouses. 3. Restoration, this is the little known component of the forgiveness process and few enter into this. The relationship is not just reconciled; but there is a certain level of trying to go back to where it once was in its physical dimensions. For example you have a dispute with you boss, get fired and then the process of forgiveness and reconciliation happen and you are both friends again, but you are still out of a job. In restoration you get your job back or something similar. In a partial restoration the boss might help you find another job with other employers or help you get something in another department; but you two would no longer have the exact same relationship you had before. That is one example of limited restoration. Full restoration would have you back at the same job you had before the misunderstanding, or something similar if that was no longer available. You might even be put in a higher position. Sadly few folks ever enter into that part of forgiveness, for various reasons. One of those reasons can simply be the length of time that occurred after an incident may make going back to your exact situation, before the incident impossible. For example in a marriage situation, you might get remarried and cannot be restored to your spouse, you could be reconciled. You can't kick out the new spouse and return to your former married life. Or another situation might be: you move, you get a new job or calling, people die, etc. Many times you cannot go back to the original circumstances, even if both parties might want this. Maybe all that gets restored is your relationship. You spend time together, again, but with clearer boundaries. Each situation is different. Rhoda and Alex could never work together again, or be the close friends they once were; but they were allotted by their spouses a limited friendship. They both accepted this; they had a limited reconciliation. It is important that in each stage of forgiveness that the parties enter into the stages willingly and have peace. If there is a forcing of moving into a stage of forgiveness or a lack of peace, then more work needs to be done. In each of the stages of forgiveness: forgiveness, reconciliation, and restoration, it is important to realize, it must come from a heartfelt desire of each of the parties. No one can make you do any of the stages or do any part of the process for you. I have said this over and over; because Pastor Stan said his church said that they reconciled for Rhoda and Alex. That is ludicrous, utterly impossible and quite frankly, a lie.

The whole "clan": my clients, their spouses, and the, now grown, children were to meet in my office at 2pm. I had contracted a caterer to come in, at about 5pm. My wife wanted to come to the get together. I told her that since Rhoda and Alex were still going to be clients that she'd have to wait, until I finished their second half of treatments. She reluctantly agreed. I told her when their second sessions were over; we could have the whole lot over for dinner. She liked that. I decided to have a Greek restaurant cater the whole thing and hoped that the liveliness of the Greek music (which was provided with the dinner) and food prep, would make anyone who might be a bit down, feel more joyful.

I got to the office around 12 o'clock just as Helen was going to lunch. I asked her to come to the dinner at 5pm; but she passed on that because her son had a baseball game. She was a bit sad about not attending, since she felt, she too, had grown to know Rhoda and Alex, over the last few months. She admitted the dynamic would be totally different. However, she had promised her son; so she had to decline. I secured Max in my personal bathroom, in my office. I wanted know where he was, during all of the excitement. Also I didn't want him to be unnecessarily stressed, by so many people, at one time. I tidied up the office and cell phoned Helen asking her to get a couple of bunches of fresh flowers on her way back from lunch and then I put out cups for tea. I was glad I had nine nice mugs and some really great pieces of fudge from Pier 39. I was also glad that I had enough seating, with some of the folding chairs I kept in the closet.

My plan was to let the "kids" talk with me first; after their parents got some tea and fudge and went back, into the front office. When they seemed done expressing themselves; I then would bring in the parents, to see if there were any loose ends or questions, from the kids for the adults. It was going to take time; but I was banking on how many young people find full expression of their emotions difficult. I thought this arrangement would give more time for the whole group to be together. At about a quarter to 2pm I heard the downstairs door open and a large excited group coming up the stairs. Alex D. and his wife Rhoda were there with their one daughter, who had flown in from LA for this. Alex and his wife Liz were next with their three kids. I had the young people sit down, in my office, and asked the parents to take a mug of tea and some fudge and go into the waiting area (part of me hoped they'd talk to each other; but they seemed rather quiet). When they left the room, I joked with the kids, a bit, and watched as they checked each other out. Alex's children didn't see each other much and they hadn't seen Rhoda's daughter in almost 13yrs. They were all good looking kids and seemed relatively well adjusted. Though Alex's daughter had had anorexia; you couldn't tell at this time. She seemed of normal weight. I asked each of them if they had a significant other and all of them said they did. I asked if they knew why they were here; they all said they did. I then asked who would like to speak first and Rhoda's daughter raised her hand. She looked a bit shy at first, but then you could see the resolve in her face.

"Basically after this whole stupid thing happened, my childhood was basically crap. I lost my mother. Before all of this happened my mother and I were always together, biking, roller blading, going to movies, swimming, everything. She was always happy and excited about living. Her whole focus was on me. She always had something planned, whether it was baking cookies or a craft. I was her whole world. I was like a princess. I got anything I wanted and my mom was a nice homey mom. She was a Christian; but didn't go to church. We'd study the bible together and that was nice and simple, no churchiness. But then we moved to California from Texas; she began to go to your dad's church. She was fine at first; we just went on Sunday mornings. She went to adult church and I went to Sunday school. My dad was happy she was getting to know people. But then she started to go to a woman's bible study and that was the beginning of her changing. She wasn't content just being my mom; she started wanting other things in her life. She wanted to work for God. She began working for your dad and got more and more involved in church work. At first, she was just working a couple of hours a day for him. As time went on, she worked 30hrs or more a week. Your dad was nice and he let me come and do my homework at church, while I waited for my mom to finish up. Eventually the head pastor came up to her and told her he was considering her for a permanent staff job. After that she worked with your dad, even more hours per week; some of the work was done from home. She was even more serious about her church work and I never saw her, unless I went to the church, too. She'd give me an option. I could go home after school or hang out with her and the other church kids. I usually chose to meet her at the church. She only worked till about 4pm and then we'd go home and make dinner for my dad. He was a bit ticked that she was working for free; but she reassured him, she was going to get a permanent staff position, in a few months. So he finally let it go. Your dad, Alex, liked me a lot and always treated me so nice, like I was one of his kids. He and my mom were always laughing. It was actually like a second home, for awhile. Things changed around Christmas. My mom and your dad were stressed, because of that seminar he was holding. She was doing even more extra work for him. Even when she was home, she worked into the night, for the church. On Christmas Eve, I was playing in the church playroom with the other kids. She came in and said that we had to get home to make Christmas Eve dinner for our family. So I ran ahead of her, to the parking lot. She came out with a bunch of papers to work on, over the holiday. Your dad was following right behind her. I was skipping and hopping about and turned around to see your dad grab my mom roughly and hug her. I couldn't hear what they were saying. She was trying to break free from his hug. I could tell she wasn't happy and thought maybe he was too rough. So I watched them out of the corner of my eye, as I played. I thought maybe your dad was trying to kiss my mom. They were talking, as they were struggling. I heard him say something to her and she got a strange look on her face. She started crying. I thought it was because her arm was twisted behind her back. I thought he didn't know he was twisting it. The she said something to him and he let her go and she grabbed my arm and we almost ran home. I thought it was because we were late. But then she threw up on the sidewalk. She was crying and wasn't her usual joyful self. As soon as she got home, she went to bed and told me she didn't feel good. I watched some cartoons, until my dad came home. We never had Christmas Eve dinner. She didn't wake up; so dad and I went to In and Out burger. That was the beginning of my troubles. My normally happy mom kept crying and praying. It could happen anytime, anywhere. When she went to work at the church, she made me come and stay with her in her office, during Christmas break. When she worked, she'd be crying; she was very depressed. She and your dad no longer joked and other people at work started to treat her impolitely, like she did something wrong. She wasn't the same. She was always sad and crying; she never laughed. My dad and I were worried. I asked him what was wrong with her. He said that mom would tell him, eventually. Pastor Stan kept yelling at her and calling her into his office; I could hear him shouting at her, from mom's office. Even after Christmas break, Pastor Stan kept taking her aside and yelling at her whenever, he got the chance. He did this at the church in front of others. I was so embarrassed; I couldn't see why she let him treat her like this. I'd have punched him. This seemed to go on forever. She was supposed to work at the church's Summer Camp and didn't come with when I went. I was kinda mad about this, since we were supposed to go to camp together, before I started Middle School. We had planned that for months. Then, when Middle school started, your cousins kept teasing me. They said my mom was in love with your dad and they kept at it in front of all the kids. I got really angry and told everyone what really happened, how your dad attacked my mom. Then they left me alone. My mom called your dad and told him off; when I told her what happened. After that, I didn't have many friends. The kids at church stayed away from me. My mom kept trying to make things right with your dad and the church.

They rejected her and said they didn't believe in reconciliation. We stayed for about two and a half more years. We ended up leaving the church and going to another one. But kids from your church also went to our new church's youth meetings. They would say bad things about my mom. The pastors made it worse because they never defended me. They'd agree with the kids and put my mom down. I never told my mom this stuff; because she was already so depressed. No matter what church we went to, some of the kids, from your church, would show up. They'd tell everyone my mom had tried to seduce your dad. My parents argued over the situation. To make matters worse, your dad would call our house and not speak and send blank emails. I knew about this, first hand, because I picked up some of the calls and used to use my mom's computer. Your church kept harassing my mom, for years later. She was sad for a long time. Your dad would sometimes come up to my mom in shops or on the street, crying, get afraid someone would see him, and run away. I tried two times to speak to your dad, for my mom. The first time and he told me he had to obey his leaders in the church. The second time he said that they forbid him to speak to me. No matter where my mom went to church there were always people, from your church, who'd come and spread rumors and put her down. After awhile, I got sick and tired of God and the church. I still believe in God; but I now have decided that I will be a Christian; but I'll never enter another church again. I'm done. I had wanted to be a pastor, at one time; but now I hate churches and pastors. They are phony. Church people are bigots and judgmental. I hate the whole church system. It is mostly artificial and superficial. I have never seen God there; I have only seen small minded, ignorant people, with agendas. That is my story."

I sat and looked at her and shook my head. People think that they do things in a vacuum; that no one else gets hurt. We may think we offended just one person, not thinking that that person has a family, career, and friends. This young woman is now an accountant and lives in LA; but her relationship with her parents is forever damaged. She mocks them for their passivity and allowing themselves to be abused. Alex's poor judgment lead to her only seeing hypocrisy. She never had a chance to see Jesus, as separate from the sins of His people. To her God's people were representatives of

Jesus, as well they should be, and she didn't have a chance to know Him for Himself. Ideally God's people should be mini-representations of Jesus. But when they are not, this destroys many people's faith. This is why this whole religious system found in many churches is so very evil and not a game. Souls are in the balance.

Alex's younger son decided to speak next, his name was Stan. "I was kind of little when the whole thing started. I was five and my dad's pal. Everywhere he went, I went, and we even looked alike at that time. I was like his Mini-me. I think he figured out, by the time I came along, that he had blown it with my brother and sister. He had always been too busy for them; so he made sure I was with him as much as possible. We'd go to the grocery and on other errands together and on occasion we'd see Mrs. Du. She used to go on daily walks and had to pass by the church to get to the park, since she lived nearby. I remember one time that dad and I had gone into Safeway; we were picking up a drug at the Pharmacy. She was coming down the aisle, headed right for us, but not seeing us till she got right up close. She saw my dad and smiled, but could not talk and neither could he. I kept pulling on his sleeve and saying, 'Dad, it's that lady; it's that lady.' He and my mom were always fighting about her. When my mom was mad at him she'd say, 'Why don't you go to Rhoda's house; she'll take your crap. I'm not going to.' Things like that. So when I saw her, I'd get all excited. Dad would only smile or even cry; but he wouldn't talk. They were kinda weird. Anyway, another time I remember he and I were in the car, stopped at a traffic light. Mrs. Du was coming down the street and he lifted me up and kept pointing to me. I didn't really know why he was doing that. Mom had said the night before; if he made things right with Mrs. Du that she'd take me away and he'd never see me again. I cried about that for a long time. Over the years dad would get into trouble for trying to speak to or communicate with her. He'd get caught and my mom would shout at him. Then Pastor Stan would come over to the house and yell at my dad. So I have to say my childhood was messed up, too. I remember dad sitting by himself, a lot, looking lonely and sad. He wasn't as funny as he used to be, for many years. That's all I have to say, really."

I just shook my head as I thought of how one stupid move destroyed two families. Sexual sin is so selfish. It is mainly done to satisfy a hunger, for a mere moment in time; and ends up destroying so many. The next one to talk was Alex's daughter. She was a bit reticent; but finally began to speak, "Wow what can I say? My life was hell, too. Some folks believed that Mrs. Du was after my dad. She wasn't very pretty or at least not the type you'd imagine that a man would want to seduce. They figured she was kind of desperate or something, that she was delusional in her attempt to seduce my dad. Like why would my dad, even consider her as a mistress. Since my dad was a nice guy, they thought he was an easy mark. But sadly, way before Mrs. Du came into the picture, my mom and dad were always arguing over him paying too much attention to the ladies and having affairs. The ones I saw them argue over, were all different types of women. He wasn't that picky. My parents had some long and rather violent fights, concerning this issue, sometimes right before we had to go to church. I used to feel so hypocritical sitting in the pastors' pew, with my family, and having to look perfect. Outside of Sunday worship time, I knew things were not so perfect in my dad's life. But I didn't really become aware of the extent his problem, until I was older. I used to blame my mom for being crabby. Sometimes I would see him standing right up close to certain ladies, when he didn't think I or anyone else was watching. That always made me uncomfortable and then they'd laugh in a special way, like two people who knew each other very well. This all bothered me; but I never had any proof that he was seeing those particular women. I was afraid to talk to my mom because she kept threatening to divorce him. They fought all the time. I didn't want to make things worse. So I got into my studies more, I tried to be the perfect student and daughter. Over time I got more quiet and detached from my family. I lived in my own world. My dad's cousin had me over to her house a lot. She had a real hang up about food. I'd go to eat some chips and she'd say, 'You know how many calories are in those? There's so much oil. You got to be careful; you don't want to get fat do you?' The way she said that kind of stuff, I knew she already thought I was fat. My mom's weight went up and down; but she was never what you'd call fat. But my second cousin was always a perfect size two and anyone would feel like a giant next to her. Her two kids were always eating and throwing up and hiding food. We'd go to the mall and eat and then come home and throw up. I think I heard her do the same thing a few times. After awhile this became a habit. Sometimes I just wouldn't eat and I'd get really thin. People would tell me how cute I looked. With this kind of a relative and my dad's problems, it somehow made me feel better to starve myself, a bit more in control. Everything around me was out of control; but food and my eating it; I could control. I was aware that my dad had gotten into trouble for trying to attack Mrs. Du. He kept denying it and saying she was too fat for him to want her. He said it was all her, but to be honest, I knew he was lying from seeing the way he'd look at her, from across the room. But when my friends would tease me about someone like Mrs. Du being after my dad, I'd pretend to think it was funny too. This made me depressed. Also I couldn't stand the way he treated my mom. When I went to college I was glad to get away from the drama. But I kept throwing up and not eating. For awhile I felt better, until my roommates and family began to say I was beyond skinny. I didn't listen to anyone and soon I was failing my classes and having a hard time doing my school work. My parents had to put me into a treatment center and it was hell. I didn't want to eat; but they made me and I kept trying to run away. But over time I did get better. I accept him now for what he is: a weak man. I did see him sit next to Mrs. Du, at a public prayer meeting, a few years ago. I think it was accidental; neither of them looked comfortable. But the way my dad acted, I could tell he still liked her. After the meeting, I encouraged him to go and speak with her and get things right. He said he couldn't do this since Pastor Stan was at the meeting. Pastor Stan was yelling about the whole thing the next day, at church, and I started to see how my dad was unable to stand up to him. I don't like Pastor Stan and am glad he is no longer a pastor. My mom is not happy with her and my dad's relationship. My dad has had more negative feedback, these last couple of years. More people now believe he was the aggressor and not Mrs. Du and there are rumors about other women. He recently got put in a new department at work. I don't think he likes his job as much as he once did. I'm not sure if my mom and dad will grow old together. I never want to turn out like them. I don't think love should be so miserable."

I turned to his oldest son and asked, "What about you?" He said, "Well, to be honest, I have tried to distance myself from my dad. I don't go for the way he has treated my mom, all of these years. He had various relationships, with other ladies and did not consider my mom and how she felt. She did fight with him a lot; but that is because he kept being irresponsible. He was bad with money and always had some lady on the side. I tried to accept him; but his whole attitude really turned me off. He only thought about himself. He works hard and has been good to us; but he didn't really see or care what his infidelities, did to my mom and us kids. Mrs. Dui was always nice to me, calling me Honey, all the time, and just being kind. But I just couldn't stand to be near one of my dad's 'women'. So I'd never smile back or be nice to her; I was afraid she might be my new mom someday. I made sure to stay away from her daughter. She was pretty; but I determined not to ever approach her. I even made fun of her and her mom. I could see dad liked Mrs. Du and she was always working with him. When she left the church, dad got kind of weird and would be more secretive. Pastor Stan was always on his back and yelling at him. He'd even come to our house and start a long session of yelling. I got sick and tired of church and hardly go today. I can't stand the phoniness of it. My dad seemed closer to my sister and little brother than me. I think I was too much like my mom. I never got the feeling he really liked me. He was a good enough dad, taking us on trips and trying to be funny. But he was always at work; only mom would come and see my baseball games. He never had time. I felt like I was in the way. I was a coach for awhile and have been trying to find myself. I don't want to be sleazy like my dad. Now I am trying to forgive him and develop a relationship with him. No, it was not easy being the son of a 'swinger', who pretended to be a perfect pastor."

Wow. Each kid in this story had some lasting scars from the Rhoda and Alex experience and from other dalliances Alex had engaged in. I wondered what would happen when I invited the parents in.

I told the young people a factual account of what happened between Alex and Rhoda, so that they'd see objectively and not have to rely on the half truths that they had gathered from their parents, people at church, and just their own imaginations. I then told them that I was so sorry that their parents had let them down. I said I'd be glad to see any of them, privately, for help in healing from the bad choices of their parents. But I also begged them to remember that their parents were human and that humans make mistakes and often regret choices that they make, later on down the road. I asked them to not judge their parents on their character flaws; but to focus more on their good qualities. I wanted them to remember the love that their parents lavished on them, over the years. I then told them that their parents were coming back into the room and that this would be a good time to politely, as possible, confront their parents on the issues that still bugged them. I told them that people were more likely to open up in the environment that therapy provided. I also told them that I hoped there would be a time of repentance and forgiveness.

I then got up from my chair and went to the door and opened it to find four people facing forward with blank expressions. I thought, "Oh, this doesn't look so good." But I put on my happy face and said, "Okay, folks, come on in and sit next to your children or should I say, your young adults." Everyone sat down; I was glad we had enough room.

"First of all I want to ask the parents, what happened out there? The looks on your faces were none too cheerful." I looked over at Rhoda, who had her hand up.

Rhoda cleared her throat, "Well, Doc, um, er, Mark, at first we were all politely sitting and not speaking. We did those nodding half smile things. You know like how you act to people at church, you don't know too well? Then my husband asked Alex why he kept calling his wife for all of these years? Sometimes there'd be two and three calls per day and my husband often picked up the phone to answer these 'mystery' calls, especially when he worked from home. So my husband wanted to know why he kept pursuing me so long. Well, Liz did not know this had occurred and so she got ticked at Alex. Alex told his wife he was sorry; but I'm not sure that went over so well. Then Liz turned to me and said that she had seen a few anonymous emails about reconciliation in her husband's email box and she wondered if they were from me. She felt they were strange, because they were all only one sentence long. I hesitated to answer that, but then I felt nothing was wrong with those one line notes thanking Alex for either a silent call or blank email. My husband got a bit ticked and thought I'd stopped thanking Alex for those ten years ago. Then I reminded my husband that he told me to do whatever I wanted in the situation, because he was done. So, I had. Well you came out right after we all had just got the latest information, on all of the things I just mentioned. But I have one comment on this. If our spouses did not want this to go on for so long, why didn't they just help us to quickly reconcile and be done with the whole matter? Why did they listen to that evil controlling church's leadership and not trust the wishes of their spouses? Even if Alex was 'off' at that time, a simple meeting would have ended the matter for me. I kept saying this and no one heard me. That would have simply ended the whole matter since, as the saying goes, it takes two to tango? Why would they, after both knowing Stan, believe that wacked out man over their own spouse? They both knew the man had mental issues and was evil. So why trust him?"

Liz said, "To be honest a couple of the pastors at our church had control and psychological issues. But we had to obey them; so Alex could keep his position. Did I ever admire, Pastor Stan or any of his cohorts? No, absolutely not. He had us over a barrel and not only did he know it; he took a weird pleasure in it. I knew that Rhoda was a nice woman. She wasn't my type to be friends with, maybe; but I had nothing against her. I was thankful she didn't sue my husband or say anything evil about him to others; she had every right to do so. She also treated me very kindly, after the incident, to show me she was on my side. She even gave me a couple of lovely gifts and apologized profusely, though she didn't need to do that. I even told her she had done nothing to apologize for. But to confront the pastors at my church, especially Pastor Stan, was something I was not strong enough to do. On top of all this I was so ticked at my husband for even getting into this mess, in the first place, that I tried to distance myself. I do thank you, Rhoda, for not letting him talk you into adultery and for thinking of me and my family. But to be honest, I was not brave enough to face the pastors there. The moment I would have done that, they would have treated me as badly or even worse than they treated Rhoda. Women were always seen as the evil person in the story, there at our church, even if they were the victims. Rhoda and I were the victims. The other pastors didn't want the donations to stop for the new building and so Rhoda was thrown in the trash, immediately. I'd have been right there with her for making a stink in anyway and coming against the male dominated leadership."

Alex D. was red in the face. "Look I'm not even a Christian and I did not want to get into any church mess. Because of the tackiness of this whole thing, I started to feel maybe this whole Jesus thing was a lie. I felt that my wife was in something evil and I did not want to get entangled in it. I did try to speak to Pastor Stan and you know what he said? He said that my wife seduced Alex and that she wanted to run off with him to Hawaii and that the situation was hopeless. He recommended for me to divorce my wife. Divorce?!! First of all I believed her and knew she had not tried to seduce Alex and I saw immediately that Pastor Stan was evil and a liar. This was obvious, even to a nonbeliever. I didn't like him; he had others at his church spread around a lot of rumors and lies about my wife. I wanted to sue the whole bunch of them. I had no desire to make nice. But the lawyer we went to said that the problem was that there were no witnesses. It was a She said/He said situation. So I just washed my hands of the whole thing. Do I regret this now? You bet. But to be honest I was afraid they'd sue me or that I'd kill Alex and have to go to jail or something like that and so I told Rhoda to handle it herself. I guess I should have asked her, over the following ten years, how she was handling the thing. But I didn't. But I do know she went through even more suffering, at different churches. She'd stay for a few years even, but would end up quitting them when the abuse got to be too much for her. She did this about four times and finally seems to like this last one, she is at. She has been at this hopefully last church, for about three years and loves it. Rumors and lies from Alex's church kept following her. I grew to hate Christianity; lately I've been reconsidering Jesus again. I don't think He was anything like the pastors at Alex's church or other bitter judgmental Christians I have met. Jesus loves and isn't so harsh and cruel."

Alex's daughter spoke out. "Mr. and Mrs. Du I'm so sorry for the way the pastors at Dad's church treated you. I knew that many of the people there were small minded and did say nasty things about Rhoda. But I felt that I could not speak out for your wife, because my medical treatment was sponsored by them and my dad needed that job. Also I tried to move past the whole thing and now I no longer go there. I can see things from all the different sides; not the narrow way I was taught to think, at church. I do want to say, on behalf of my family, I'm sorry and really sorry I didn't stand up for you, Mrs. Du. I do have a question. It's for my mom. Mom, why didn't you divorce Dad or at least separate from him, until he got help for his problem? Why did you keep letting him walk on you? We know Dad has a bit of a temper; but you are a smart woman and you let him take advantage of you. Why did you keep accepting him back in this case and in all of the others?"

Liz was shocked that her daughter would bring this up, in this manner. "Well to be honest, Honey, I was thinking of you kids. I wanted you all to have a home that was intact and I wanted all of you to love and respect your dad. So I tried to get past this, defect in his character. In between his infidelity he was great to be with, even fun. He did get easily angered but this was only on occasion. So in the good times; I forgot the bad. But as far as the separation thing goes, I wanted to do that. But I felt, if I did it, it would be best to have some sort of therapy for your dad or that that would not help him heal; it would just destroy our marriage. But your Dad was not allowed to get therapy. Pastor Stan said that if he got therapy and it got out about why he was getting it, the church would be ruined. Also he told your dad that his career would be over; that pastors don't need to get therapy. He said that pastors were not like regular people. They no longer sinned, like regular folks, and therefore for your dad to get therapy would imply that he still was capable of sinning. I thought that was crazy; but your dad believed anything Stan told him, for a long time period. So I gave up the therapy idea. So without the therapy part, the threat of separation thing, had no back bone. I sometimes wish I had had tough love towards your dad and I think I'd love him more today; if I'd have made him respect me more in the past. I feel disrespected in all of this."

Liz started to cry and her daughter went over to her mom and laid her head on her mom's lap and also cried silently. Alex's youngest son was the next to ask a question. "Mrs. Du, how come you never spoke to my dad when you bumped into him at the grocery or at other Christian services at other churches? You could have and then this all would have ended years ago. But all you and Dad did was stand and stare at each other. I've been thinking that was a little weird. It confused me as a kid."

Rhoda answered, "Well, first of all, the times I saw your dad were so few and far between that I was literally too shocked to speak. Sometimes, I was trying to speak and hoped your dad would say something first. When he didn't, I saw that he still had that stupid church restriction on him. I backed off, hoping he'd set himself free from their religious controls, by speaking to me. But each time we bumped into each other; he didn't do that. I'd just leave and cry my heart out, because he was still in their grasp. Today, if that type of thing would have happened; I'd definitely speak to him. I no longer fear evil leaders and their threats."

Alex joined in, "They made me sign a bunch of papers, to make a written vow to God, not to go against their commands. One of the commands, clearly stated, that I should never speak to you again. If I broke this command I'd have to lose my job and pay back all benefits they'd given me. I signed it under duress. Stan actually held my hand and forced me to sign them; because I was not able to do it. I felt if I spoke to you; I'd lose my soul and also be sued."

"I'm never going to go back to that church again and I don't want anything to do with Jesus either." Alex's youngest son looked out the window, crossed his arms, and became silent.

Alex's older son said, "Do you see why I moved away from all of this? The church was f....d up and my parents were totally brainwashed by it. I had to get away. My question is for both of my parents. Was there any time that you guys saw that that place was evil and that you should leave; that you needed help? I can't believe you thought that place was normal Christianity."

"Okay, son", Alex said, "to be honest we both felt like leaving a few times; but they would not give me a recommendation. Every church I applied to said without one they wouldn't hire me. I thought of getting other jobs; but none of them would have helped with all of your college tuitions or your sister's medical bills. I got help with those with programs from the church. Also none of them had a retirement home, for your mom and I; I did not save enough to retire. I just gave up and accepted my fate. I thought there were ways to make my being at the church less evil. I determined to lie, as little as possible; if I remained in my position. I also determined to not really listen to any of the sermons or special seminars, we attended; so my mind would not be polluted. I still let them make me lie about Rhoda; say everything was fine, when it wasn't. I knew your mom was ready to leave me and the church, at least ten times. I am ashamed of my lack of character. I was a horrible example to you kids on so many levels."

Lastly Rhoda's daughter spoke. "Look everyone the problem is not that church; it's all churches. I no longer trust any church or any pastor or leader. I find they are all religious, legalistic bigots. I, for one, never want to be part of organized religion again. As for my mom, I think she was weak, because she should have demanded that Alex talk to her. I wish my dad had fought harder to protect her honor. So I do think both of my parents were way too passive or cowardly in this thing. I and Alex's kids ended up suffering for it. Pastor Alex it is hard for me to believe you were ever me or my mom's friend. That is not how a friend treats a friend. That's all I have to say on this."

"Well, wait I have one more thing to say to Pastor Alex or Alex. I don't believe you are a pastor, sorry I called you one. But I want to know what kind of love you had for my mom? Real love tries to protect the person they love and doesn't want to see that person suffer. Yet you let my mother be degraded, first by yourself, then by your church, and then by other churches. You didn't try to protect her. You knew she simply wanted to reconcile with you. So why did you not do this, even secretly, for so many years. You made her suffer and that is not love. We won't even go into the fact that you were both married and how this hurt both of your spouses. Do you know how you hurt me? I cannot ever trust a Christian leader again and I hated God for years. I also don't have a close relationship with my family, any more. This is all your doing. I admit I'm angry. I'm angry at you. On top of this you befriended me, when I was a child, and I feel betrayed. I think you are the really bad guy in this story and not Pastor Stan. He's crazy, true. But you started this whole mess."

Alex went over to her chair and looked her in the eyes. "You have every right to hate me. I deserve whatever you have said to me and more. I truly beg your forgiveness and hope in time you can be at peace with me. I was evil. I do truly repent. But please don't think that every leader is cut from the same cloth I was. There are good men out there who do serve and honor God. Maybe you will find a good leader. But what I beg you is to at least have a relationship with God; He is not at fault here. I chose to sin. So did the leaders at my church."

She looked out the window. "I'll consider this."

Rhoda replied, "Honey, I agree with you, for the most part, about your dad and I being weak. But you have to realize that that church had lawyers, police, and other members come to me and make threats, about what they'd do to me if I ever tried to contact Alex. They didn't want me to tell my story to anyone. They said if I did; they'd sue me. They threatened me with jail. Pastor Stan said he'd make your dad divorce me. He said he'd make up anything so your dad would think I not only wanted to seduce Alex, but that I had actually done the deed. They even printed up a false document saying it was an "Order of Protection", that was ordered by Alex. I took it to a lawyer friend of mine, a year later; he said it was a phony document. They called me every day and made psychological and physical threats. I just could not take the violence coming from them. I didn't want to see you or your dad hurt, in any way by them. I was not sure if they'd go beyond threats and maybe kill or maim one of us or take legal action of some sort. Yet I knew God wanted the reconciliation; so I felt I had to keep trying to go forward in this. I know I should have still made Alex accountable and damned the results. But it was all too much for me. So sorry, I disappointed you and messed up being a mom to you."

"Hmmph, if it was me, I'd have stopped trying to reconcile and just dumped the whole bunch of them and moved on. They were a bunch of slobs anyway. I am still a believer; but I'll never go to church again. They are all the same."

Rhoda, "Like Alex just said, there are some good people in the church and there are real churches. I hope you can find such a place someday. I'm so sorry, Honey. Forgive me."

I thought this was the time to pray and so I told everyone that we needed to bring God into the situation and pray. We all bowed our heads and I prayed, "Father, show up in this situation. So many lies and hurts have destroyed these young people and their parents. We come to you today and ask you to bring healing, to bring repentance, and to bring forgiveness. Help each of us to love each other, more than we ever have before."

After I prayed this and there was soft crying from almost everyone in the room. I began to feel the presence of God descend on the room and there was stillness. Each of the children went to their parents and began to repeat a prayer after me, "Lord, I know my parents aren't perfect. Each of them made mistakes that hurt me deeply. I lost respect for them, along the way; because of their choices. I know what it is like to be human and make mistakes. Today, before God, I want to forgive. I forgive Rhoda, for not standing up more to the church. I forgive Liz, for not taking a stand with her husband. I forgive Alex D., for not being more forceful with the church to clear his wife's name. I forgive Alex, for breaking his marriage vows and for letting the church abuse Rhoda and forcing him to lie in order to keep his job. Each of them has done these and other sins. We their children, now forgive our parents." The young people wept as they repeated the words and told their parents privately how they were forgiven.

Then the parents did the same, repeating this prayer after me, "We the parents of these precious children, ask humbly for their forgiveness for violating their trust and for making them ashamed of us. We each have areas of weakness. We each have failed each other and our dear children. We beg you to forgive us and give us a chance to reestablish trust." They too started to cry and we all knelt down and put our arms around each other in a circle of love. We sang 'Amazing Grace'. Alex D. actually began the song. We stayed silent, for about a half an hour, and then we got up. I invited anyone who wanted to see me privately, to schedule an appointment. I also reminded them that though this time was blessed; there would be many times ahead of them all, when they'd have to forgive, again and again, as they tried to reestablish connection and trust. I told them to go slowly and pray about anything that came to their minds. All anger and unforgiveness, should be taken to God as it came into their minds, and not stored up. I also said I was available by phone to give any help, they might need. I told them this would take time; but that we had made a grand start. Then we all went into the front office and had a rather silent dinner, despite the Greek music and food preparations. People were contemplating all that had just happened. When our dinner time was over, I said goodbye to all of them. I didn't clean up the mess; I went into my office, too overcome for words. I lay prostrate on the floor, my face in the carpet, weeping silent thanks to God.

Epilogue

I learned a couple of important lessons, from my time counseling Alex and Rhoda:

1. The church was never meant to be an ultra controlling organization. Jesus was never like this. He told people what their sin was; but respected them enough to then let them choose, for themselves, when and if they would repent and change. If Jesus respected the free will choice of men, then how much more should the leaders of the church? Morality cannot be legislated. Moral choices not made from an inner conviction, are not choices; they are rote obedience to religion. The leaders of the church are to serve and not demand mindless obedience to their commands. People need to hear from God first and then evaluate if the leaders words are God's or the leaders'. Blind obedience is not God's way. When all is done in love and by free choice, then there is less hypocrisy. The world sees the hypocrisy in the church, quite clearly. The Church cannot keep people from sinning by running rough shod over them. It must trust that God will ultimately be able to keep and direct His people. If a member goes off track, the Church can guide; but it cannot beat the person into total submission. God is the one to bring back the lost sheep. Leaders are to treat the flock

with gentleness and help them come into their best. The Church, should never be a corrupt corporation, that behaves like the World, or worse. The object isn't to look perfect, but to be holy. Religious rules don't make people holy; holiness comes through knowing the Lord and His love. The love of God and for God, makes people holy, not the enforcing of legalistic controls.

2. Forgiveness is a beautiful thing and it is the beginning of God's plan to restore relationships. In all, except a few rare cases, the next step, after forgiveness should be reconciliation. Reconciliation looks different, in each case. For some it will be a time to make things right and clarify past confusions. Then when this is done, the parties may just decide to end it there and go in peace. For others, reconciliation will go further into relationship; but will have boundaries to be decided by all parties involved. For the blessed few, it will mean a total restoration of relationship and perhaps going to an even higher level of commitment. Reconciliation should not be thought of as, just a fancy form of forgiveness. It is a real second step in the forgiveness process. Churches would do well to encourage this and not stand in the way of it. Our churches are full of people who have never mended broken relationships, either in or out of the church. God's people need to be taught it is honorable: to apologize, to repent, to forgive, to ask for forgiveness, and to reconcile. Wounded and angry people will never be able to manifest Christ to the world. Of course, all must be done in safety and honor, respecting the wishes of those involved. No one can reconcile for someone else and no one can tell someone not to reconcile. God's people need to be at peace with each other and those they come into contact with outside the church.

As for the people in this story, they are just a small example of stories going on in the Church, at large. If legalism and control almost destroyed their lives, how many other lives are being destroyed? If churches are more concerned about how they look and donations and not about immorality and abuse, then there is something terribly wrong. Church should be a place of safety and healing, not abuse and cover-up. How many Alexes and Rhodas are being kept from their destinies by corruption and legalism? How many families are losing their faith and being crushed by Religion? The Church needs to do self introspection, repent, and purge out hidden sin. The wounded need to be cared for and healed, not beaten down. God is love.

Now as for, Alex and Liz, they made a commitment to see me for the next two years, so that their marriage will be totally healed. They told me that they have hope that they will finally love each other, as they were meant to. They had a grandchild, soon after the first set of meetings ended. They want to be sure they will enjoy their 'golden years' together and set a new example for their family and the next generation to come.

Alex D. and Rhoda made a commitment to see me for about a year. Rhoda will be seeing me first, to deal with her feelings about the Assembly, the first cult she was in, before Alex's church. They then want to come for a couple of sessions together to make sure Alex D. has no confusion about Rhoda's time in the first cult and other issues in their marriage. Both are looking forward to exciting second careers and to growing old together.

My life has been made richer by meeting people, who finally obeyed God and stopped obeying legalistic rules. Reconciliation is the heart of God. I will tell my wife all about this, in two years; unless she reads this book first.

About the author

I became a Christian over 43yrs ago and have had many good and bad experiences in the church. I was involved in many ministries, over the years, and have sadly seen some things in the Church that are shameful: adultery, violence, backbiting, etc. Things that might even go far beyond what any nonbeliever might be capable of doing. Because of this I have determined to try and rid the church of some of these unsavory practices. I did an exhaustive study on what forgiveness is and in the course of this study I also learned about reconciliation. I have read over 110 books, on these two subjects, and have both taken and given classes on them. I believe that teaching on the subjects of forgiveness and reconciliation is my life calling.

I was involved in a couple of church scandals, as the victim, and have had to learn to forgive the malicious Christian leaders who tried to destroy me. It was a very difficult experience for me since I was taught to trust people in authority, especially in the Church.

I live in Danville, California; most folks here are affluent; but I'm not. I am of Italian descent. I went to the University of Illinois and graduated with a degree in Elementary Education, with a minor in Social Services. I met and married a Taiwanese man at the University. He is a computer "genius" and specializes in Data Architecture, Data Warehousing, and ETL. We have recently purchased an old home which we are remodeling together. We have one daughter, in her late twenties, who is an accountant and lives in LA. We also have two cats, Mimi and Jingles; they make us laugh. My family lives in the Chicago area and my husband's lives near Taipei, Taiwan. I occasionally travel to see them. I am therefore an international traveler. We've also been to Japan. I no longer work outside the home. I spend my time remodeling and caring for our rather large home and writing, of course. I attend a large Charismatic Christian Church and most of my friends are from there. I am preparing to get more seriously into writing and will be doing speaking engagements. My husband and I are planning to start a business and don't believe in retirement. We are just starting our lives, at almost 60yrs old.